Advance Praise for Timothy Dinoman

"Timothy Dinoman is a delightful new action star whose charm is far from extinct. A thrilling read for anyone looking for adventure."

–Jarad Greene, author, *Scullion* and *A-Okay*

"Timothy Dinoman is the secret agent we've been waiting for! Every page is not only wonderfully vibrant but brimming with action, humor, and most importantly, kindness."

–Robyn Smith, artist, *Nubia: Real One*

For Rachel

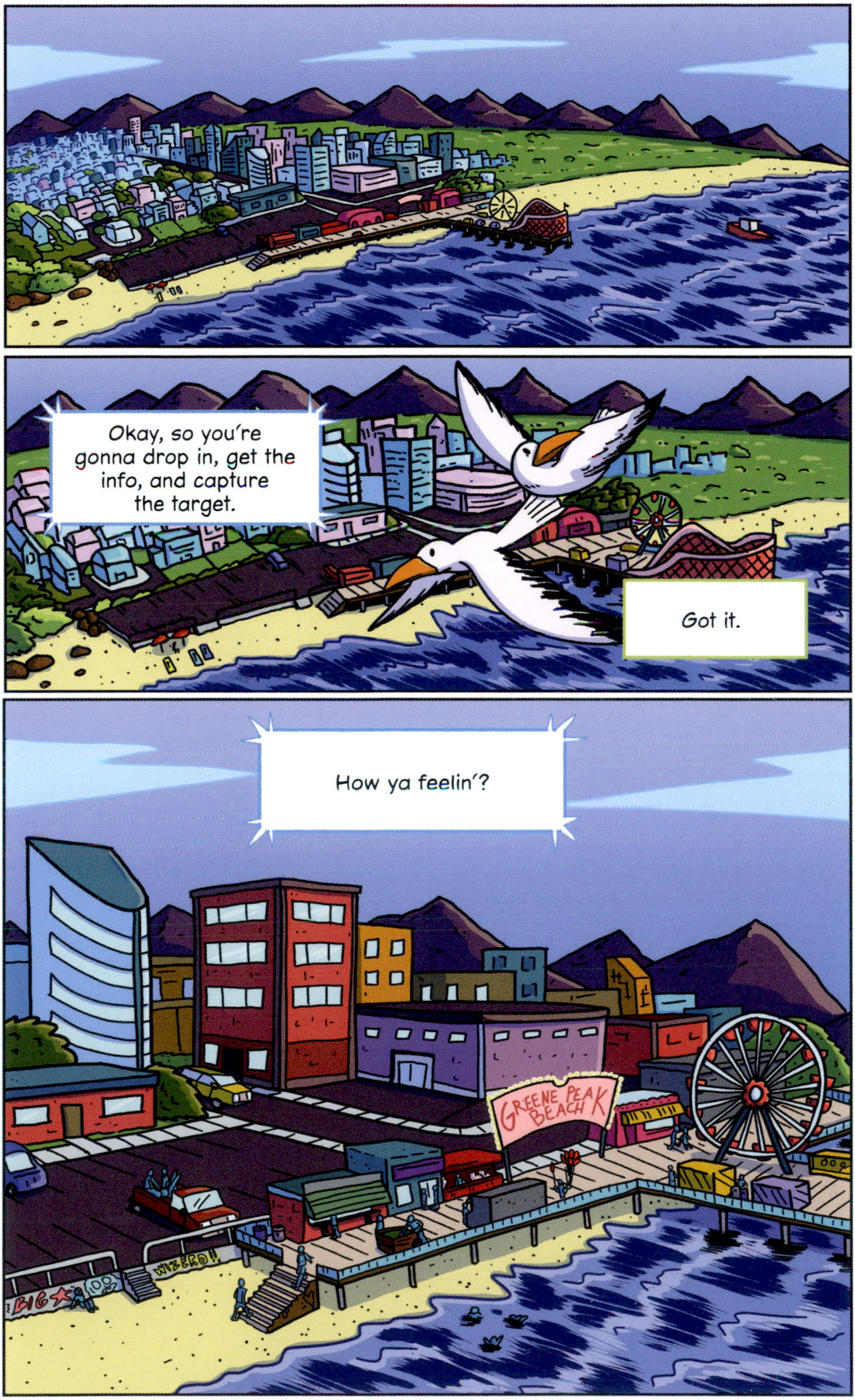
Okay, so you're gonna drop in, get the info, and capture the target.
Got it.
How ya feelin'?
GREENE PEAK BEACH
BIG

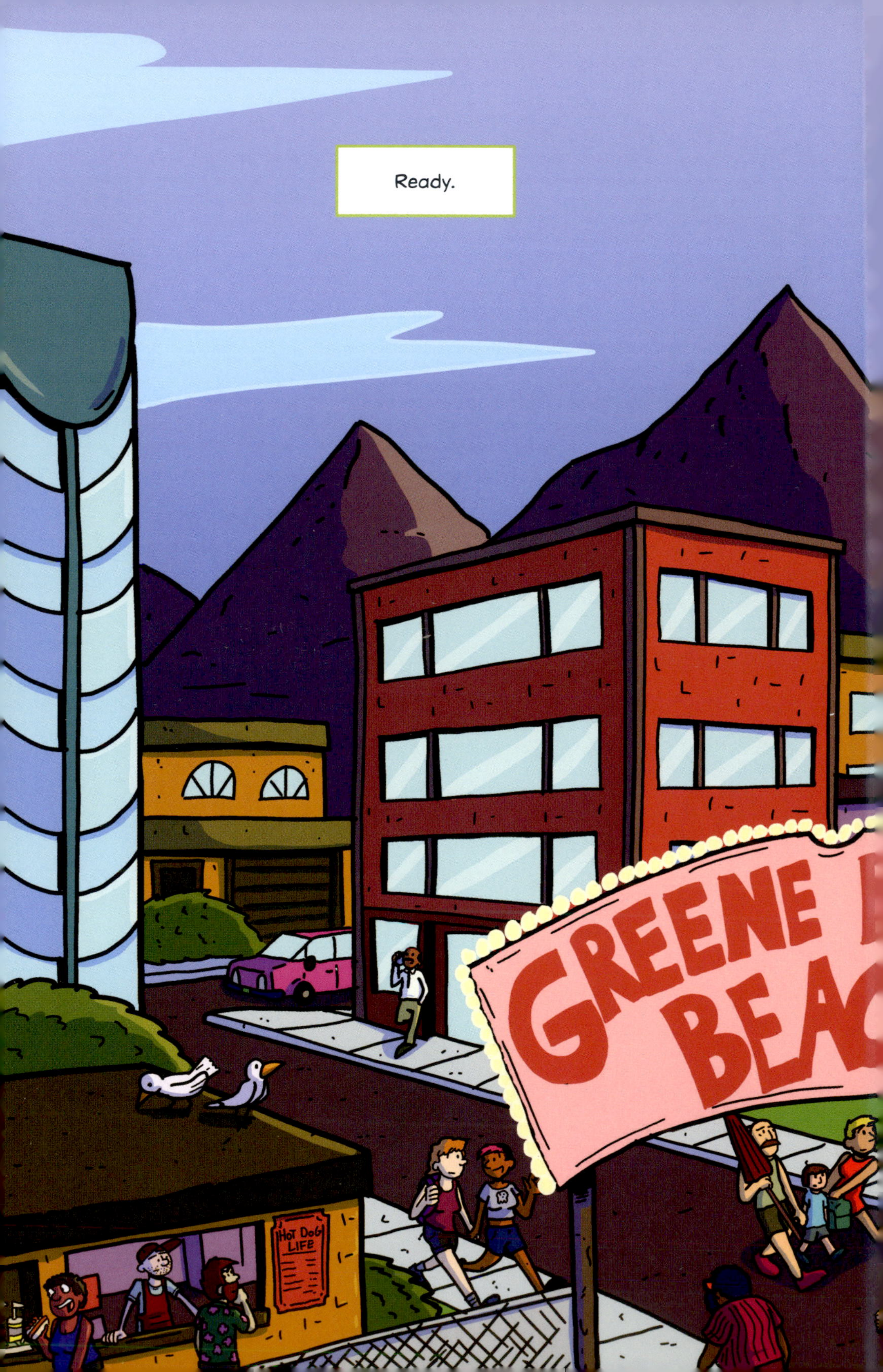
Ready.
GREENE
BEAC
HOT DOG LIFE

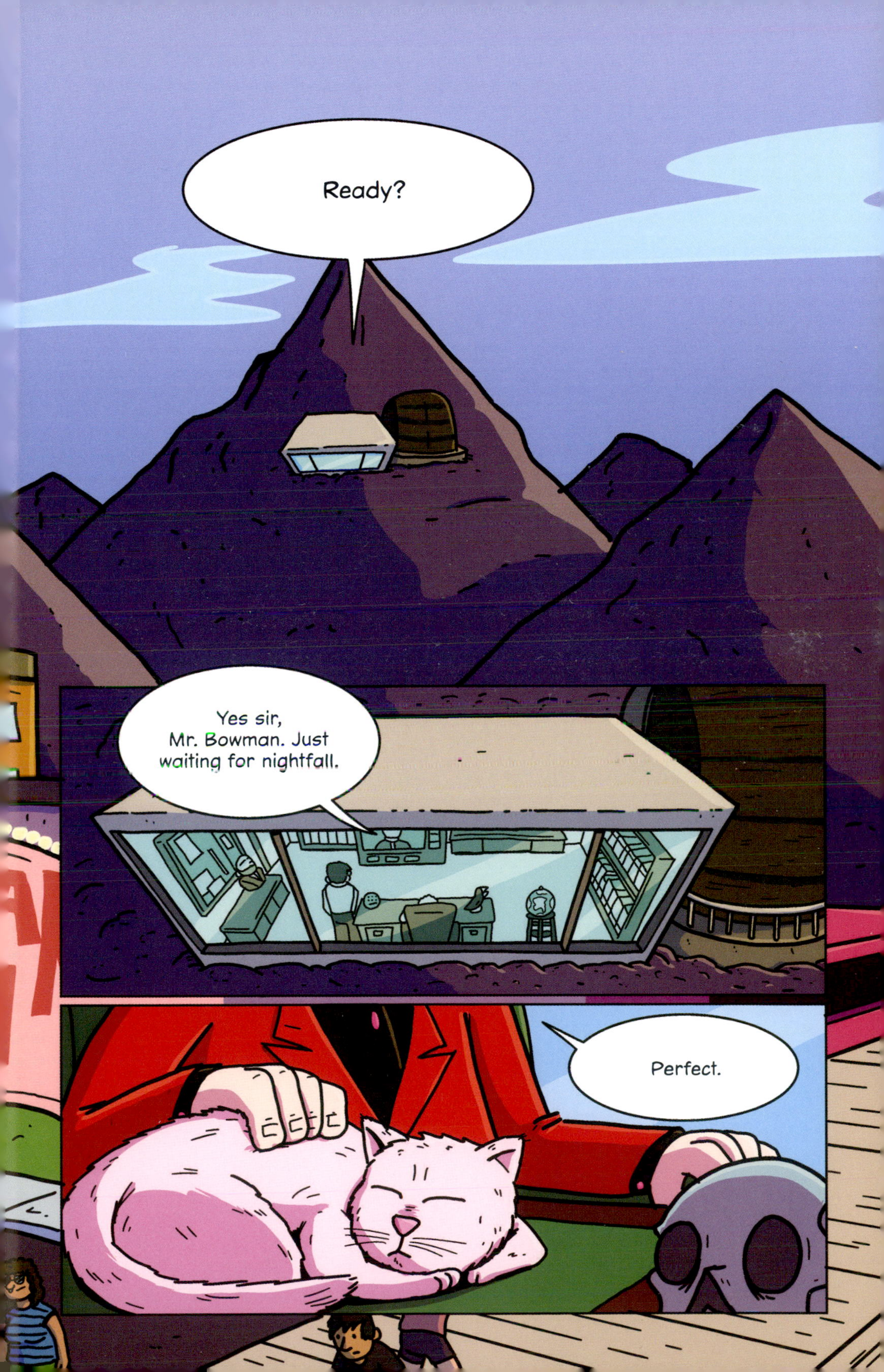
Ready?
Yes sir, Mr. Bowman. Just waiting for nightfall.
Perfect.

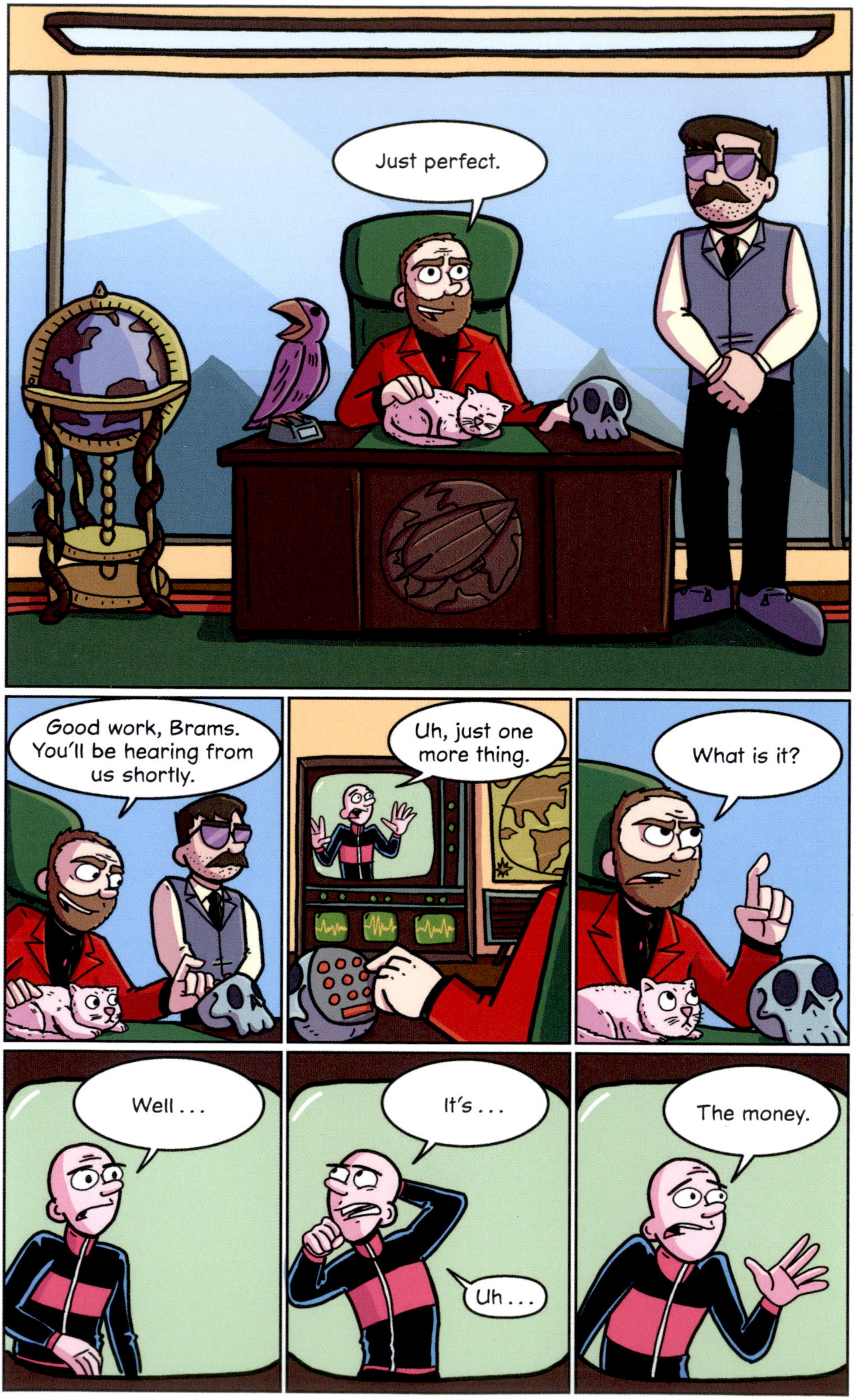
Just perfect.
Good work, Brams. You'll be hearing from us shortly.
Uh, just one more thing.
What is it?
Well . . .
It's . . .
Uh . . .
The money.

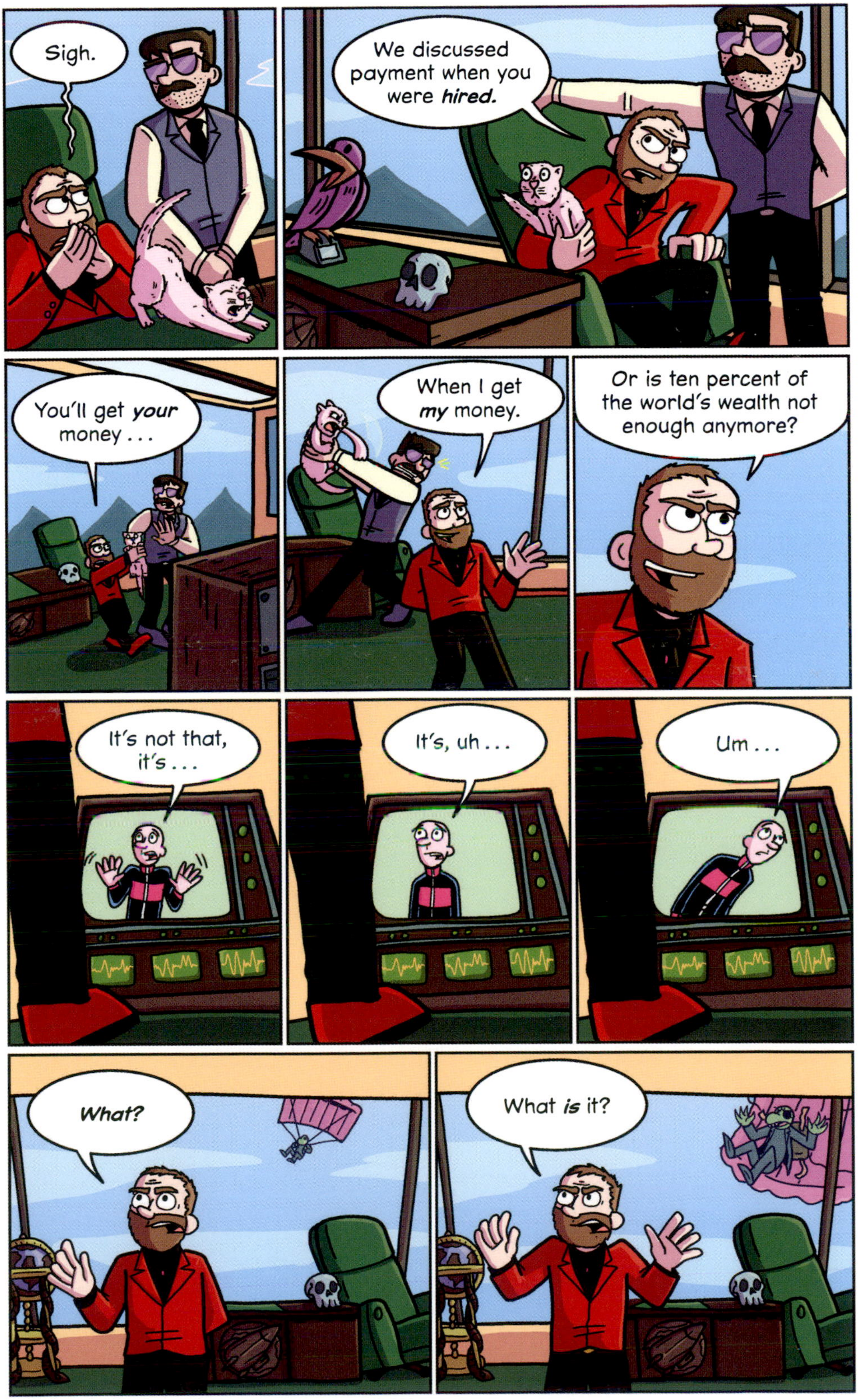
Sigh.
We discussed payment when you were *hired.*
You'll get *your* money . . .
When I get *my* money.
Or is ten percent of the world's wealth not enough anymore?
It's not that, it's . . .
It's, uh . . .
Um . . .
What?
What *is* it?

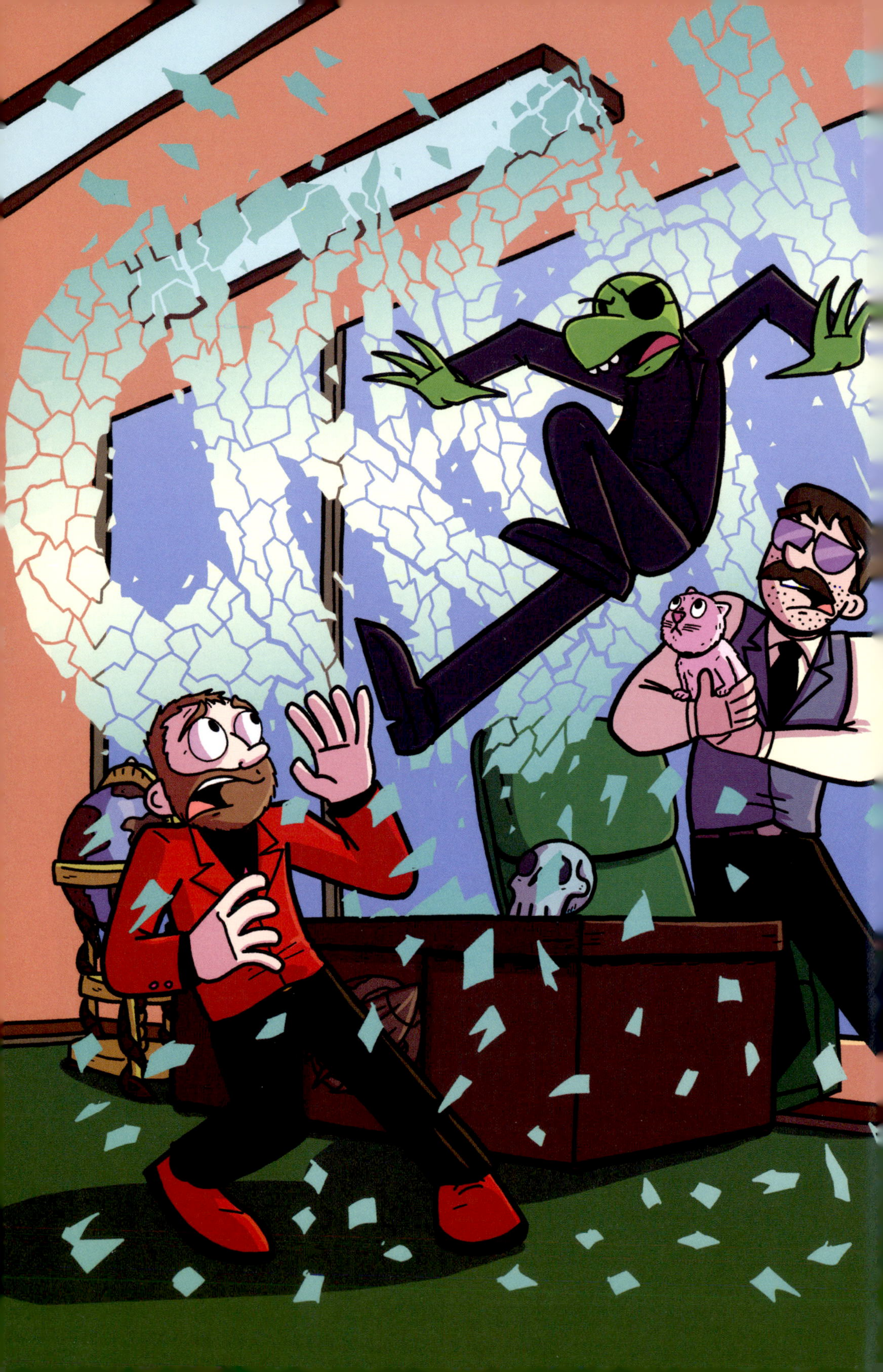

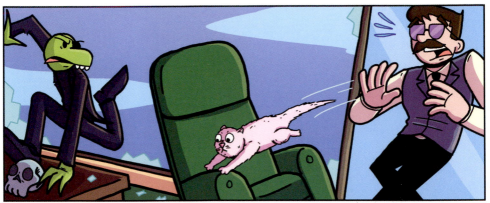

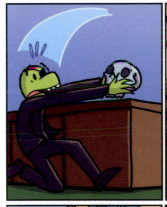

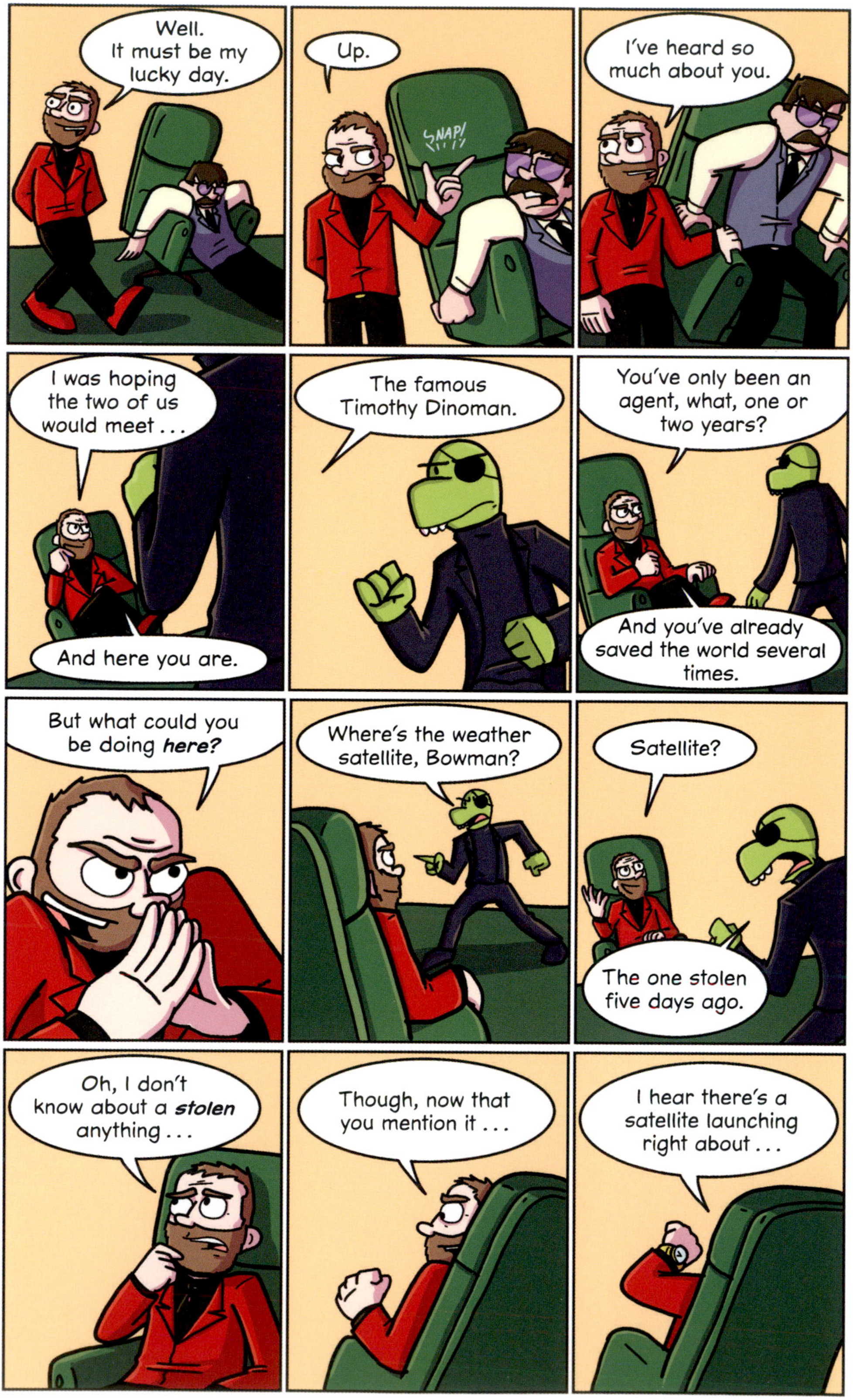
Well.
It must be my lucky day.
Up.
SNAP!
I've heard so much about you.
I was hoping the two of us would meet . . .
And here you are.
The famous Timothy Dinoman.
You've only been an agent, what, one or two years?
And you've already saved the world several times.
But what could you be doing *here?*
Where's the weather satellite, Bowman?
Satellite?
The one stolen five days ago.
Oh, I don't know about a *stolen* anything . . .
Though, now that you mention it . . .
I hear there's a satellite launching right about . . .

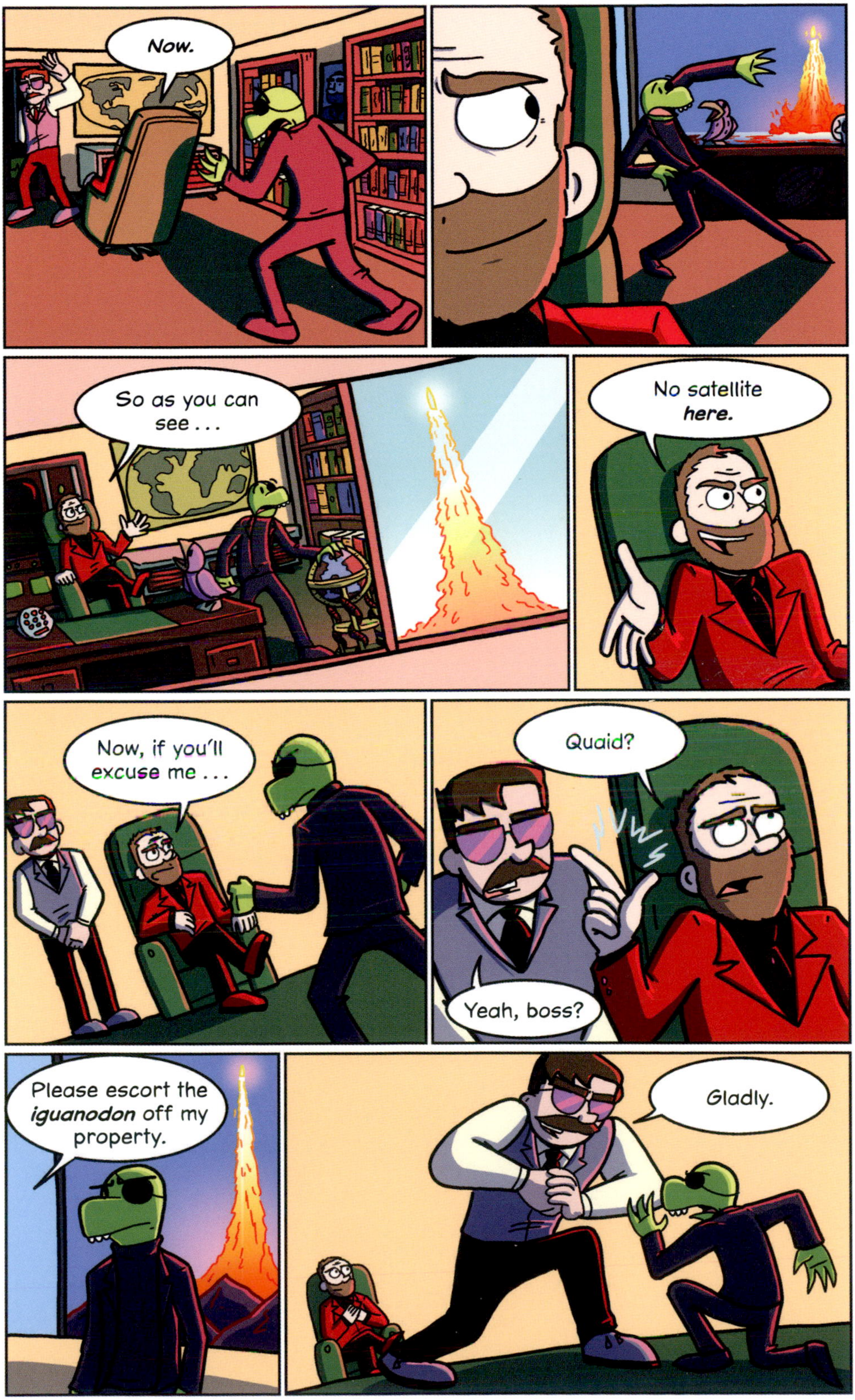
Now.
So as you can see . . .
No satellite *here.*
Now, if you'll excuse me . . .
Quaid?
Yeah, boss?
Please escort the *iguanodon* off my property.
Gladly.

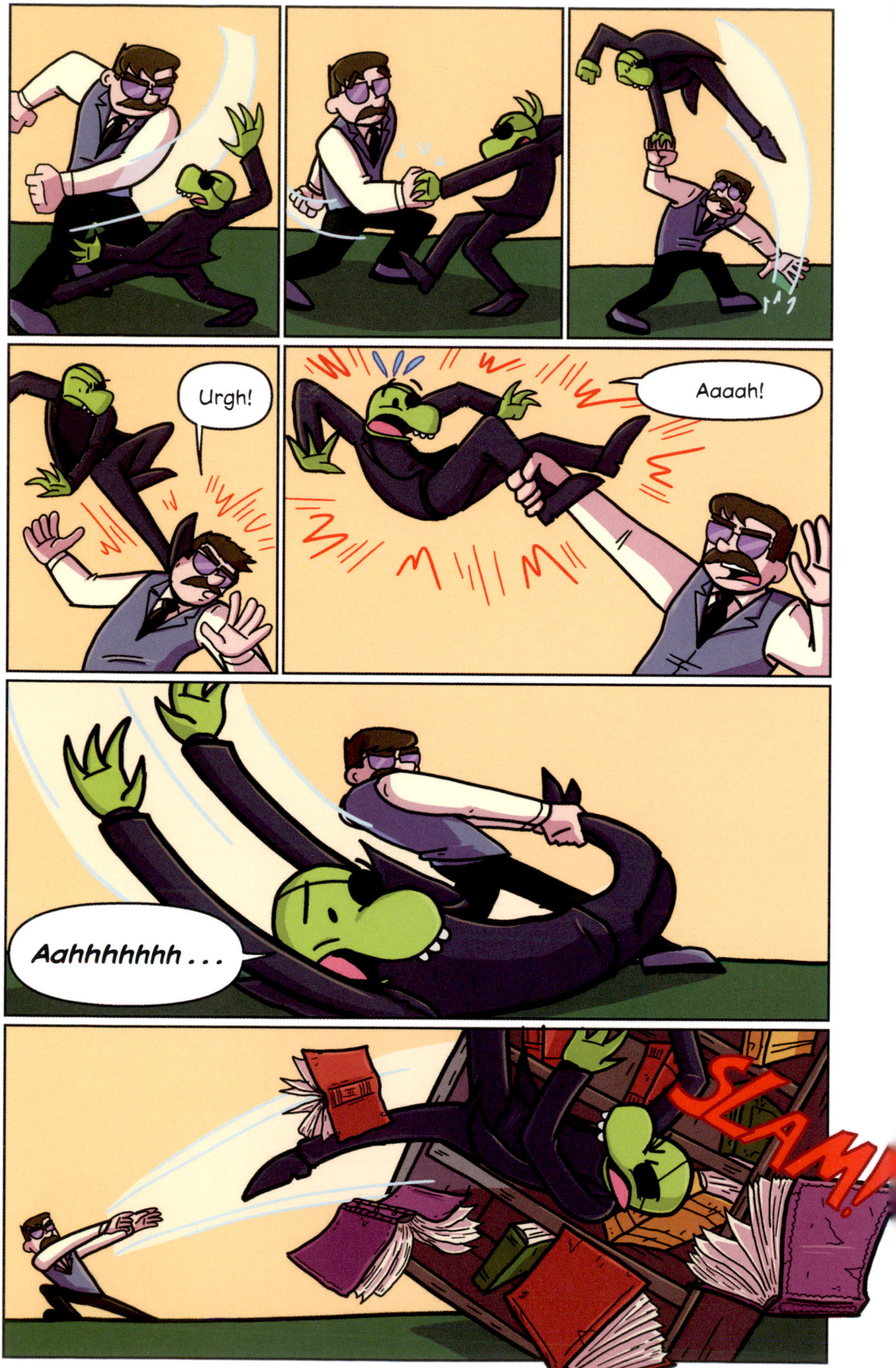
Urgh!
Aaaah!
Aahhhhhhh . . .
SLAM!

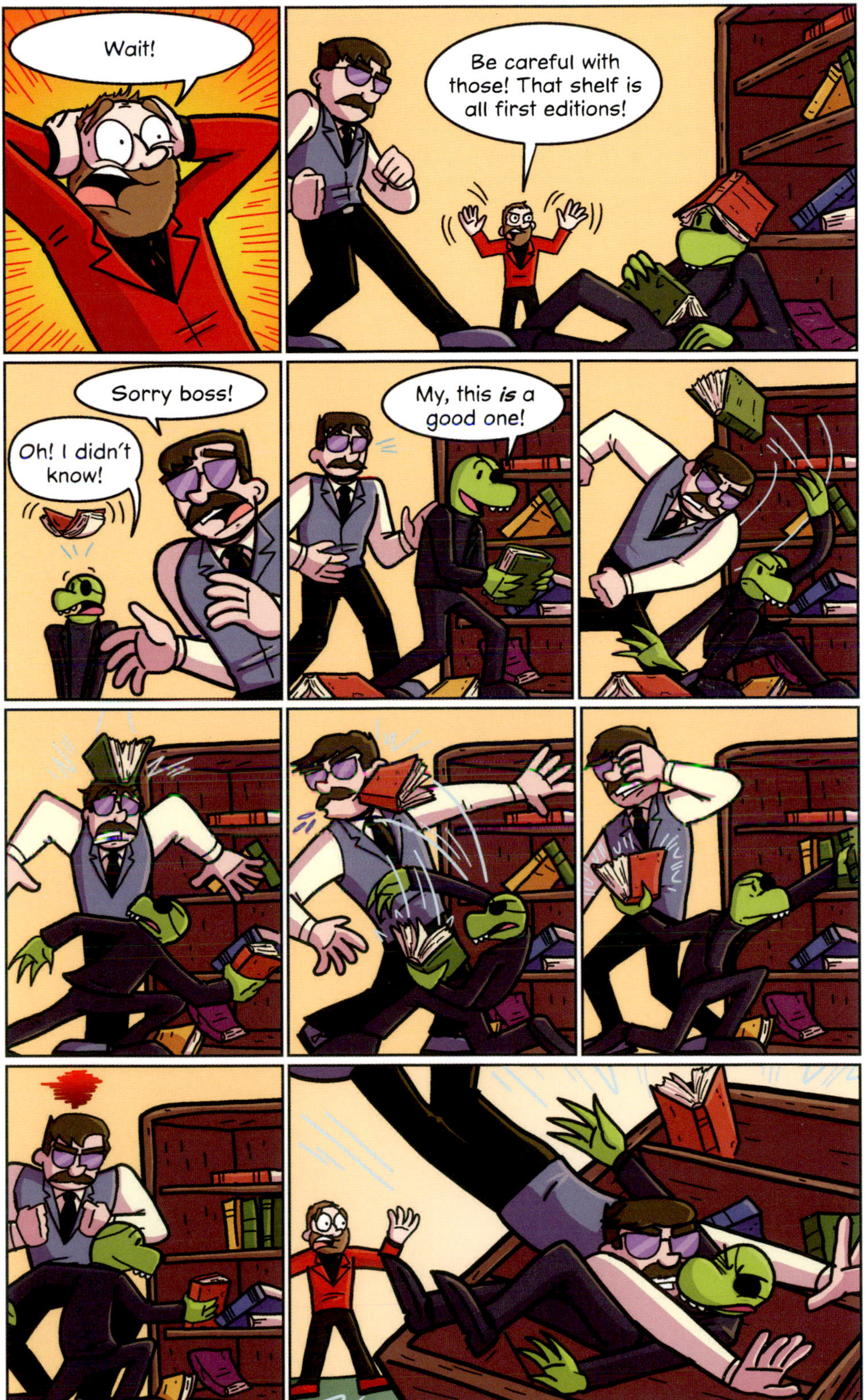
Wait!
Be careful with those! That shelf is all first editions!
Sorry boss!
Oh! I didn't know!
My, this *is* a good one!

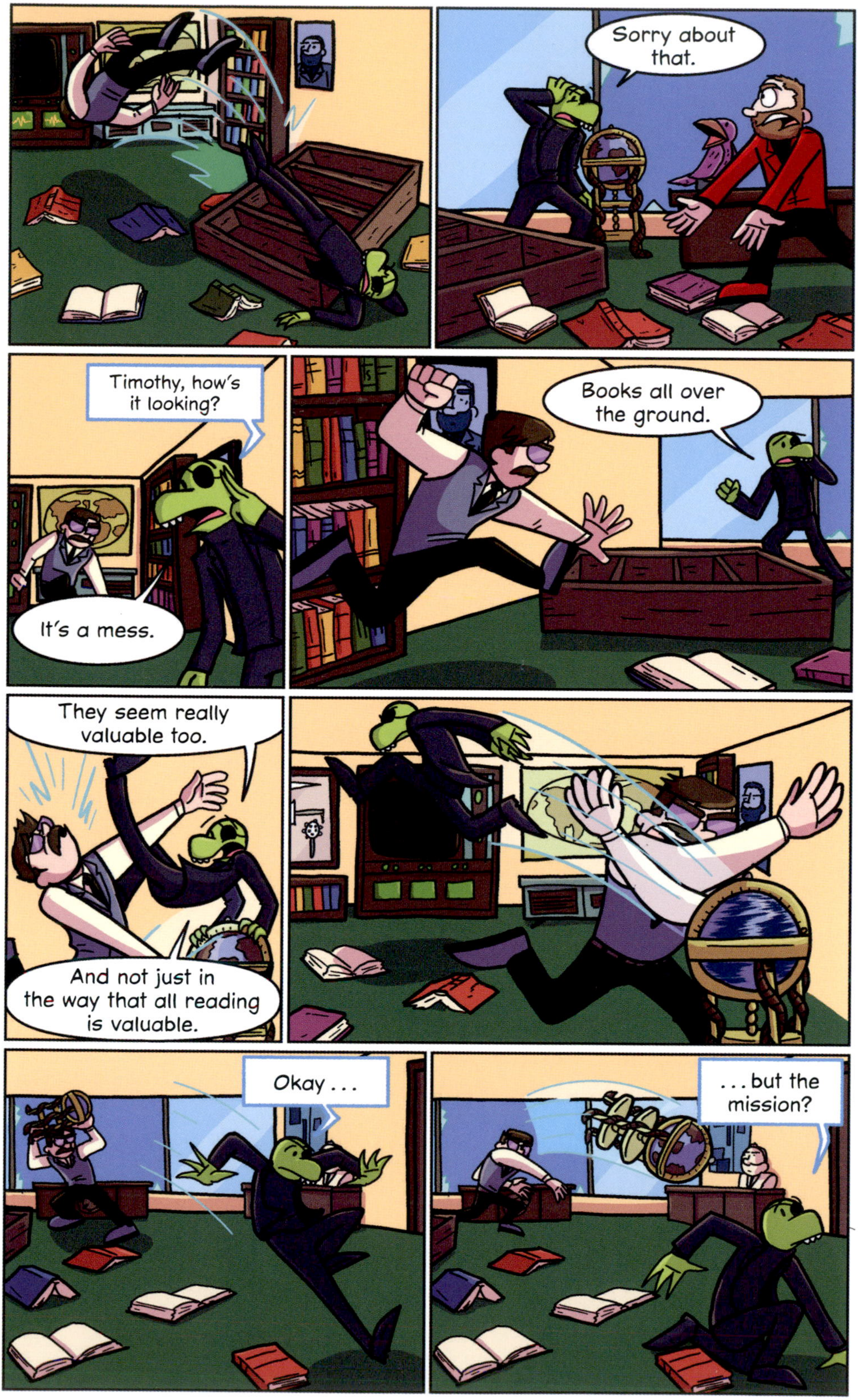
Sorry about that.
Timothy, how's it looking?
It's a mess.
Books all over the ground.
They seem really valuable too.
And not just in the way that all reading is valuable.
Okay . . .
. . . but the mission?

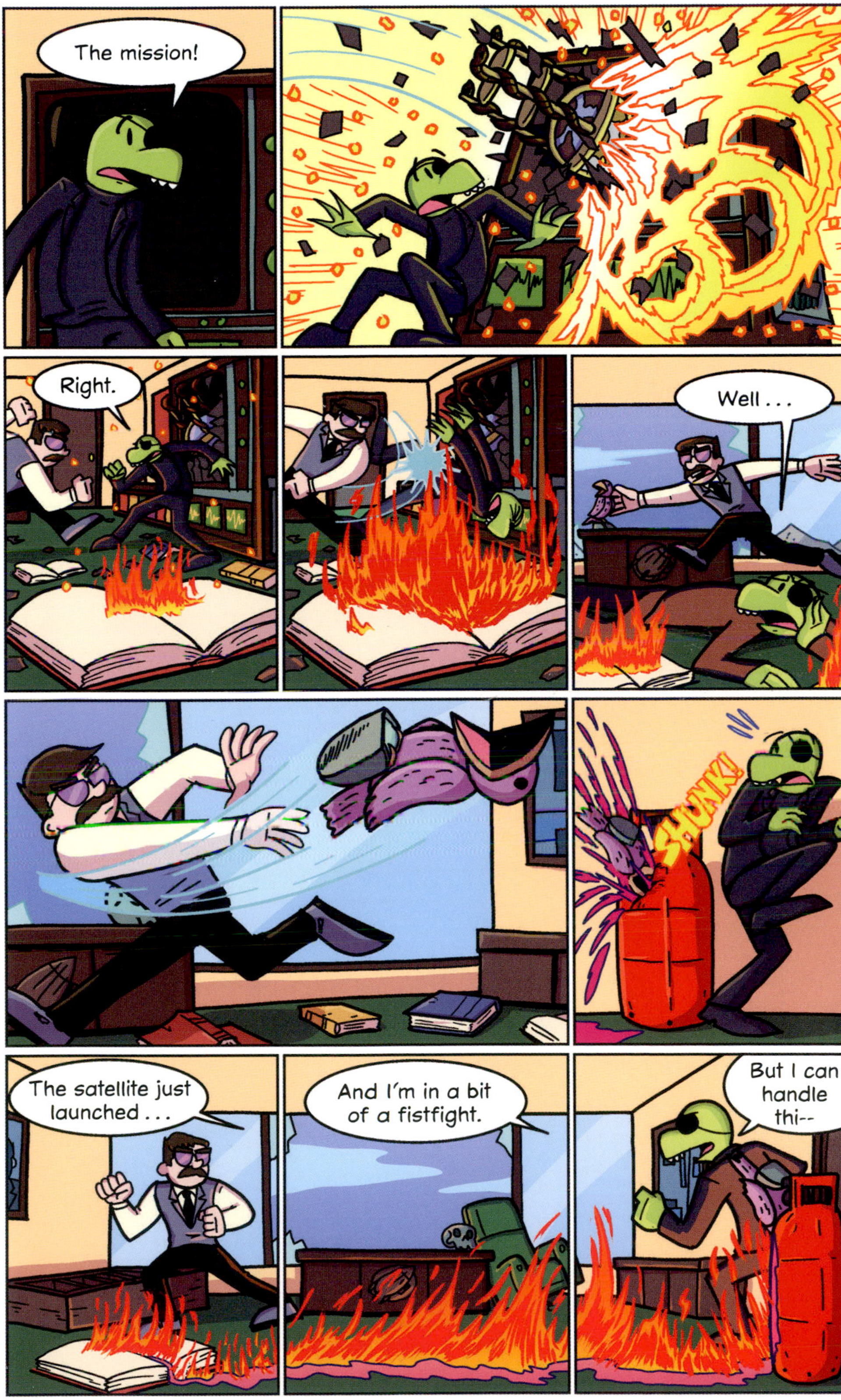

The mission!
Right.
Well . . .
SHUNK!
The satellite just launched . . .
And I'm in a bit of a fistfight.
But I can handle thi--

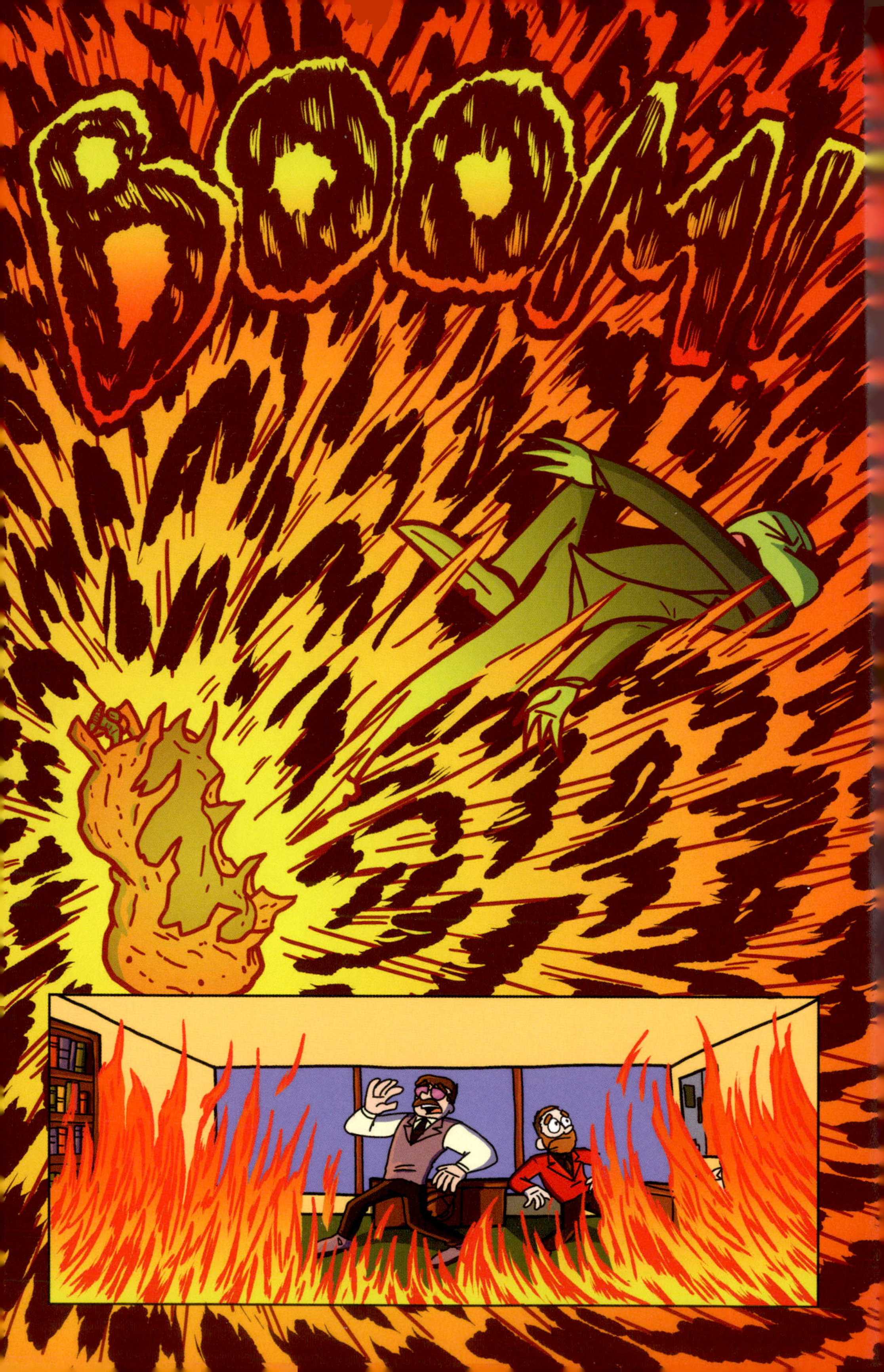
BOOM!!

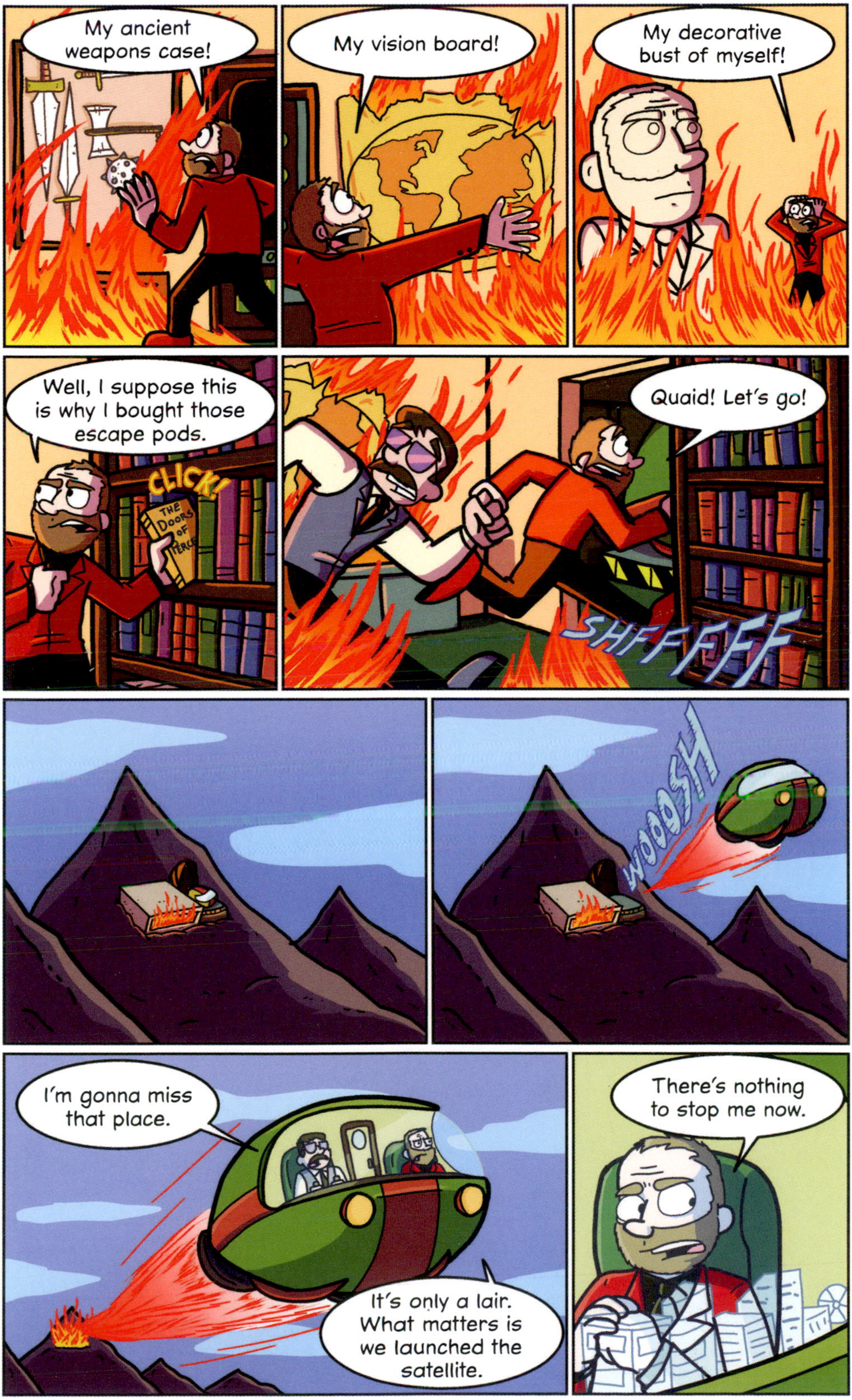
My ancient weapons case!
My vision board!
My decorative bust of myself!
Well, I suppose this is why I bought those escape pods.
CLICK!
THE DOORS OF PERCE
Quaid! Let's go!
SHFFFFFF
WOOOSH
I'm gonna miss that place.
It's only a lair. What matters is we launched the satellite.
There's nothing to stop me now.

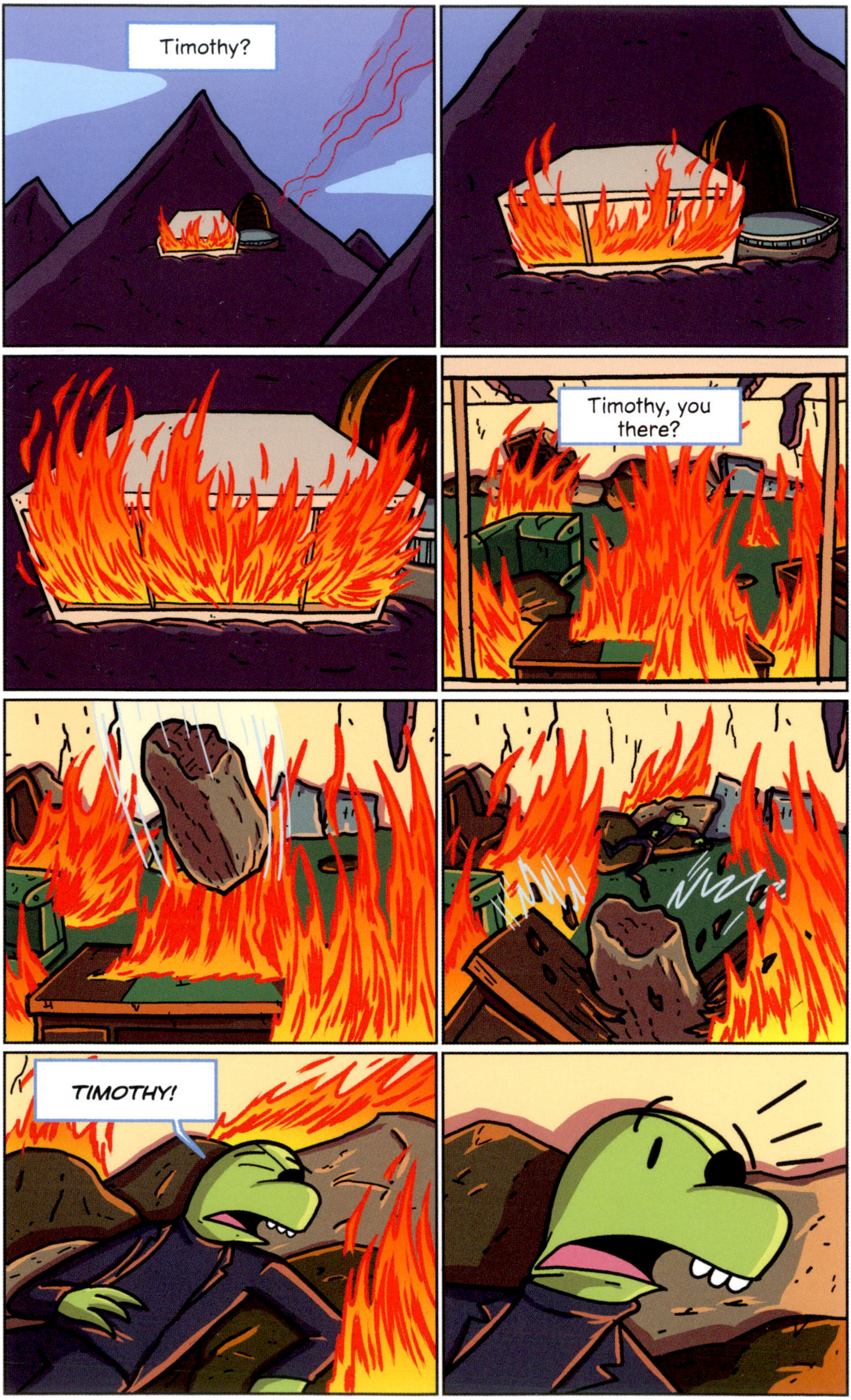
Timothy?
Timothy, you there?
TIMOTHY!

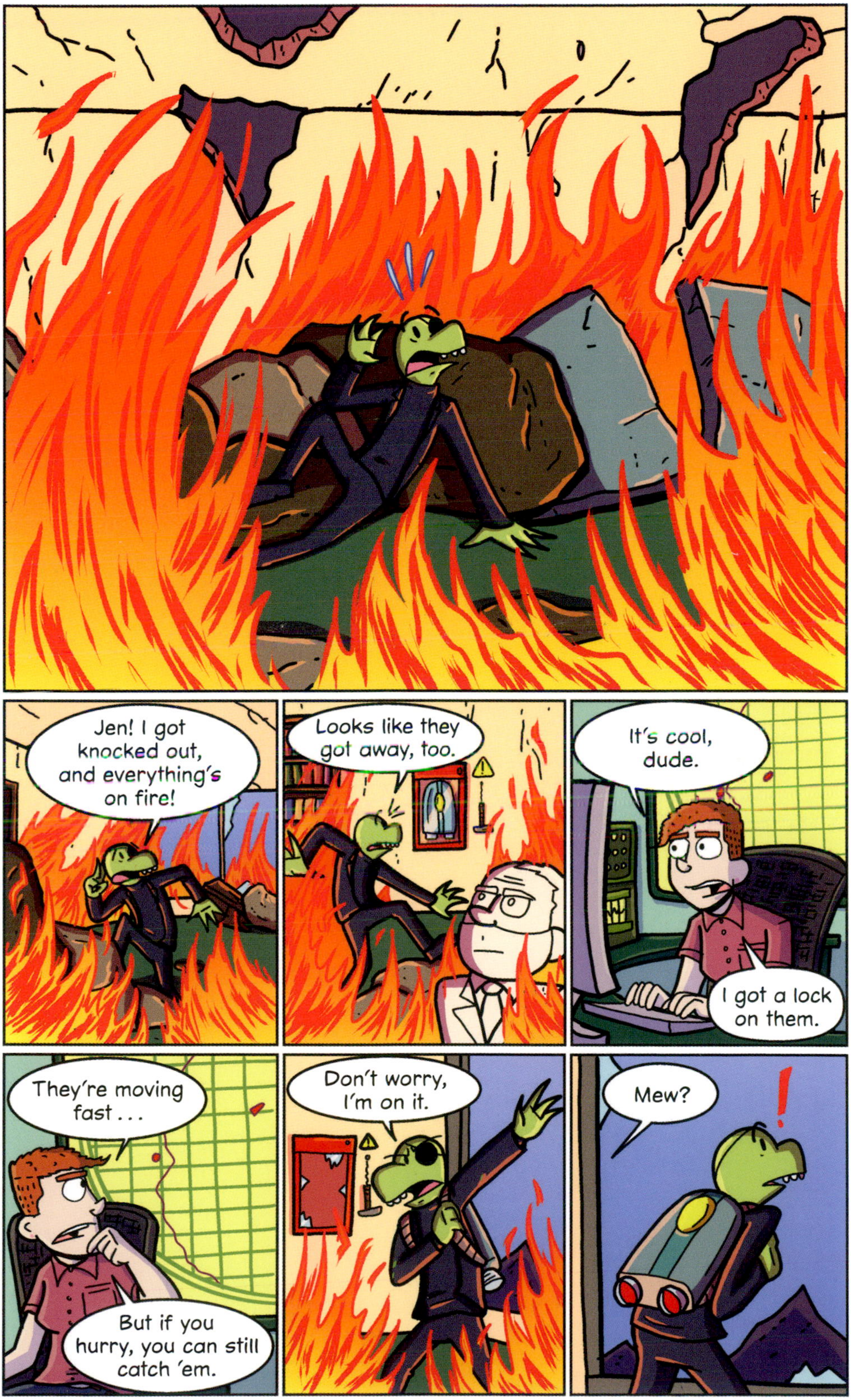
Jen! I got knocked out, and everything's on fire!
Looks like they got away, too.
It's cool, dude.
I got a lock on them.
They're moving fast . . .
But if you hurry, you can still catch 'em.
Don't worry, I'm on it.
Mew?

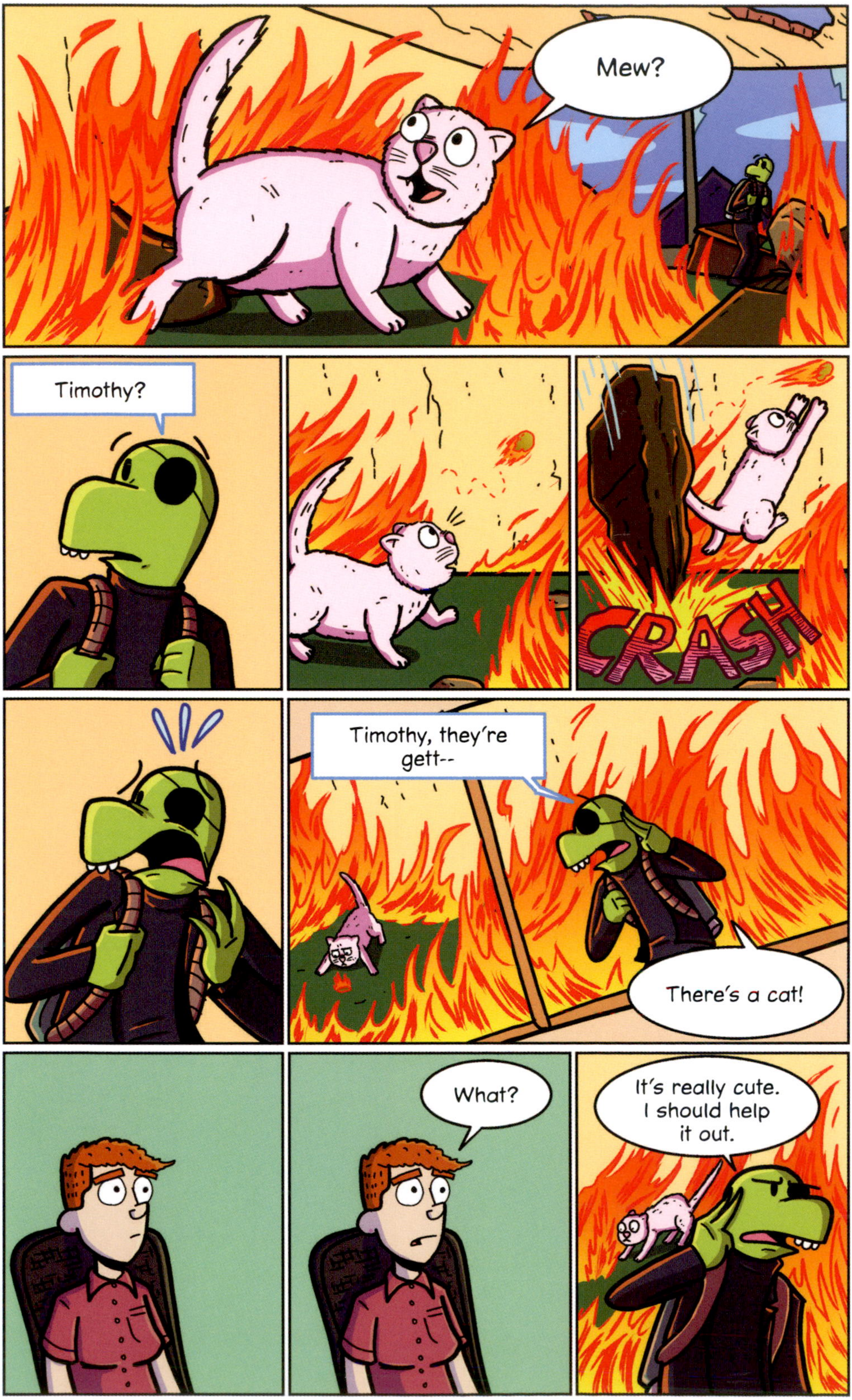

Mew?
Timothy?
CRASH
Timothy, they're gett--
There's a cat!
What?
It's really cute. I should help it out.

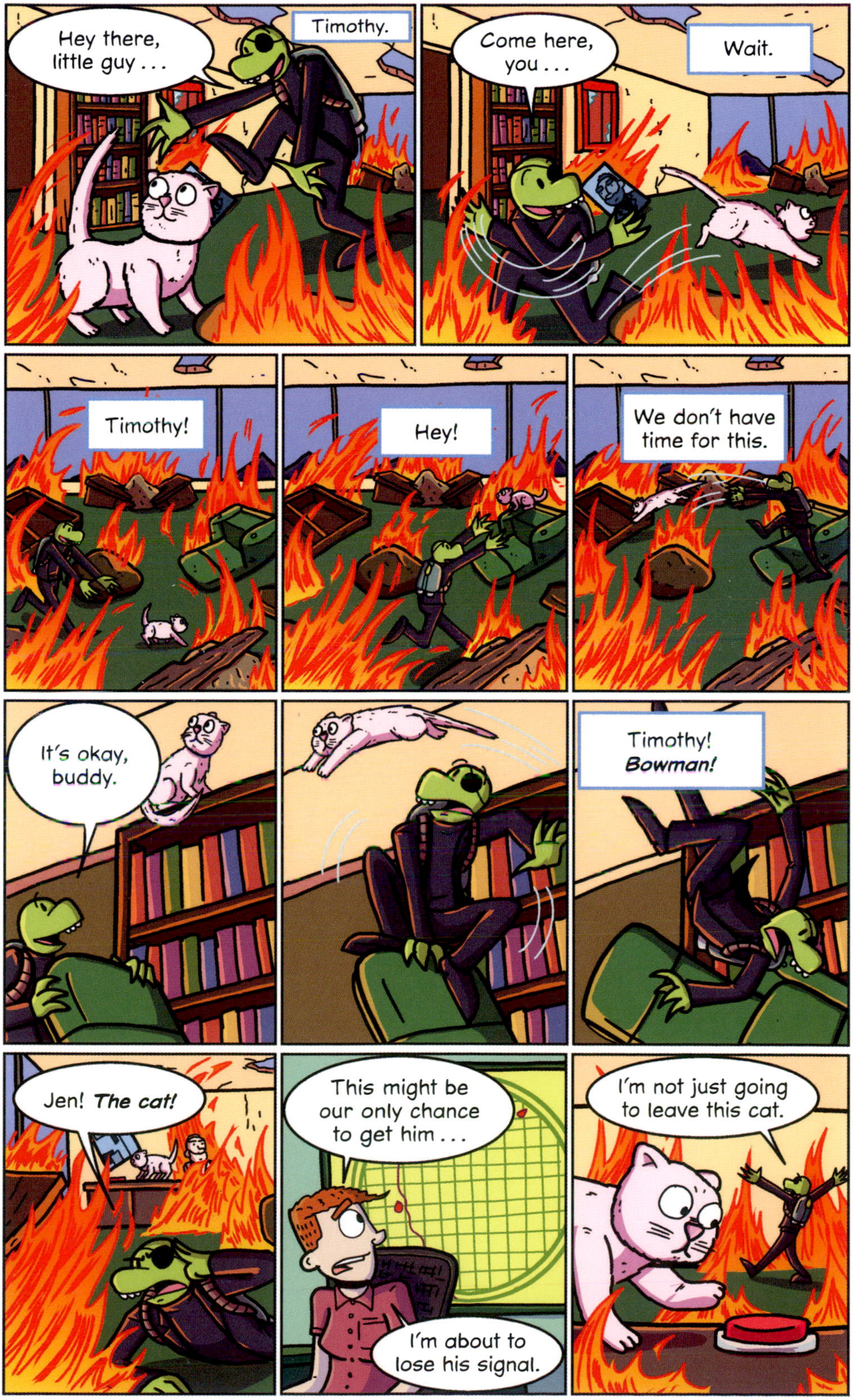
Hey there, little guy . . .
Timothy.
Come here, you . . .
Wait.
Timothy!
Hey!
We don't have time for this.
It's okay, buddy.
Timothy! **Bowman!**
Jen! ***The cat!***
This might be our only chance to get him . . .
I'm about to lose his signal.
I'm not just going to leave this cat.

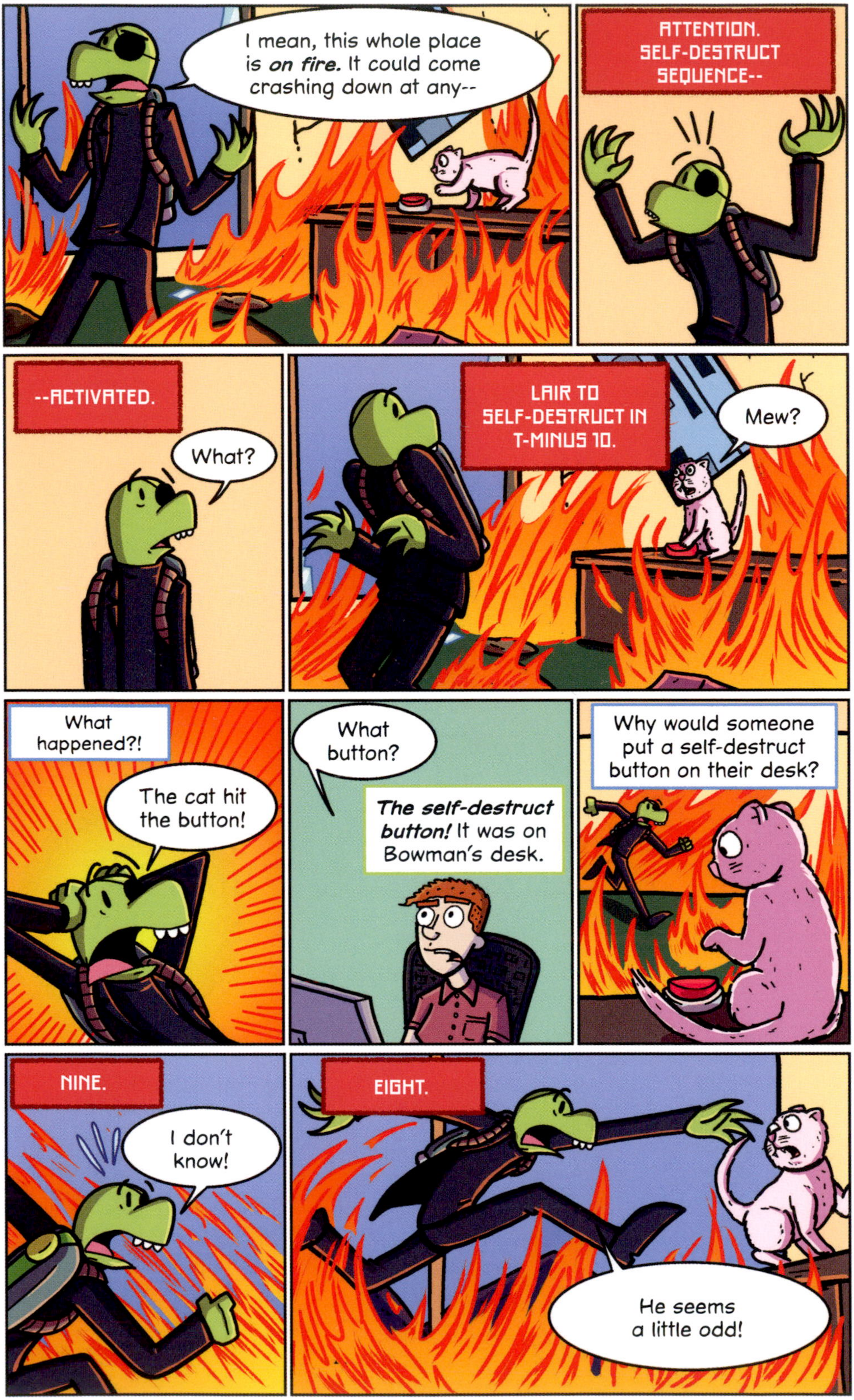

I mean, this whole place is *on fire.* It could come crashing down at any--
ATTENTION. SELF-DESTRUCT SEQUENCE--
--ACTIVATED.
What?
LAIR TO SELF-DESTRUCT IN T-MINUS 10.
Mew?
What happened?!
The cat hit the button!
What button?
The self-destruct button! It was on Bowman's desk.
Why would someone put a self-destruct button on their desk?
NINE.
I don't know!
EIGHT.
He seems a little odd!

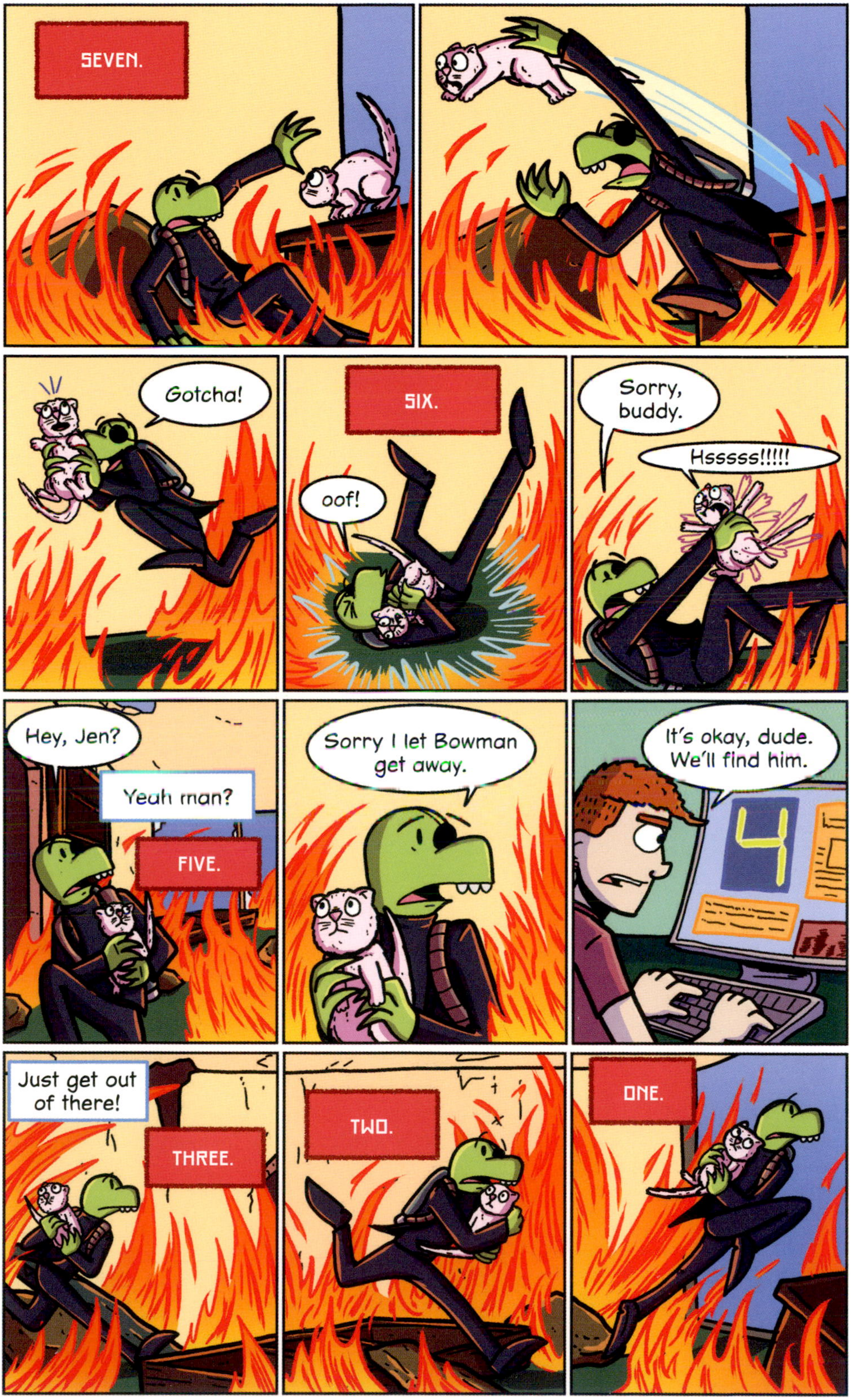
SEVEN.
Gotcha!
SIX.
oof!
Sorry, buddy.
Hsssss!!!!!
Hey, Jen?
Yeah man?
FIVE.
Sorry I let Bowman get away.
It's okay, dude. We'll find him.
4
Just get out of there!
THREE.
TWO.
ONE.

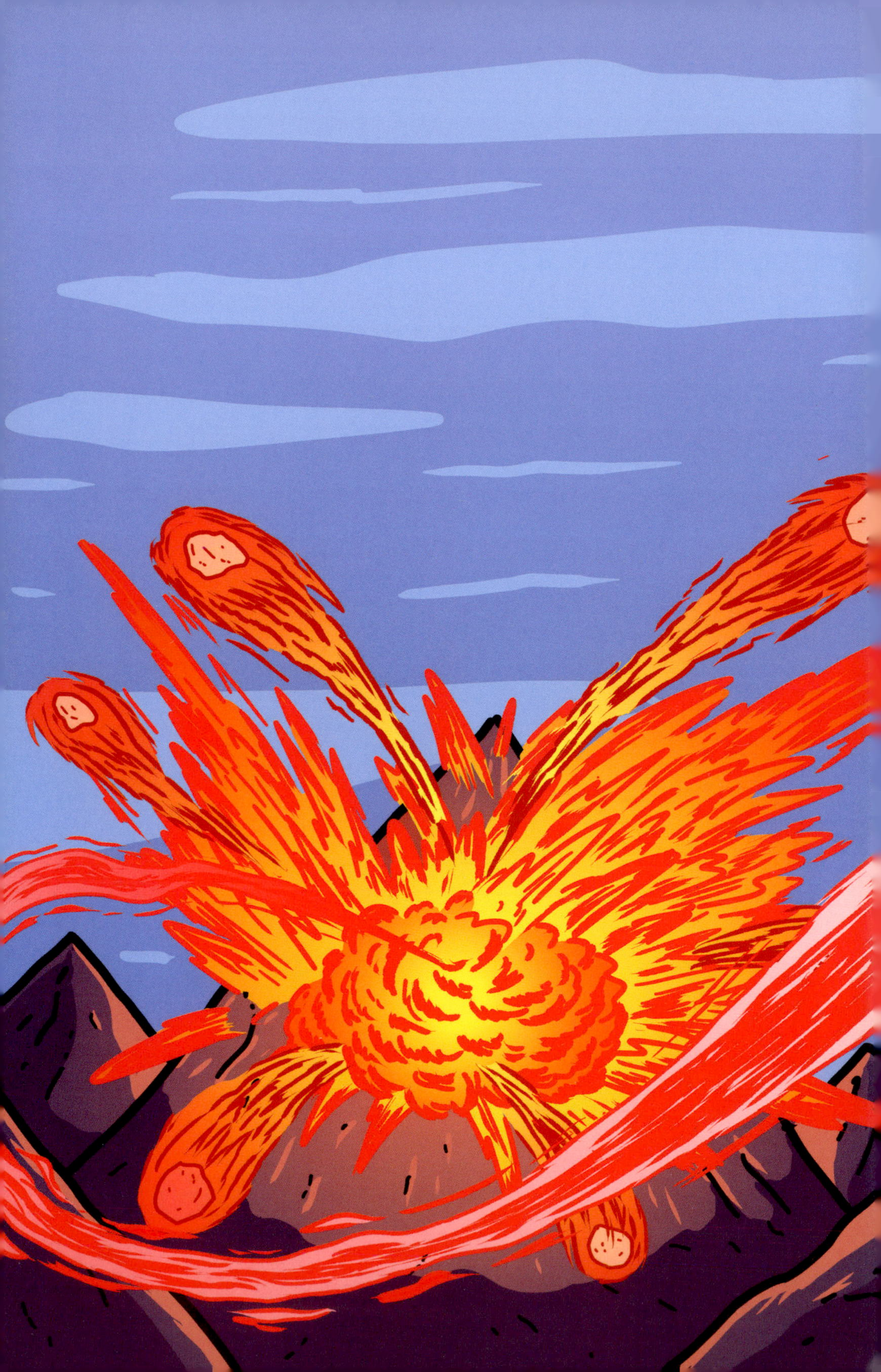

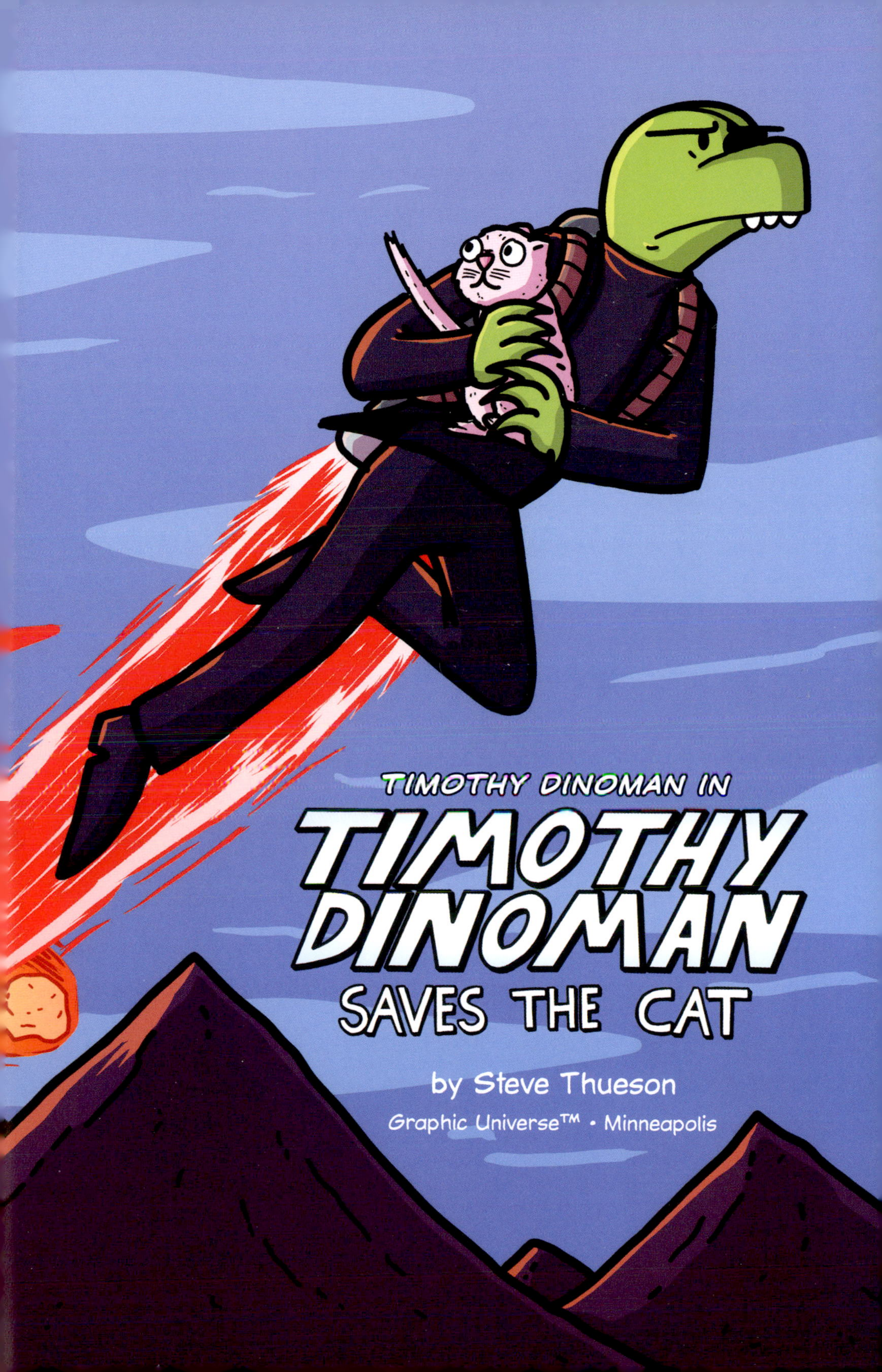

TIMOTHY DINOMAN IN

TIMOTHY DINOMAN SAVES THE CAT

by Steve Thueson

Graphic Universe™ • Minneapolis

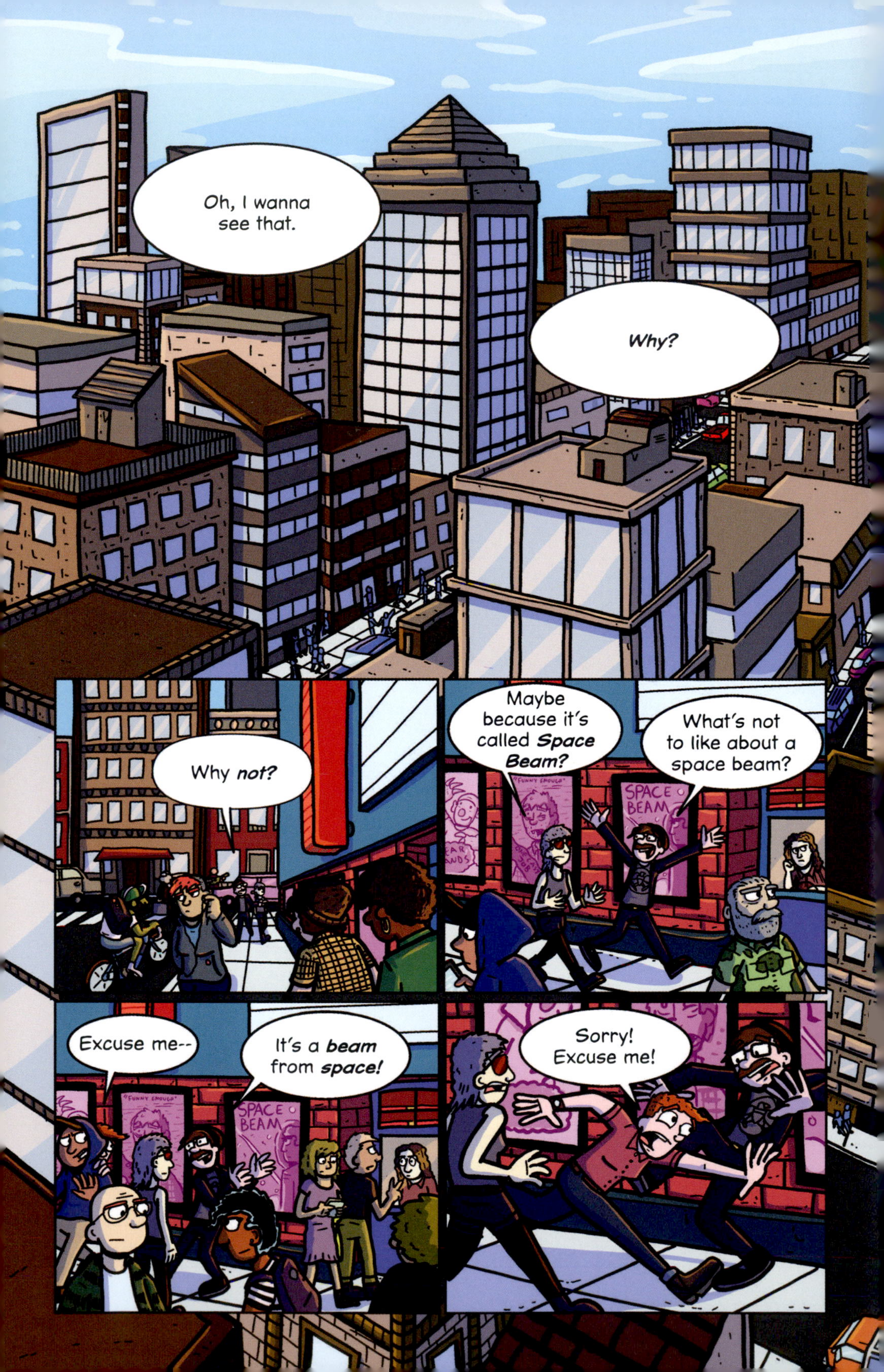
Oh, I wanna see that.
Why?
Why *not?*
Maybe because it's called *Space Beam?*
What's not to like about a space beam?
"FUNNY ENOUGH"
SPACE BEAM
Excuse me--
It's a *beam* from *space!*
"FUNNY ENOUGH"
SPACE BEAM
Sorry! Excuse me!

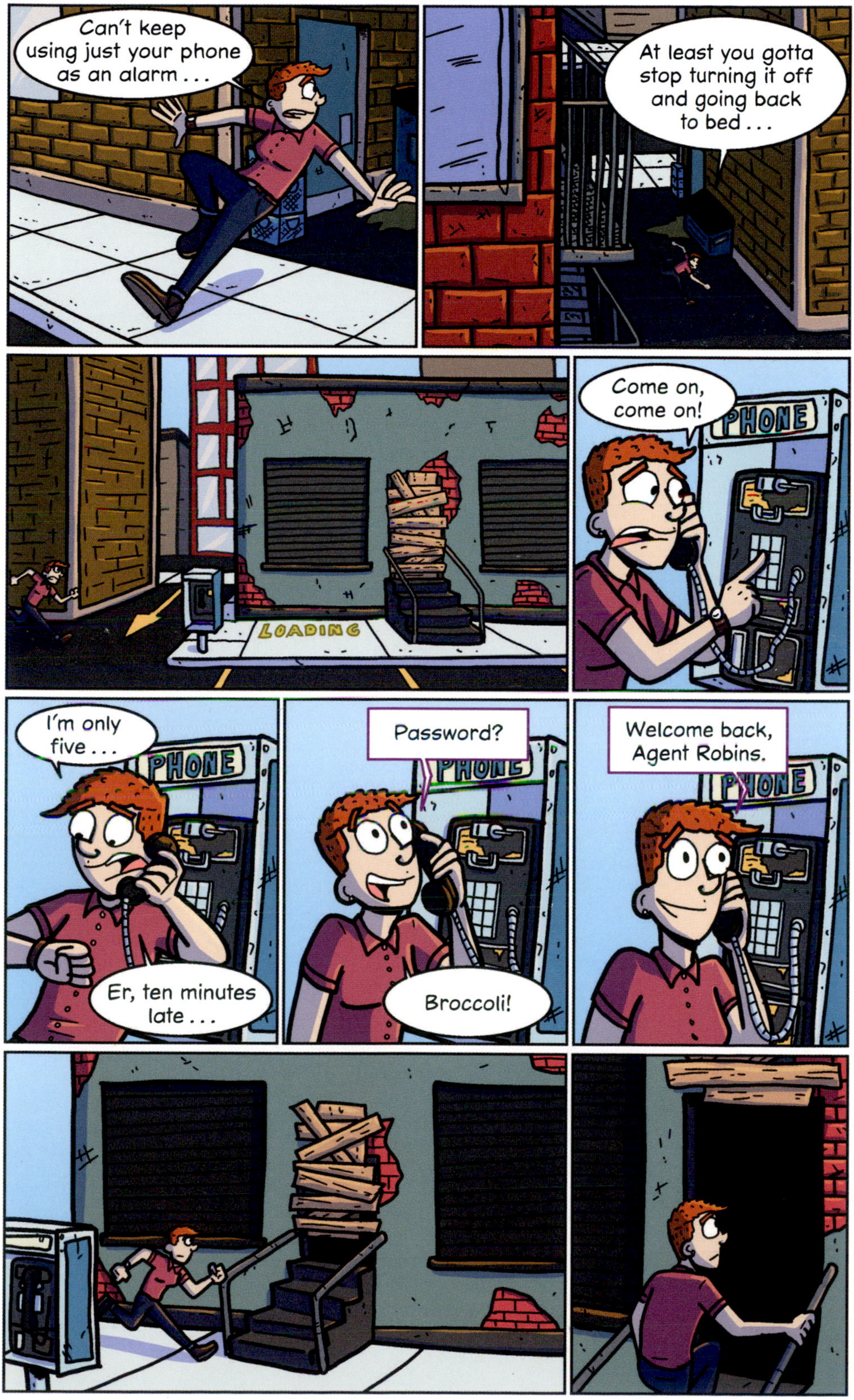
Can't keep using just your phone as an alarm . . .
At least you gotta stop turning it off and going back to bed . . .
LOADING
Come on, come on!
PHONE
I'm only five . . .
Er, ten minutes late . . .
Password?
Broccoli!
Welcome back, Agent Robins.

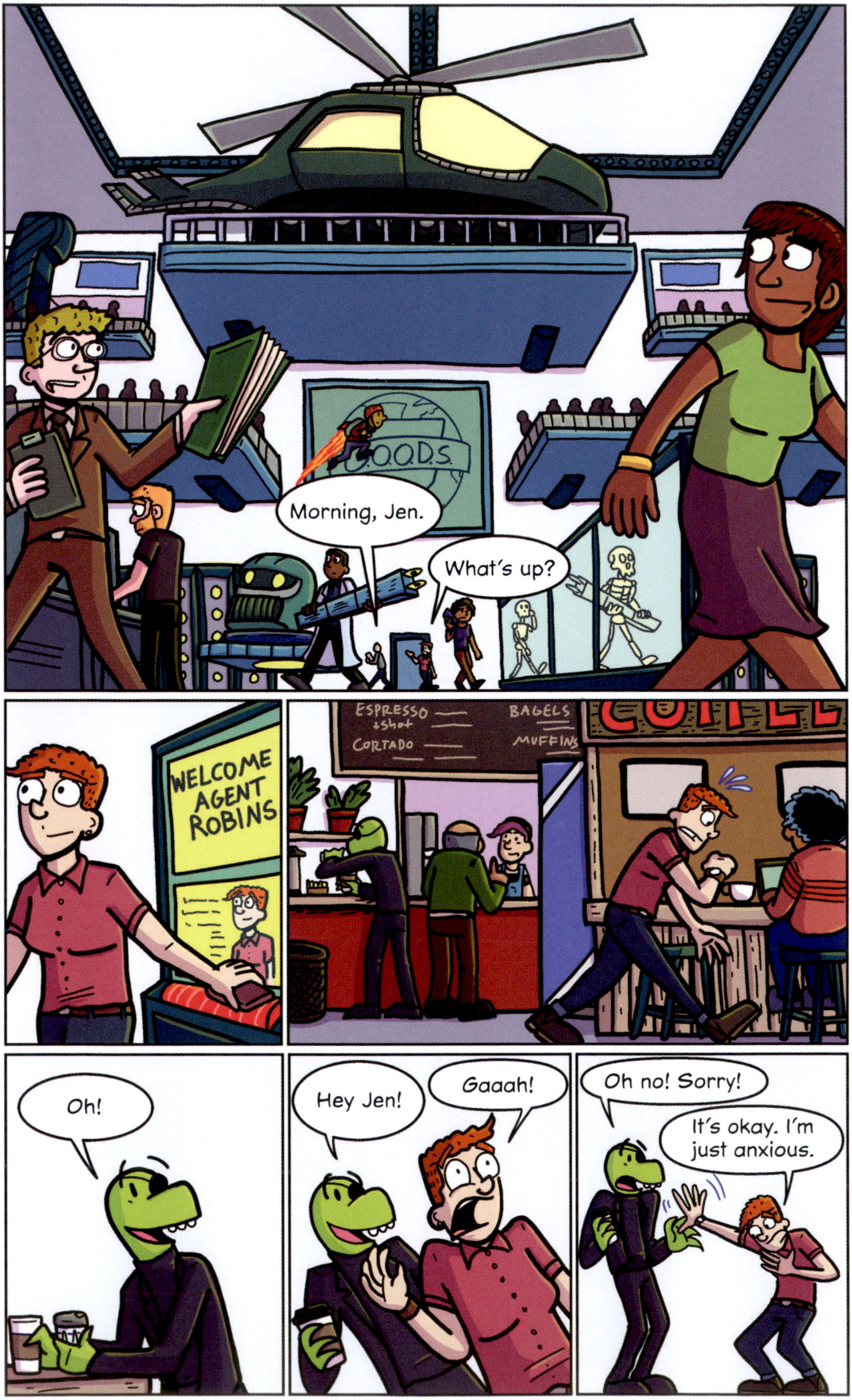
G.O.O.D.S.
Morning, Jen.
What's up?
ESPRESSO +shot
CORTADO
BAGELS
MUFFINS
WELCOME AGENT ROBINS
Oh!
Hey Jen!
Gaaah!
Oh no! Sorry!
It's okay. I'm just anxious.

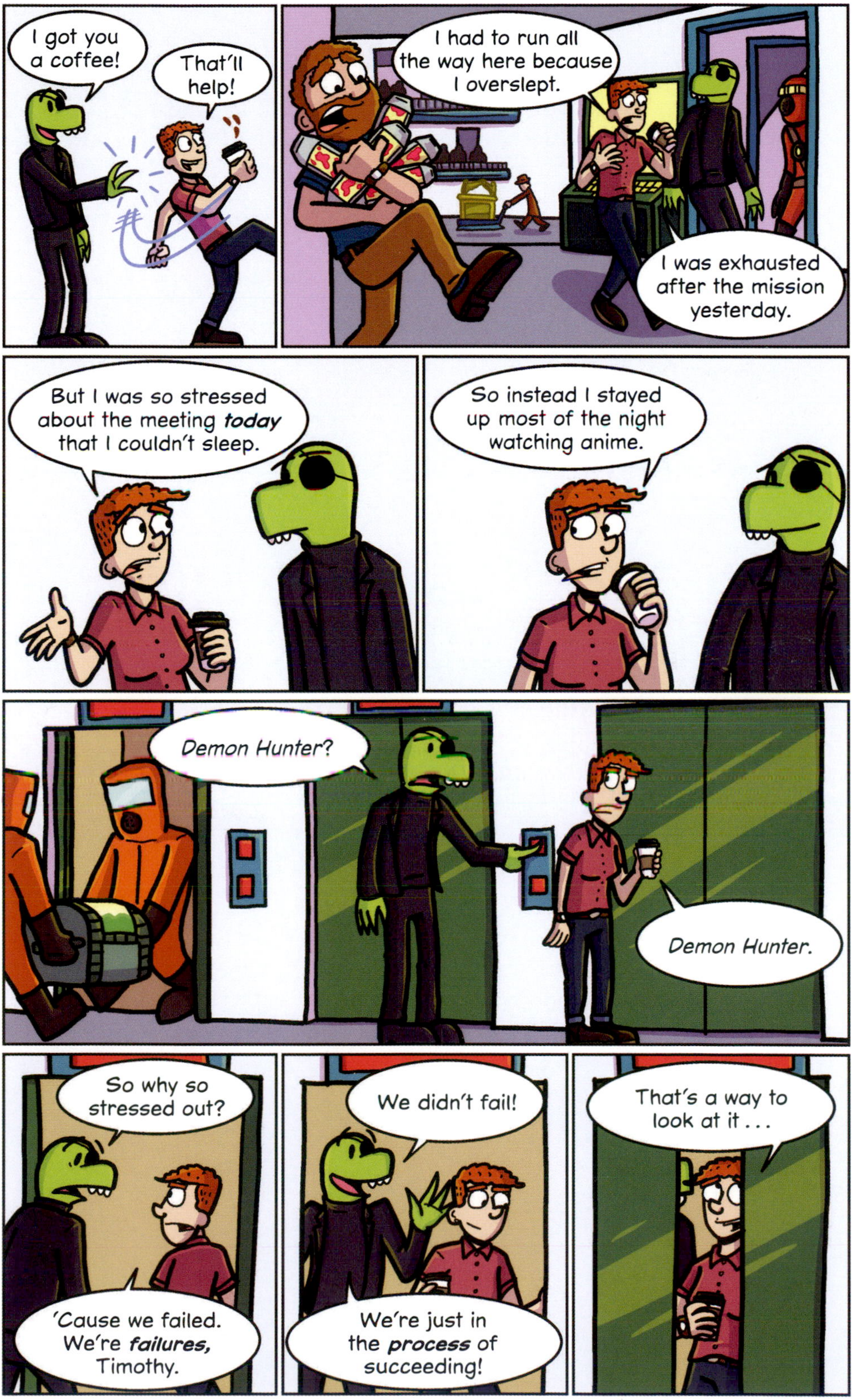
I got you a coffee!
That'll help!
I had to run all the way here because I overslept.
I was exhausted after the mission yesterday.
But I was so stressed about the meeting *today* that I couldn't sleep.
So instead I stayed up most of the night watching anime.
Demon Hunter?
Demon Hunter.
So why so stressed out?
'Cause we failed. We're ***failures,*** Timothy.
We didn't fail!
We're just in the ***process*** of succeeding!
That's a way to look at it . . .

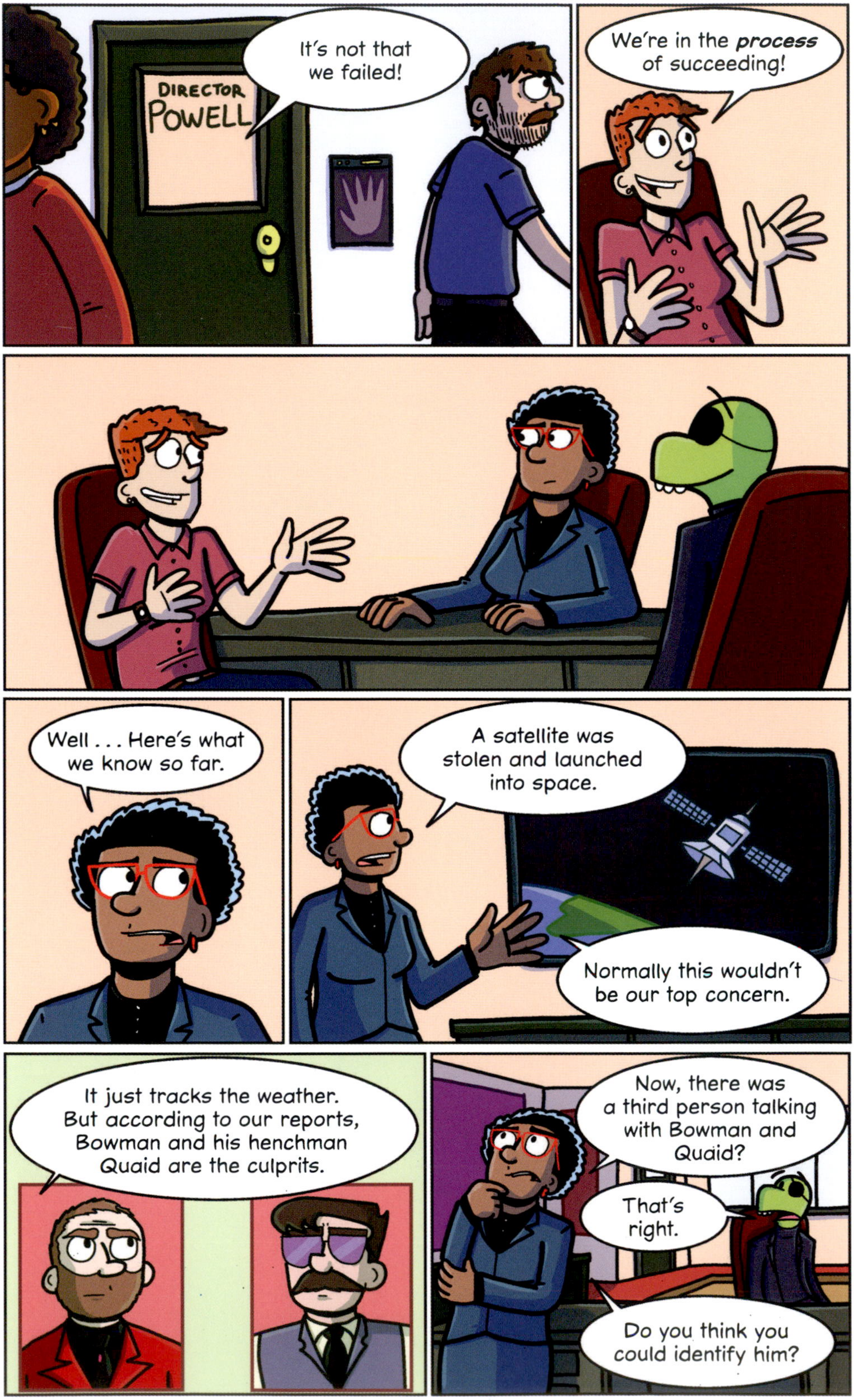

DIRECTOR POWELL
It's not that we failed!
We're in the *process* of succeeding!
Well . . . Here's what we know so far.
A satellite was stolen and launched into space.
Normally this wouldn't be our top concern.
It just tracks the weather. But according to our reports, Bowman and his henchman Quaid are the culprits.
Now, there was a third person talking with Bowman and Quaid?
That's right.
Do you think you could identify him?

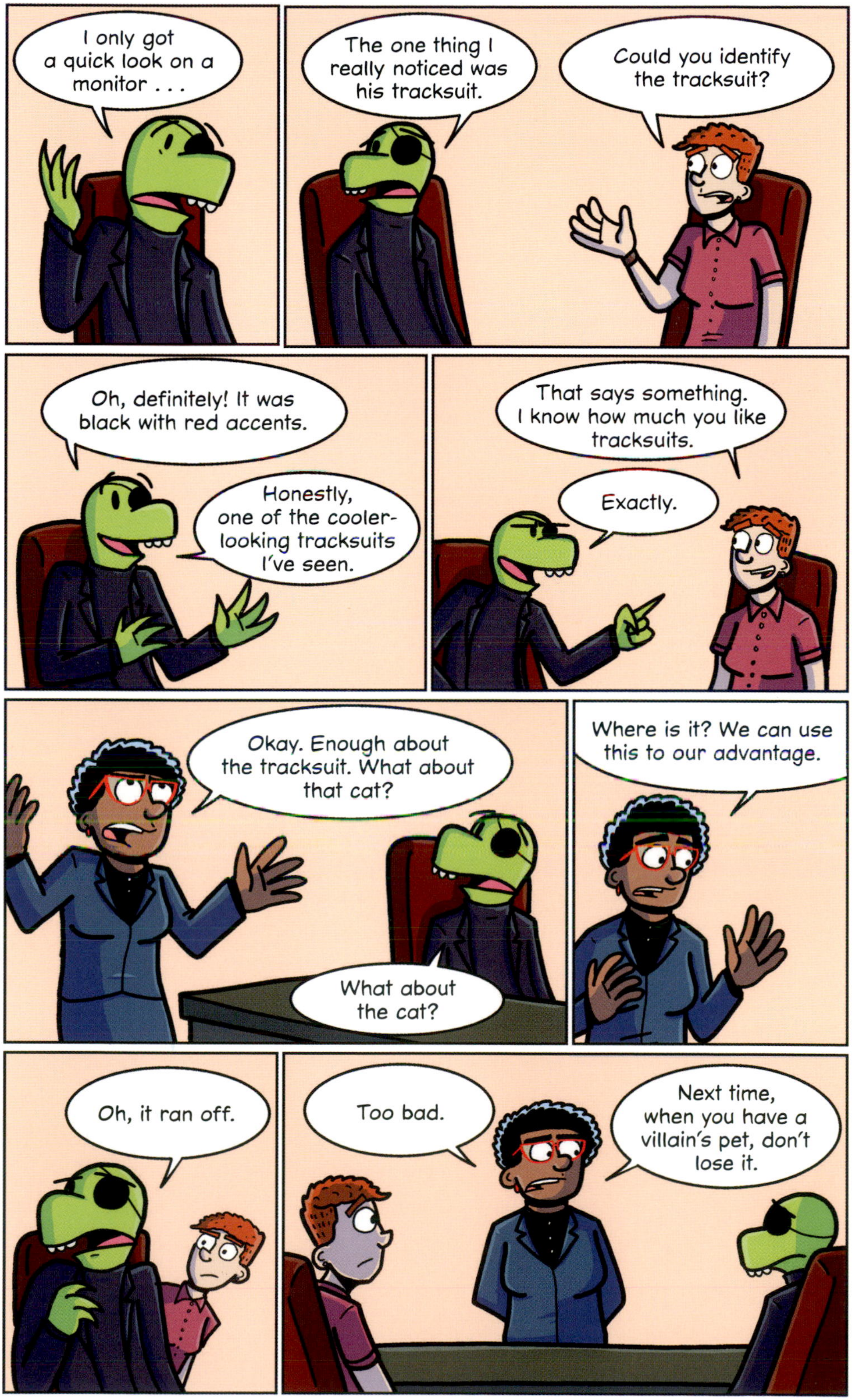
I only got a quick look on a monitor . . .
The one thing I really noticed was his tracksuit.
Could you identify the tracksuit?
Oh, definitely! It was black with red accents.
Honestly, one of the cooler-looking tracksuits I've seen.
That says something. I know how much you like tracksuits.
Exactly.
Okay. Enough about the tracksuit. What about that cat?
What about the cat?
Where is it? We can use this to our advantage.
Oh, it ran off.
Too bad.
Next time, when you have a villain's pet, don't lose it.

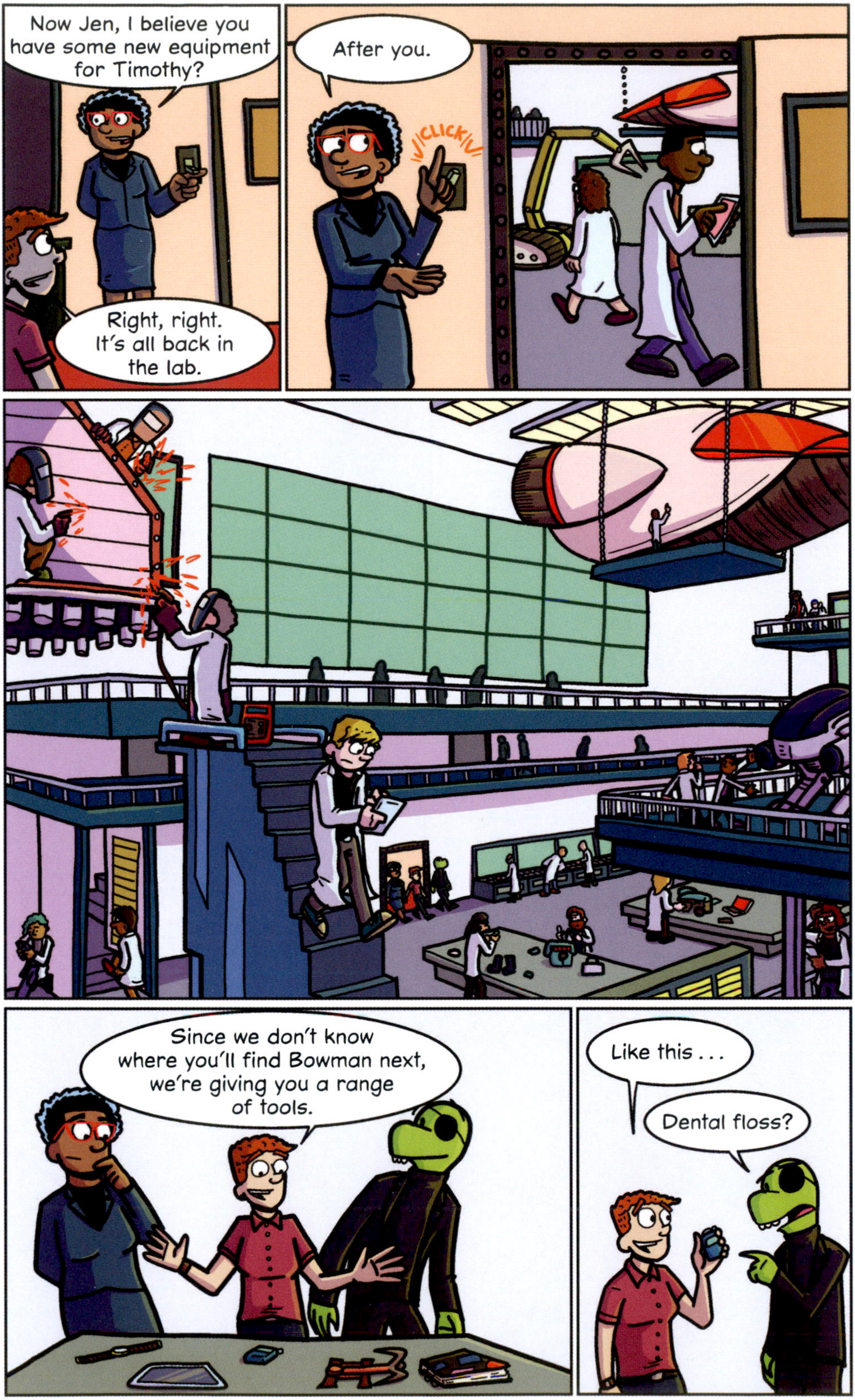
Now Jen, I believe you have some new equipment for Timothy?
Right, right. It's all back in the lab.
After you.
CLICK
Since we don't know where you'll find Bowman next, we're giving you a range of tools.
Like this . . .
Dental floss?

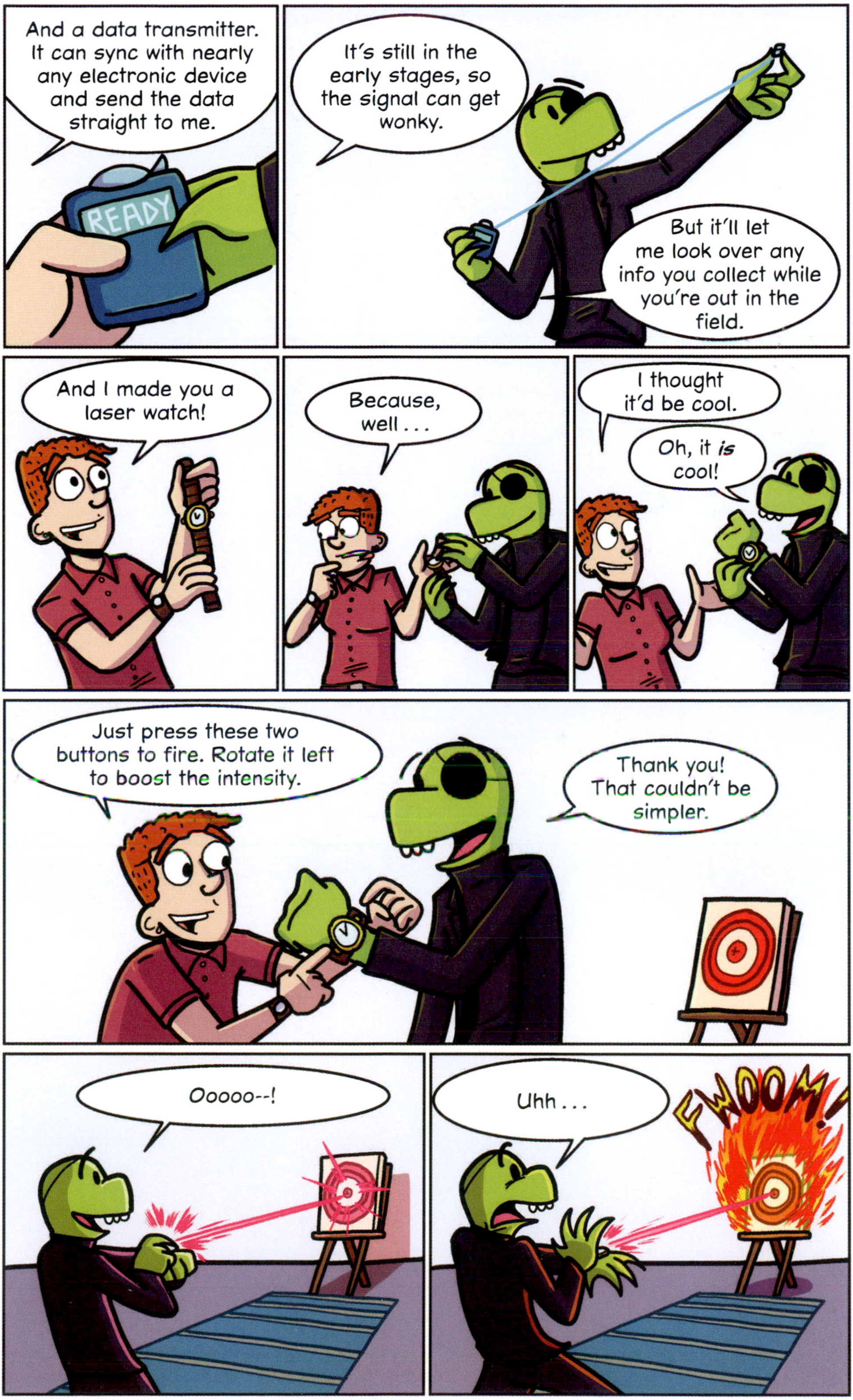

And a data transmitter. It can sync with nearly any electronic device and send the data straight to me.
READY
It's still in the early stages, so the signal can get wonky.
But it'll let me look over any info you collect while you're out in the field.
And I made you a laser watch!
Because, well . . .
I thought it'd be cool.
Oh, it *is* cool!
Just press these two buttons to fire. Rotate it left to boost the intensity.
Thank you! That couldn't be simpler.
Ooooo--!
Uhh . . .
FWOOM!

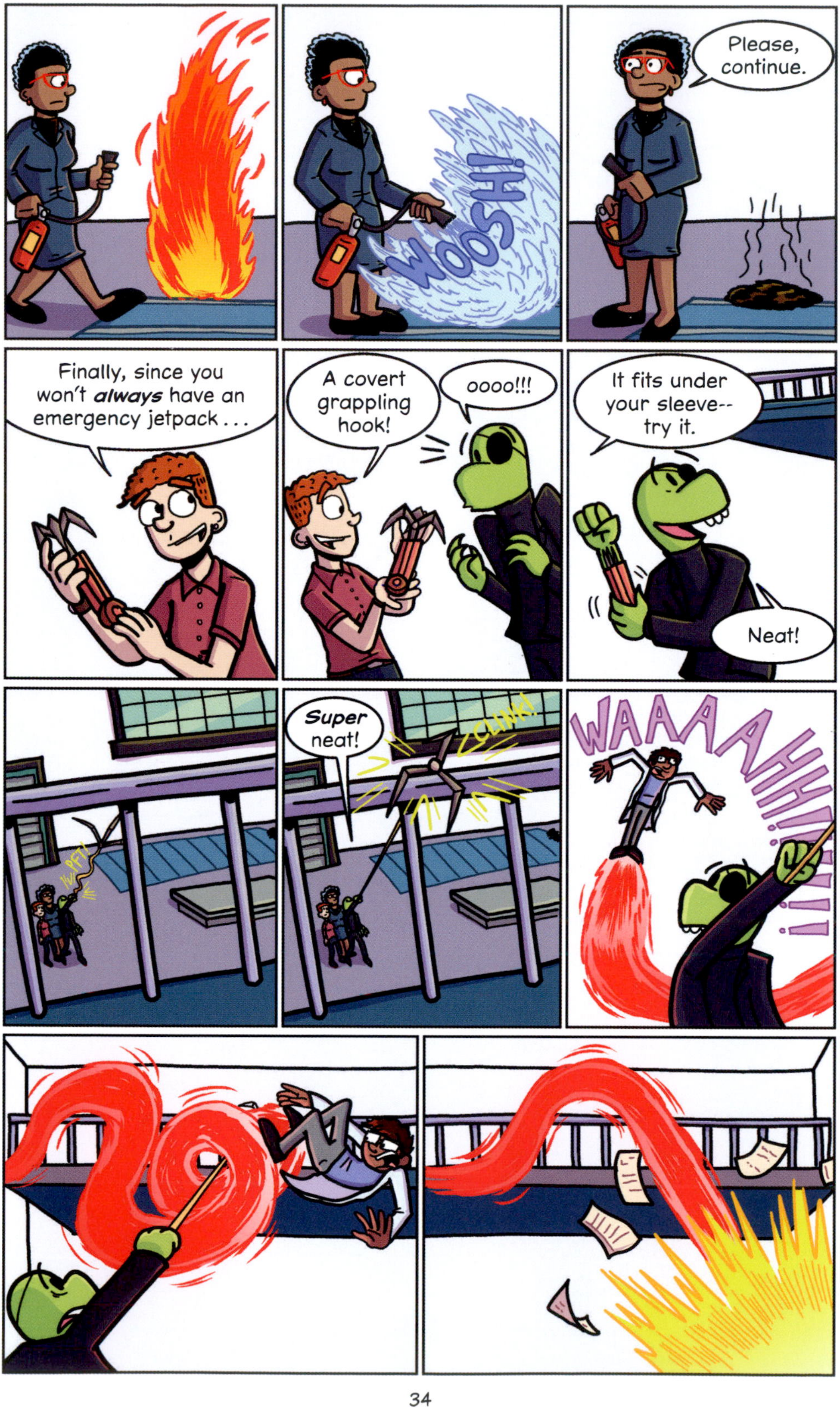
WOOSH!
Please, continue.
Finally, since you won't ***always*** have an emergency jetpack . . .
A covert grappling hook!
oooo!!!
It fits under your sleeve-- try it.
Neat!
FFT!
Super neat!
CLINK!
WAAAAHHH!!!!!!!

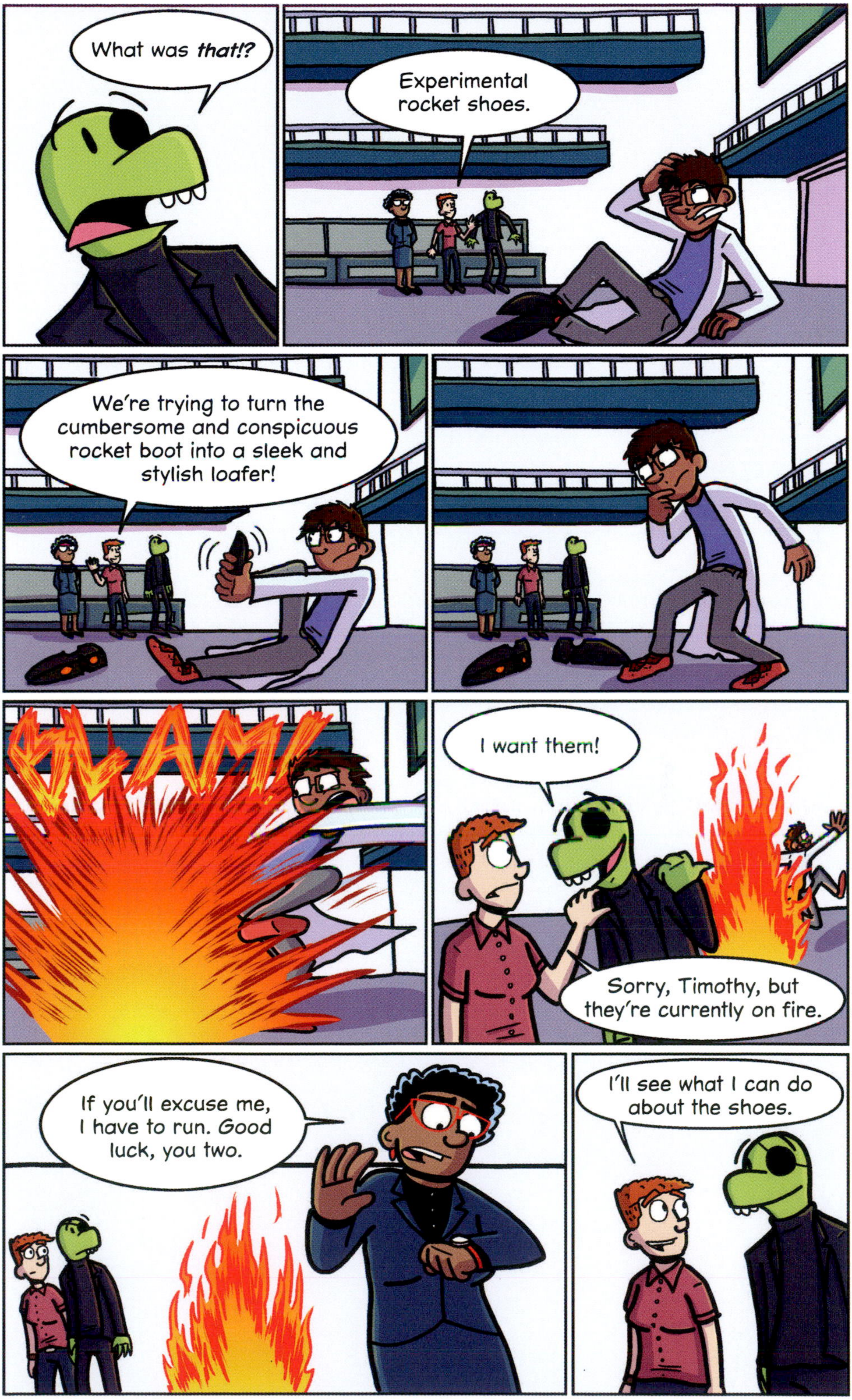
What was *that!?*
Experimental rocket shoes.
We're trying to turn the cumbersome and conspicuous rocket boot into a sleek and stylish loafer!
BLAM!
I want them!
Sorry, Timothy, but they're currently on fire.
If you'll excuse me, I have to run. Good luck, you two.
I'll see what I can do about the shoes.

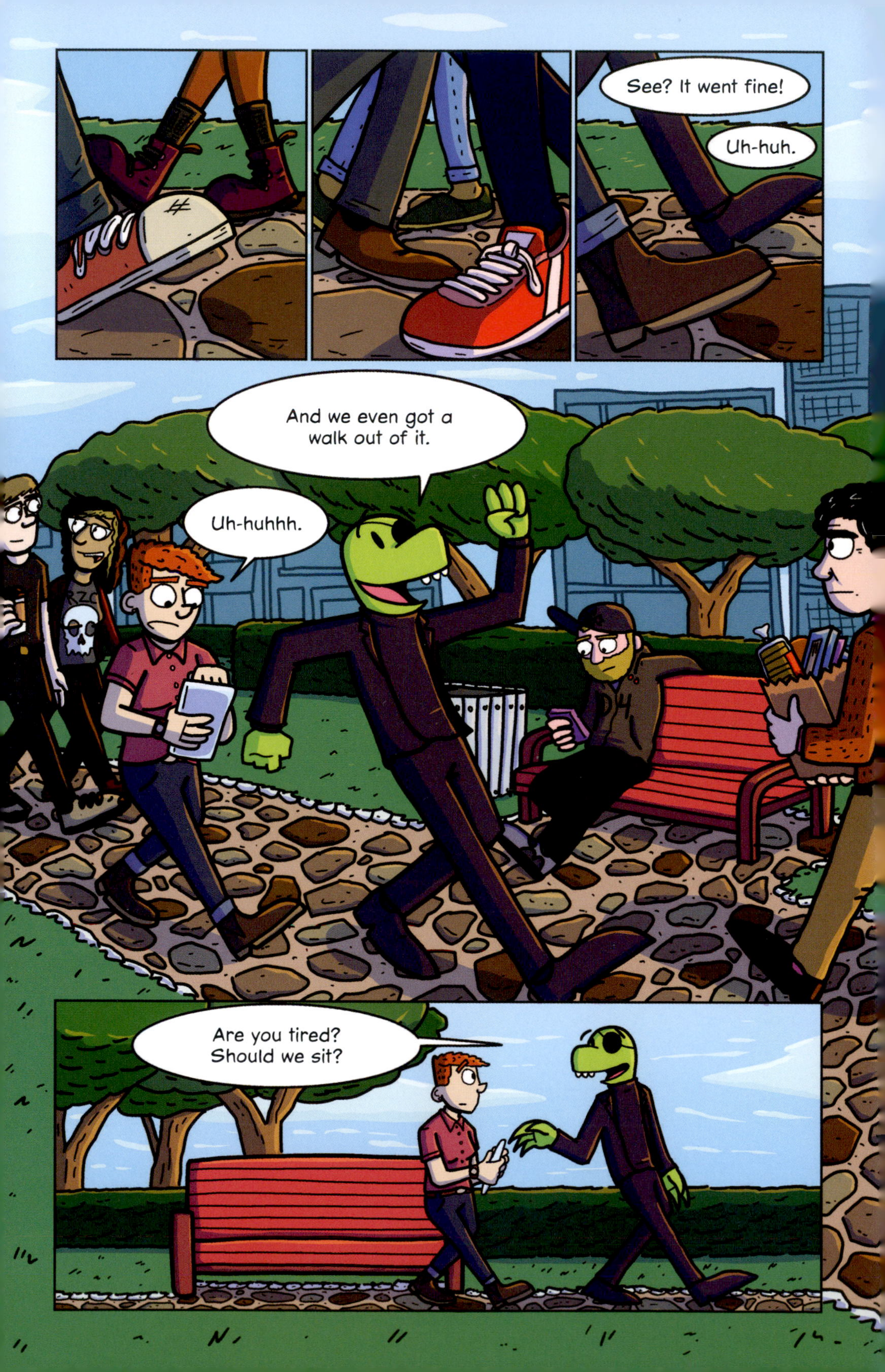
See? It went fine!
Uh-huh.
And we even got a walk out of it.
Uh-huhhh.
Are you tired? Should we sit?

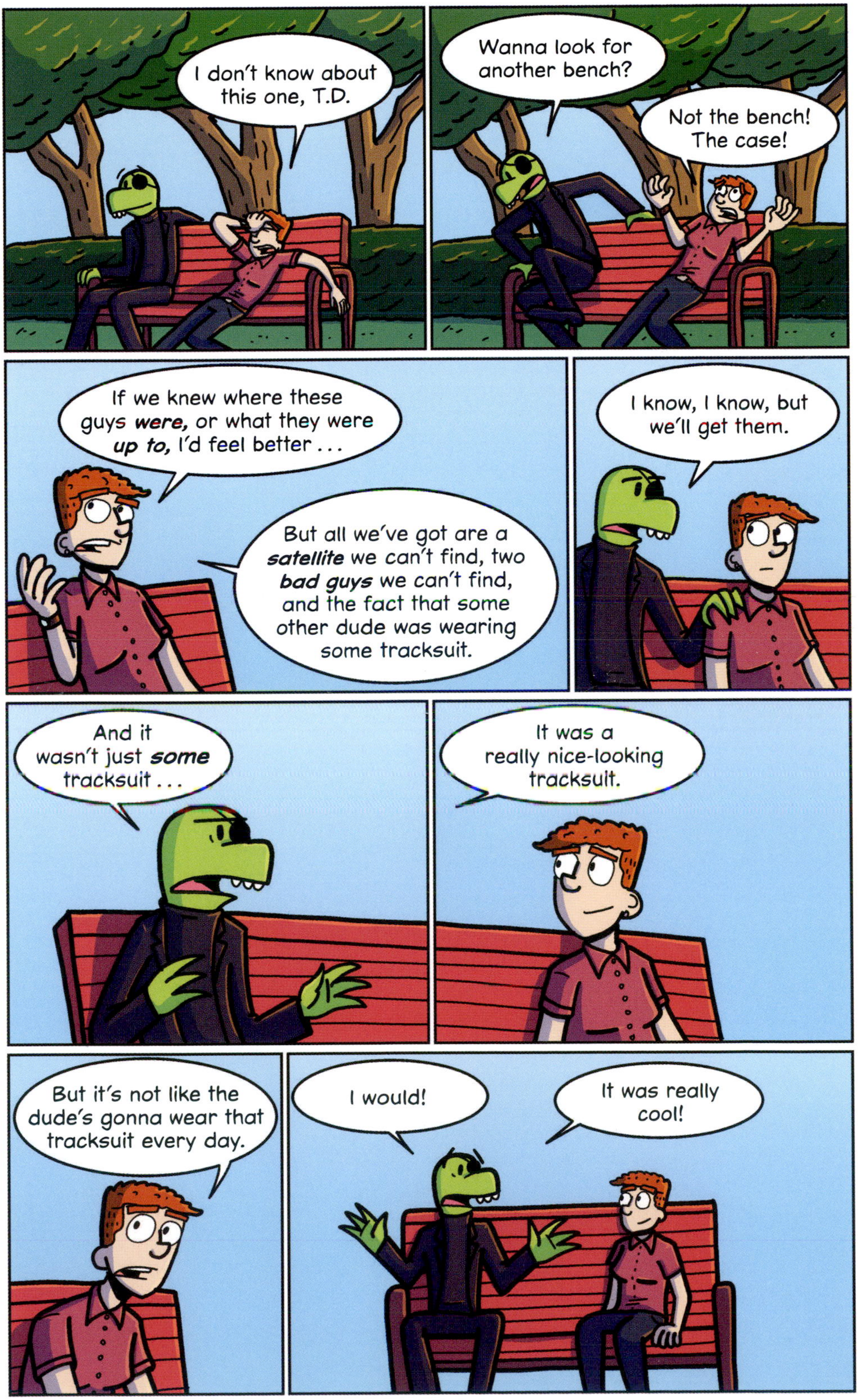
I don't know about this one, T.D.
Wanna look for another bench?
Not the bench! The case!
If we knew where these guys ***were,*** or what they were ***up to,*** I'd feel better . . .
But all we've got are a ***satellite*** we can't find, two ***bad guys*** we can't find, and the fact that some other dude was wearing some tracksuit.
I know, I know, but we'll get them.
And it wasn't just ***some*** tracksuit . . .
It was a really nice-looking tracksuit.
But it's not like the dude's gonna wear that tracksuit every day.
I would!
It was really cool!

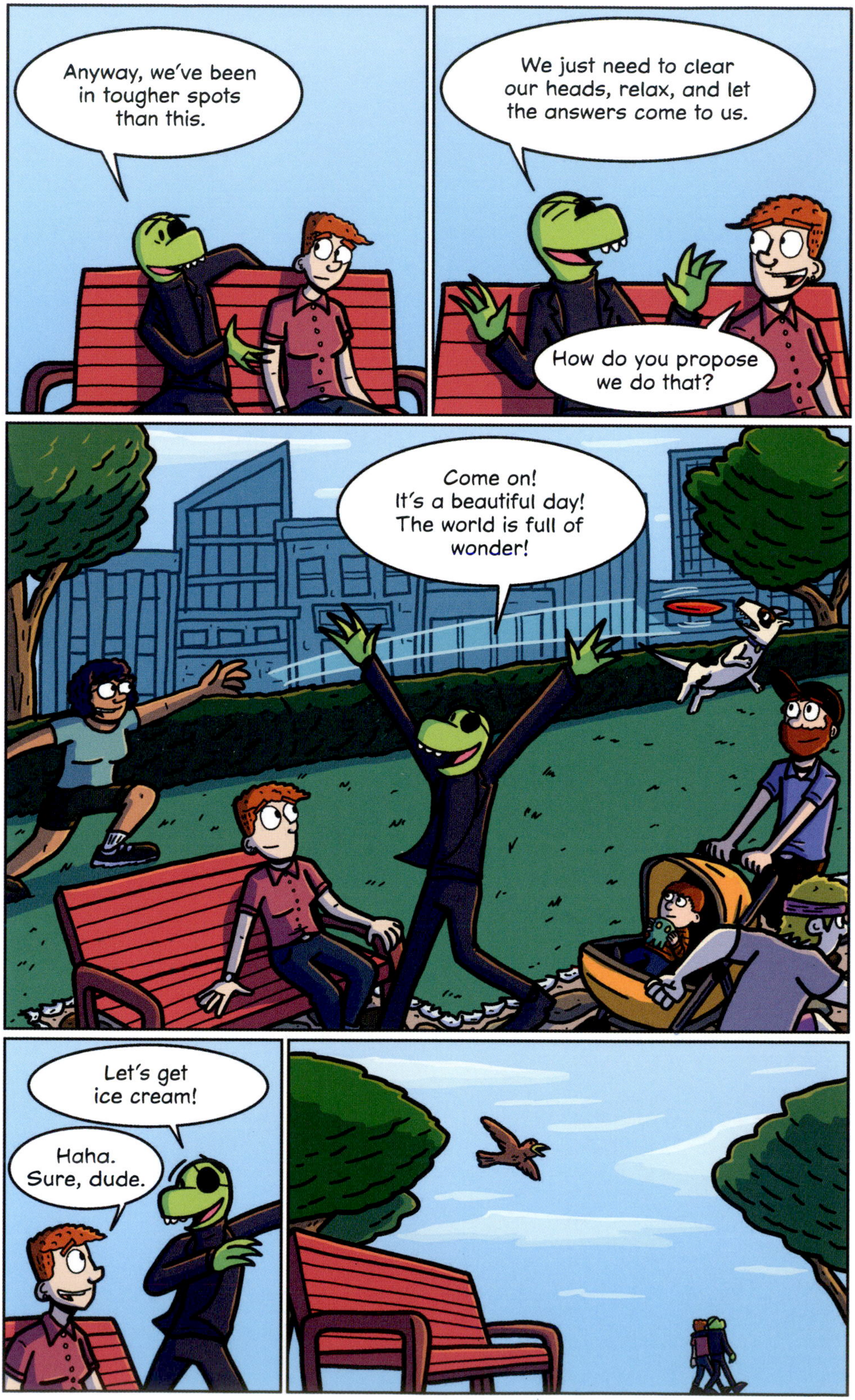
Anyway, we've been in tougher spots than this.
We just need to clear our heads, relax, and let the answers come to us.
How do you propose we do that?
Come on! It's a beautiful day! The world is full of wonder!
Let's get ice cream!
Haha. Sure, dude.

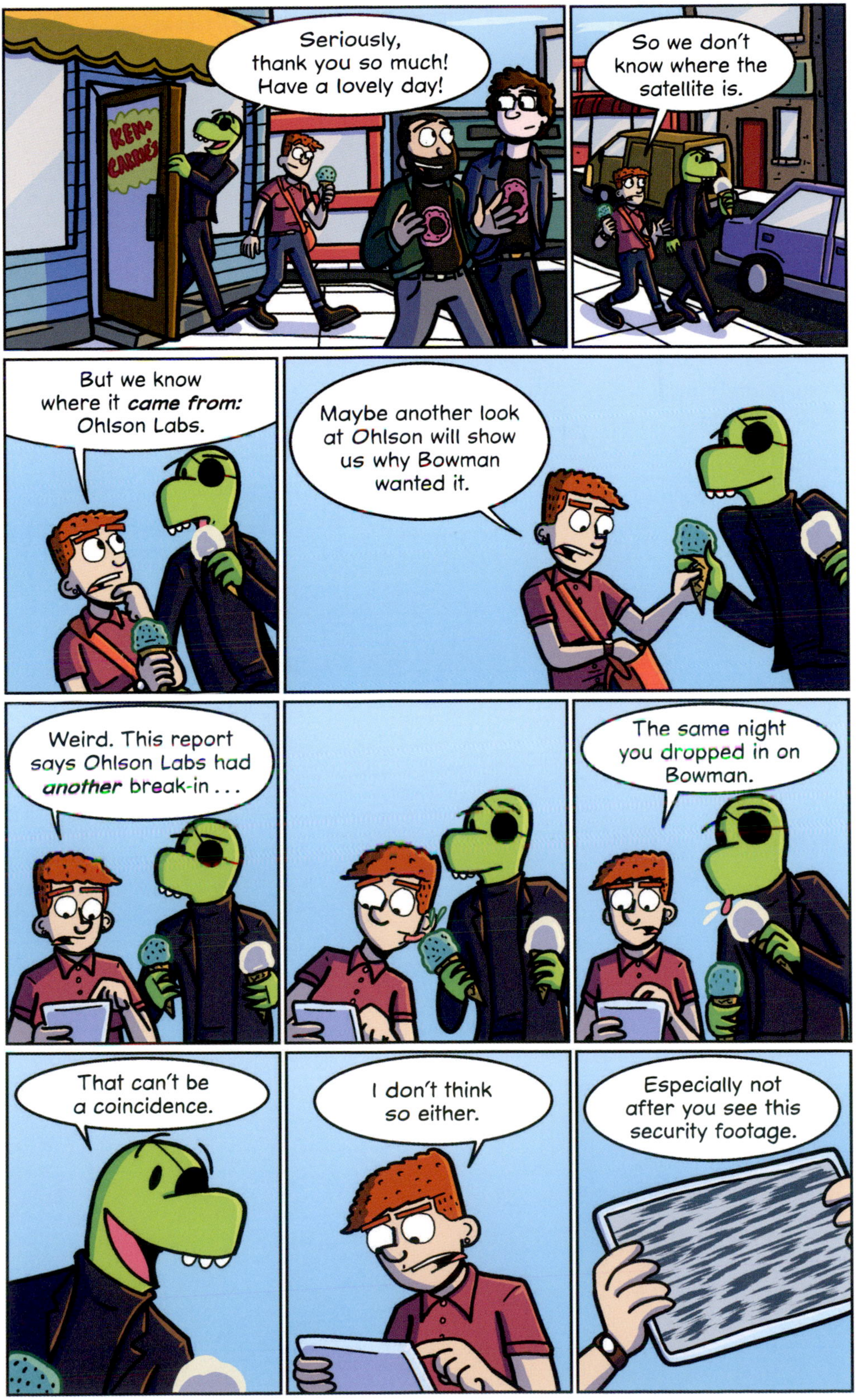
KEN+CARRIE'S
Seriously, thank you so much! Have a lovely day!
So we don't know where the satellite is.
But we know where it *came from:* Ohlson Labs.
Maybe another look at Ohlson will show us why Bowman wanted it.
Weird. This report says Ohlson Labs had *another* break-in . . .
The same night you dropped in on Bowman.
That can't be a coincidence.
I don't think so either.
Especially not after you see this security footage.

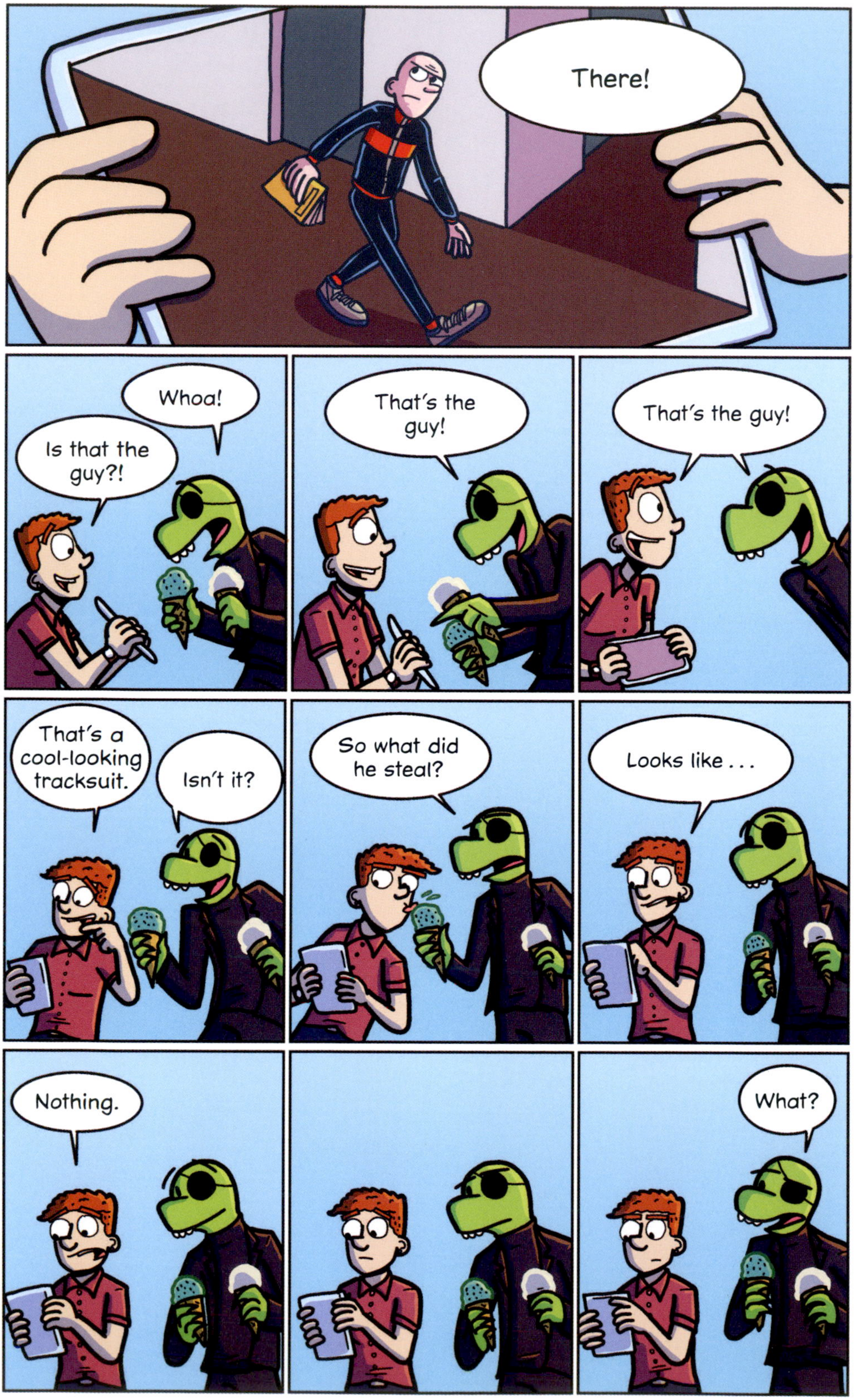
There!
Whoa!
Is that the guy?!
That's the guy!
That's the guy!
That's a cool-looking tracksuit.
Isn't it?
So what did he steal?
Looks like . . .
Nothing.
What?

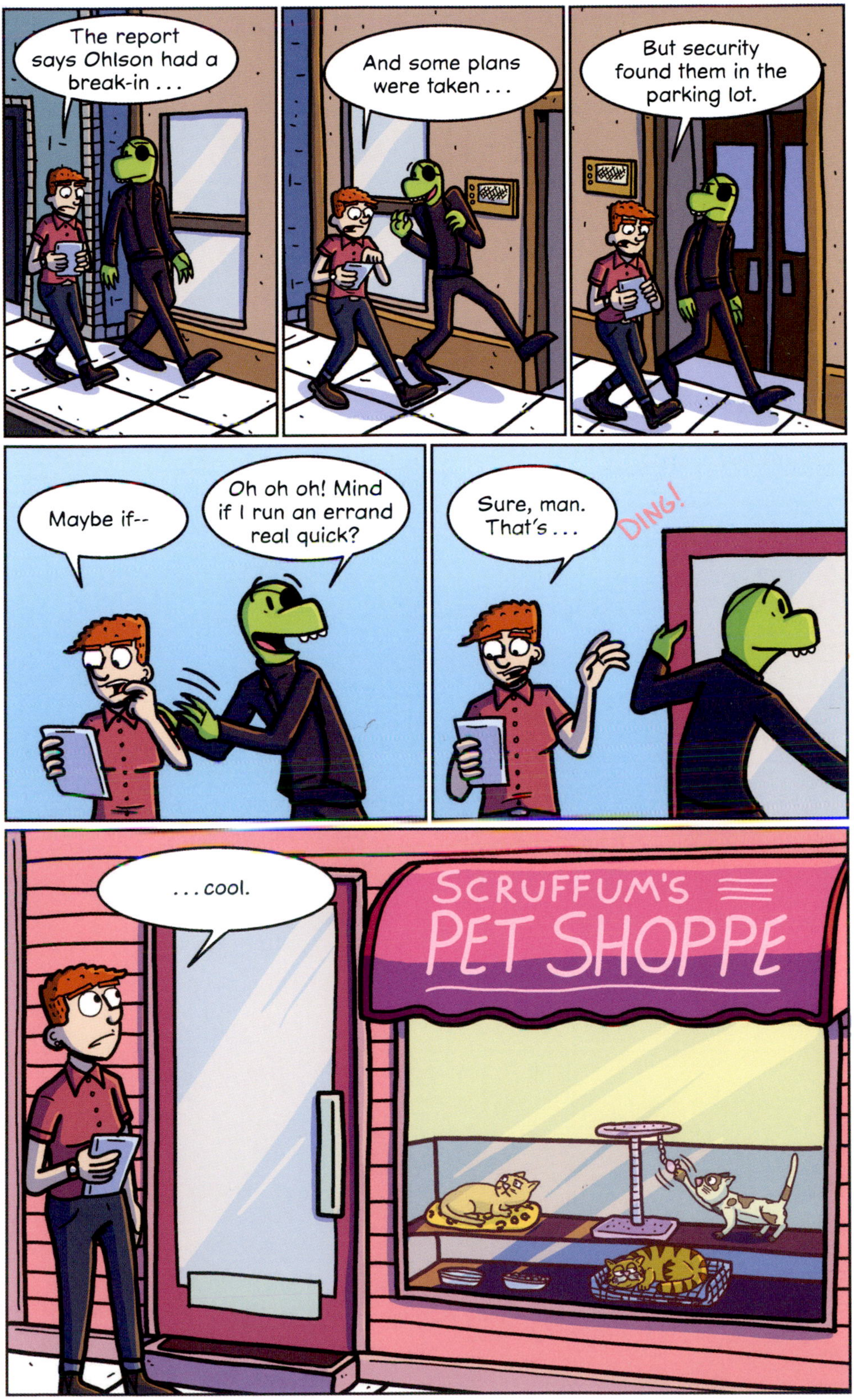

The report says Ohlson had a break-in . . .
And some plans were taken . . .
But security found them in the parking lot.
Maybe if--
Oh oh oh! Mind if I run an errand real quick?
Sure, man. That's . . .
DING!
. . . cool.
SCRUFFUM'S PET SHOPPE

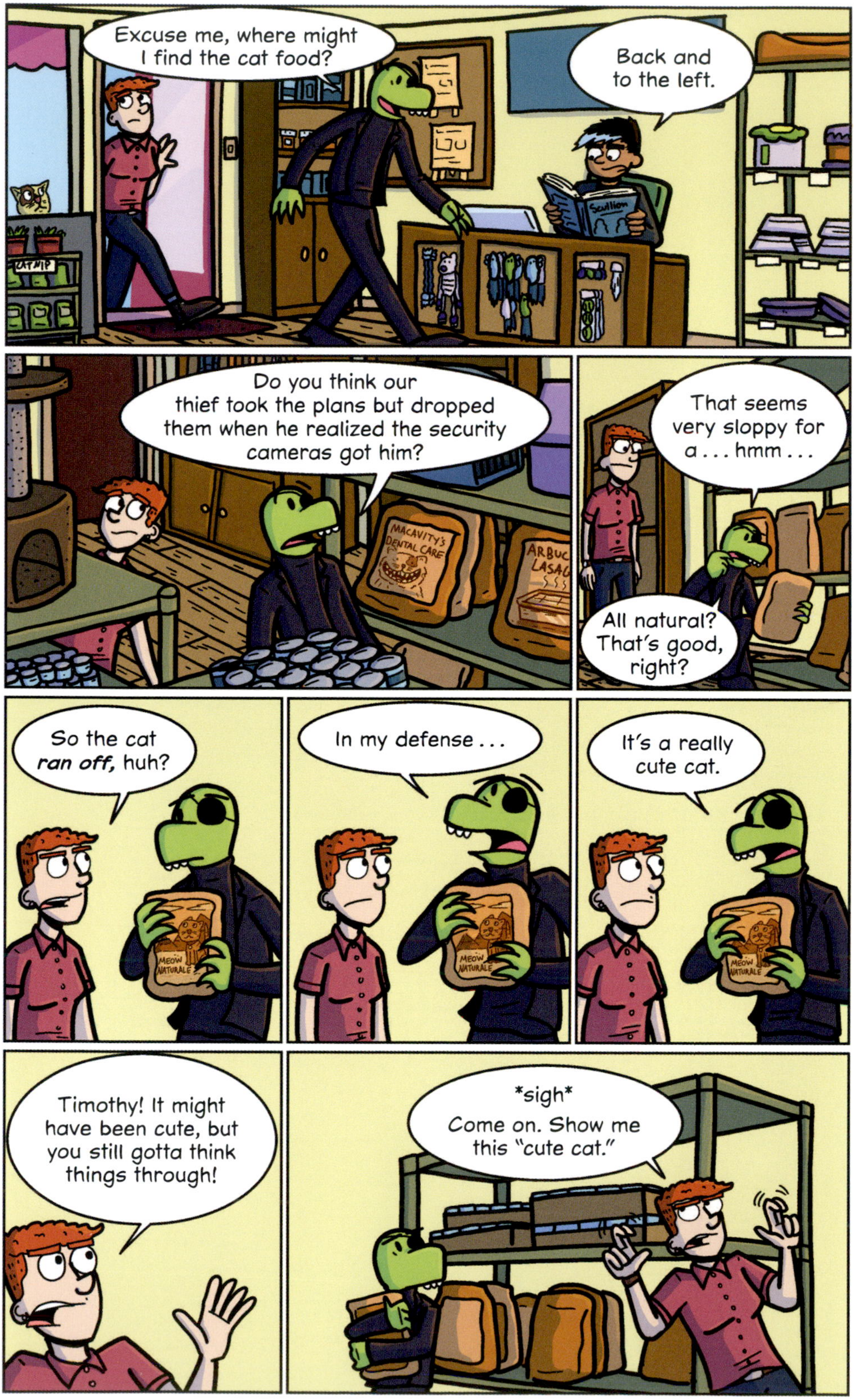
Excuse me, where might I find the cat food?
Back and to the left.
Scullion
CATNIP
Do you think our thief took the plans but dropped them when he realized the security cameras got him?
MACAVITY'S DENTAL CARE
That seems very sloppy for a . . . hmm . . .
All natural? That's good, right?
So the cat *ran off,* huh?
MEOW NATURALE
In my defense . . .
It's a really cute cat.
Timothy! It might have been cute, but you still gotta think things through!
sigh
Come on. Show me this "cute cat."

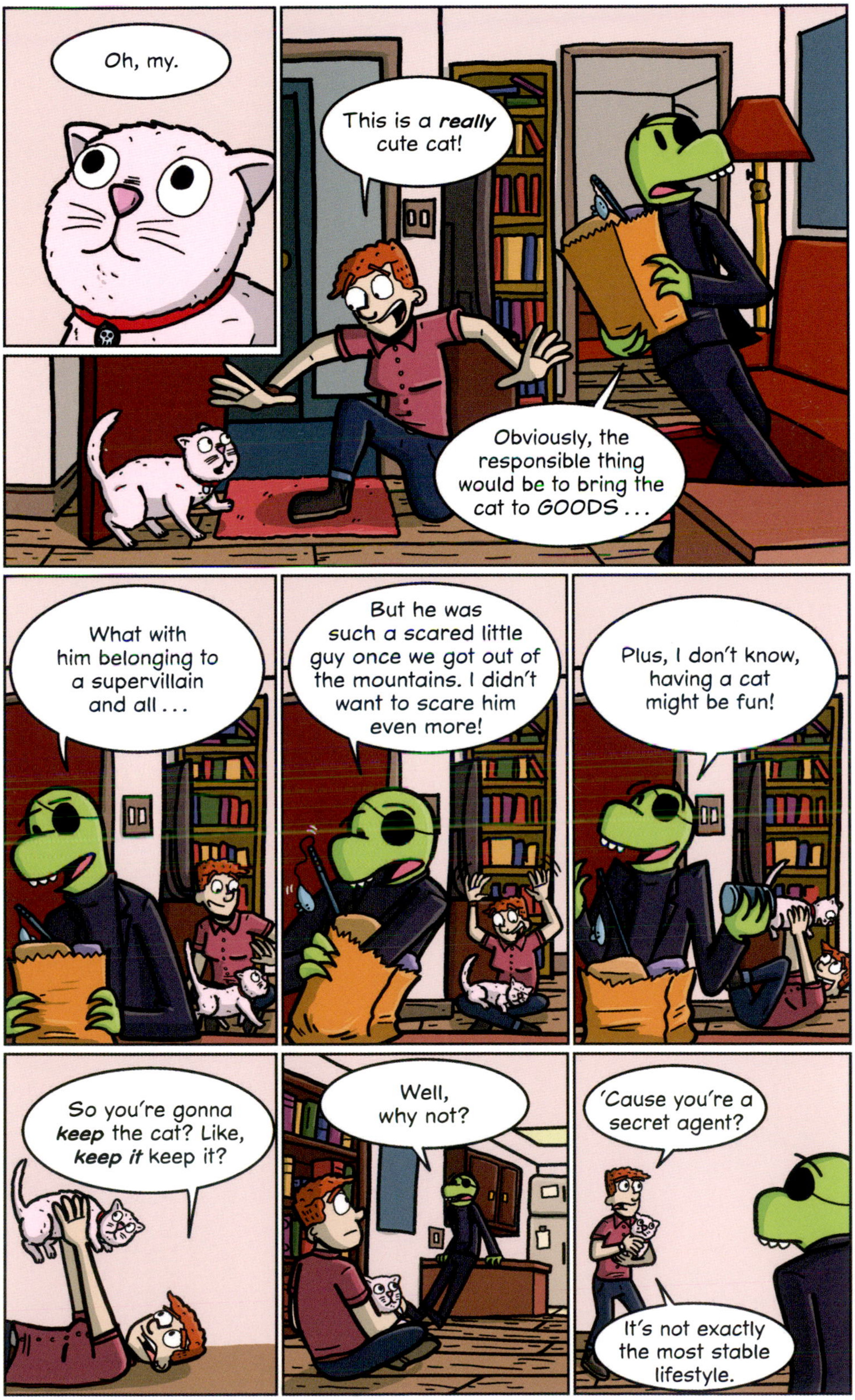
Oh, my.
This is a *really* cute cat!
Obviously, the responsible thing would be to bring the cat to GOODS . . .
What with him belonging to a supervillain and all . . .
But he was such a scared little guy once we got out of the mountains. I didn't want to scare him even more!
Plus, I don't know, having a cat might be fun!
So you're gonna *keep* the cat? Like, *keep it* keep it?
Well, why not?
'Cause you're a secret agent?
It's not exactly the most stable lifestyle.

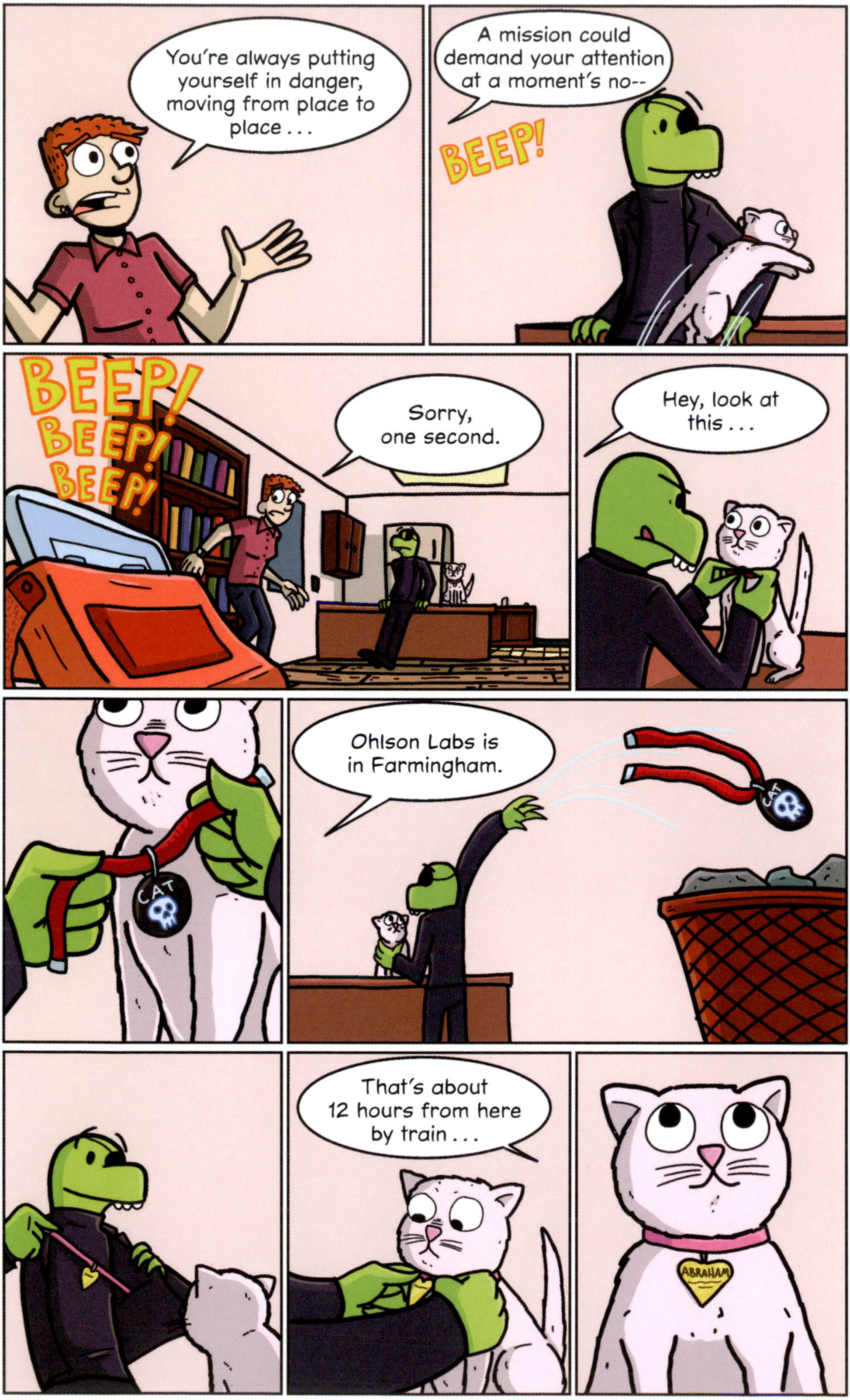
You're always putting yourself in danger, moving from place to place . . .
A mission could demand your attention at a moment's no--
BEEP!
BEEP! BEEP! BEEP!
Sorry, one second.
Hey, look at this . . .
CAT
Ohlson Labs is in Farmingham.
CAT
That's about 12 hours from here by train . . .
ABRAHAM

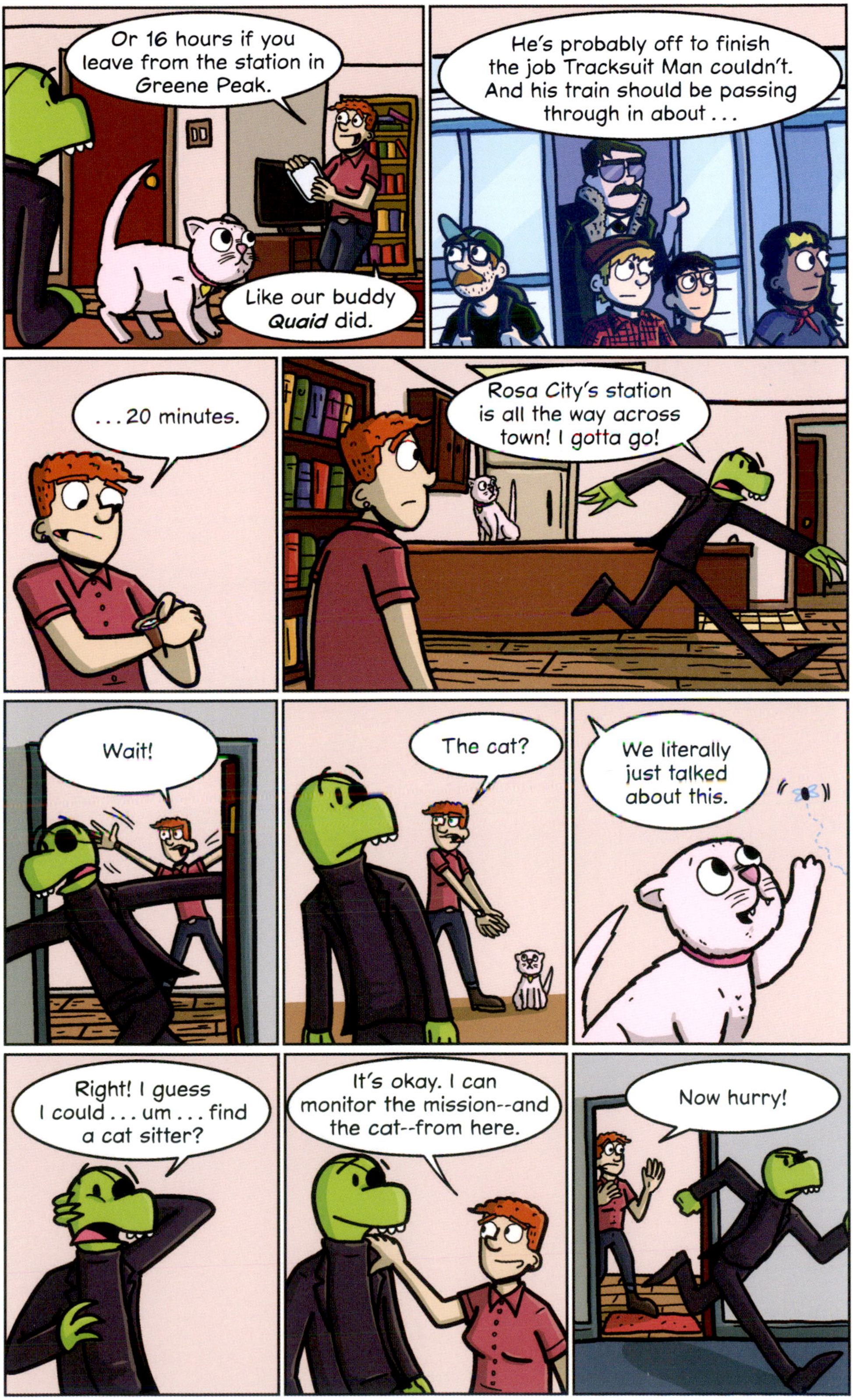
Or 16 hours if you leave from the station in Greene Peak.
Like our buddy *Quaid* did.
He's probably off to finish the job Tracksuit Man couldn't. And his train should be passing through in about . . .
. . . 20 minutes.
Rosa City's station is all the way across town! I gotta go!
Wait!
The cat?
We literally just talked about this.
Right! I guess I could . . . um . . . find a cat sitter?
It's okay. I can monitor the mission--and the cat--from here.
Now hurry!

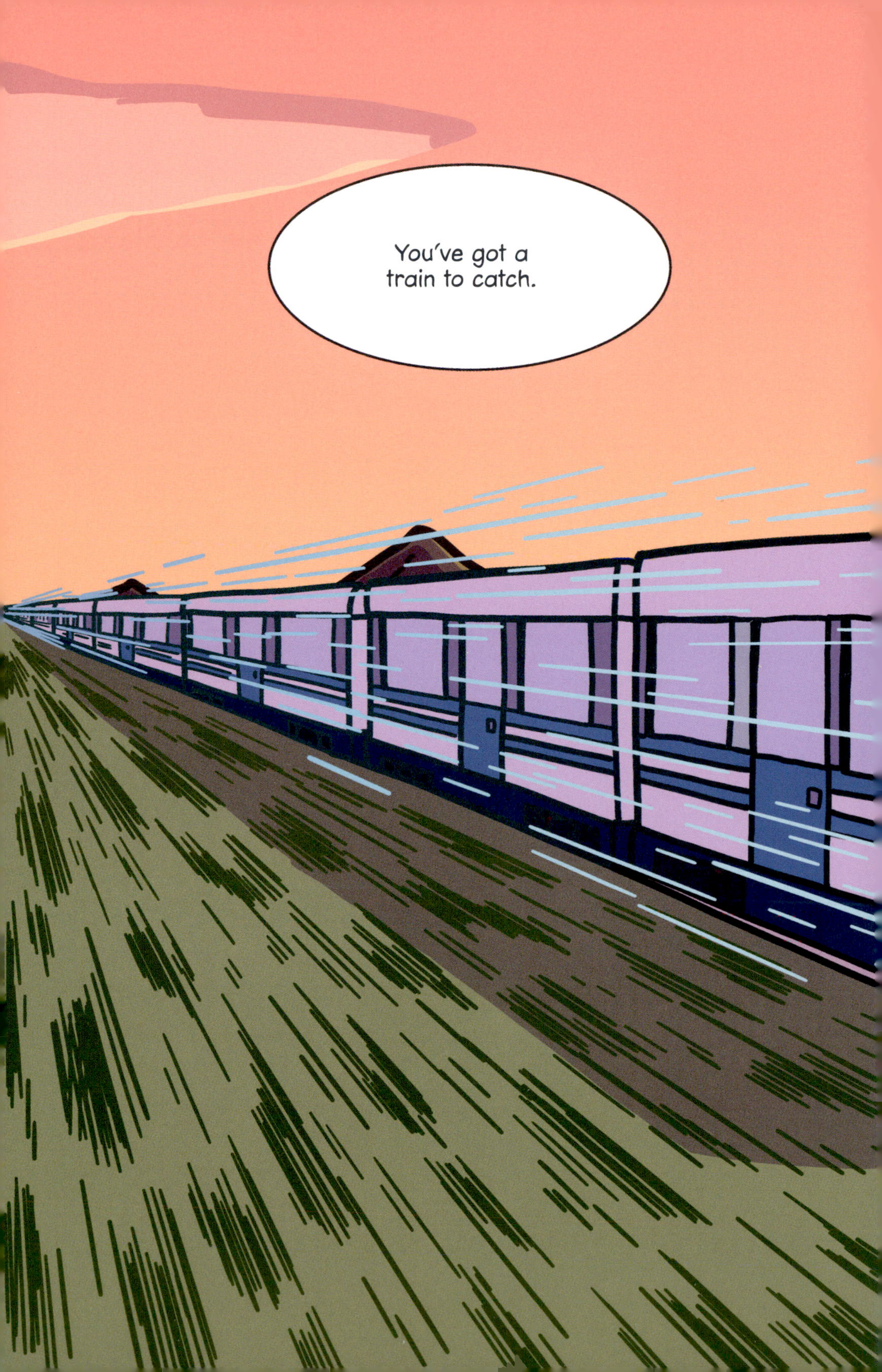
You've got a train to catch.

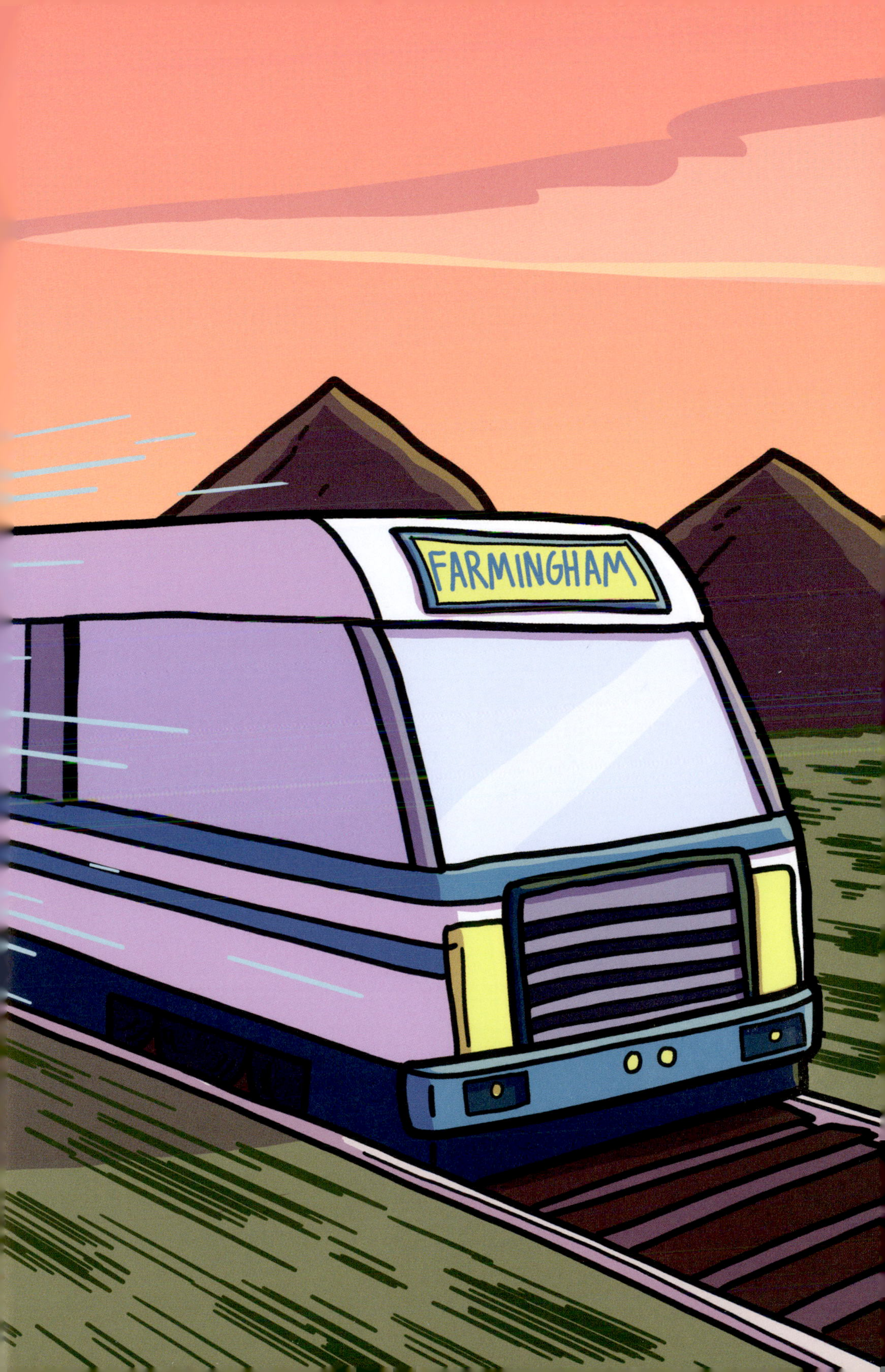
FARMINGHAM

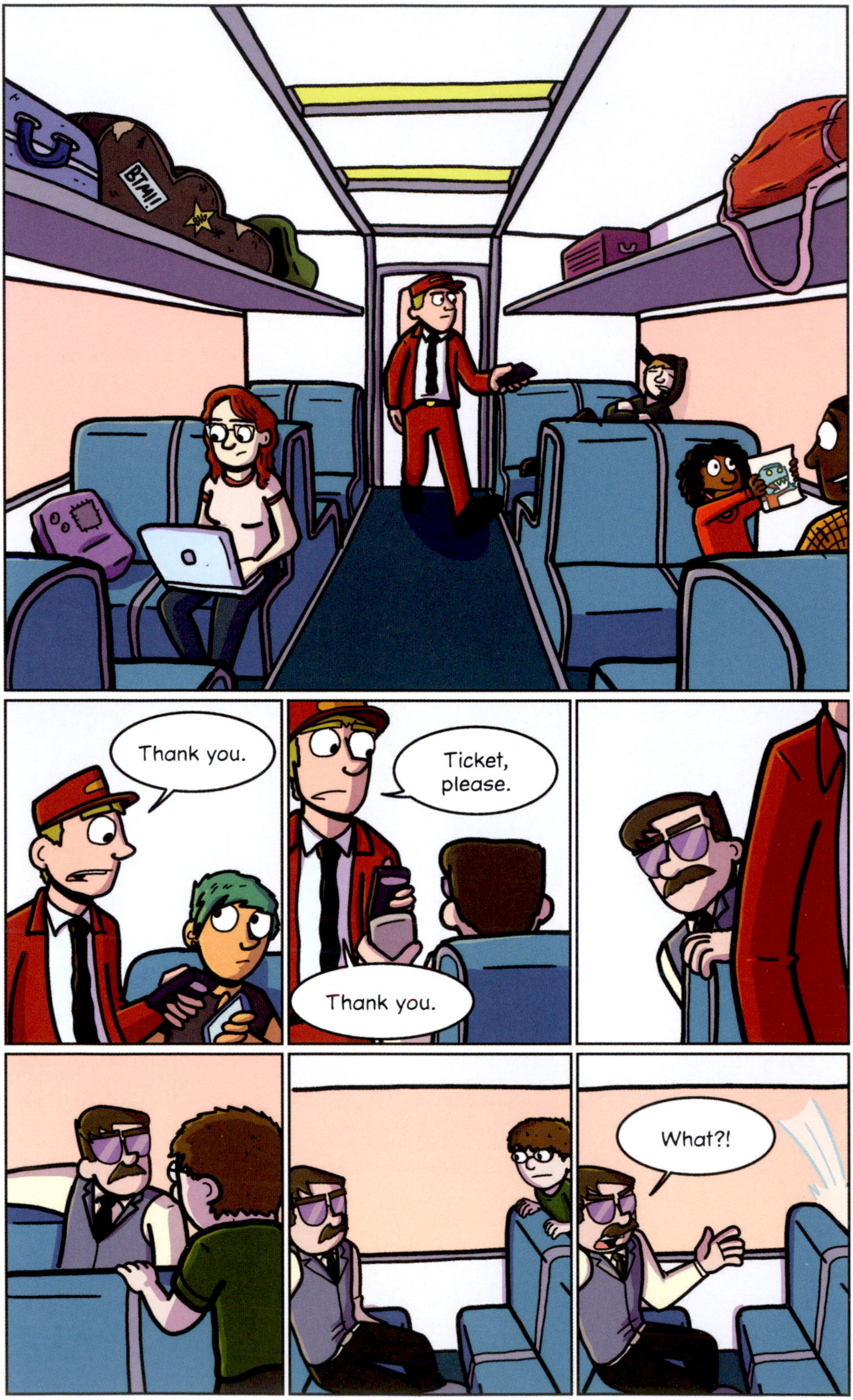
Thank you.
Ticket, please.
Thank you.
What?!

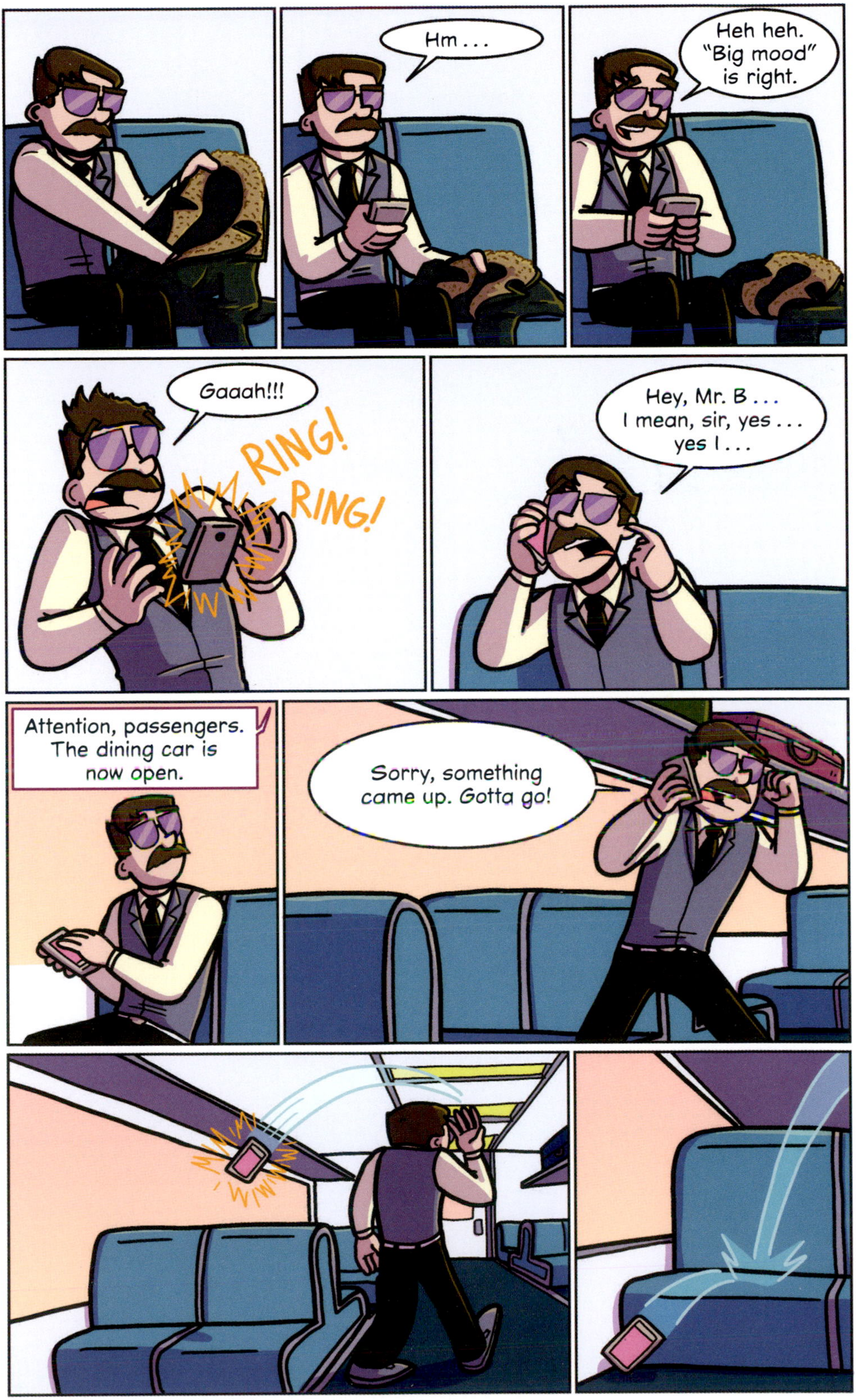
Hm . . .
Heh heh. "Big mood" is right.
Gaaah!!!
RING! RING!
Hey, Mr. B . . . I mean, sir, yes . . . yes I . . .
Attention, passengers. The dining car is now open.
Sorry, something came up. Gotta go!

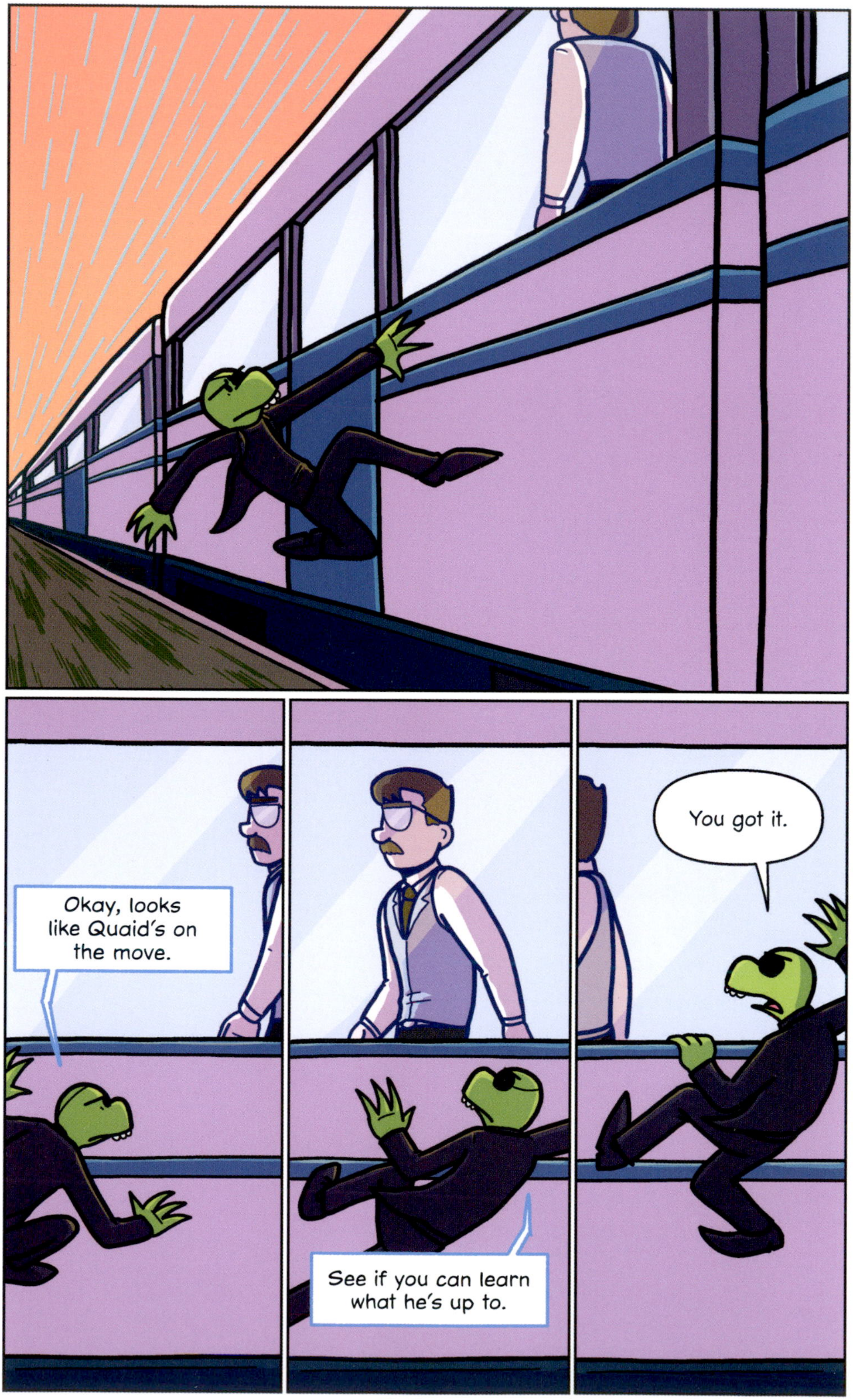
Okay, looks like Quaid's on the move.
See if you can learn what he's up to.
You got it.

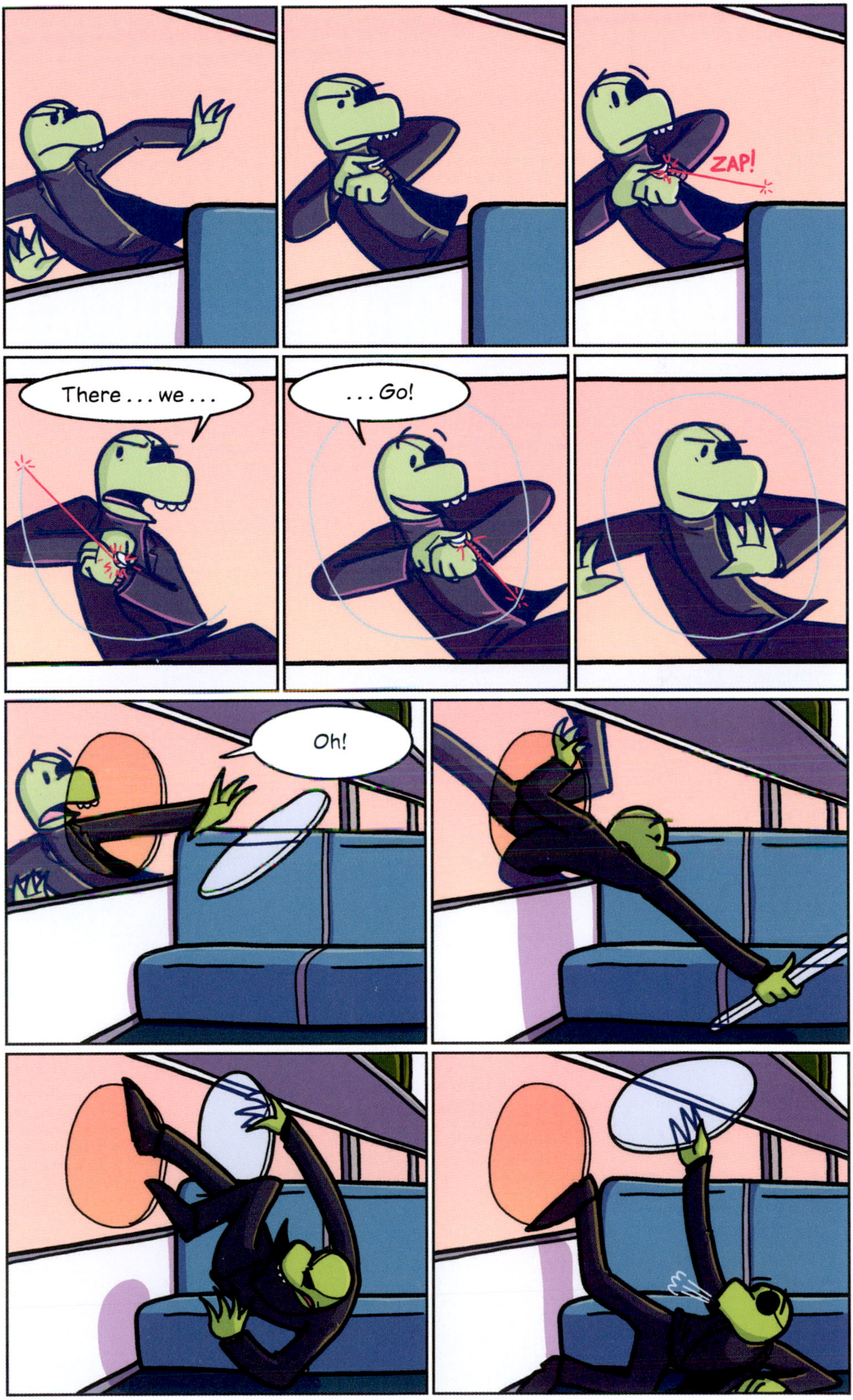
ZAP!
There . . . we . . .
. . . Go!
Oh!

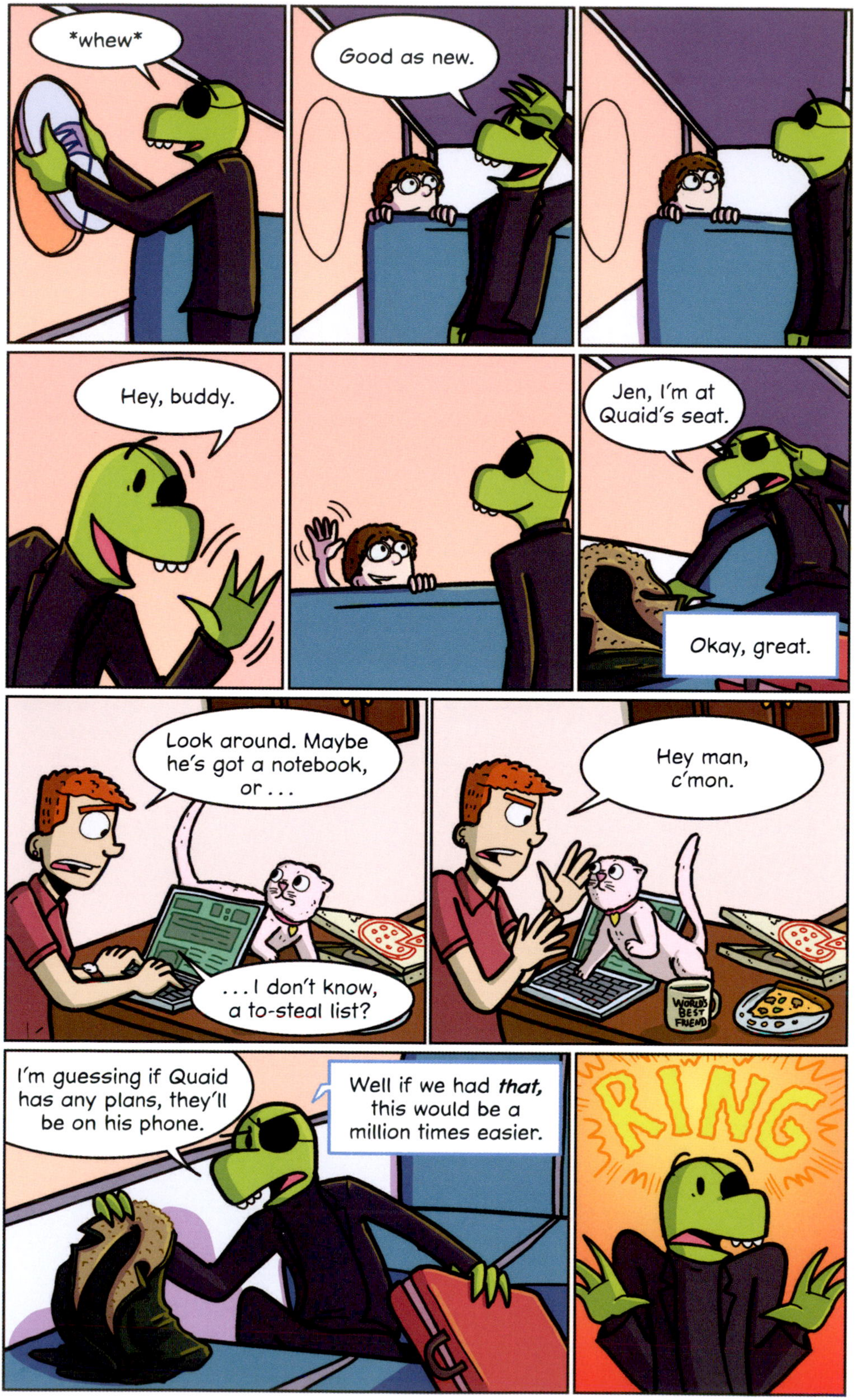
whew
Good as new.
Hey, buddy.
Jen, I'm at Quaid's seat.
Okay, great.
Look around. Maybe he's got a notebook, or . . .
. . . I don't know, a to-steal list?
Hey man, c'mon.
I'm guessing if Quaid has any plans, they'll be on his phone.
Well if we had *that,* this would be a million times easier.
RING

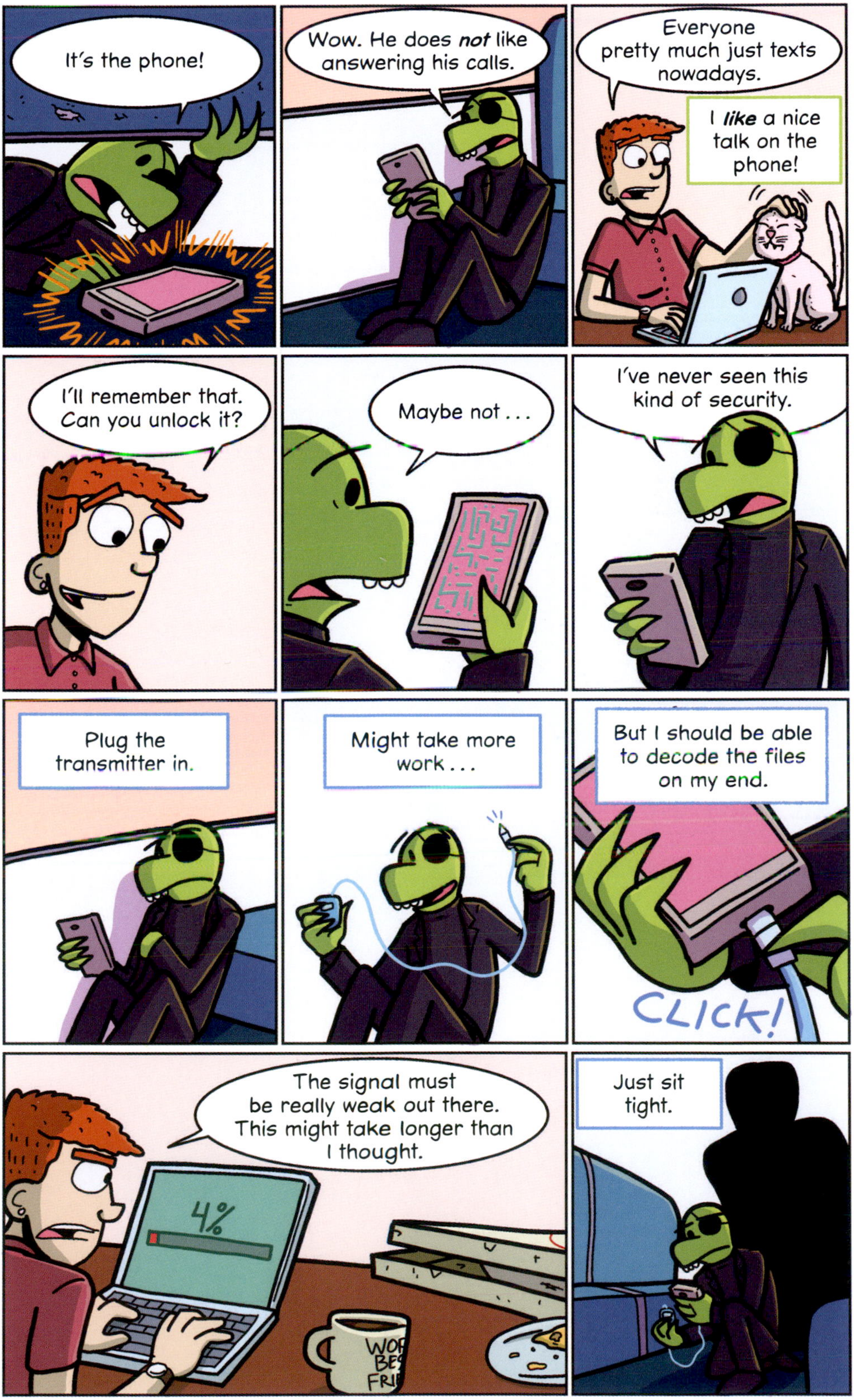
It's the phone!
Wow. He does *not* like answering his calls.
Everyone pretty much just texts nowadays.
I *like* a nice talk on the phone!
I'll remember that. Can you unlock it?
Maybe not . . .
I've never seen this kind of security.
Plug the transmitter in.
Might take more work . . .
But I should be able to decode the files on my end.
CLICK!
The signal must be really weak out there. This might take longer than I thought.
4%
Just sit tight.

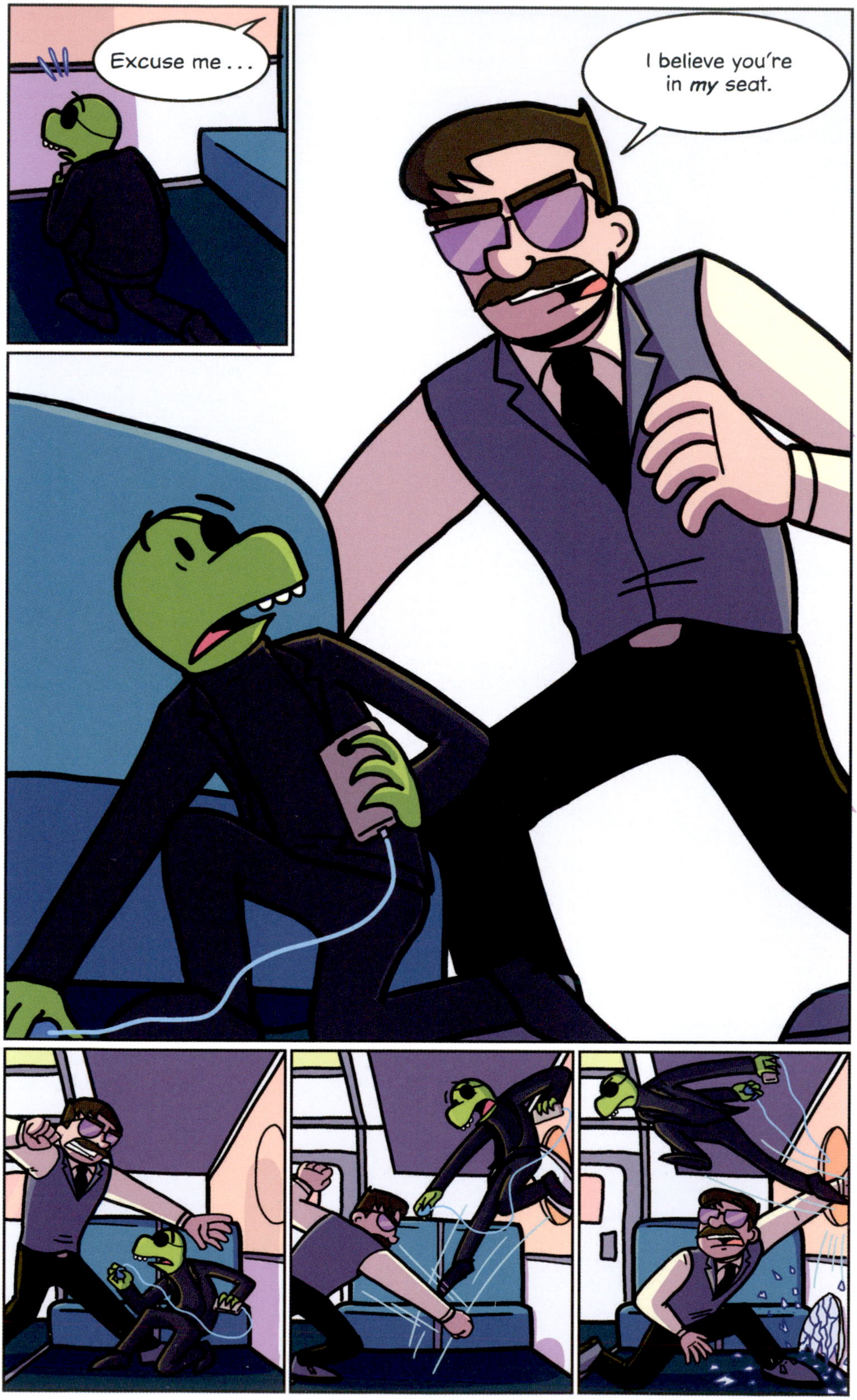
Excuse me . . .
I believe you're in *my* seat.

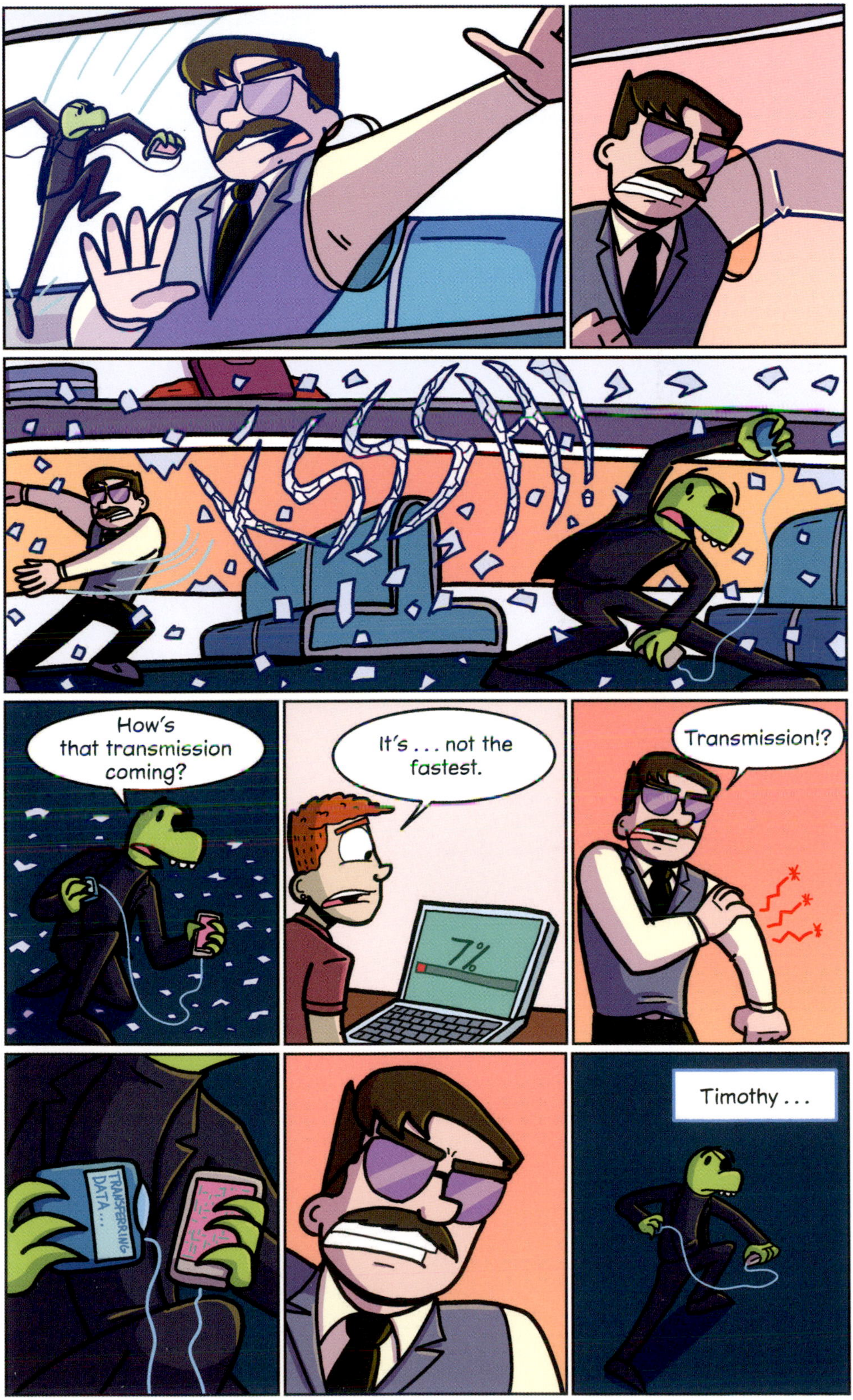
KSSSH!
How's that transmission coming?
It's . . . not the fastest.
7%
Transmission!?
TRANSFERRING DATA...
Timothy . . .

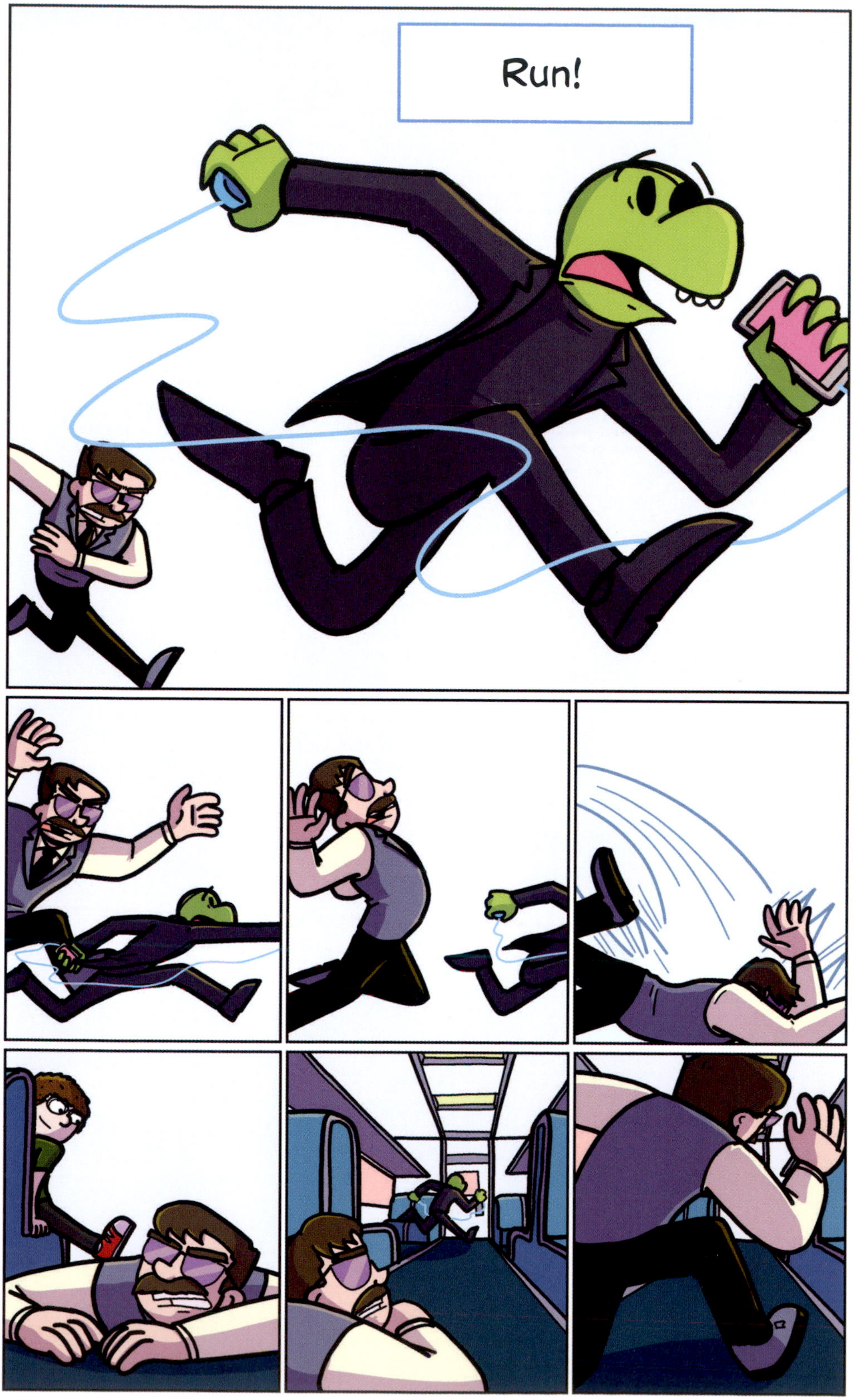
Run!

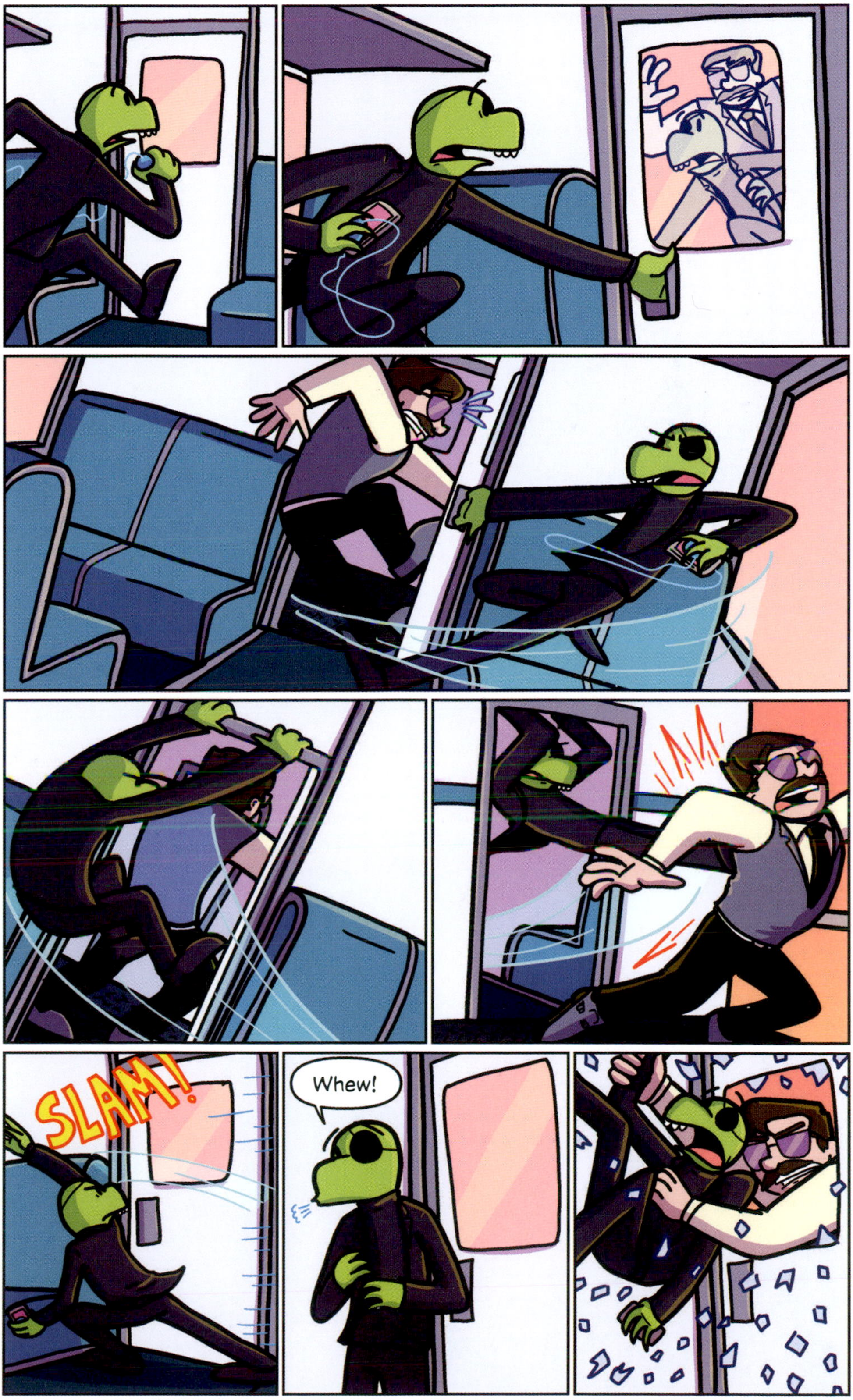
SLAM!
Whew!

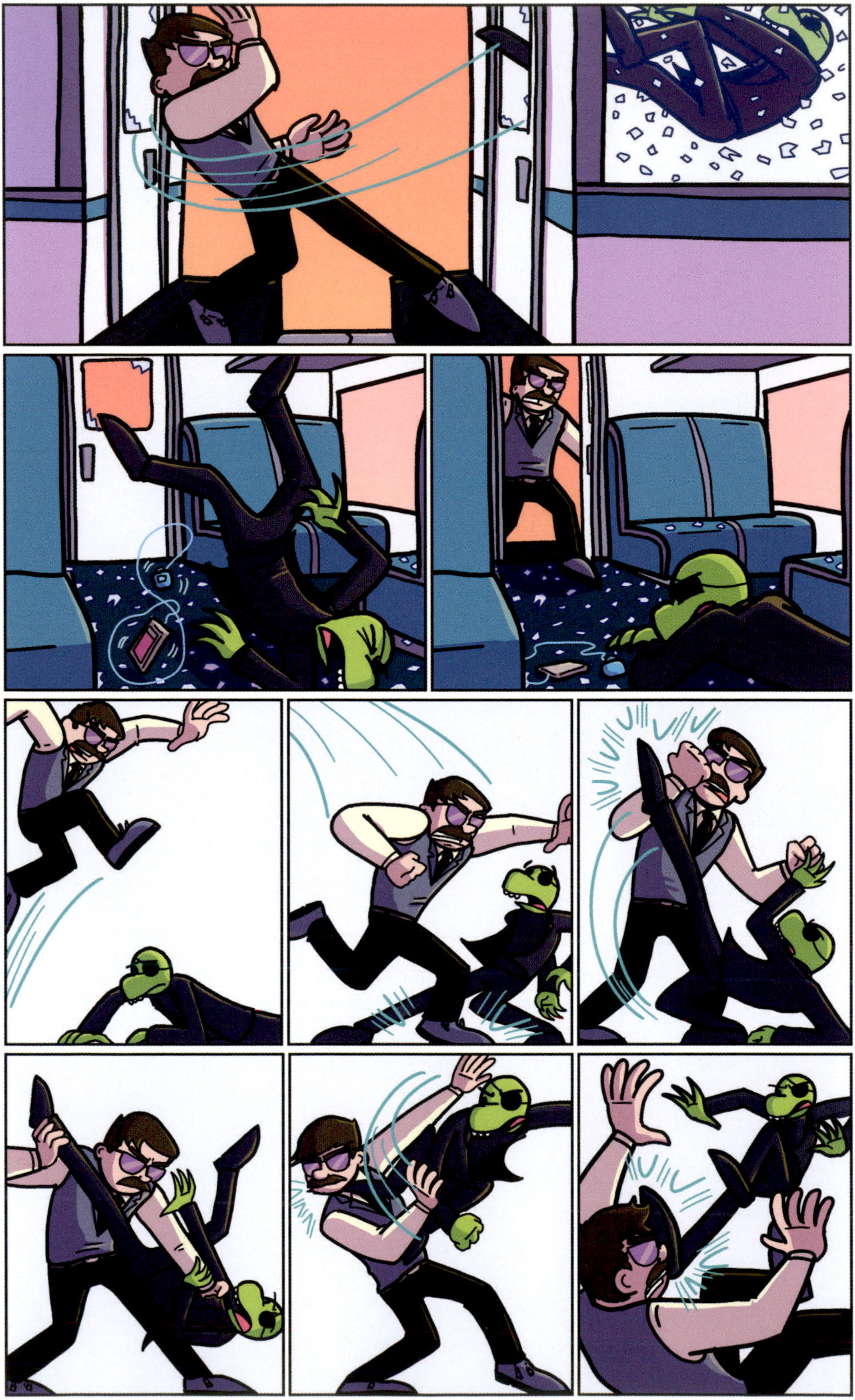

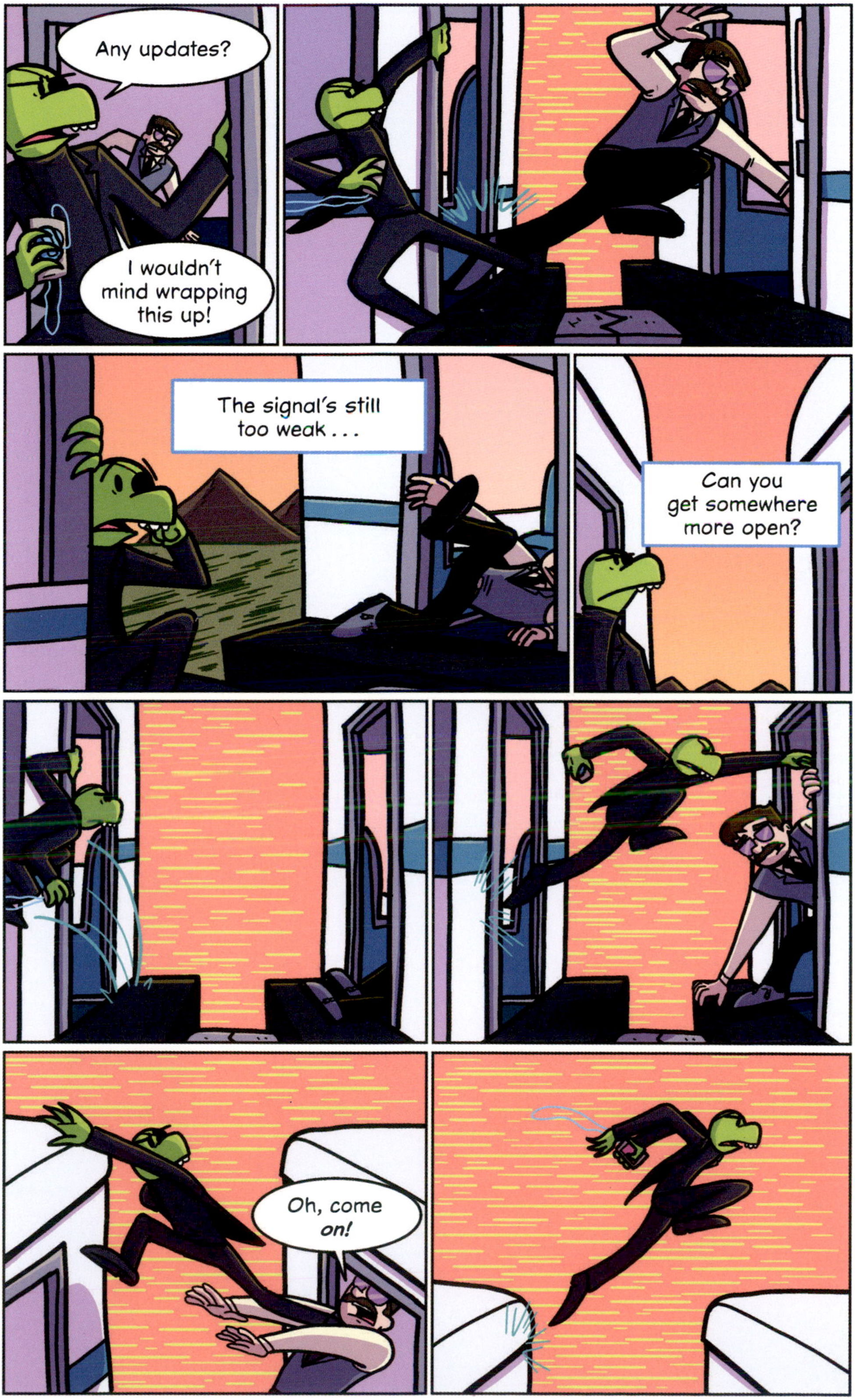
Any updates?
I wouldn't mind wrapping this up!
The signal's still too weak . . .
Can you get somewhere more open?
Oh, come *on!*

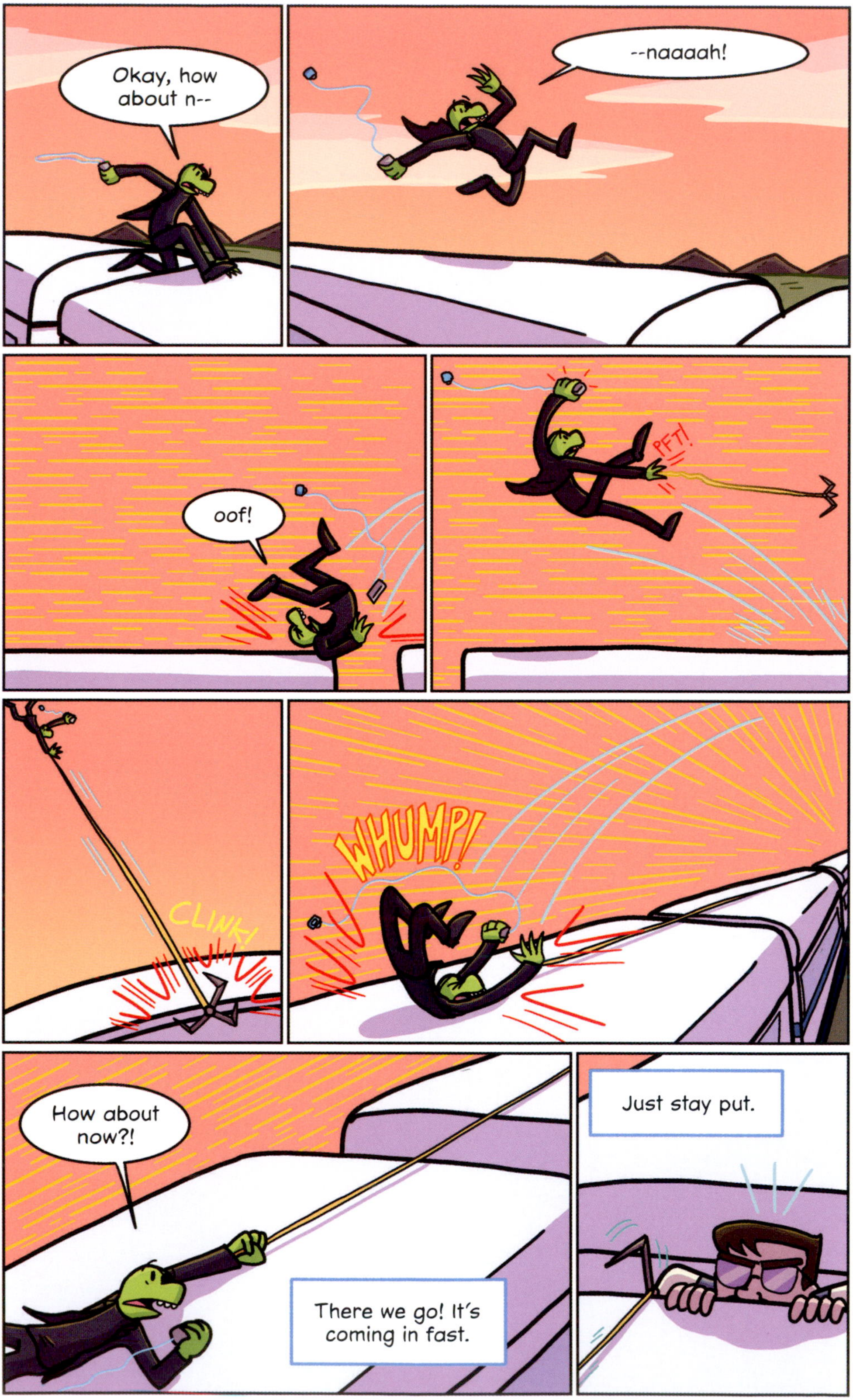
Okay, how about n--
--naaaah!
oof!
PFT!
CLINK!
WHUMP!
How about now?!
There we go! It's coming in fast.
Just stay put.

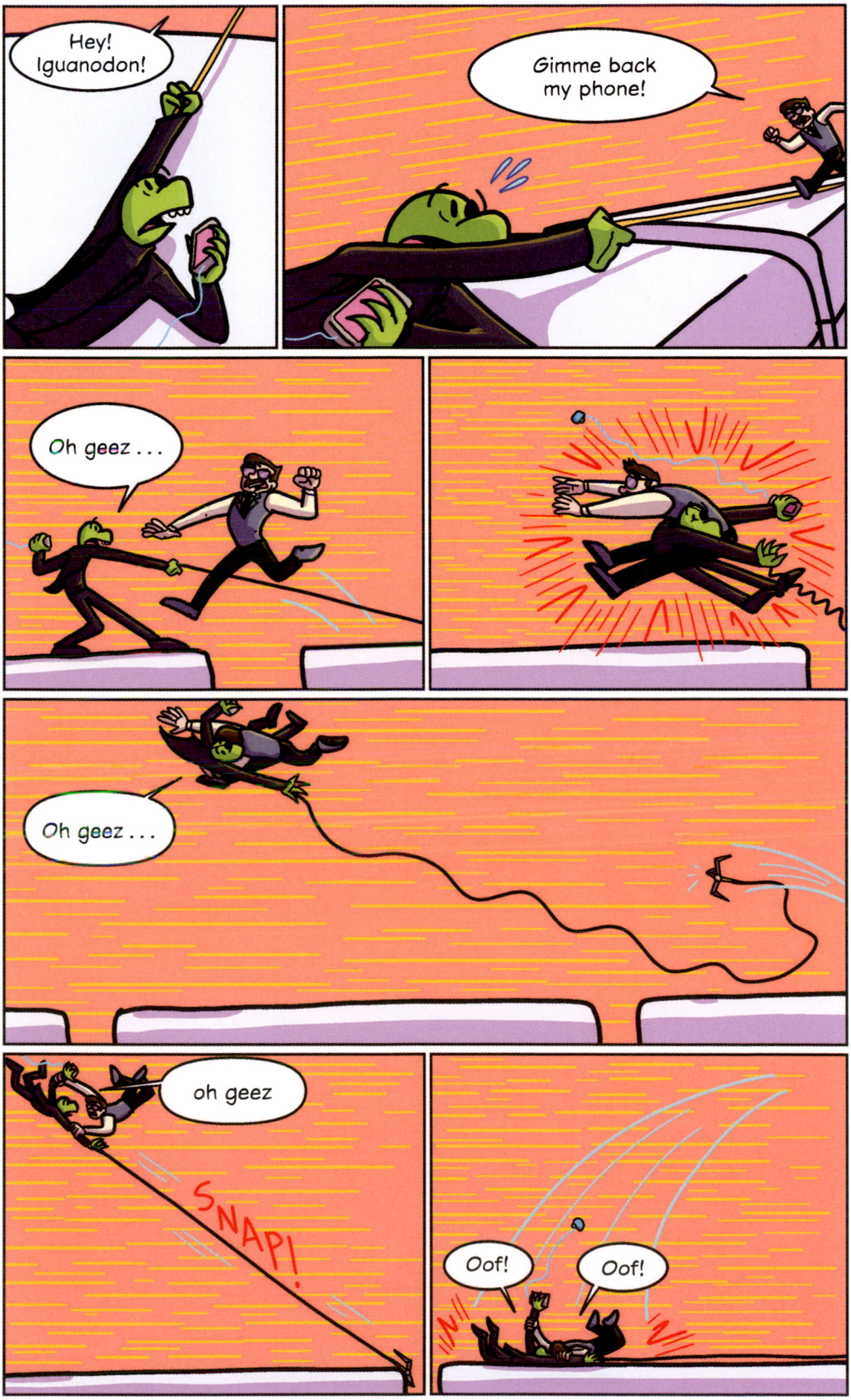
Hey! Iguanodon!
Gimme back my phone!
Oh geez . . .
Oh geez . . .
oh geez
SNAP!
Oof!
Oof!

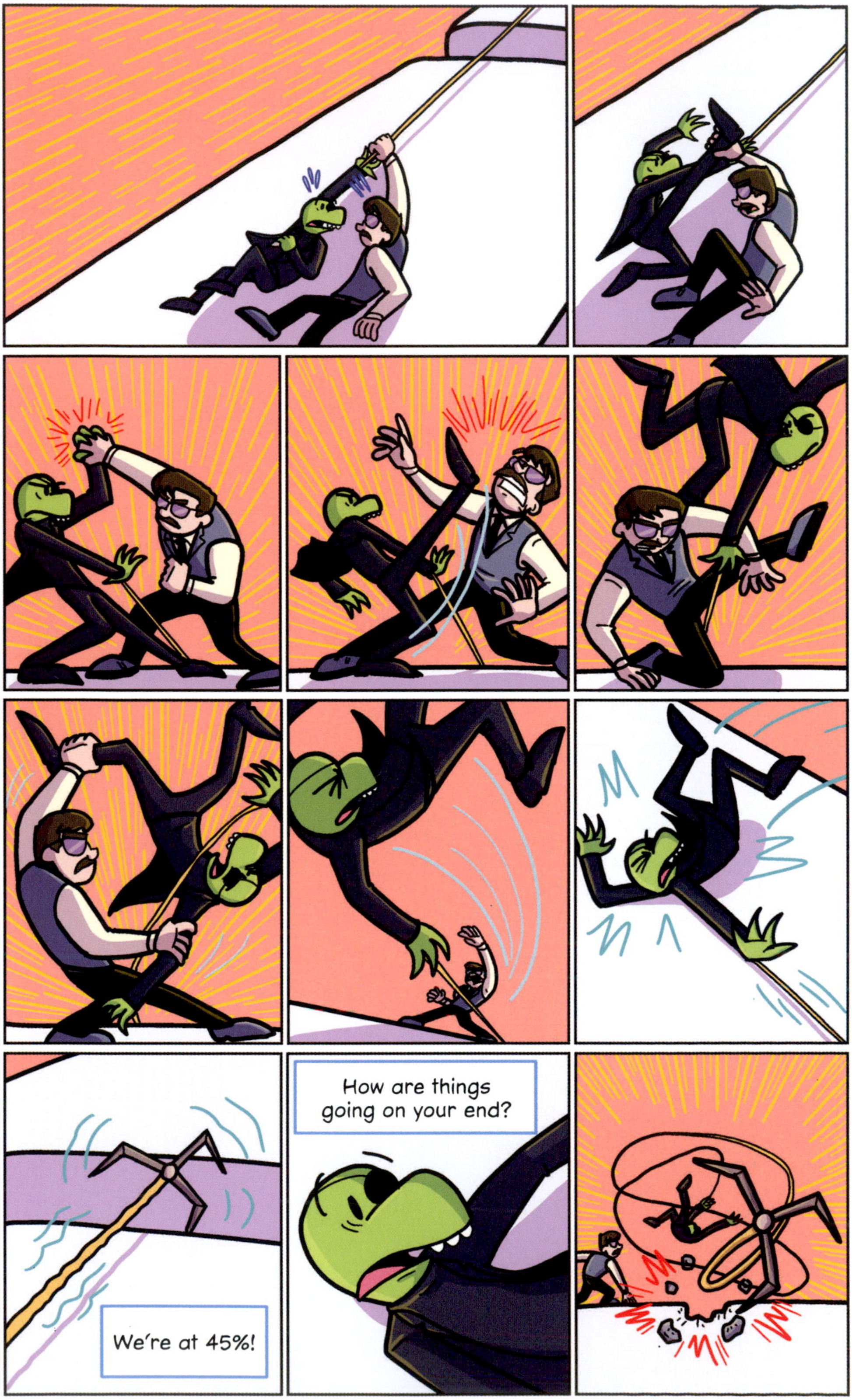
We're at 45%!
How are things going on your end?

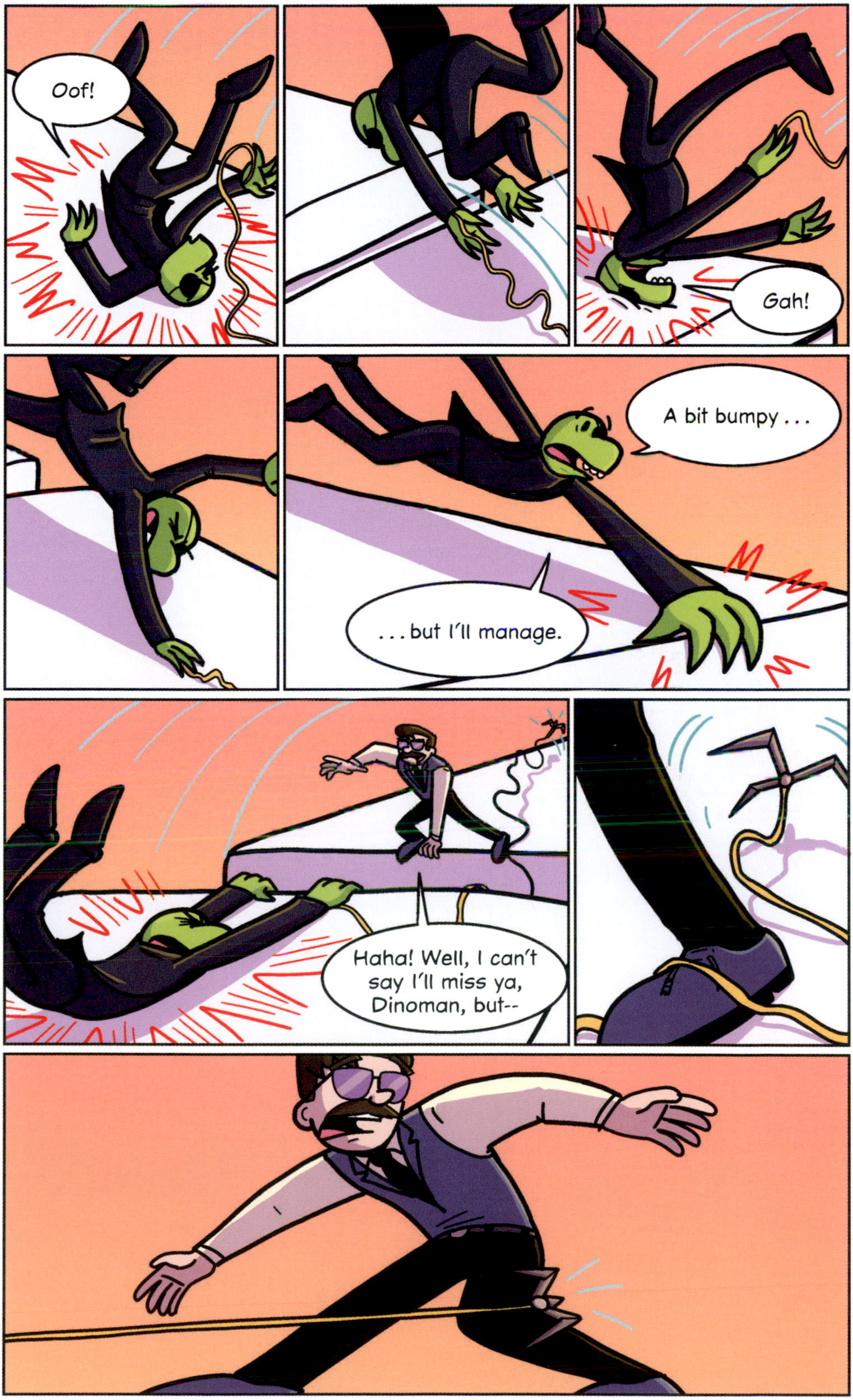
Oof!
Gah!
A bit bumpy . . .
. . . but I'll manage.
Haha! Well, I can't say I'll miss ya, Dinoman, but--

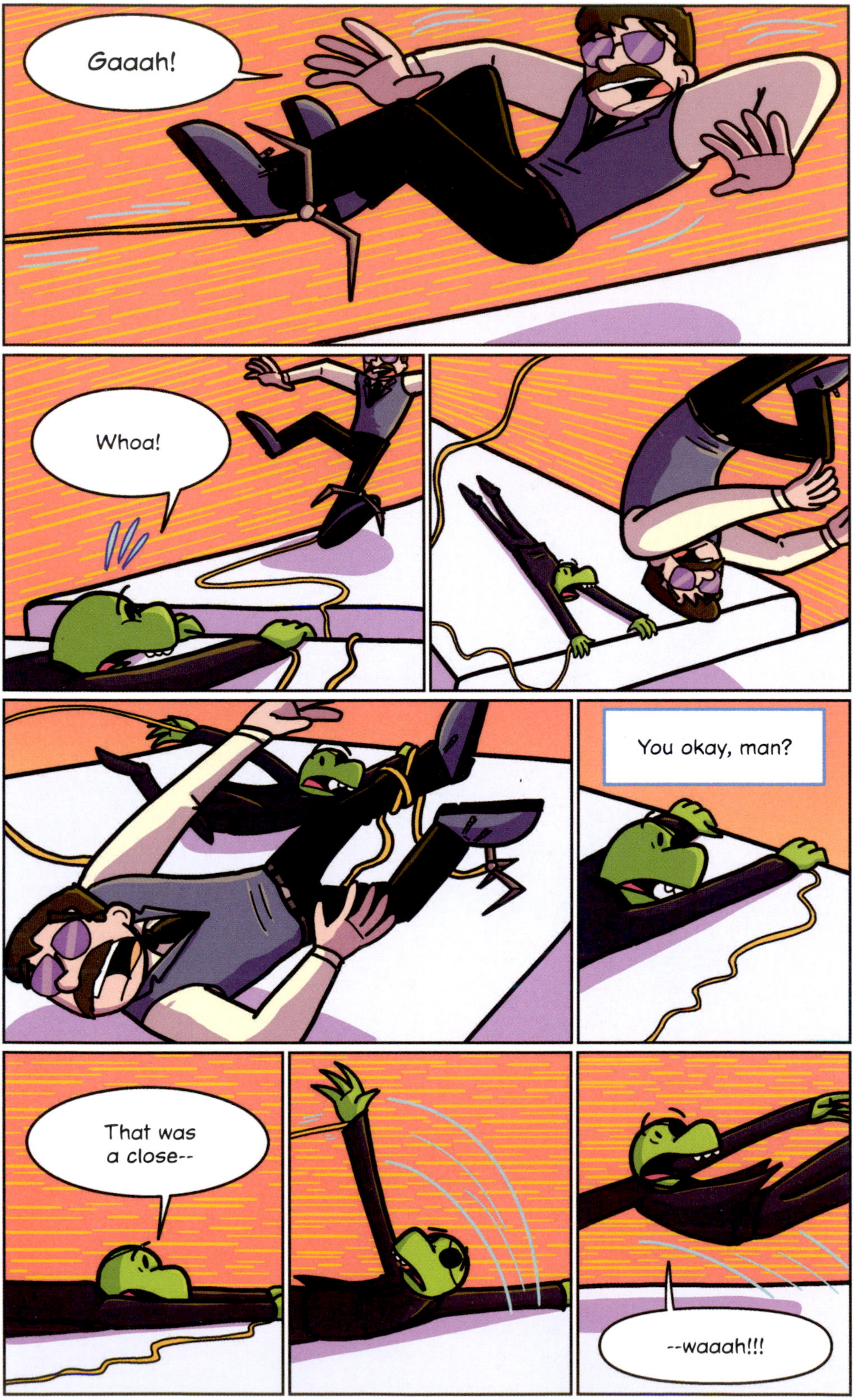
Gaaah!
Whoa!
You okay, man?
That was a close--
--waaah!!!

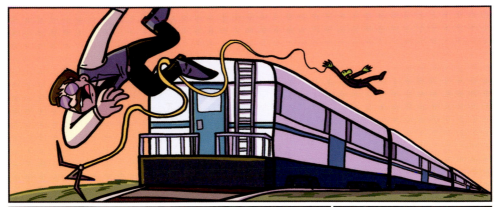

We're at 70%-- it's moving fast!

Hey, Jen?

How would going through a tunnel affect the transmission?

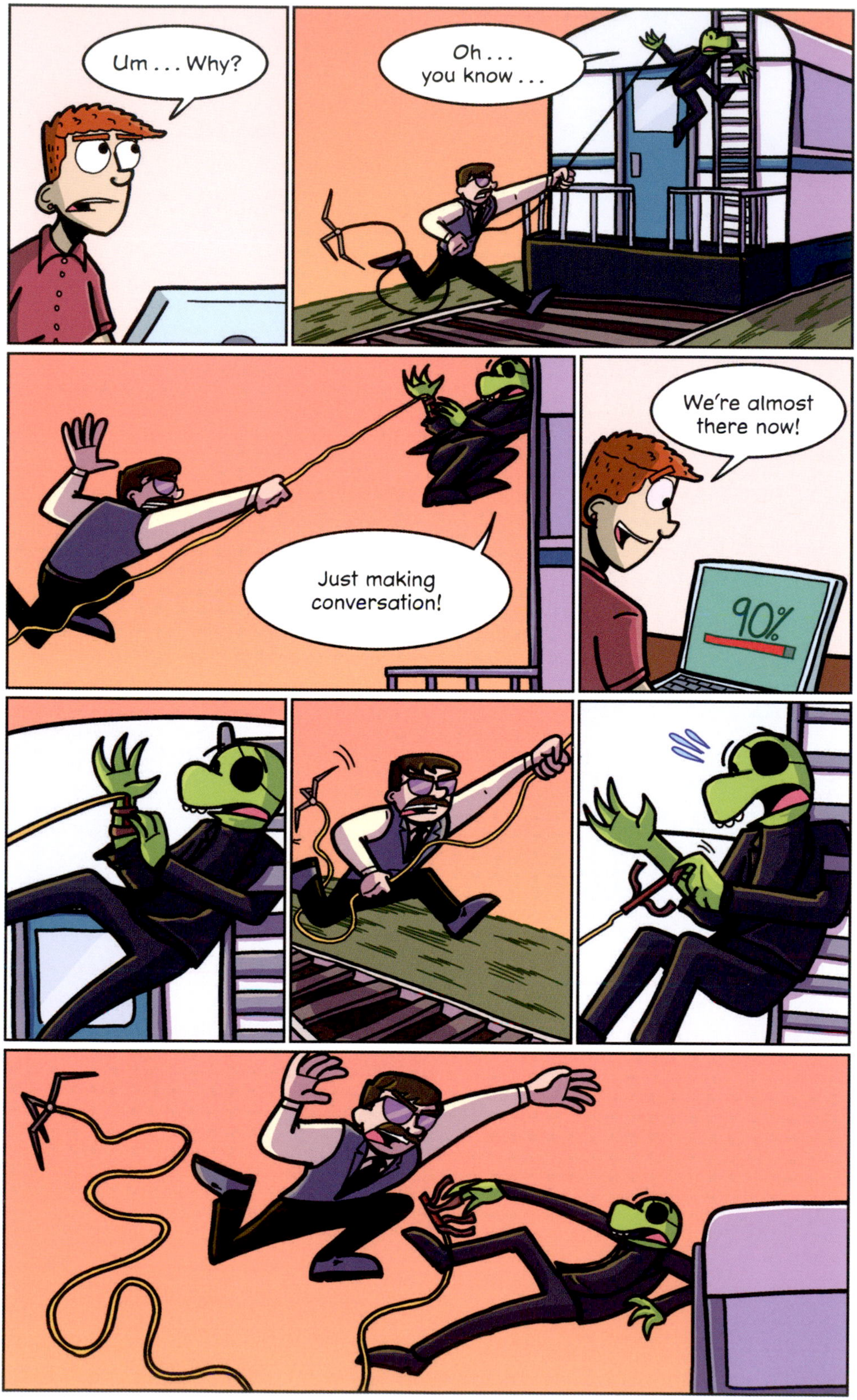
Um . . . Why?
Oh . . .
you know . . .
We're almost
there now!
Just making
conversation!
90%

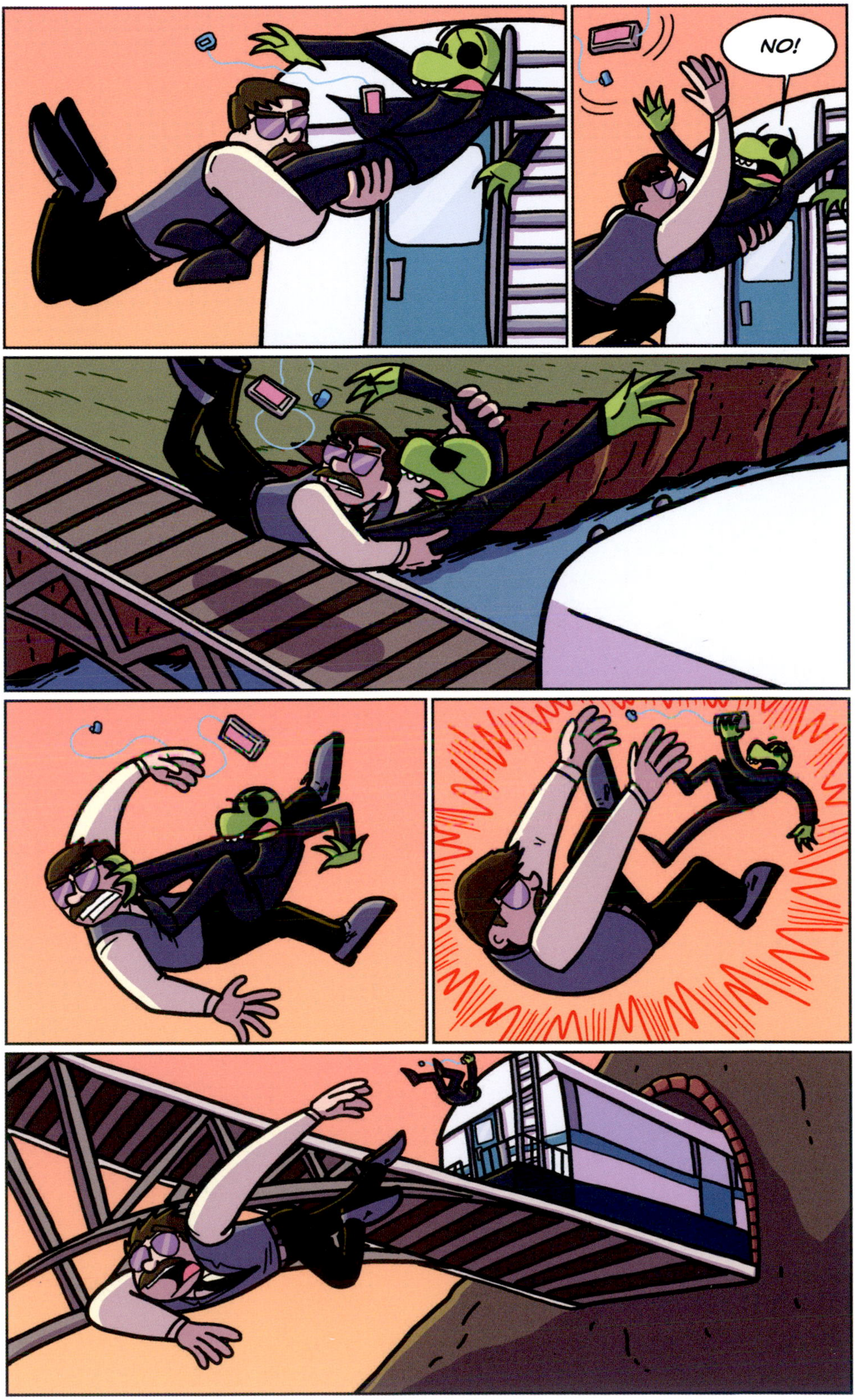
NO!

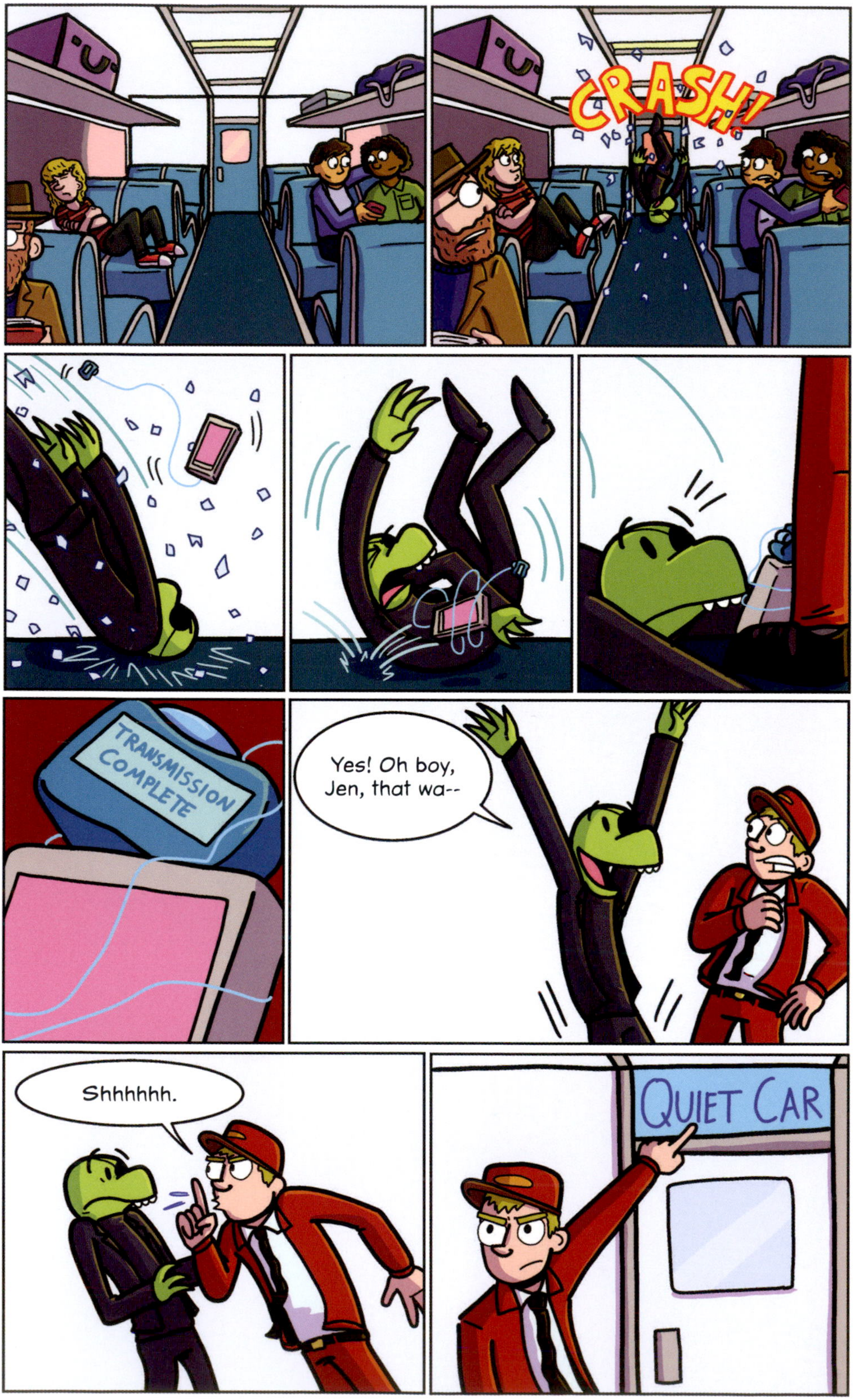
CRASH!
TRANSMISSION COMPLETE
Yes! Oh boy, Jen, that wa--
Shhhhhh.
QUIET CAR

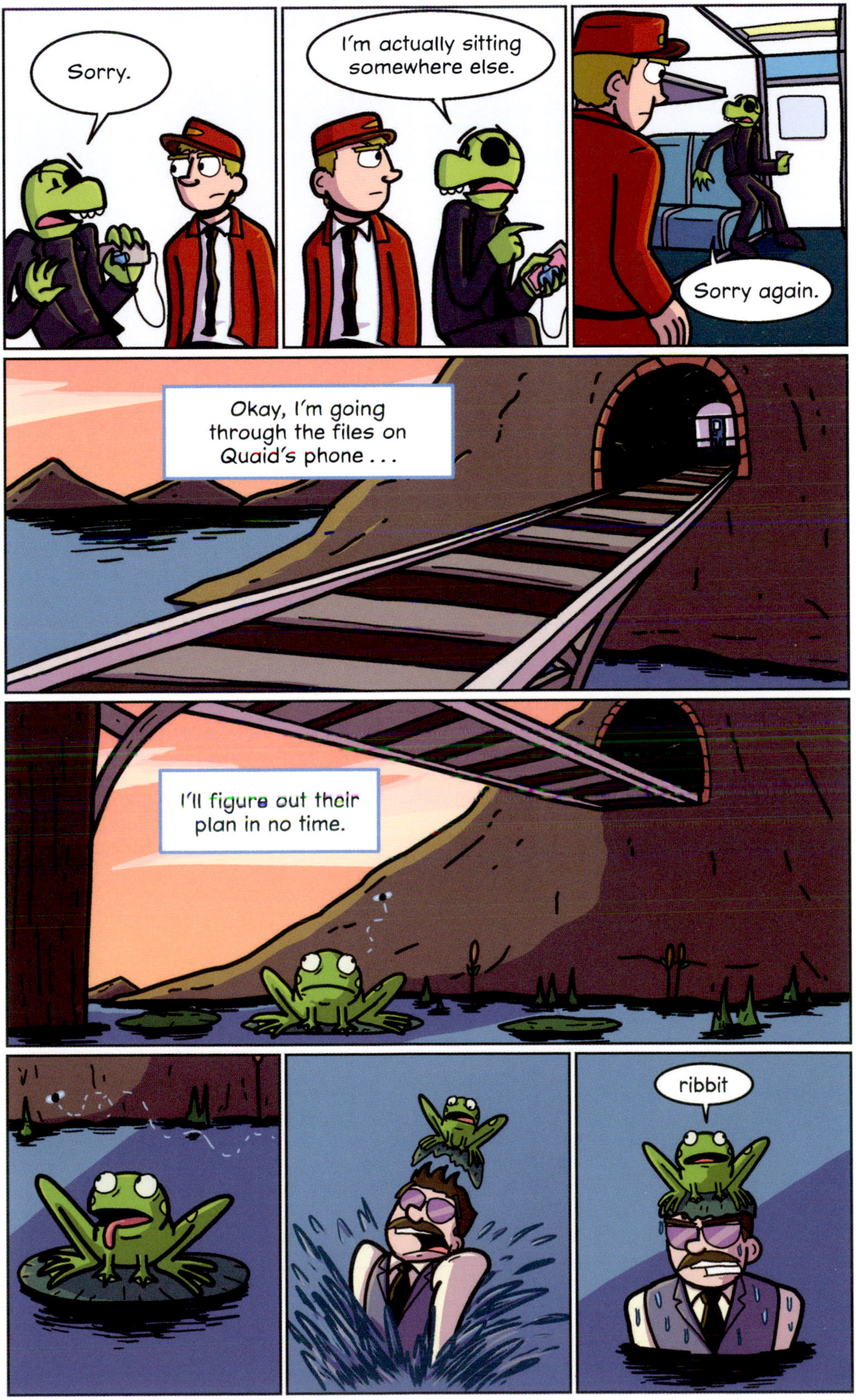
Sorry.
I'm actually sitting somewhere else.
Sorry again.
Okay, I'm going through the files on Quaid's phone . . .
I'll figure out their plan in no time.
ribbit

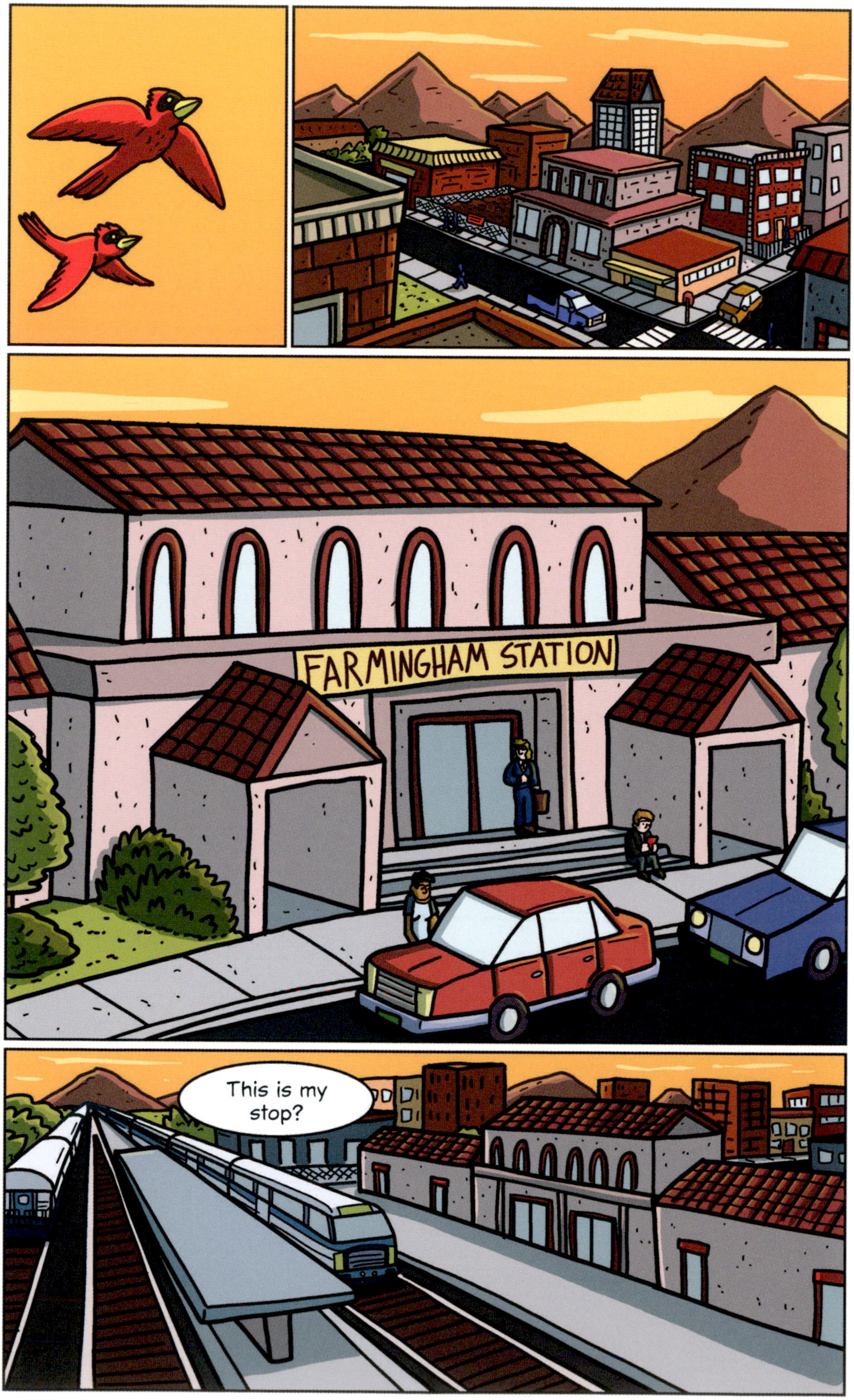
FARMINGHAM STATION
This is my stop?

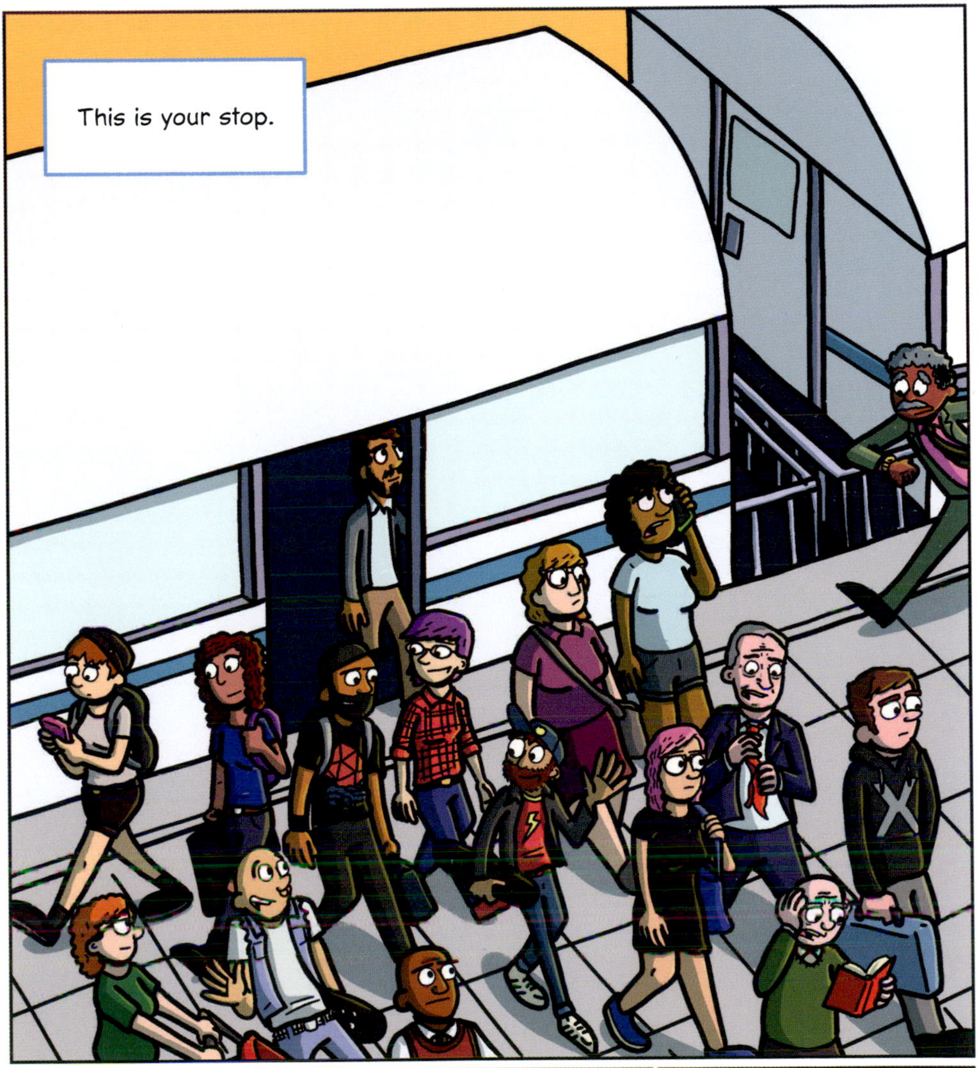
This is your stop.

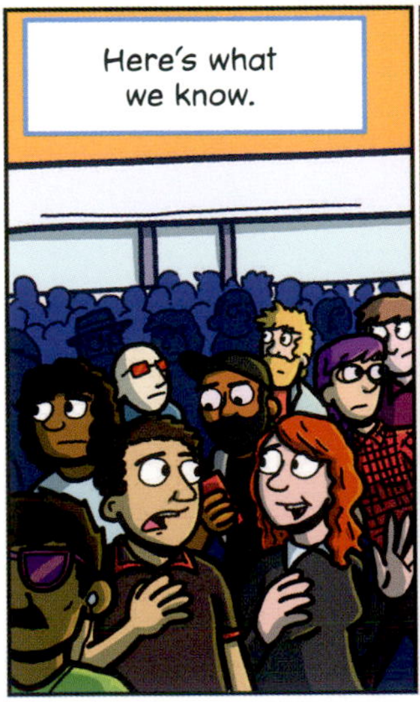
Here's what we know.

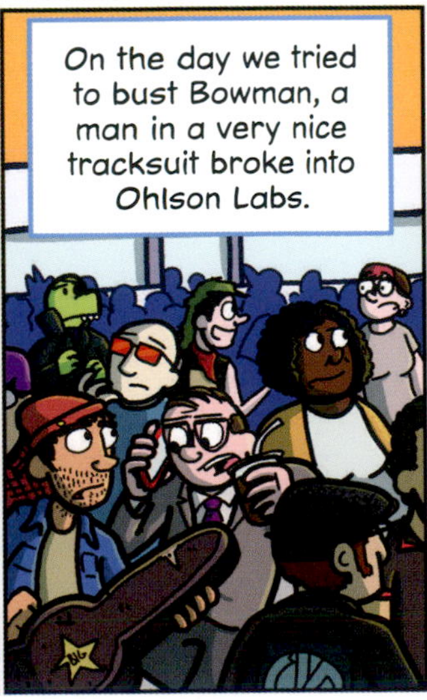
On the day we tried to bust Bowman, a man in a very nice tracksuit broke into Ohlson Labs.

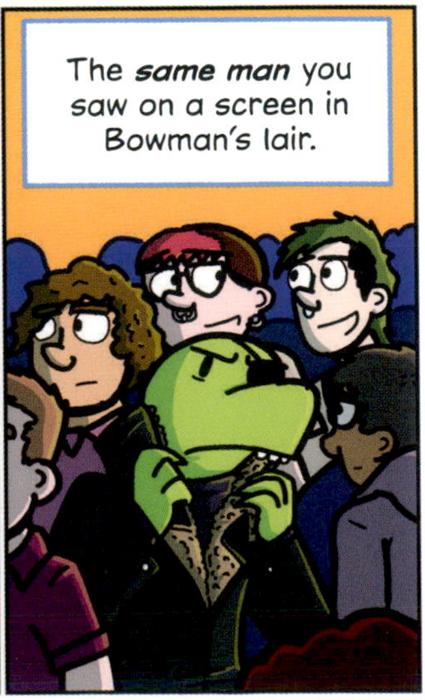
The *same man* you saw on a screen in Bowman's lair.

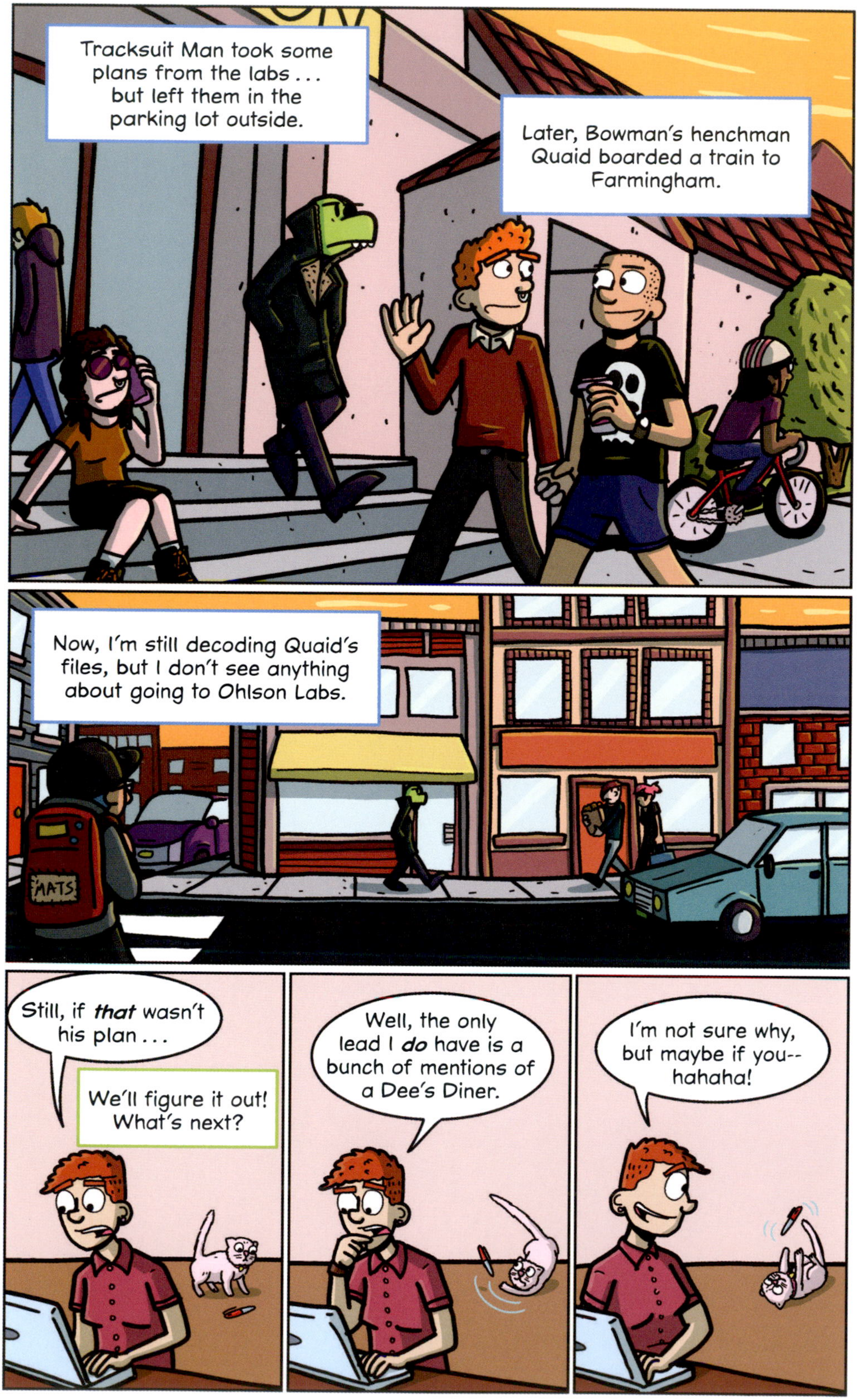
Tracksuit Man took some plans from the labs . . . but left them in the parking lot outside.
Later, Bowman's henchman Quaid boarded a train to Farmingham.
Now, I'm still decoding Quaid's files, but I don't see anything about going to Ohlson Labs.
MATS
Still, if *that* wasn't his plan . . .
We'll figure it out! What's next?
Well, the only lead I *do* have is a bunch of mentions of a Dee's Diner.
I'm not sure why, but maybe if you-- hahaha!

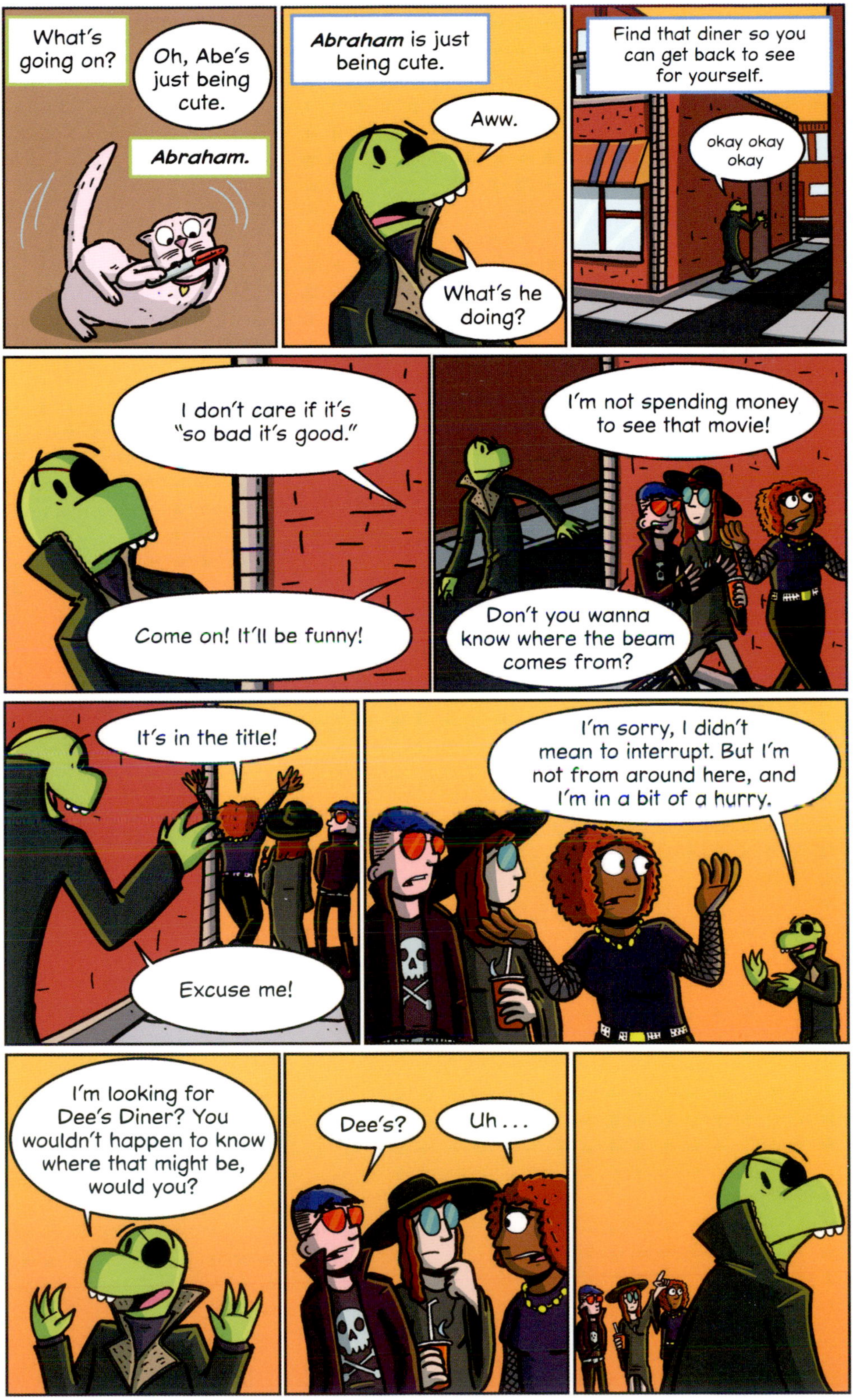
What's going on?
Oh, Abe's just being cute.
Abraham.
Abraham is just being cute.
Aww.
What's he doing?
Find that diner so you can get back to see for yourself.
okay okay okay
I don't care if it's "so bad it's good."
Come on! It'll be funny!
I'm not spending money to see that movie!
Don't you wanna know where the beam comes from?
It's in the title!
Excuse me!
I'm sorry, I didn't mean to interrupt. But I'm not from around here, and I'm in a bit of a hurry.
I'm looking for Dee's Diner? You wouldn't happen to know where that might be, would you?
Dee's?
Uh . . .

Well, would you look at that!

Jen, some helpful teens showed me the way! I'm here now!

Unless Dee's is a local chain. Which is honestly really inspiring!

Considering how many small businesses fail, especially restau--

Sure, sure. No idea what Quaid had planned, but he was headed here.

For all we know, he was just getting lunch.

I'll keep decoding these messages. You go inside and scope it out.

Got it. This shouldn't be too--

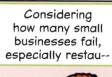

Oh geez!

What's wrong?

It's Tracksuit Guy! He's even wearing the tracksuit!

He's *still* wearing the tracksuit?

I told you, it's an everyday outfit!

He must be waiting for Quaid. What's the plan, T.D.?

Don't worry . . .

I've trained for this.

74

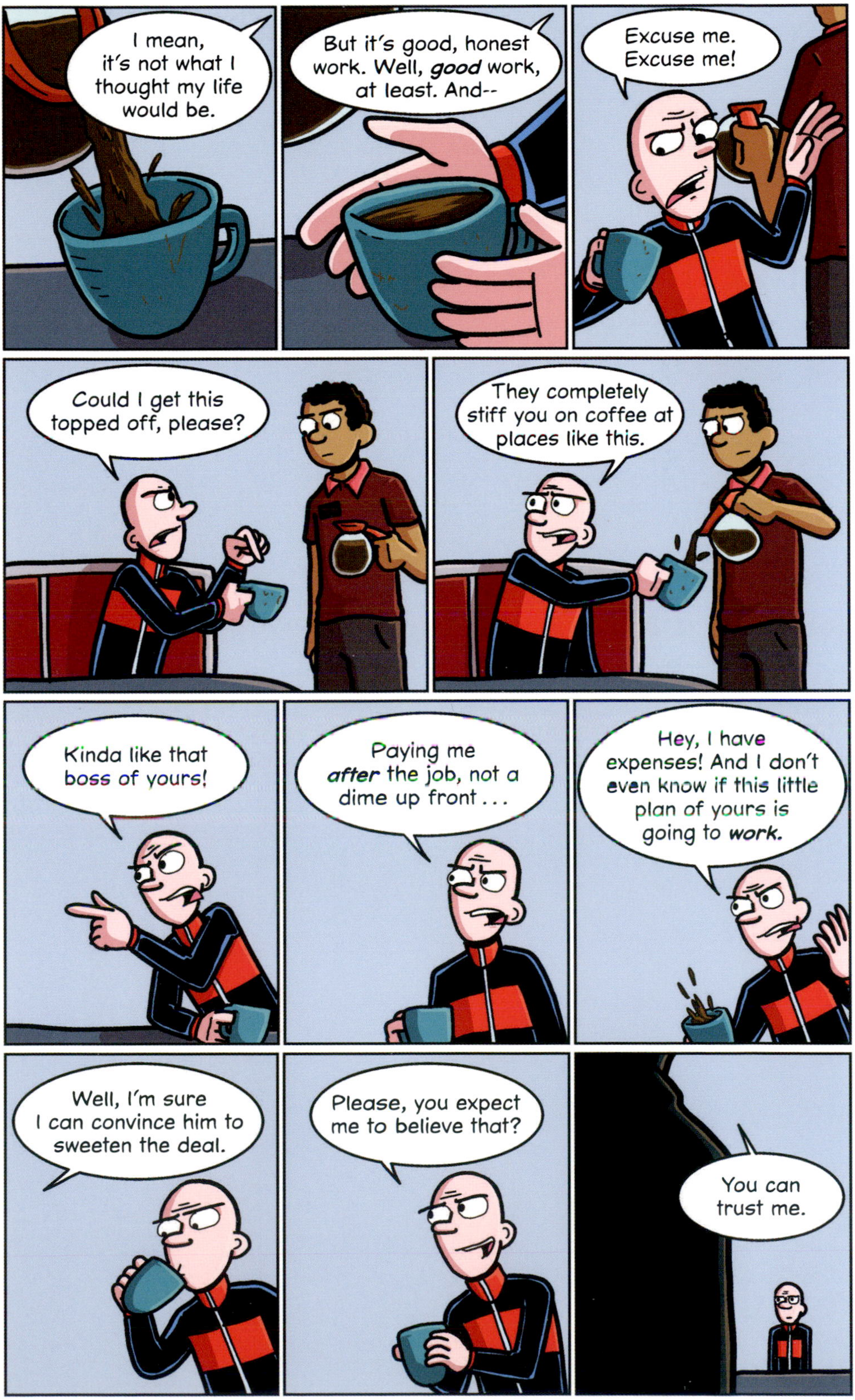
I mean, it's not what I thought my life would be.
But it's good, honest work. Well, *good* work, at least. And--
Excuse me. Excuse me!
Could I get this topped off, please?
They completely stiff you on coffee at places like this.
Kinda like that boss of yours!
Paying me *after* the job, not a dime up front . . .
Hey, I have expenses! And I don't even know if this little plan of yours is going to *work.*
Well, I'm sure I can convince him to sweeten the deal.
Please, you expect me to believe that?
You can trust me.

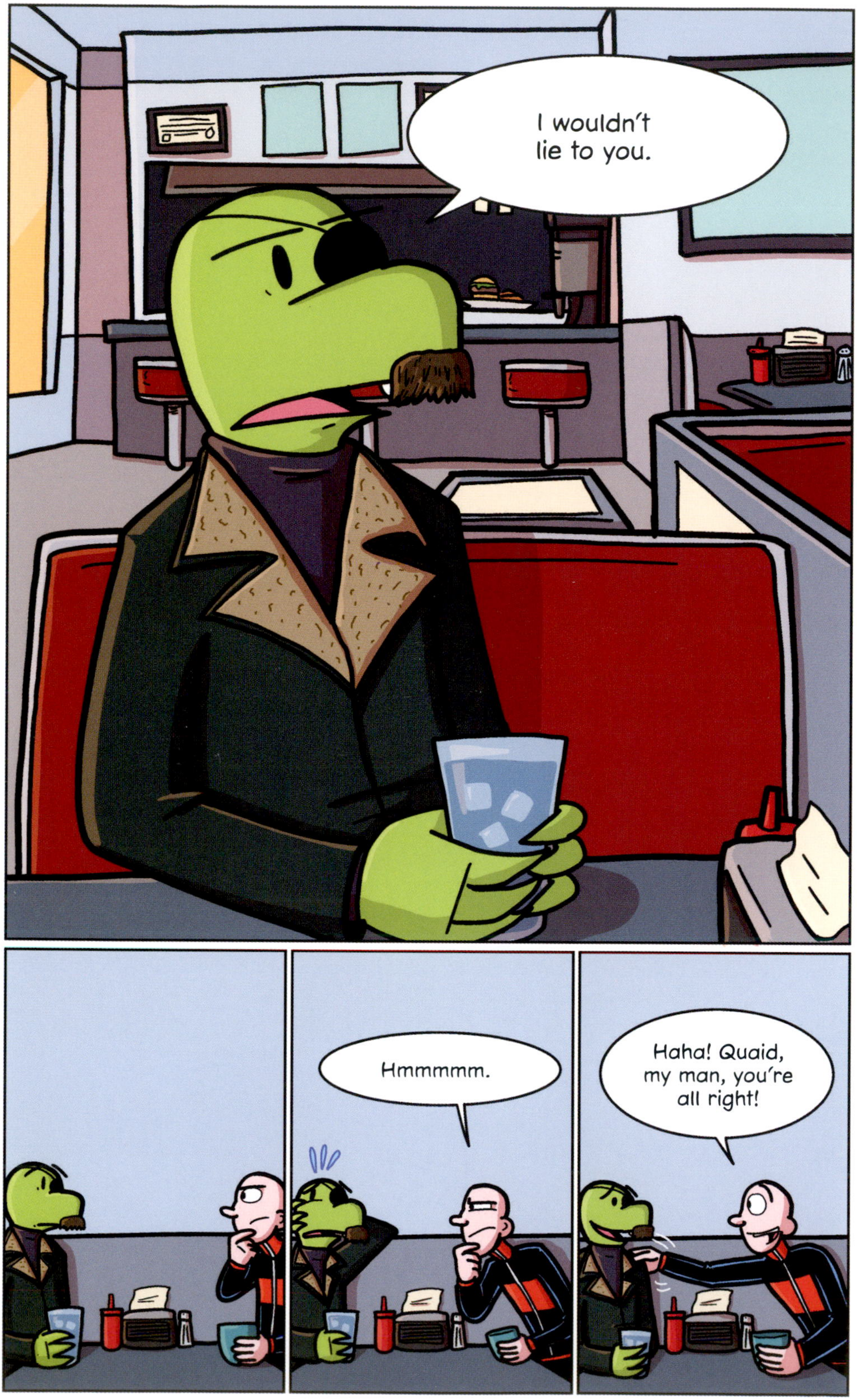
I wouldn't lie to you.
Hmmmmm.
Haha! Quaid, my man, you're all right!

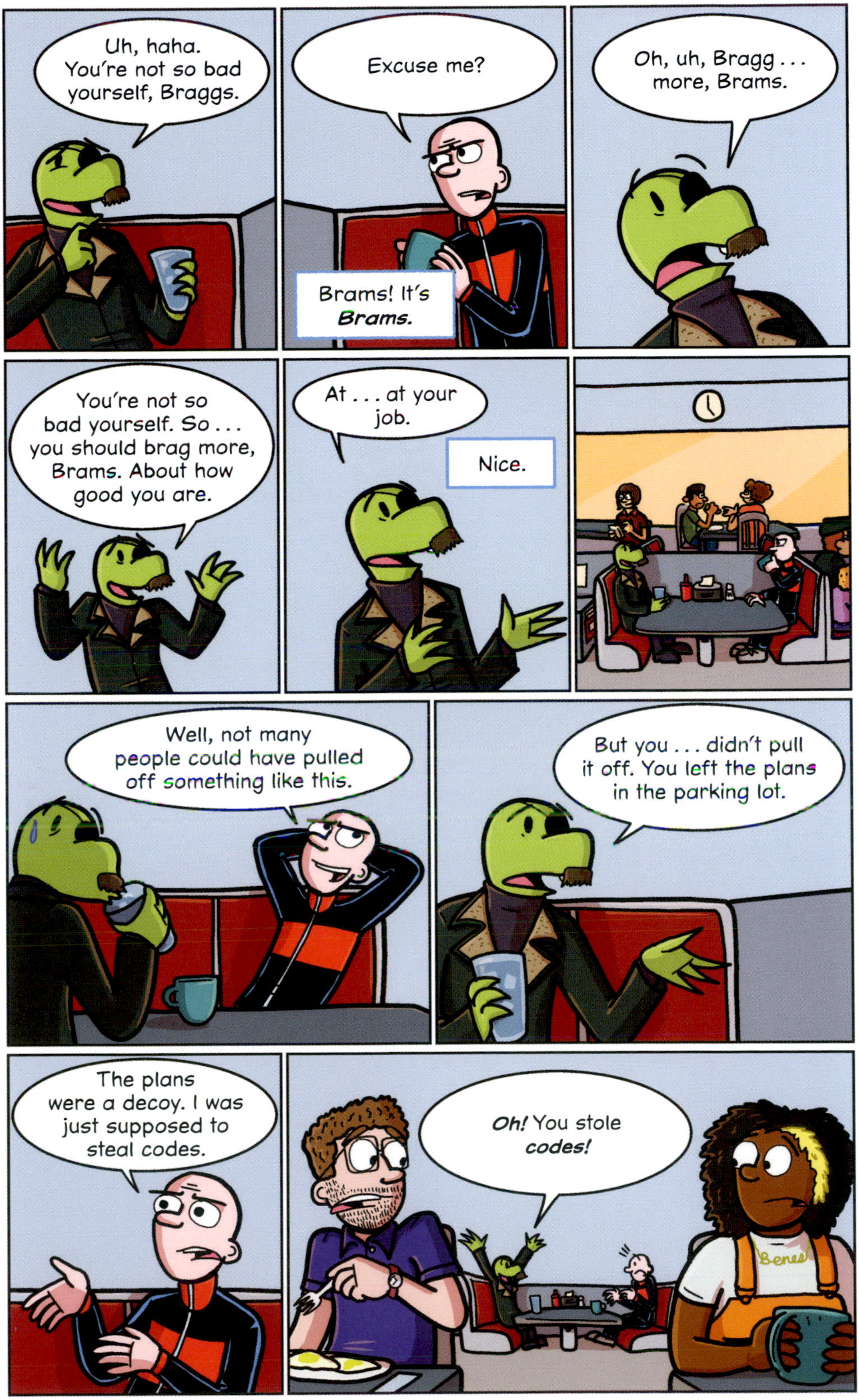
Uh, haha. You're not so bad yourself, Braggs.
Excuse me?
Brams! It's *Brams.*
Oh, uh, Bragg . . . more, Brams.
You're not so bad yourself. So . . . you should brag more, Brams. About how good you are.
At . . . at your job.
Nice.
Well, not many people could have pulled off something like this.
But you . . . didn't pull it off. You left the plans in the parking lot.
The plans were a decoy. I was just supposed to steal codes.
Oh! You stole *codes!*
Benes

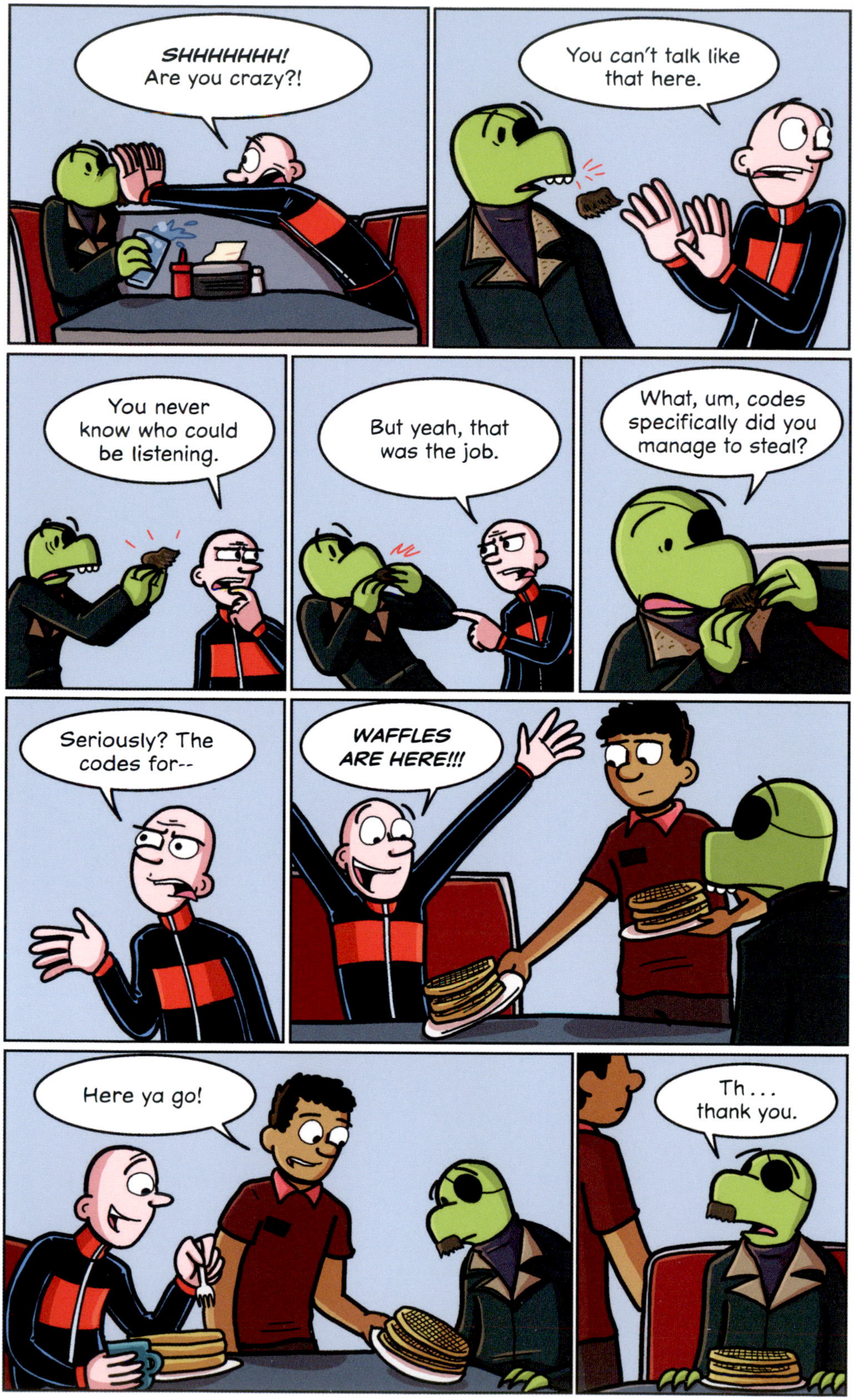
SHHHHHHH!
Are you crazy?!
You can't talk like that here.
You never know who could be listening.
But yeah, that was the job.
What, um, codes specifically did you manage to steal?
Seriously? The codes for--
WAFFLES ARE HERE!!!
Here ya go!
Th . . . thank you.

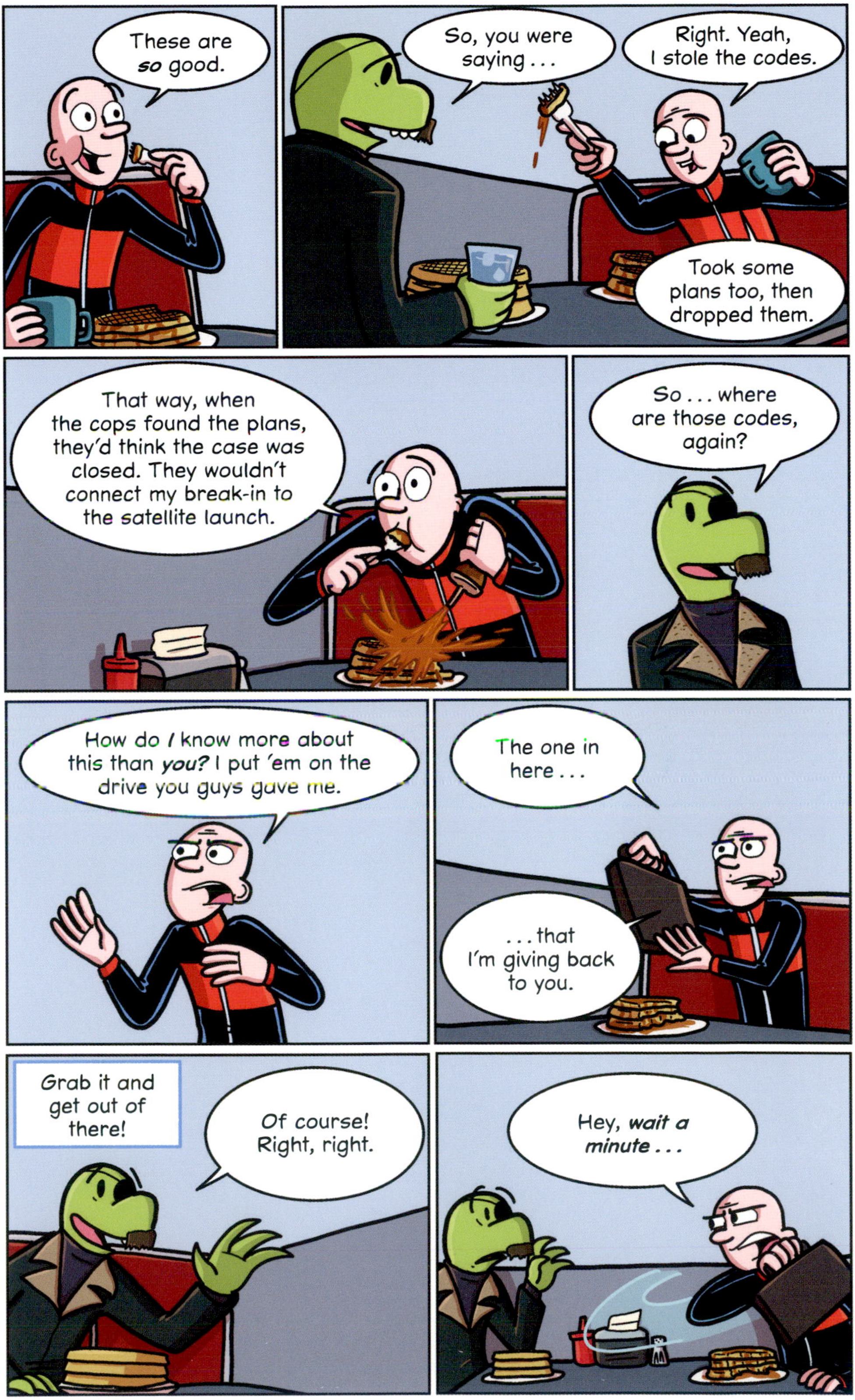
These are *so* good.
So, you were saying . . .
Right. Yeah, I stole the codes.
Took some plans too, then dropped them.
That way, when the cops found the plans, they'd think the case was closed. They wouldn't connect my break-in to the satellite launch.
So . . . where are those codes, again?
How do *I* know more about this than *you?* I put 'em on the drive you guys gave me.
The one in here . . .
. . . that I'm giving back to you.
Grab it and get out of there!
Of course! Right, right.
Hey, ***wait a minute . . .***

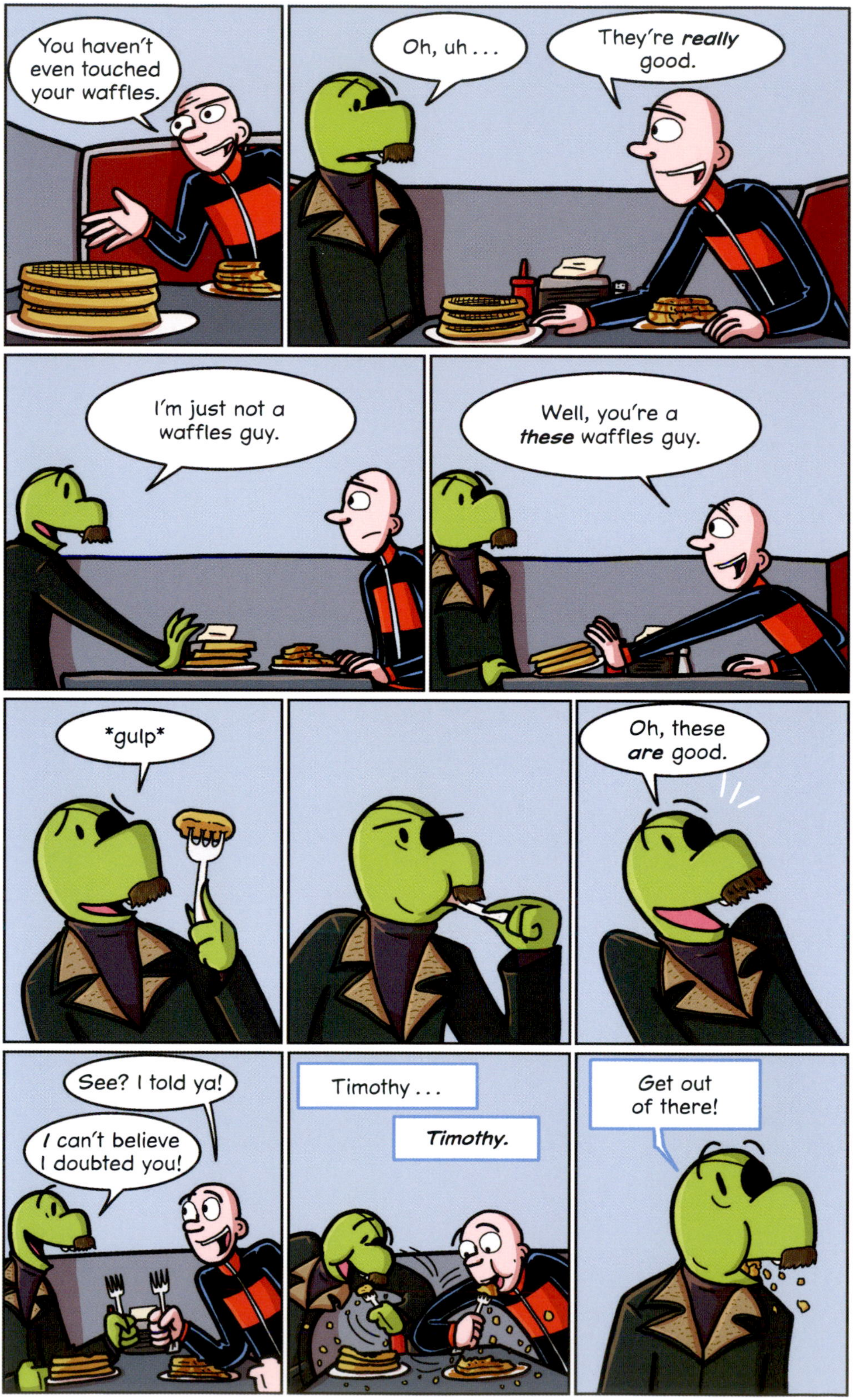
You haven't even touched your waffles.
Oh, uh . . .
They're *really* good.
I'm just not a waffles guy.
Well, you're a *these* waffles guy.
gulp
Oh, these *are* good.
See? I told ya!
I can't believe I doubted you!
Timothy . . .
Timothy.
Get out of there!

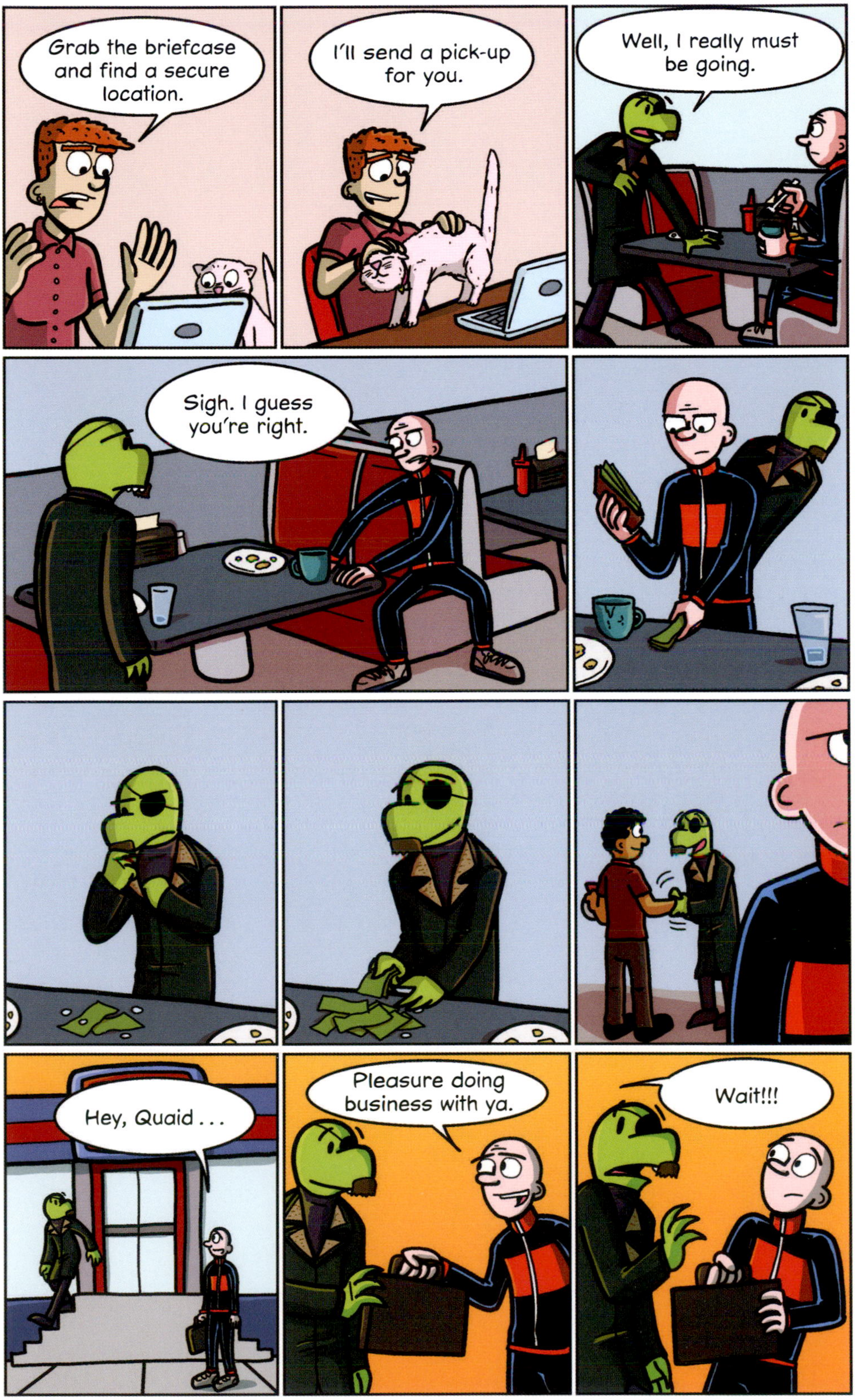
Grab the briefcase and find a secure location.
I'll send a pick-up for you.
Well, I really must be going.
Sigh. I guess you're right.
Hey, Quaid . . .
Pleasure doing business with ya.
Wait!!!

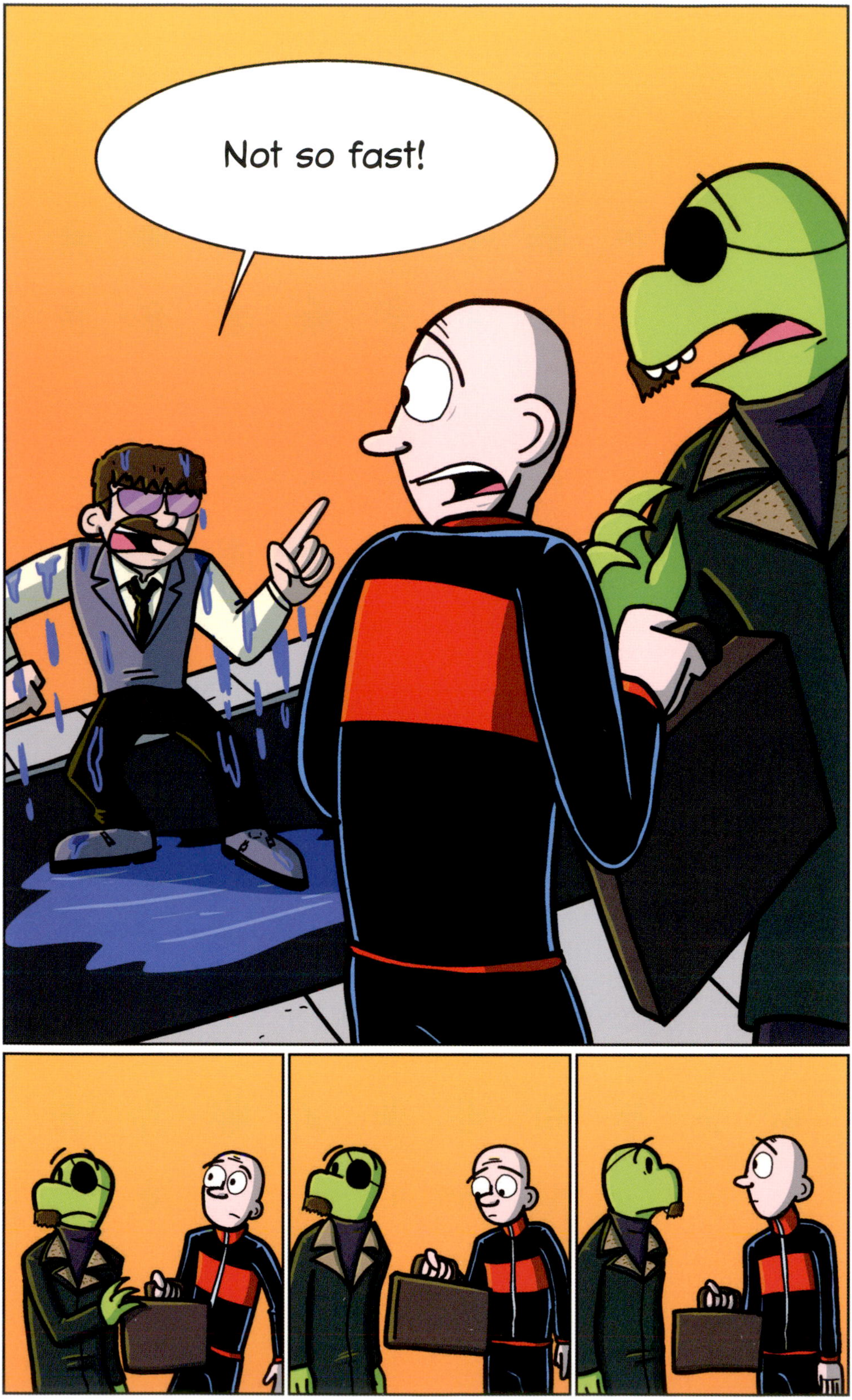
Not so fast!

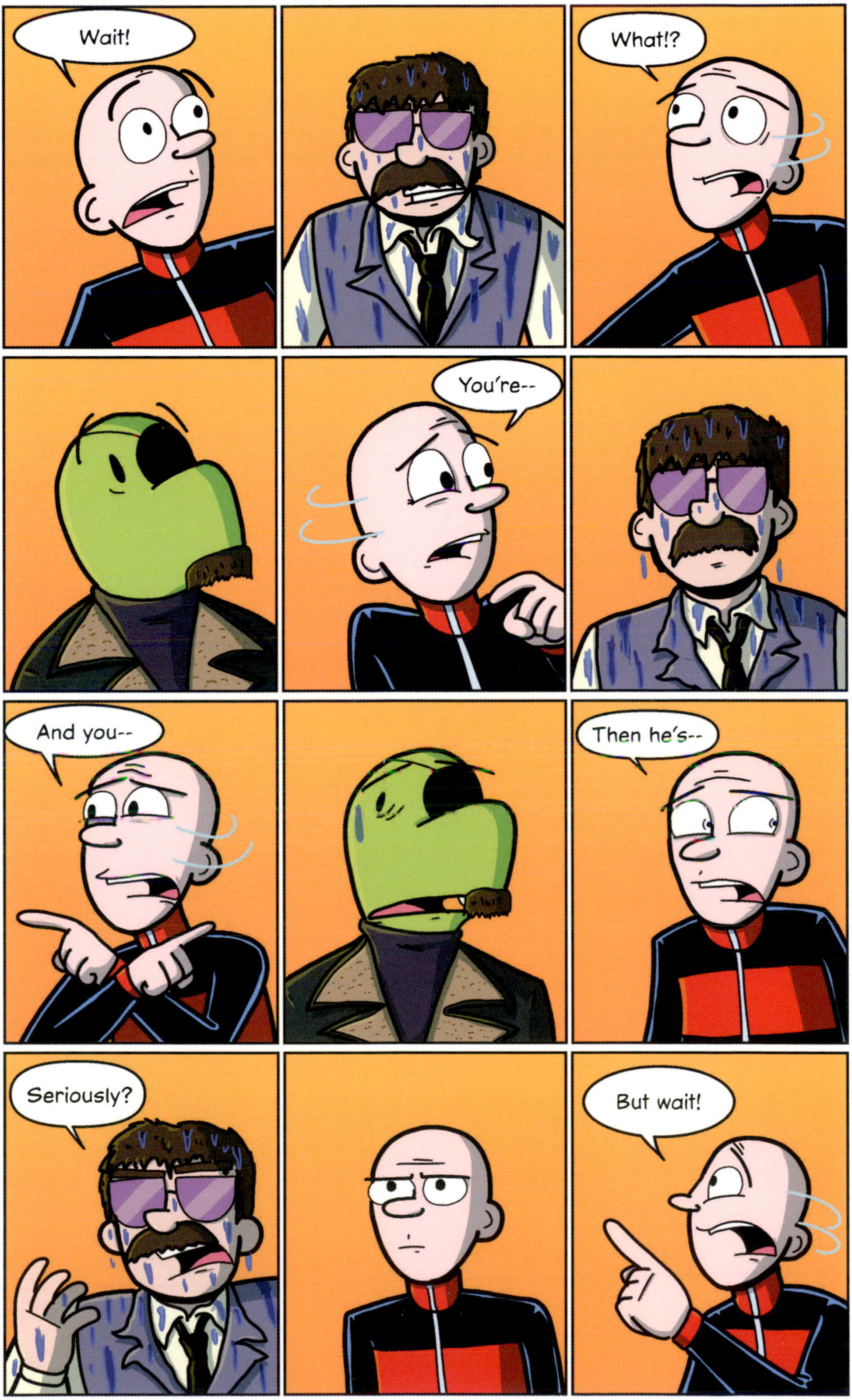
Wait!
What!?
You're--
And you--
Then he's--
Seriously?
But wait!

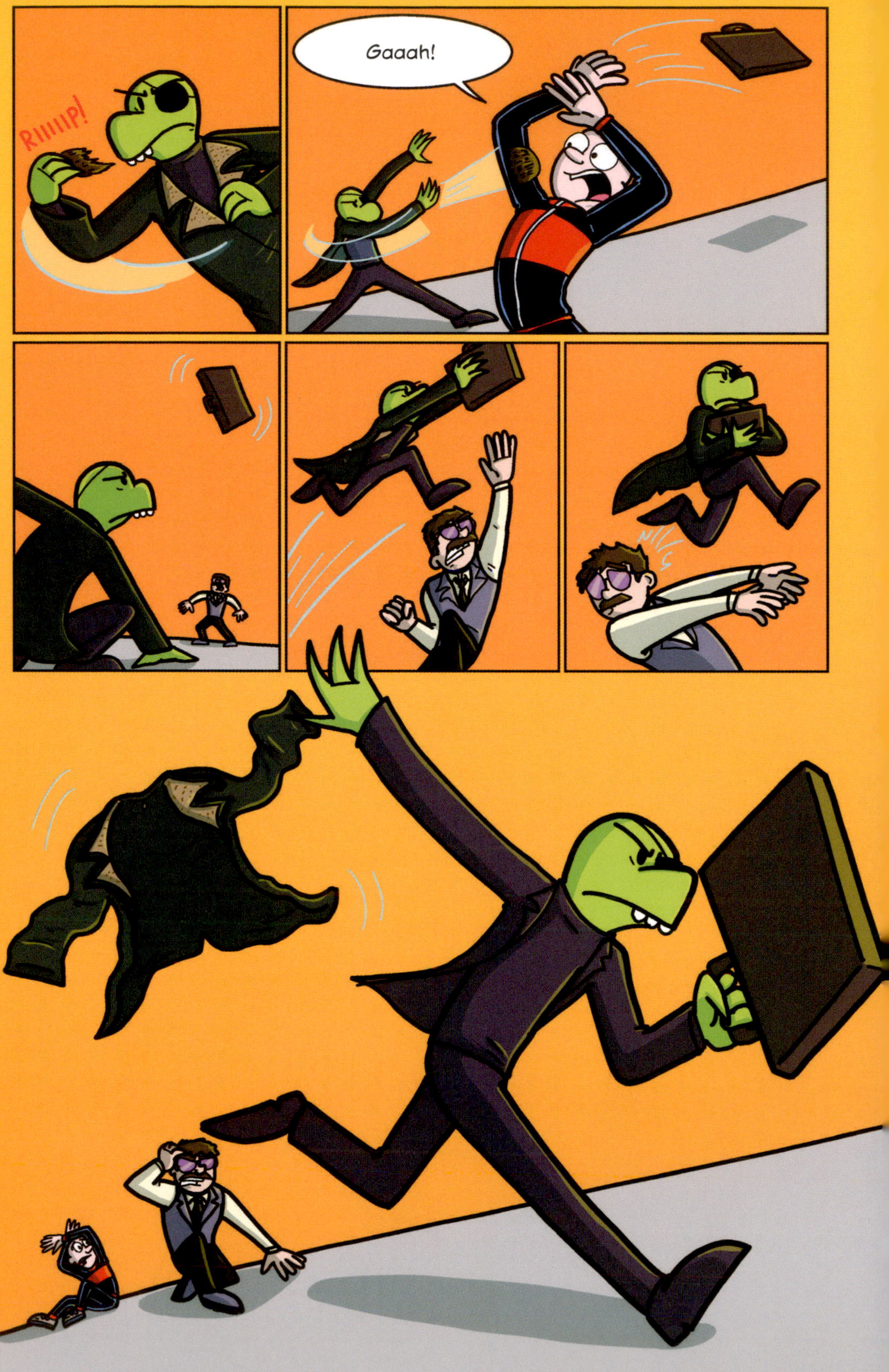
RIIIIIP!
Gaaah!

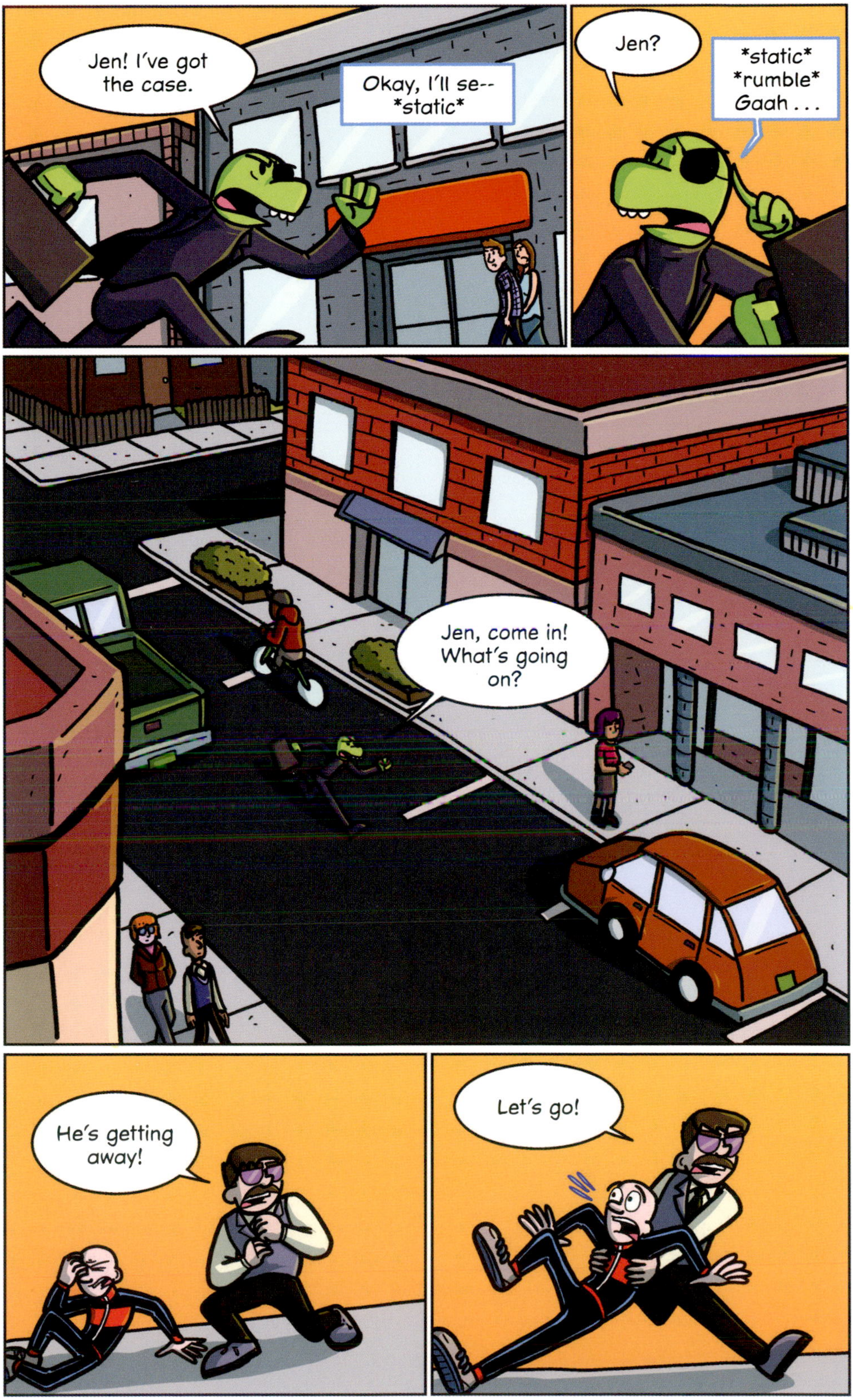
Jen! I've got the case.
Okay, I'll se-- *static*
Jen?
static *rumble* Gaah . . .
Jen, come in! What's going on?
He's getting away!
Let's go!

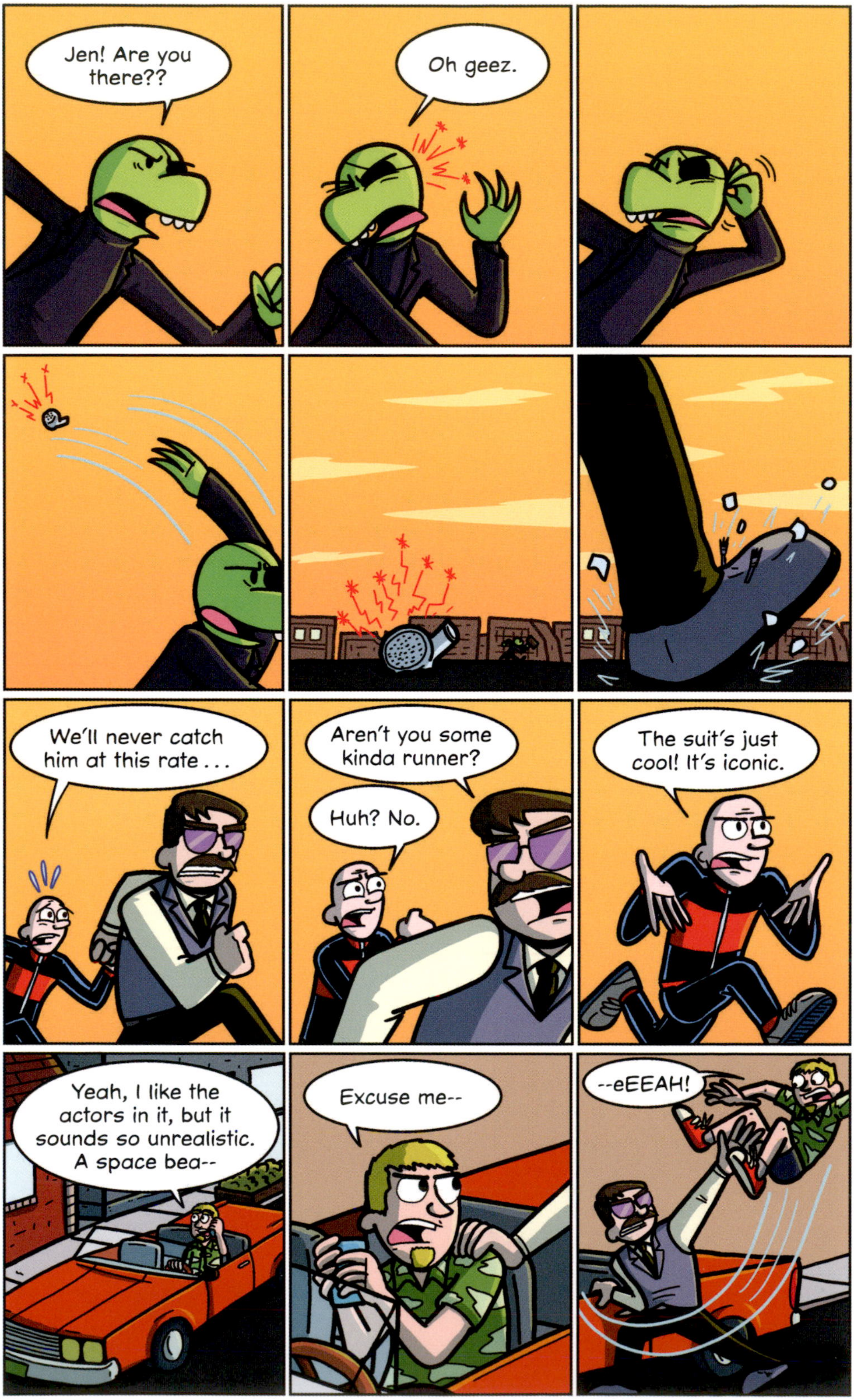
Jen! Are you there??
Oh geez.
We'll never catch him at this rate . . .
Aren't you some kinda runner?
Huh? No.
The suit's just cool! It's iconic.
Yeah, I like the actors in it, but it sounds so unrealistic. A space bea--
Excuse me--
--eEEAH!

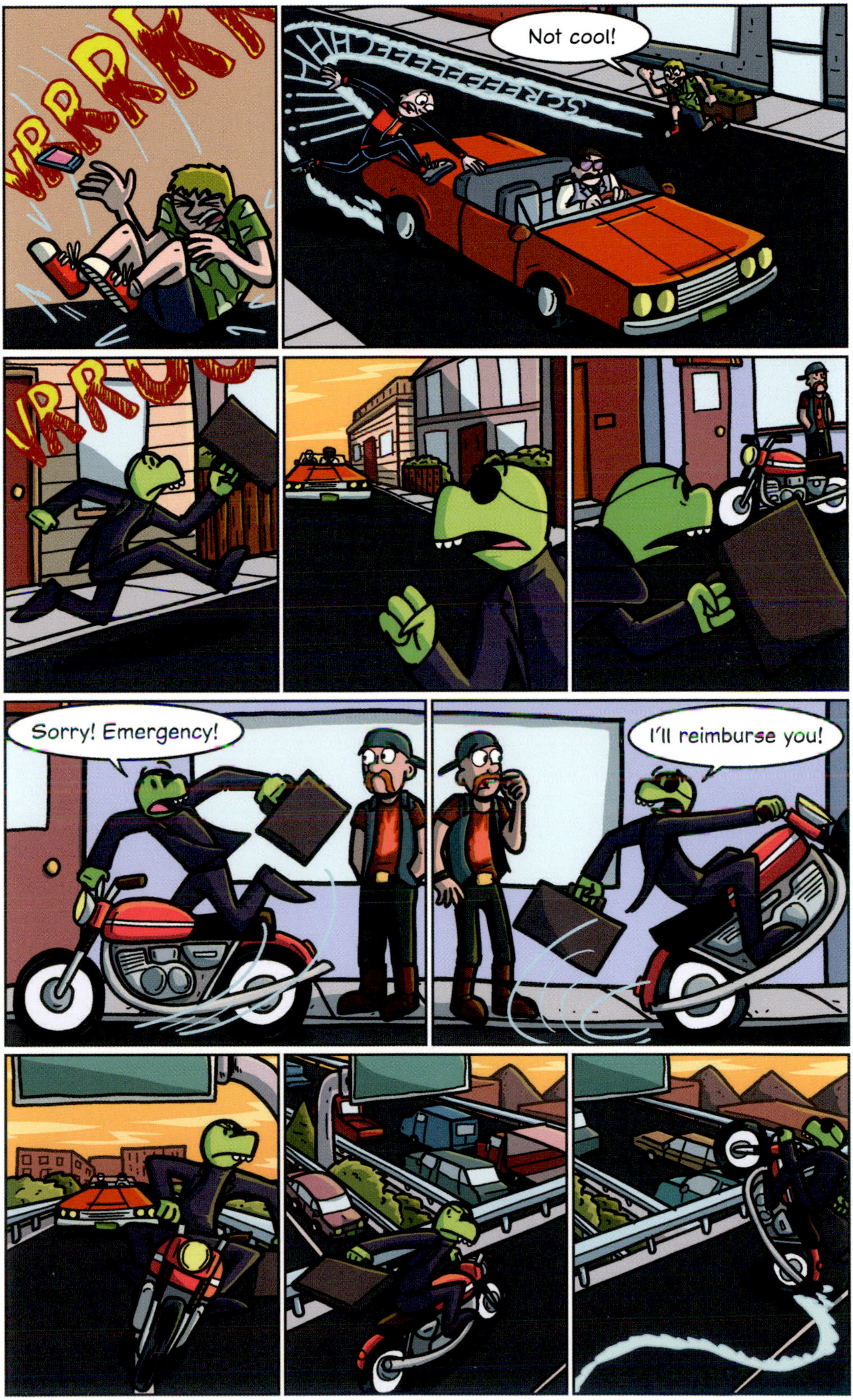
VRRRKK
SCREEEEEEEECH
Not cool!
VRRO
Sorry! Emergency!
I'll reimburse you!

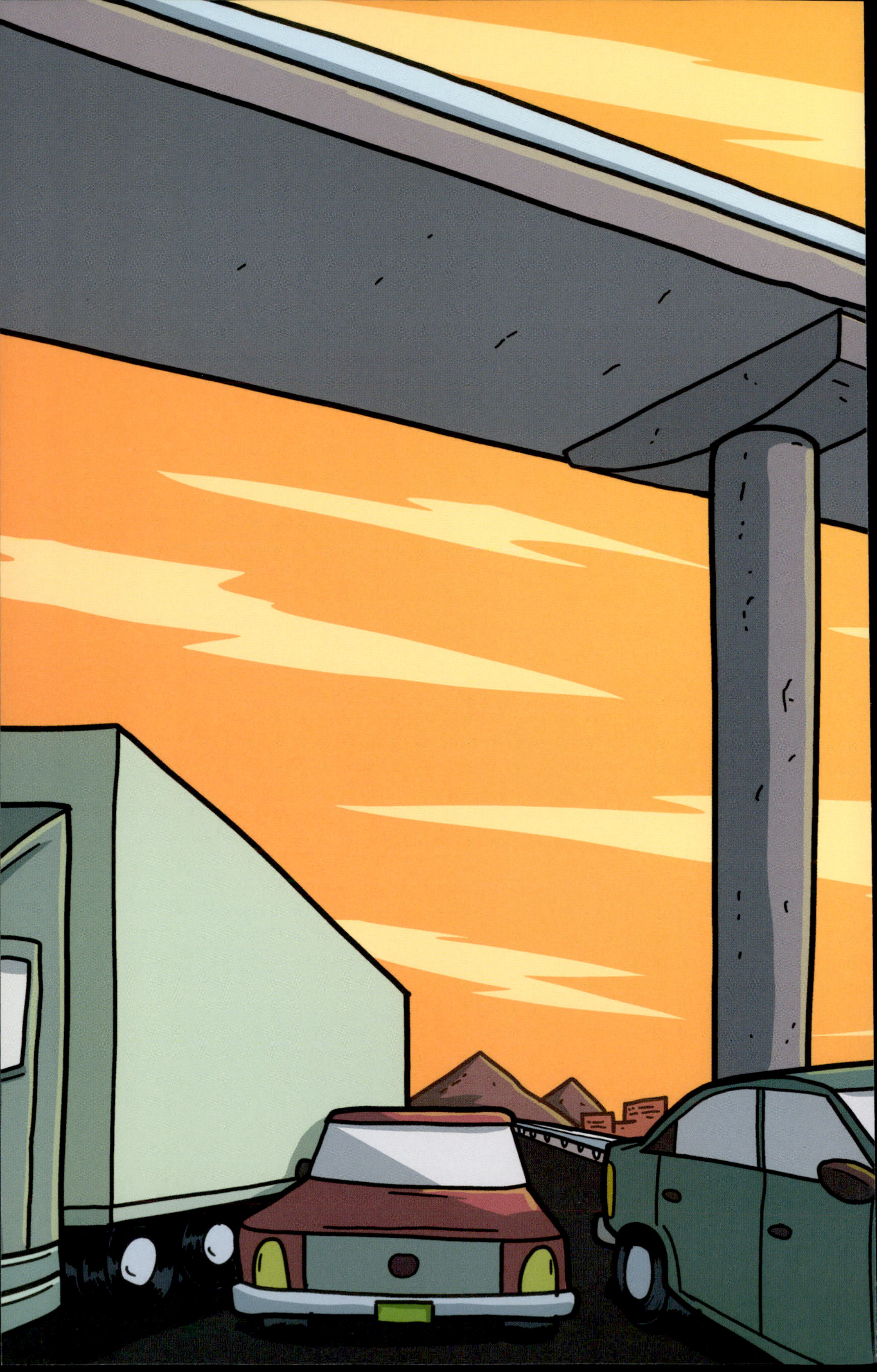

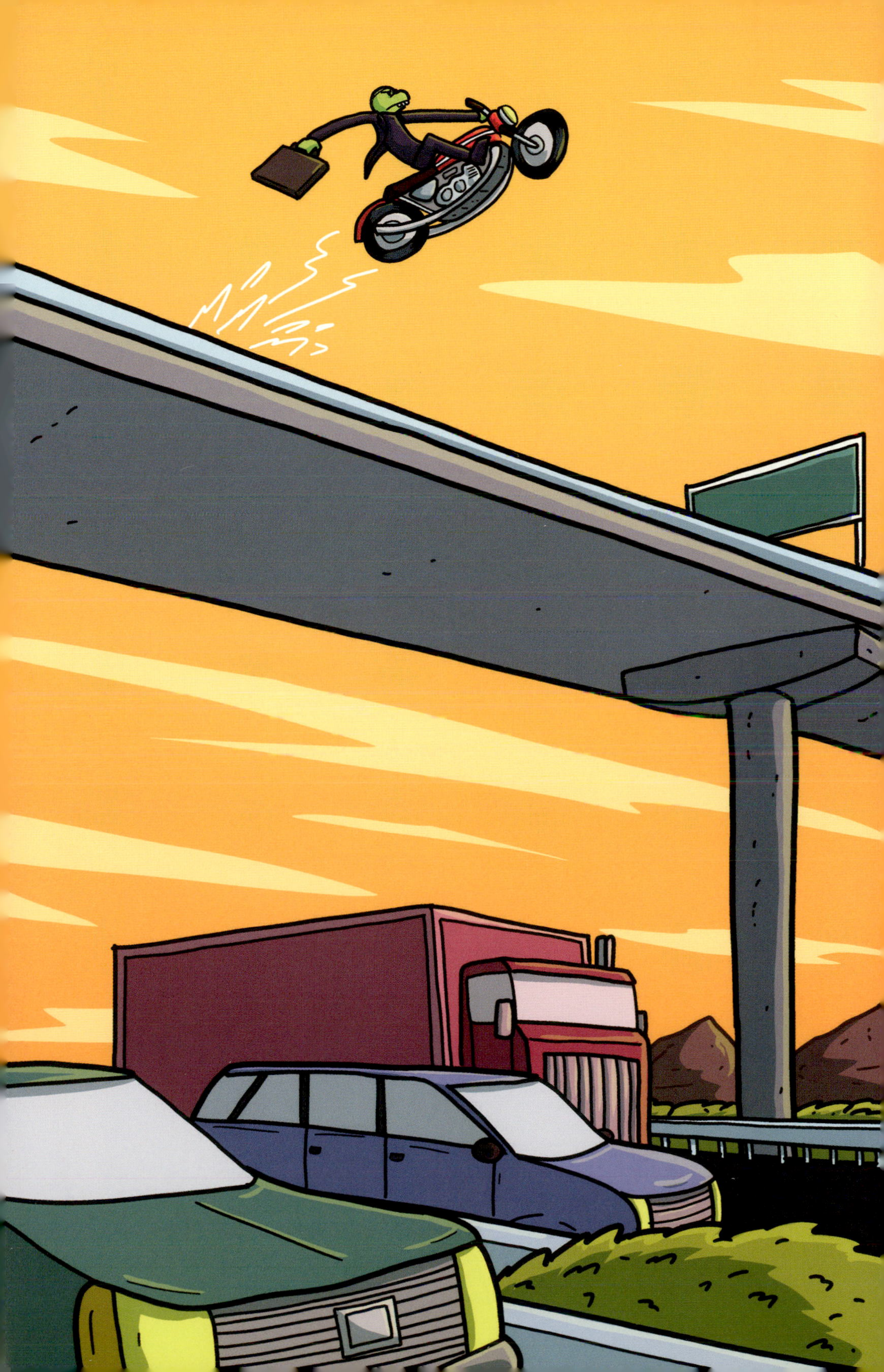

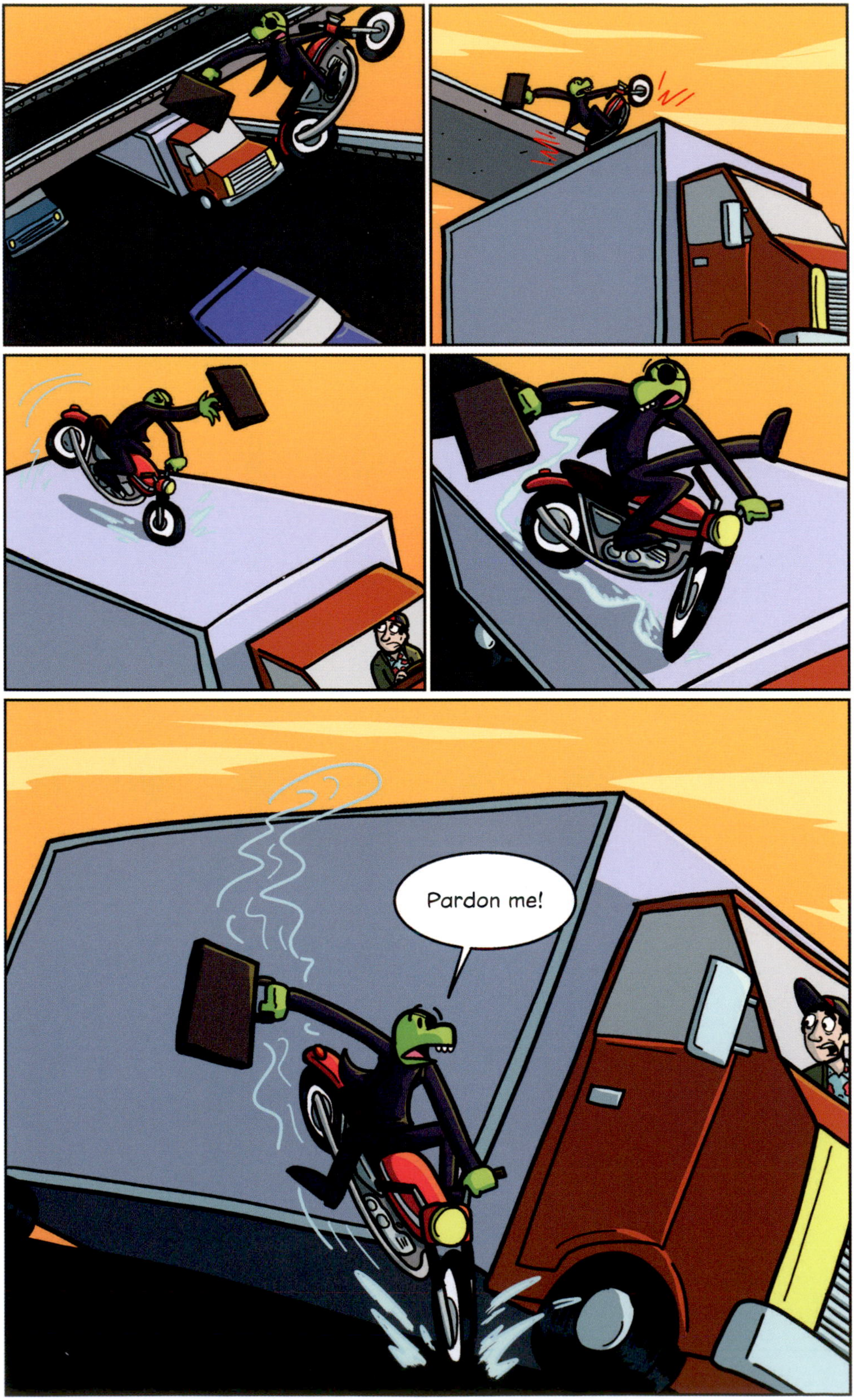
Pardon me!

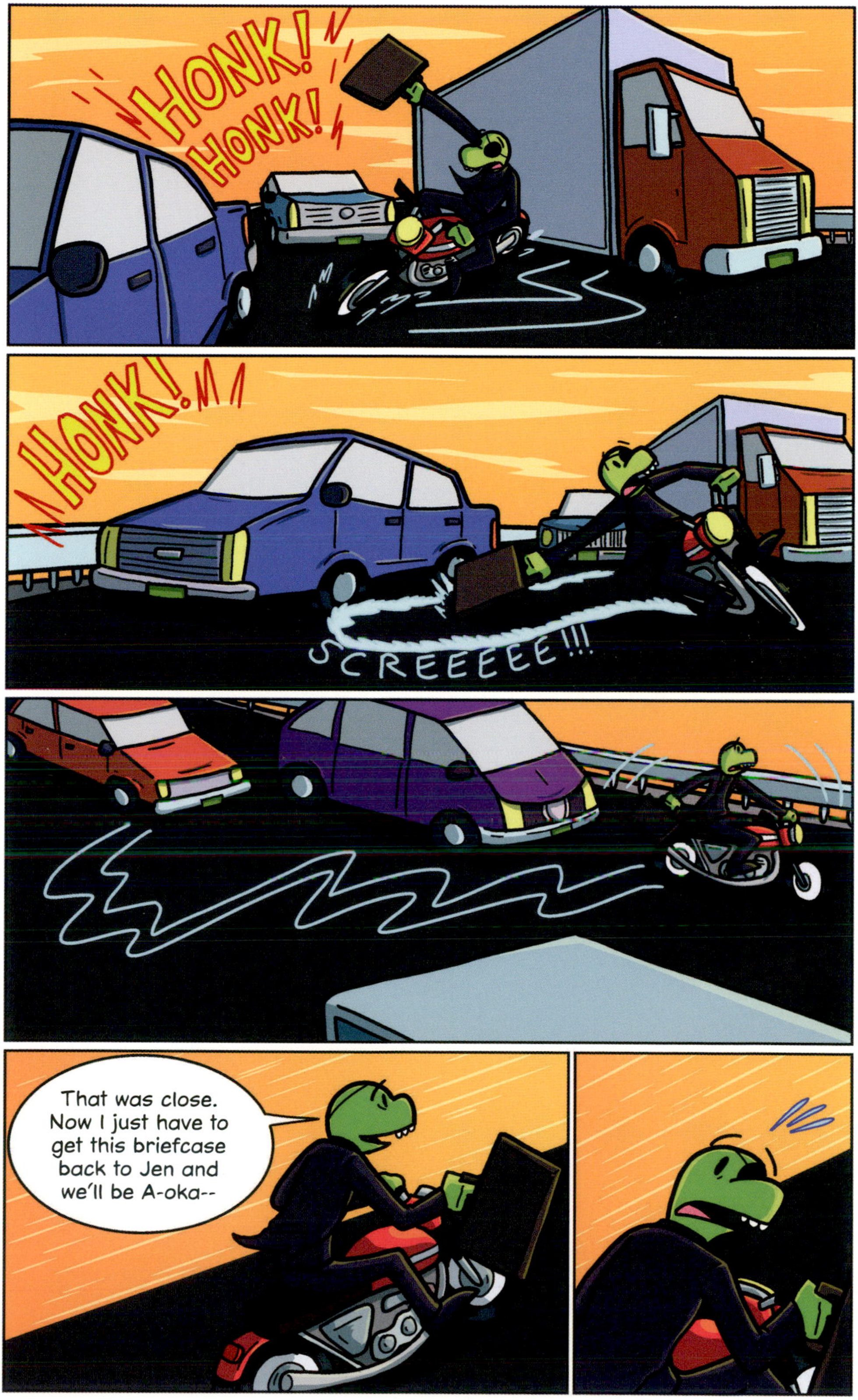
HONK! HONK!
HONK!
SCREEEEEE!!!
That was close. Now I just have to get this briefcase back to Jen and we'll be A-oka--

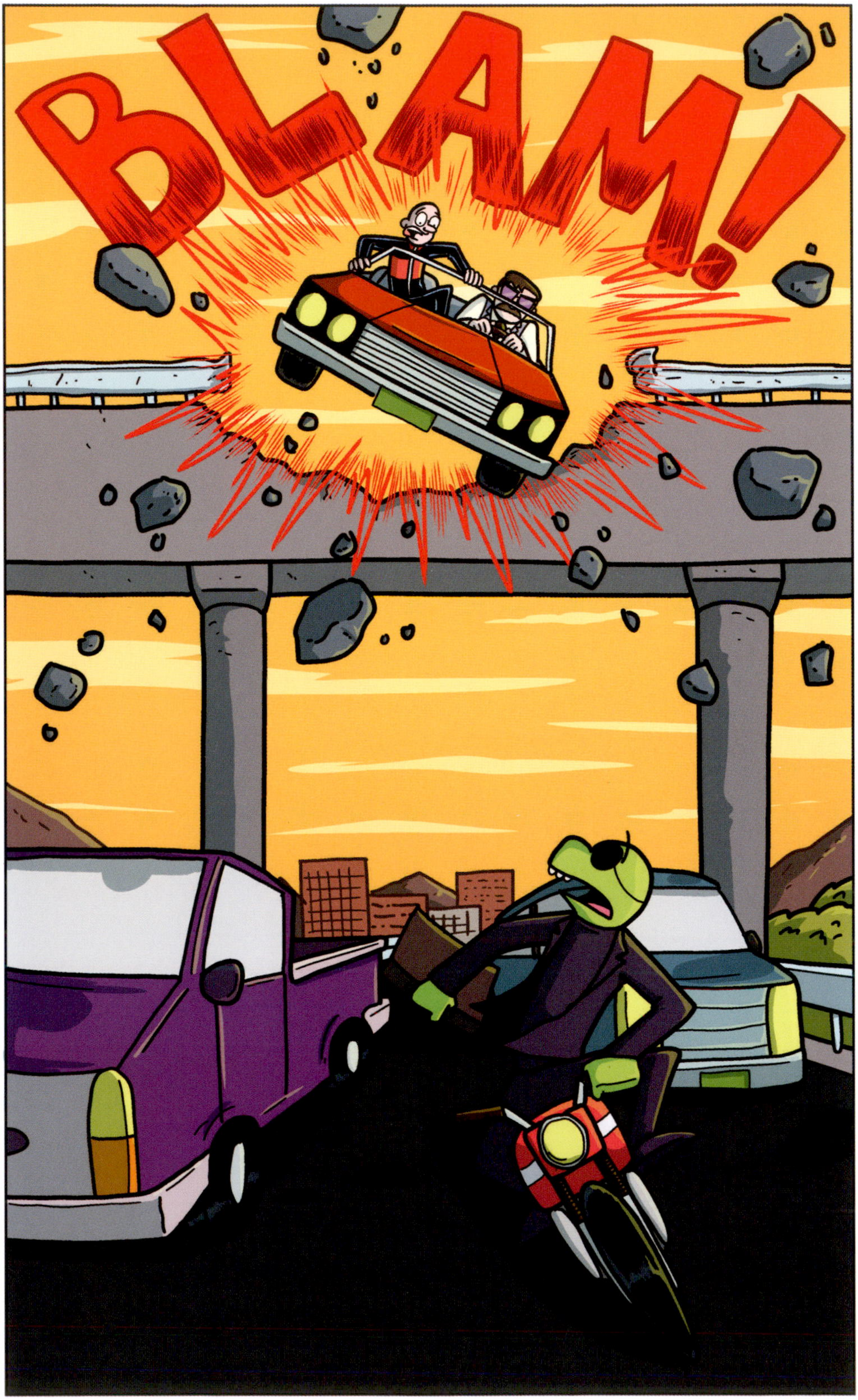
BLAM!

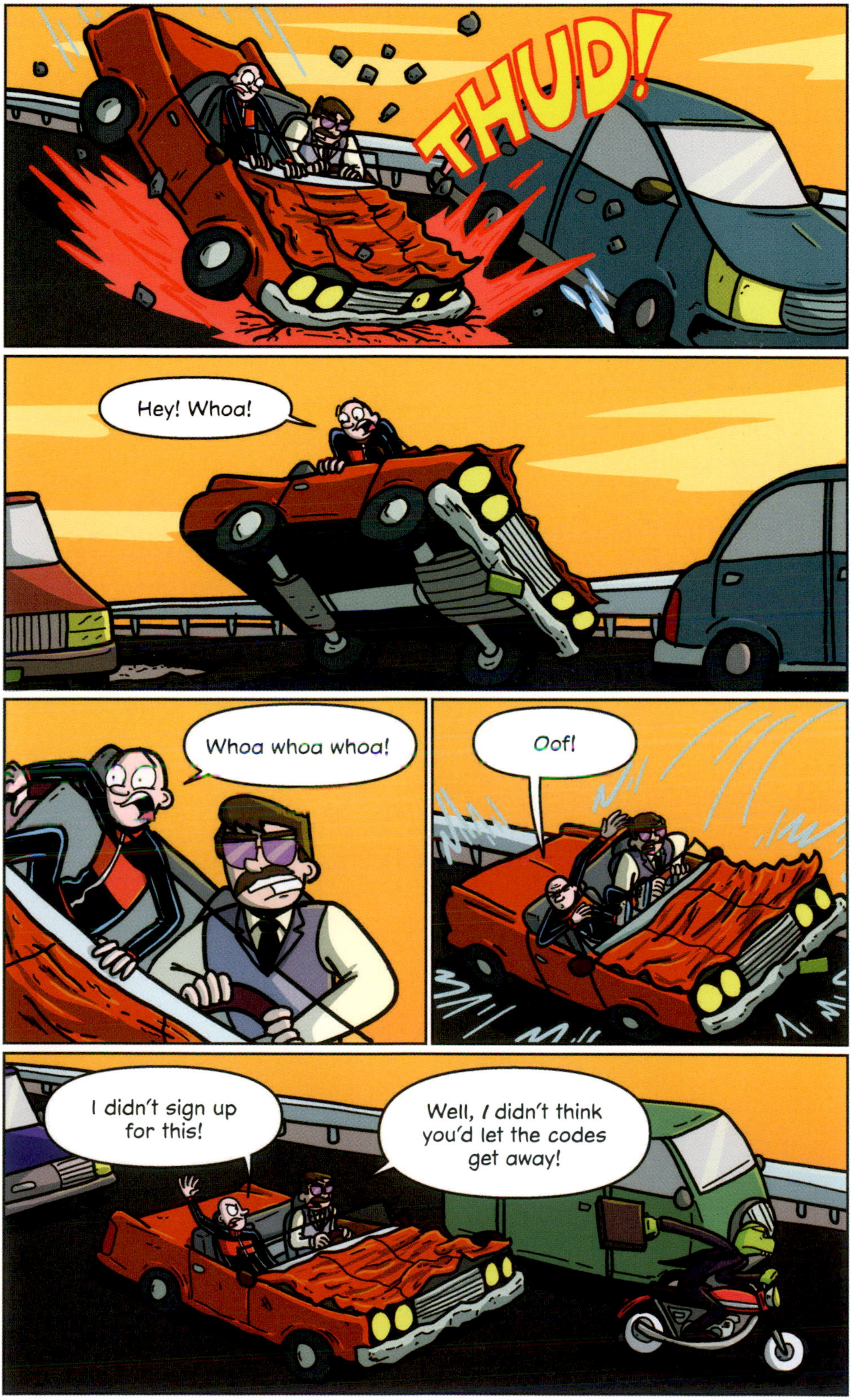
THUD!
Hey! Whoa!
Whoa whoa whoa!
Oof!
I didn't sign up for this!
Well, *I* didn't think you'd let the codes get away!

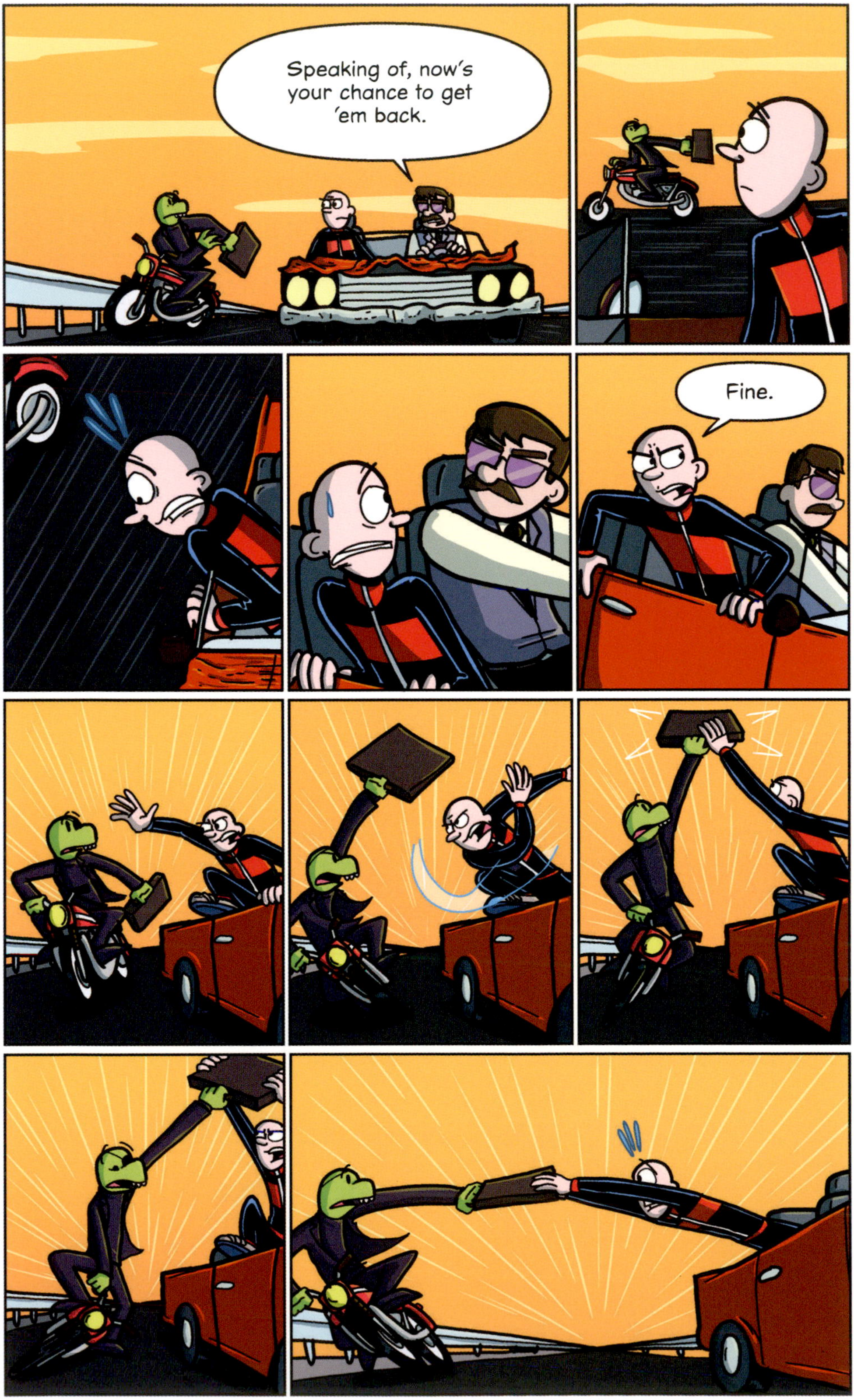
Speaking of, now's your chance to get 'em back.
Fine.

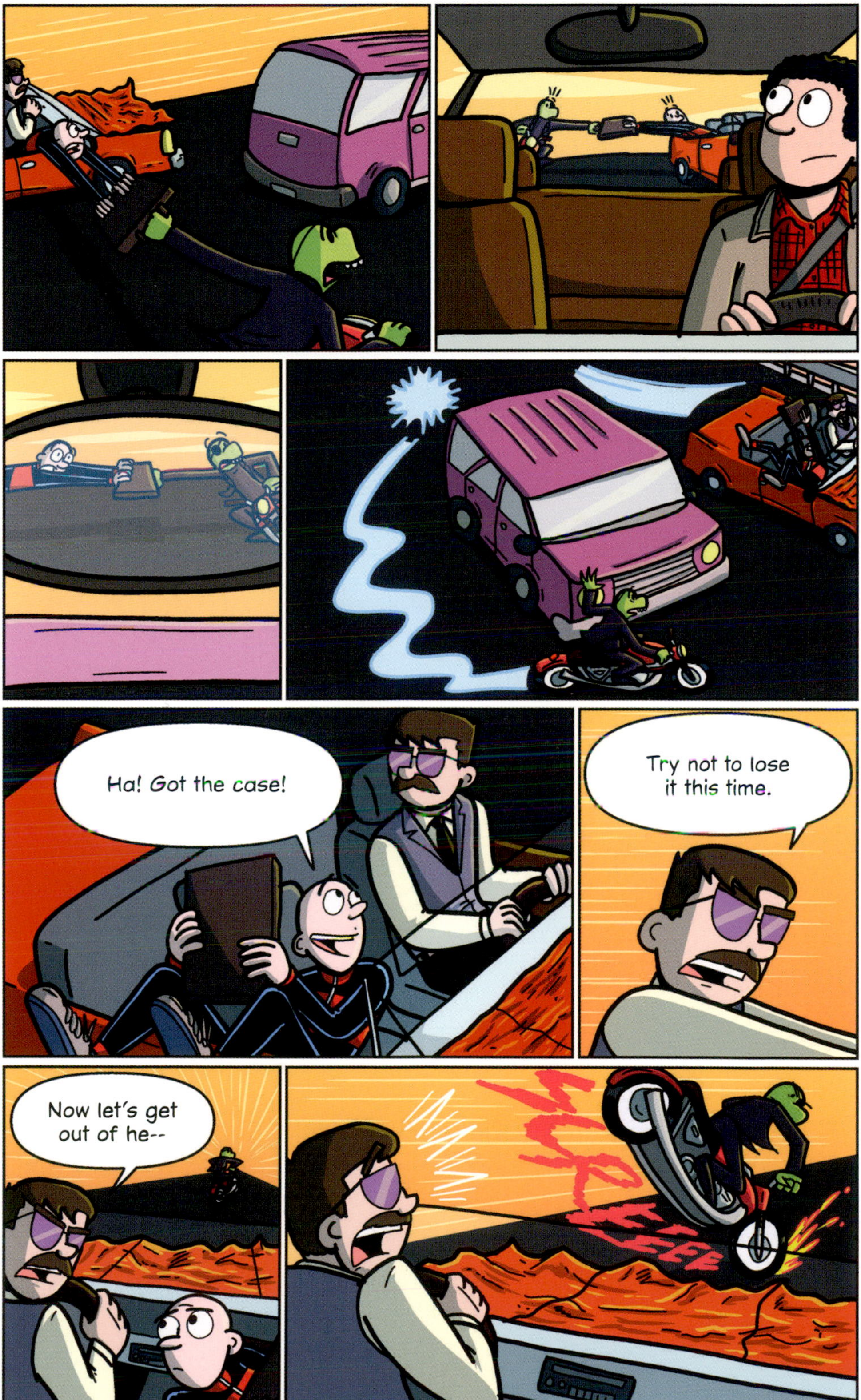
Ha! Got the case!
Try not to lose it this time.
Now let's get out of he--
SCREEEE

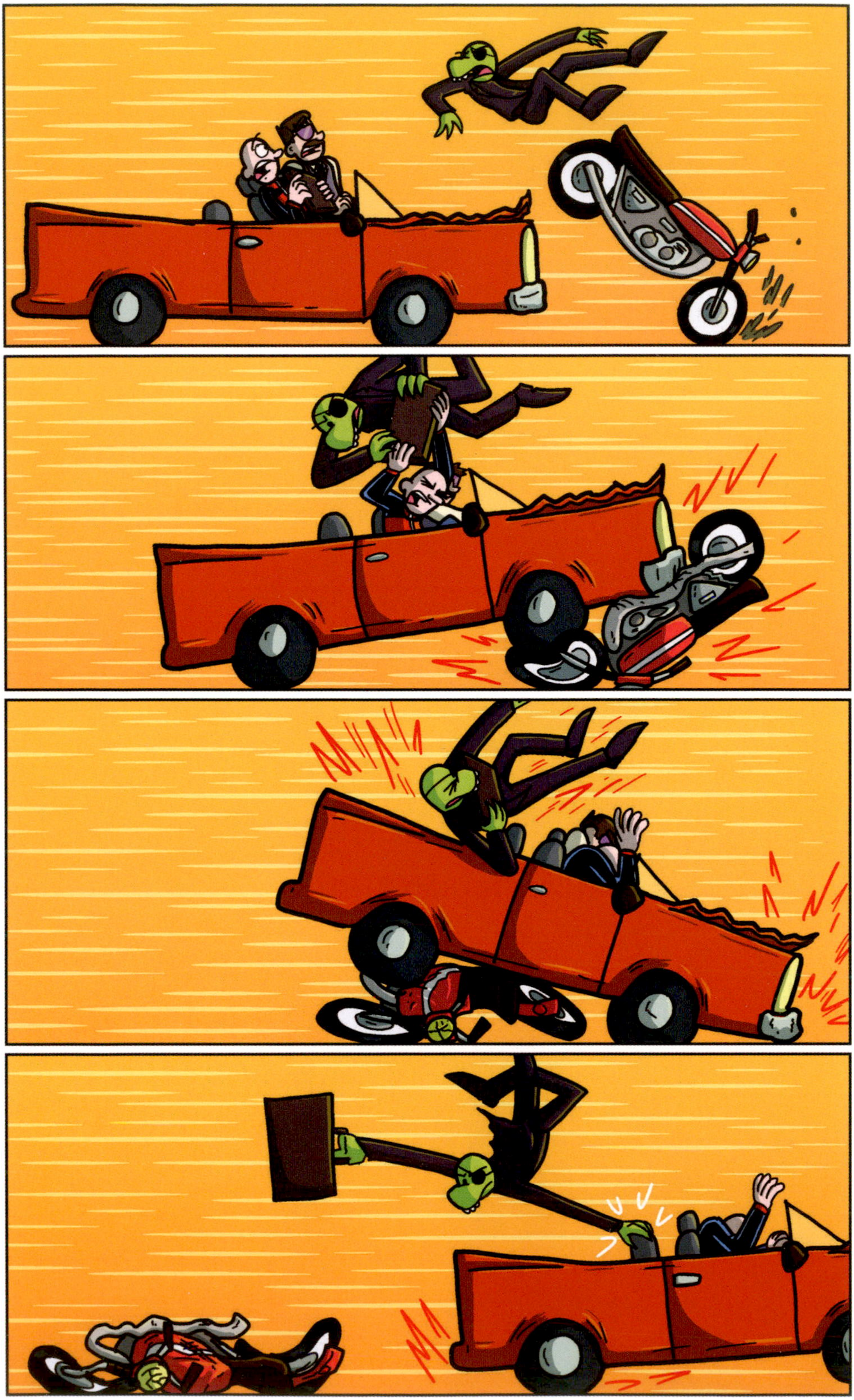

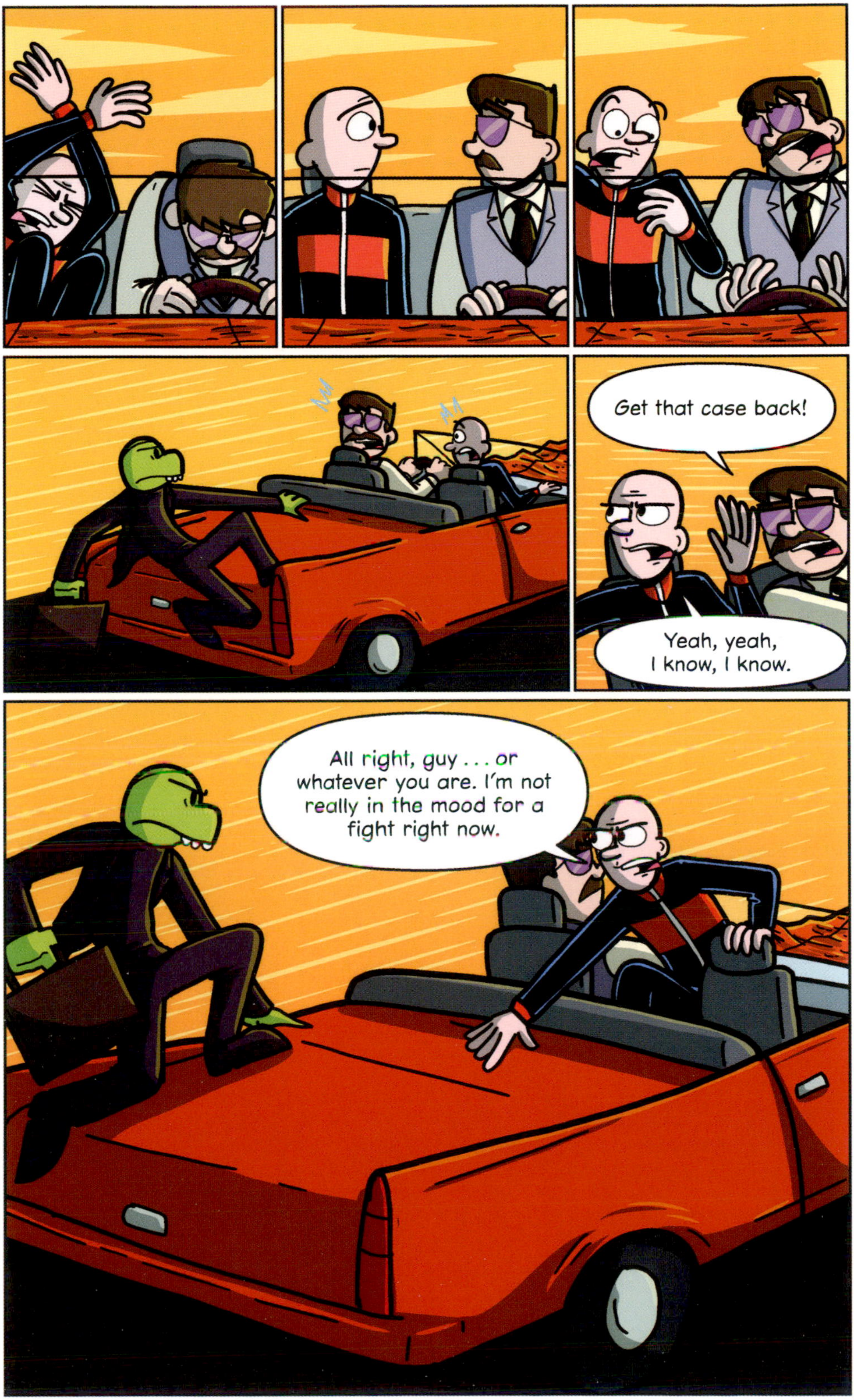
Get that case back!
Yeah, yeah, I know, I know.
All right, guy . . . or whatever you are. I'm not really in the mood for a fight right now.

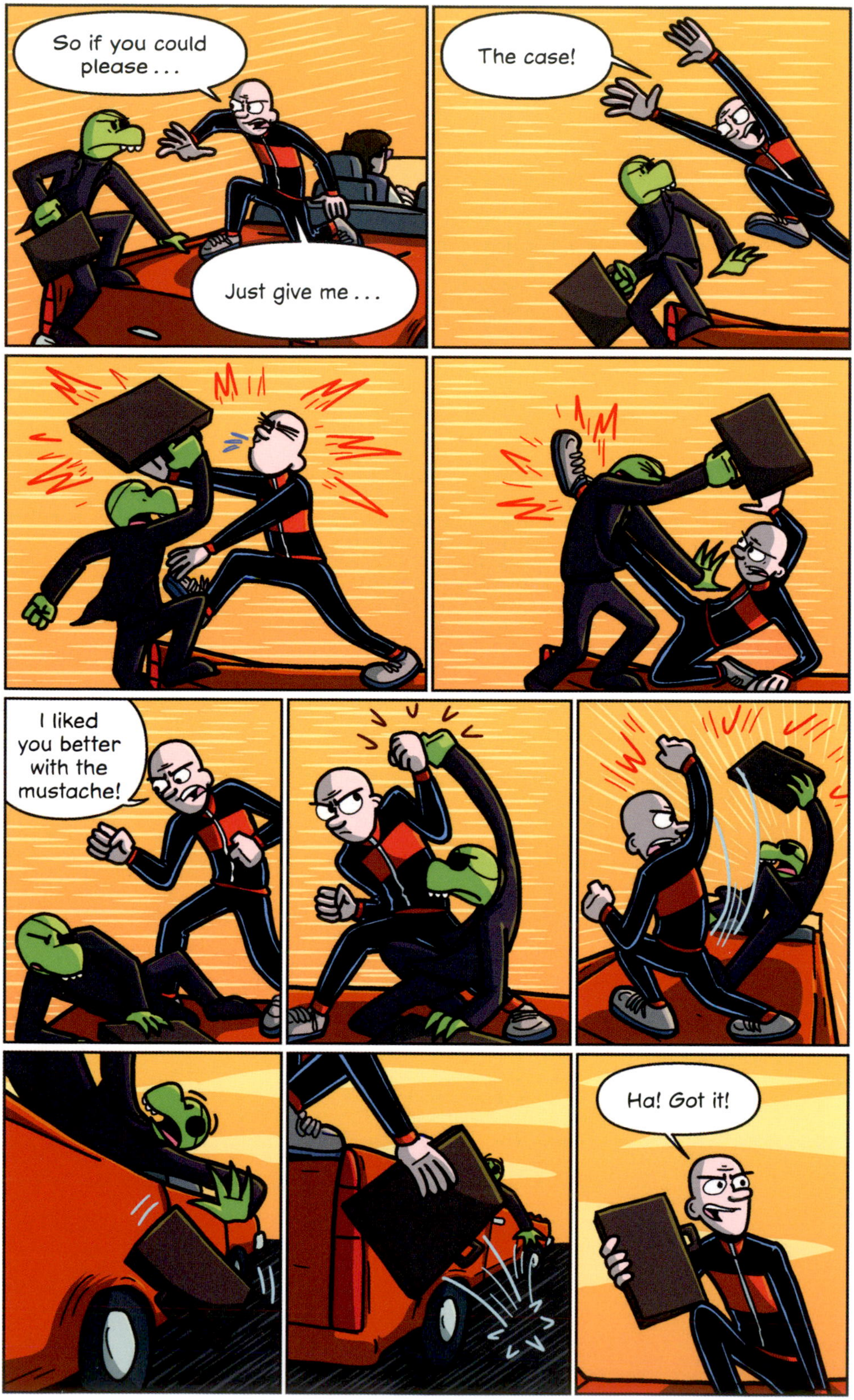
So if you could please . . .
Just give me . . .
The case!
I liked you better with the mustache!
Ha! Got it!

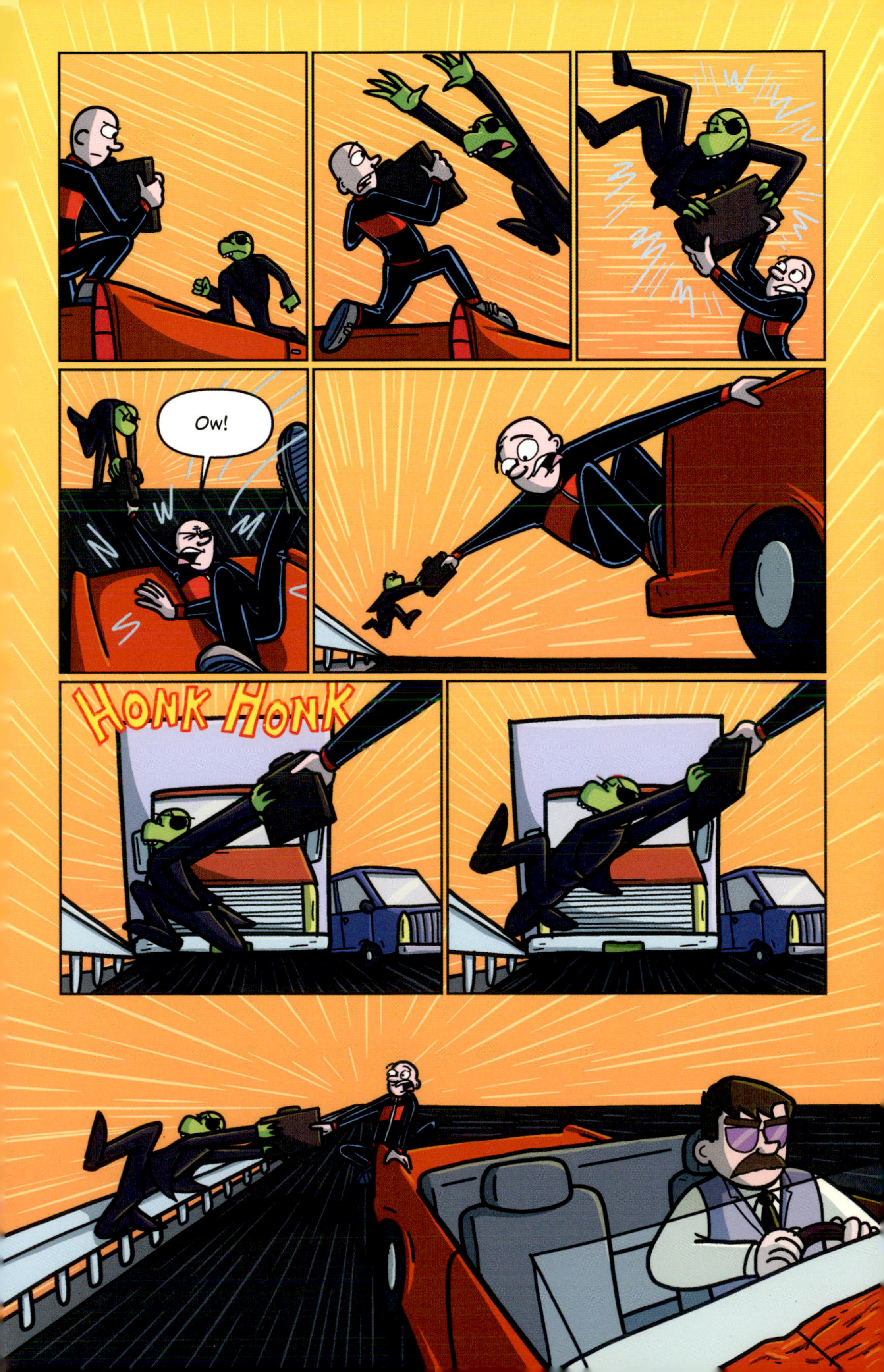
Ow!
HONK HONK

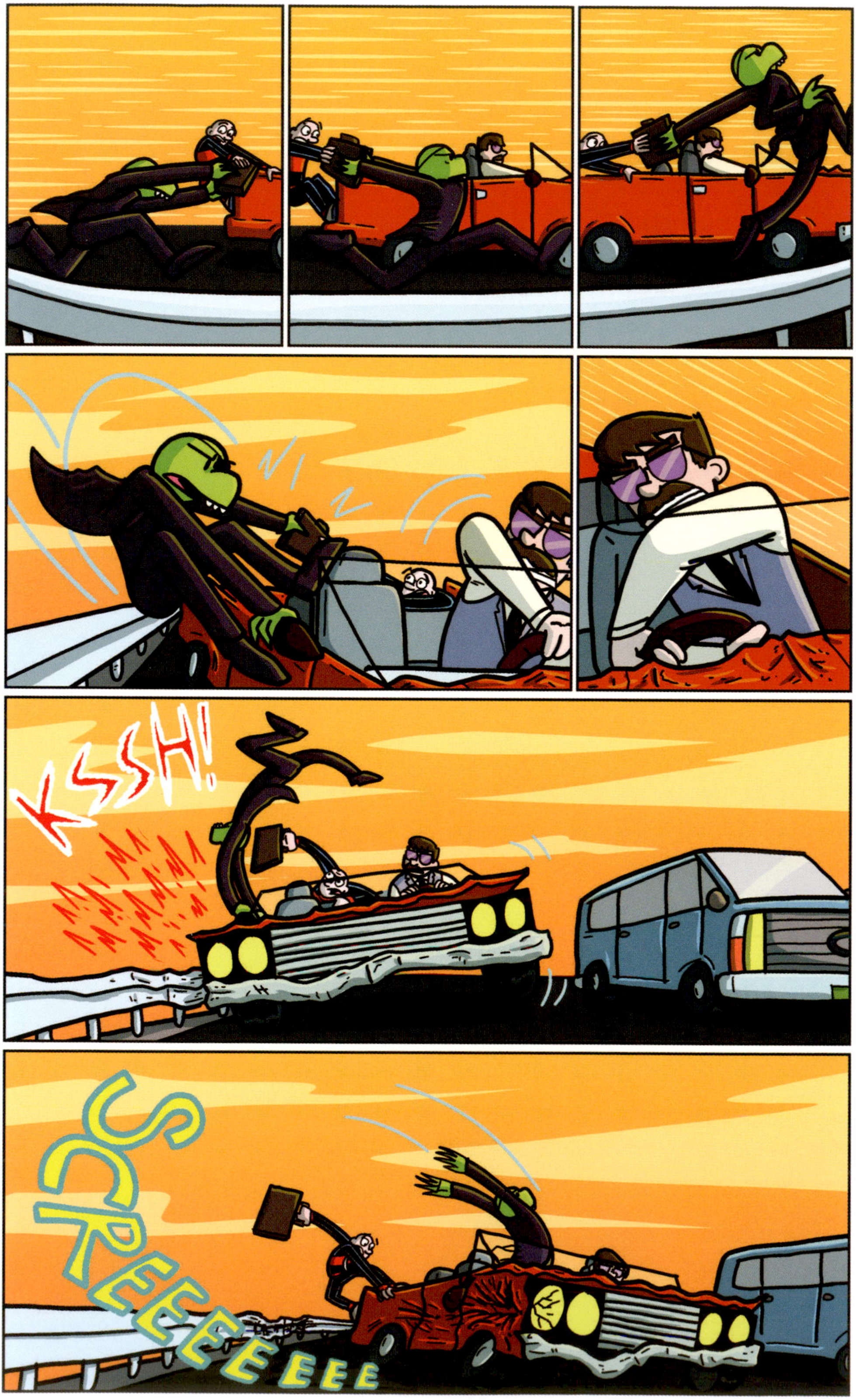
KSSH!
SCREEEEEEE

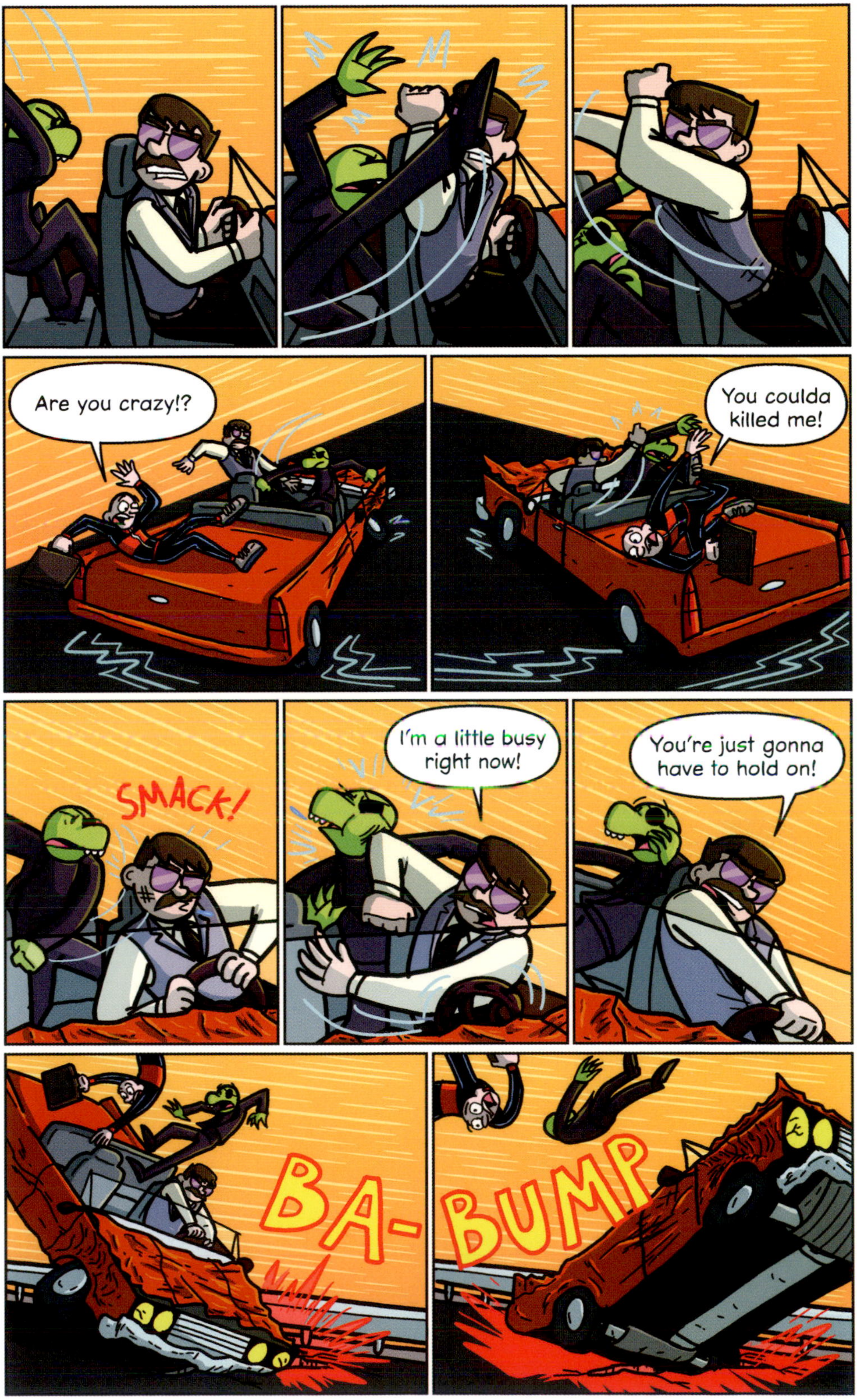
Are you crazy!?
You coulda killed me!
SMACK!
I'm a little busy right now!
You're just gonna have to hold on!
BA-BUMP

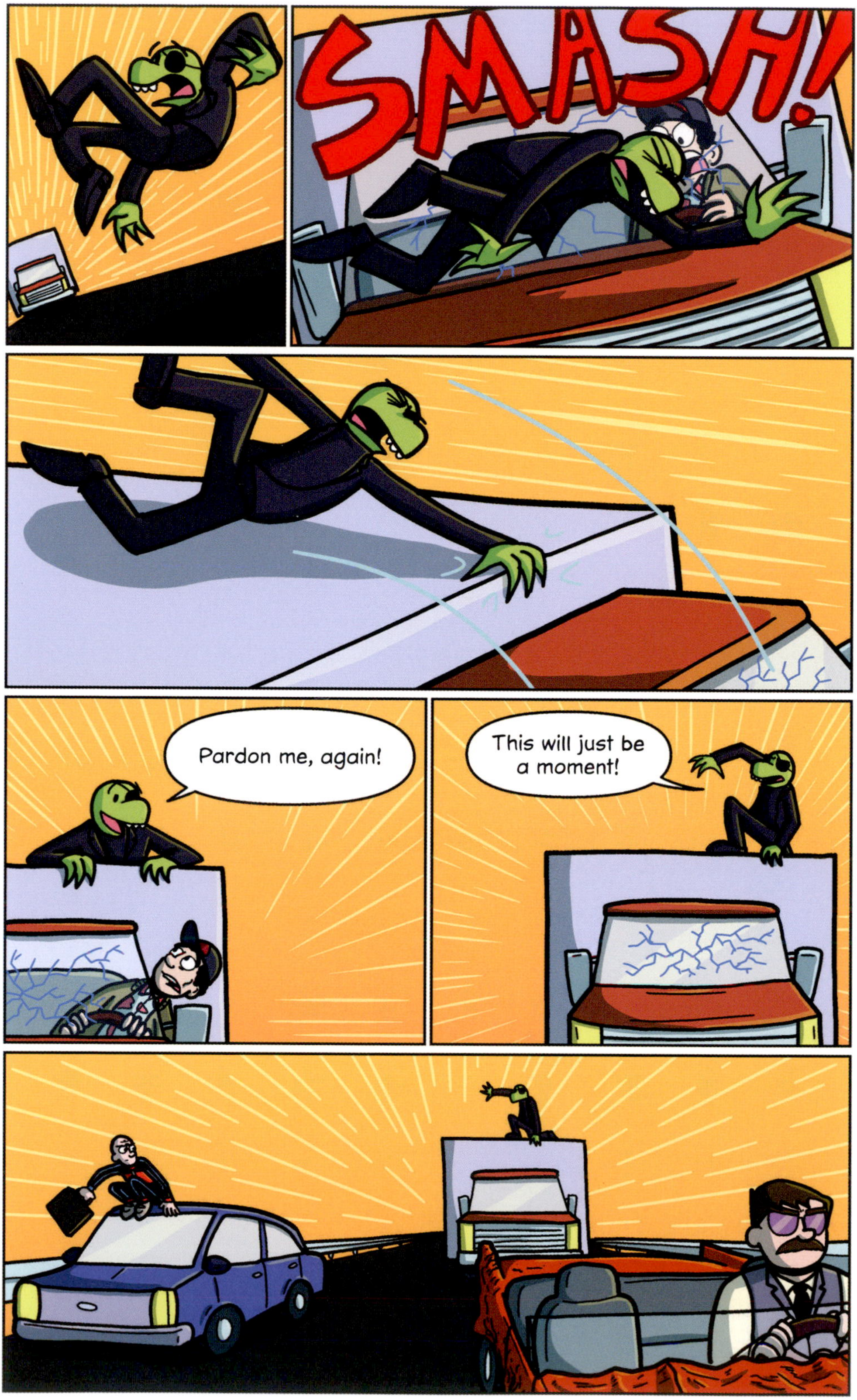
SMASH!
Pardon me, again!
This will just be a moment!

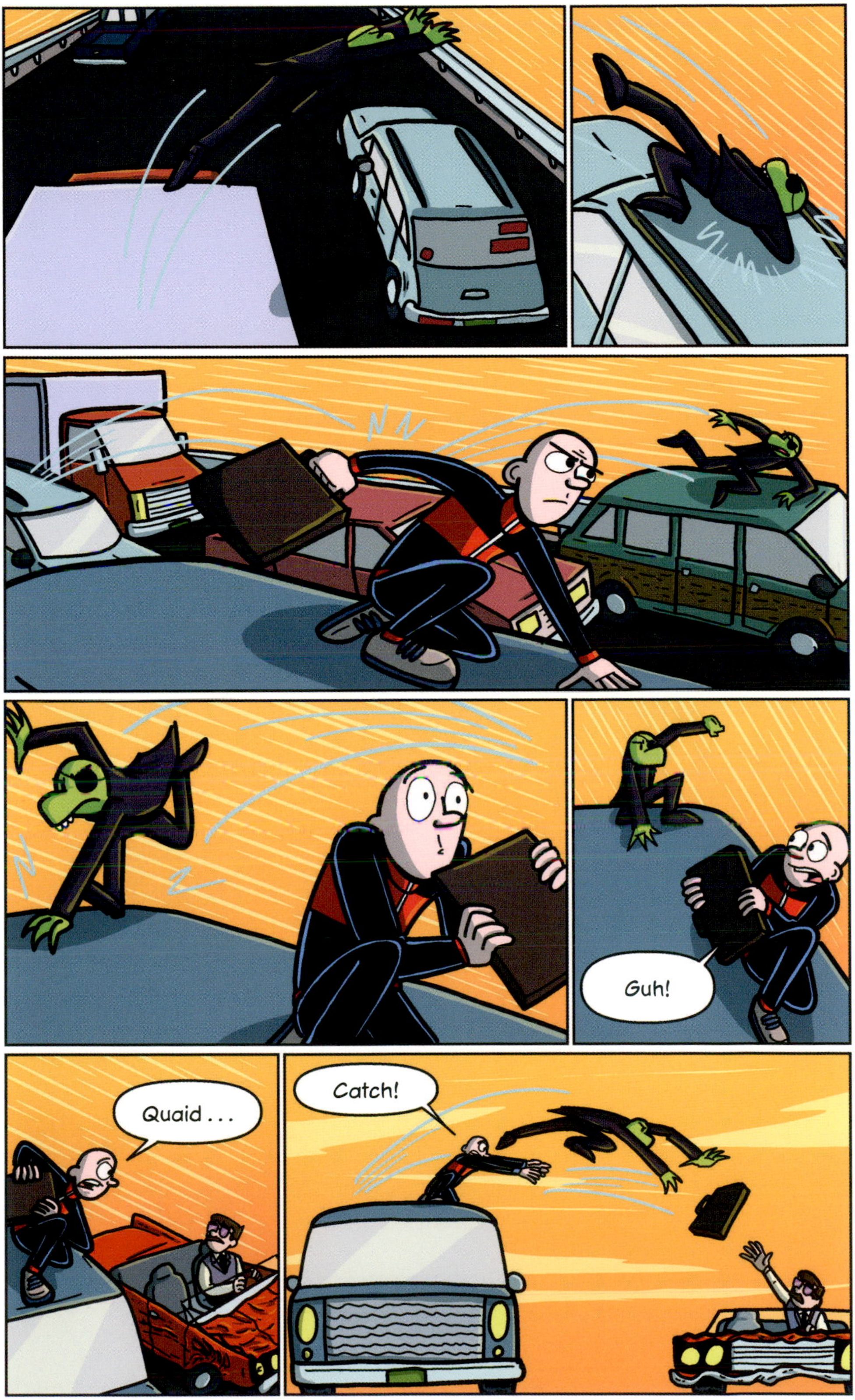
Guh!
Quaid . . .
Catch!

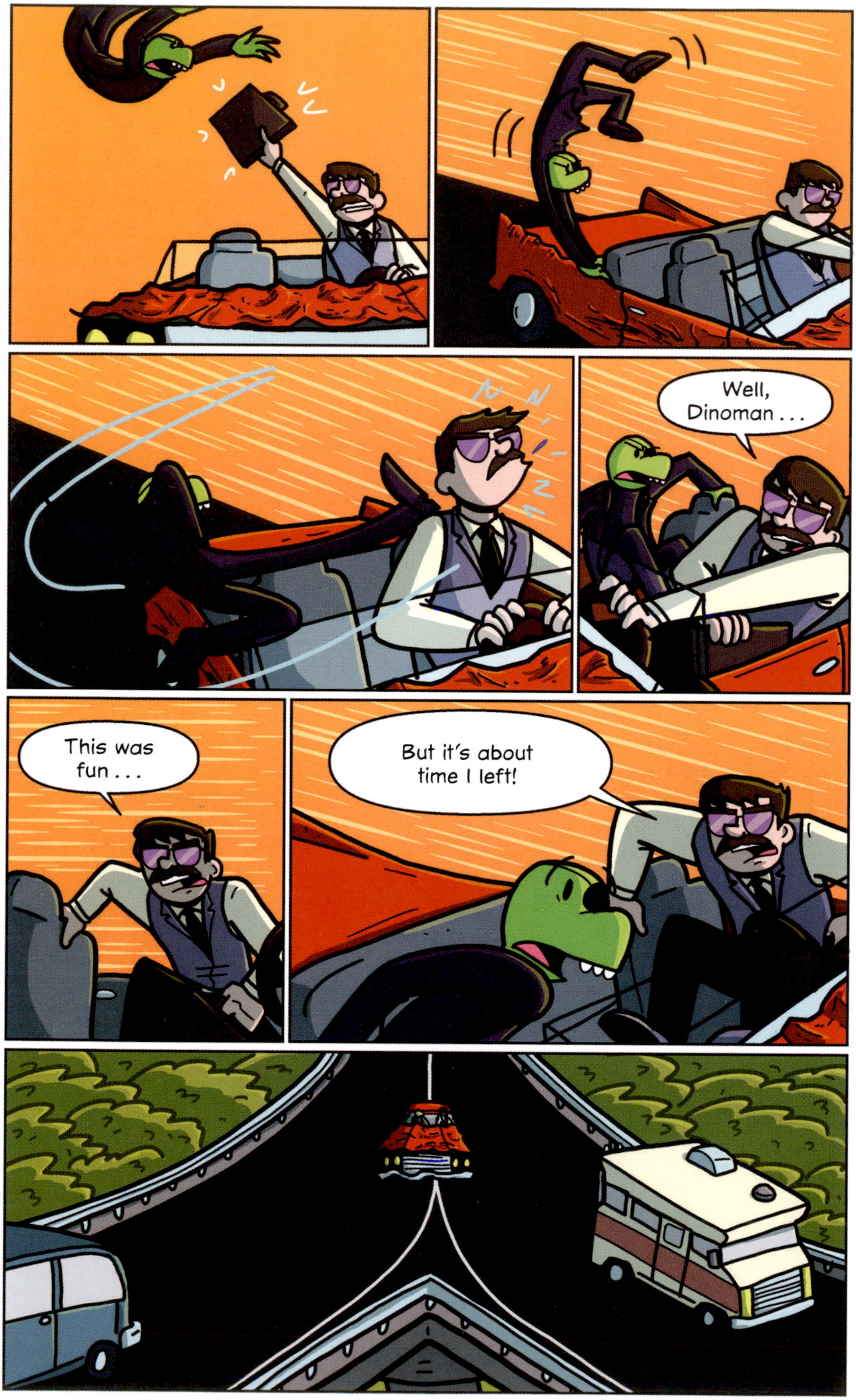
Well, Dinoman . . .
This was fun . . .
But it's about time I left!

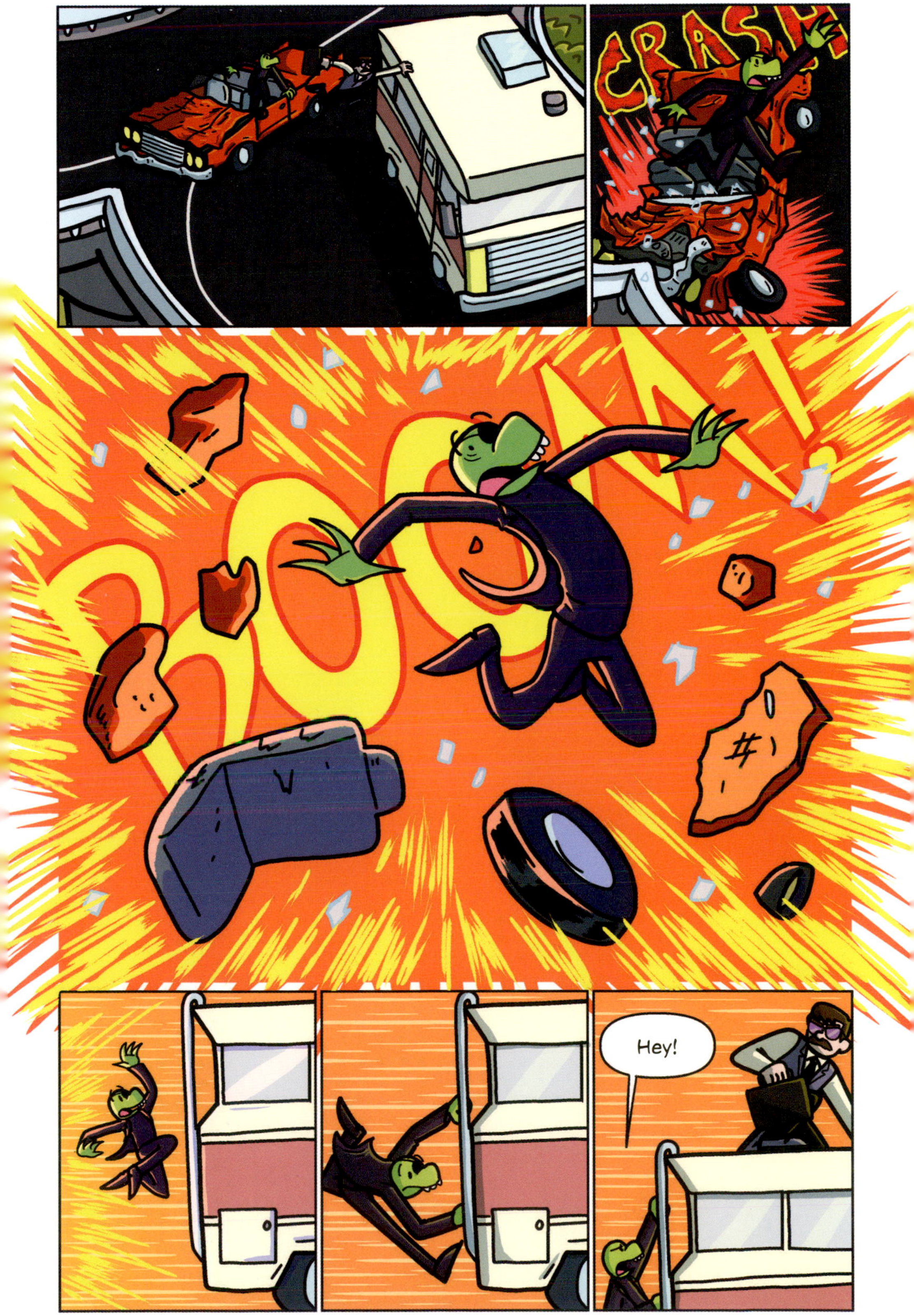
CRASH!
BOOM!
#1
Hey!

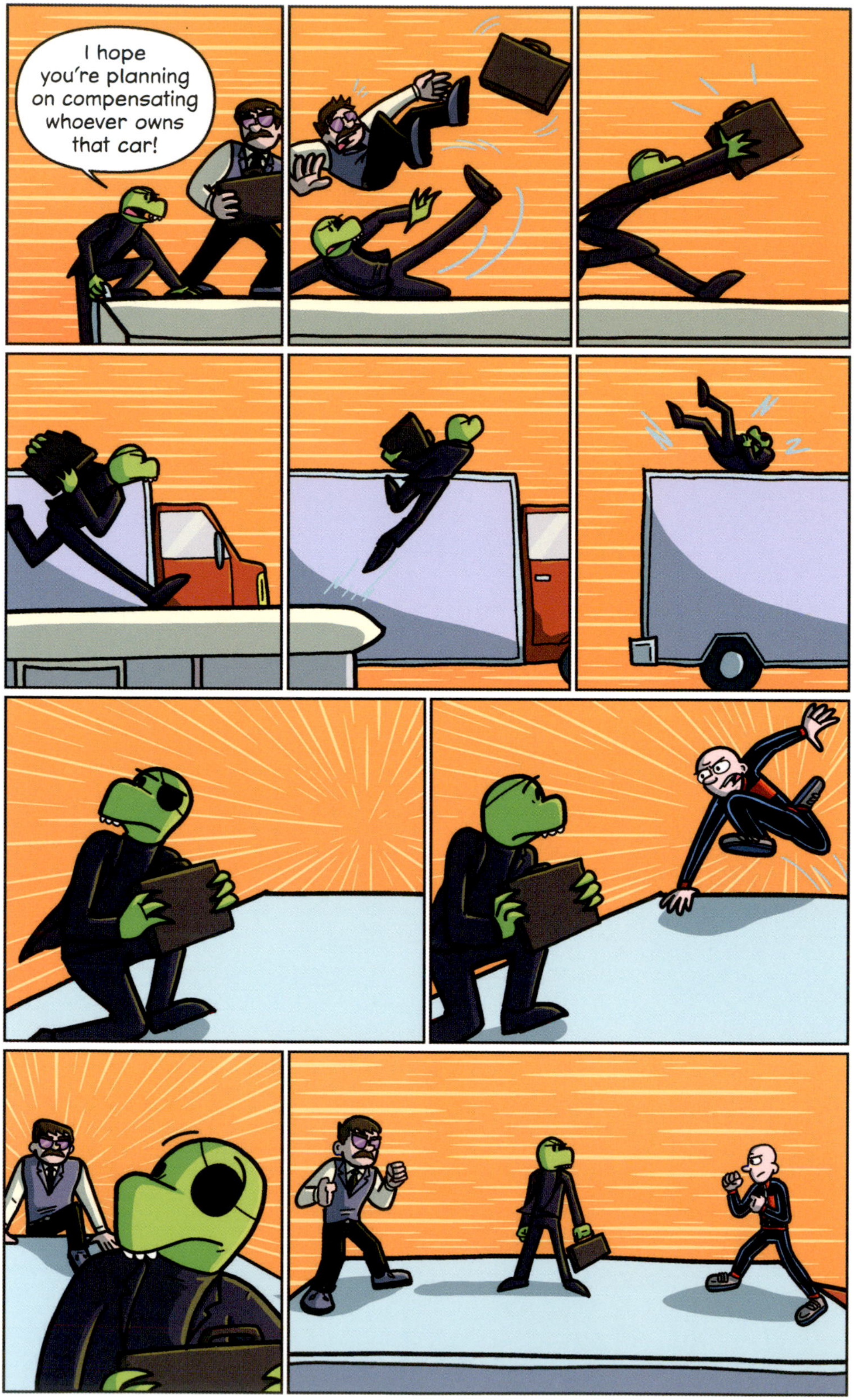
I hope you're planning on compensating whoever owns that car!

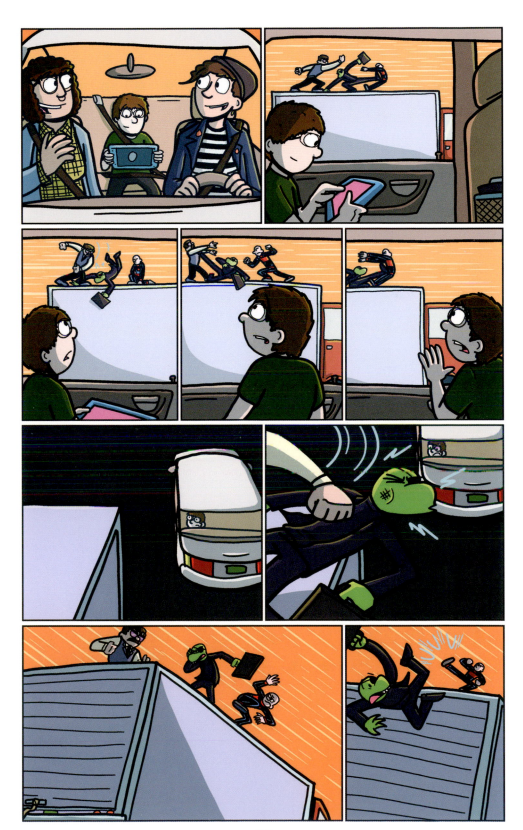

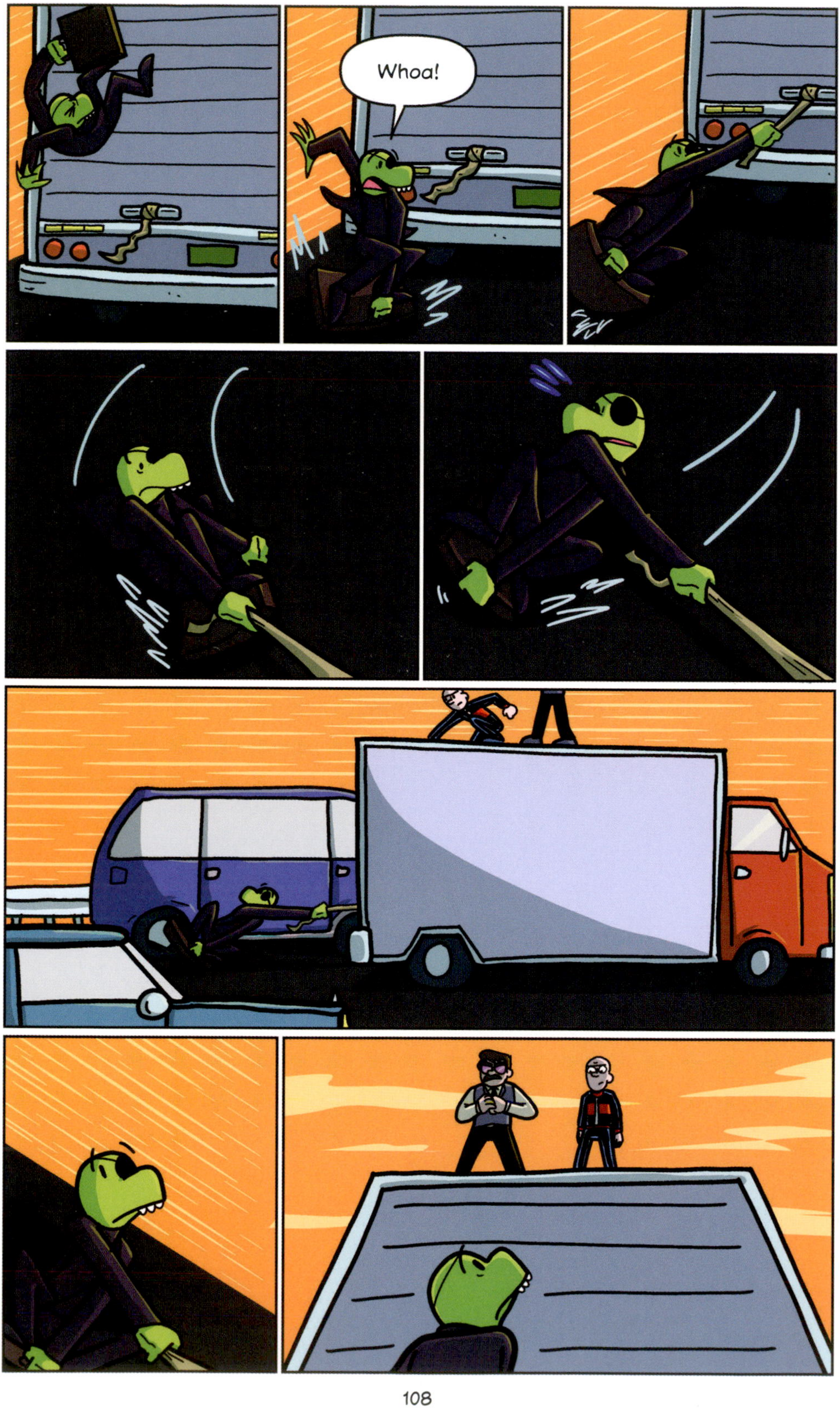
Whoa!

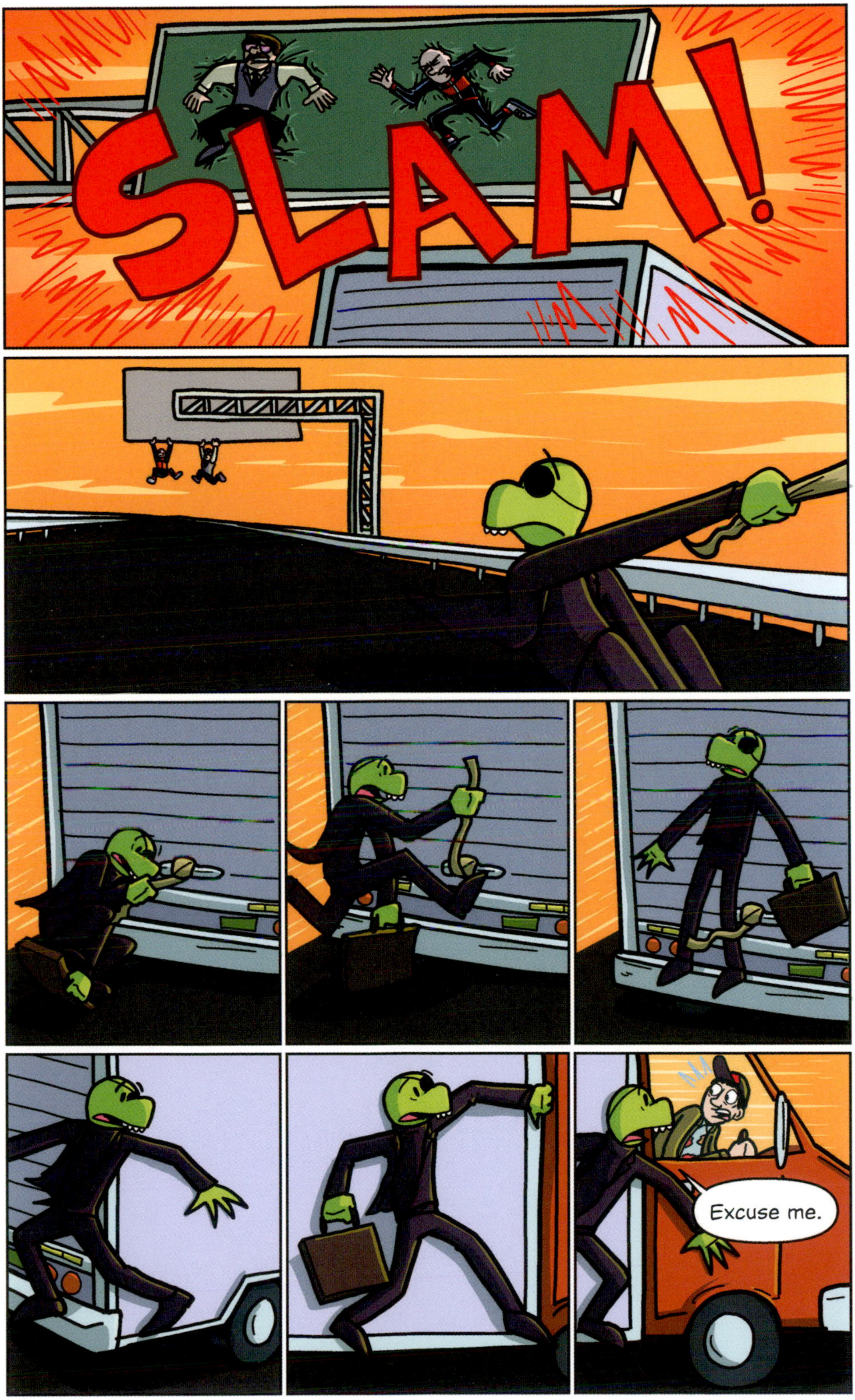
SLAM!
Excuse me.

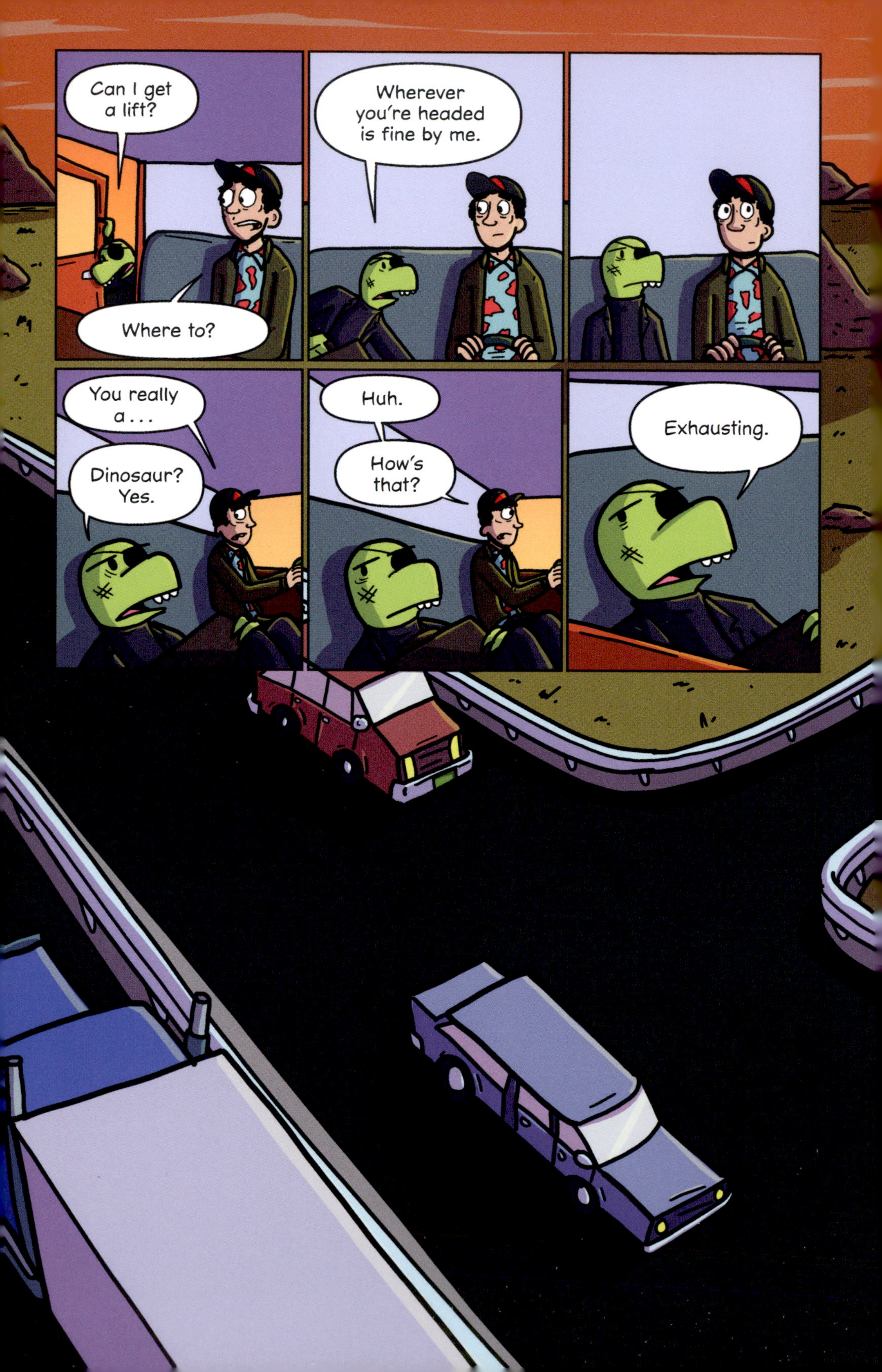
Can I get a lift?
Where to?
Wherever you're headed is fine by me.
You really a . . .
Dinosaur? Yes.
Huh.
How's that?
Exhausting.

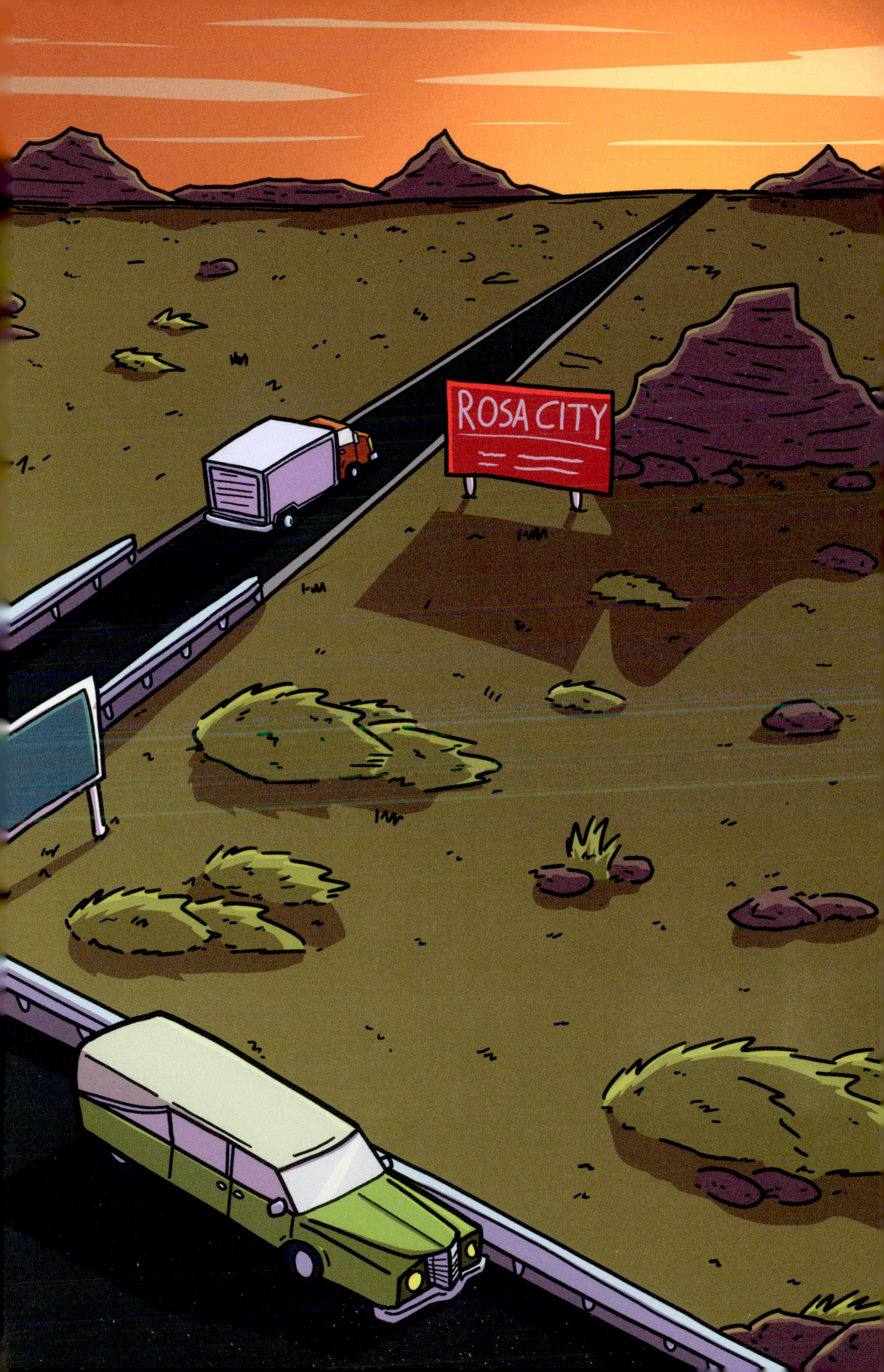
ROSA CITY

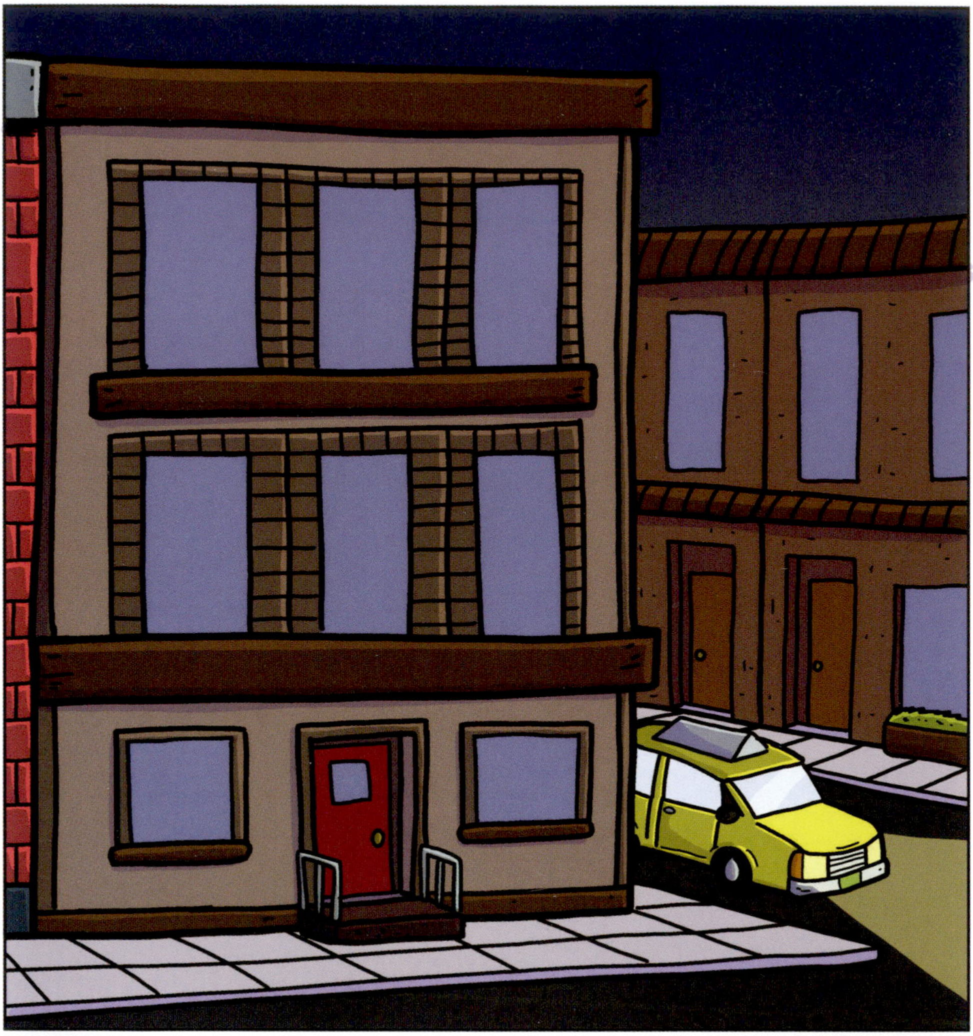

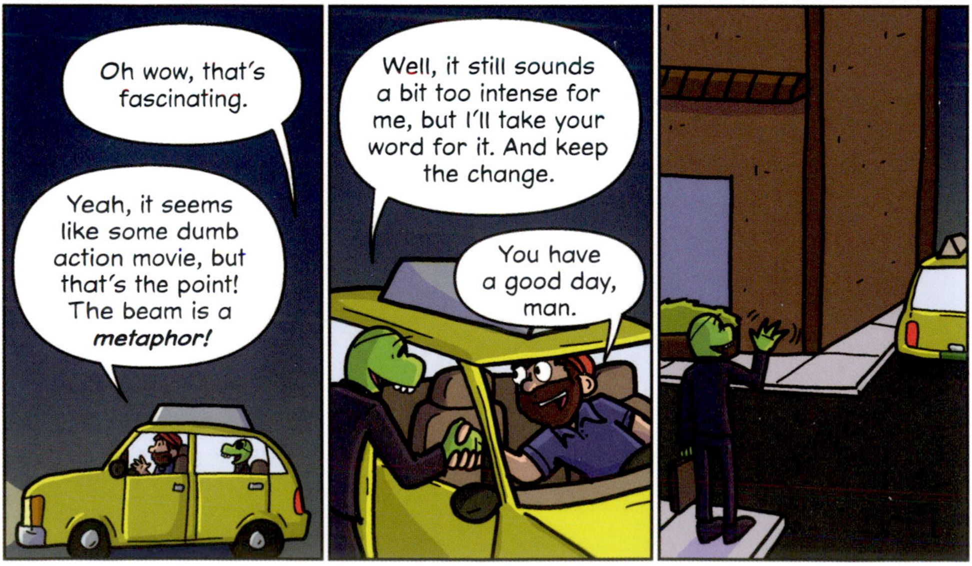

Oh wow, that's fascinating.
Yeah, it seems like some dumb action movie, but that's the point! The beam is a ***metaphor!***
Well, it still sounds a bit too intense for me, but I'll take your word for it. And keep the change.
You have a good day, man.

All right, Jen . . .
I hope you're okay . . .
At least I got the codes.
Maybe Abe was distracting her. Not a big deal . . .
It's all probably fi--

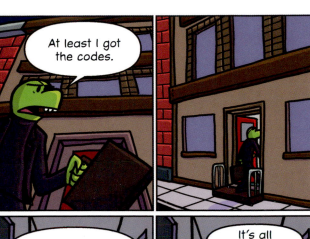

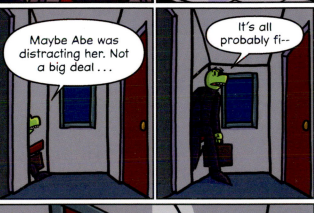

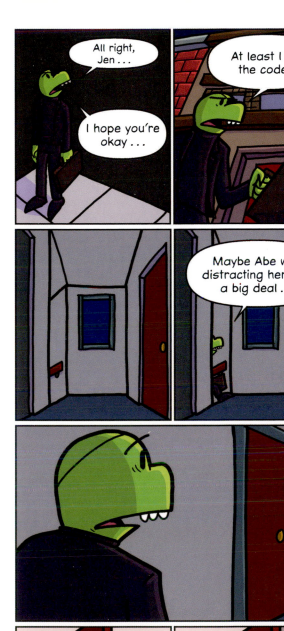

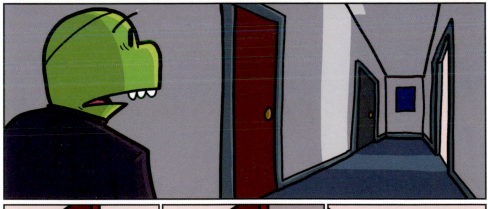

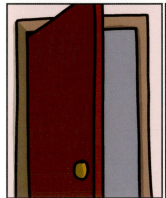

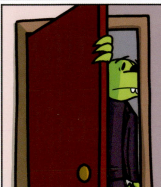

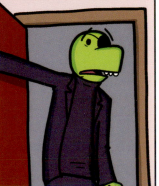

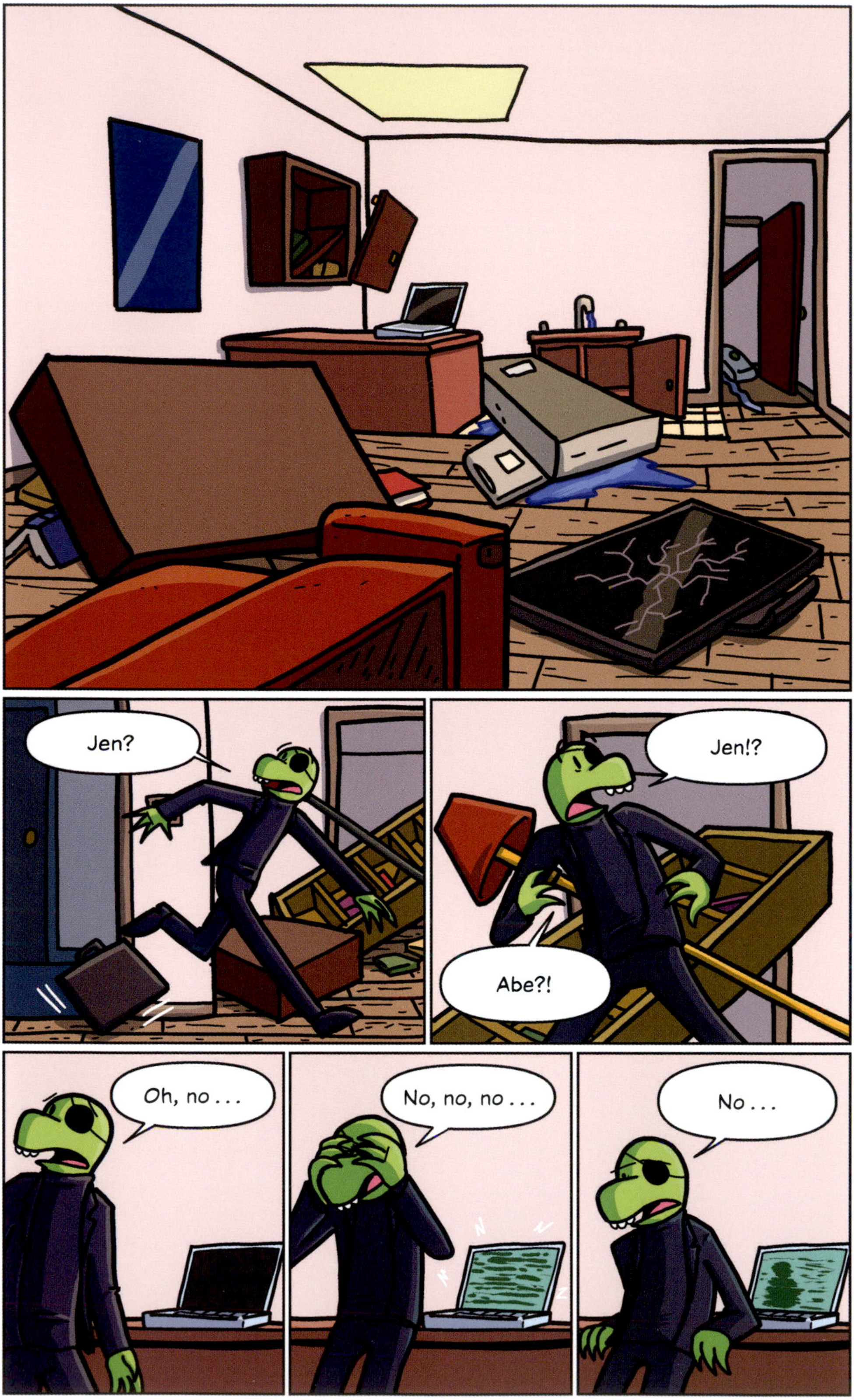
Jen?
Jen!?
Abe?!
Oh, no . . .
No, no, no . . .
No . . .

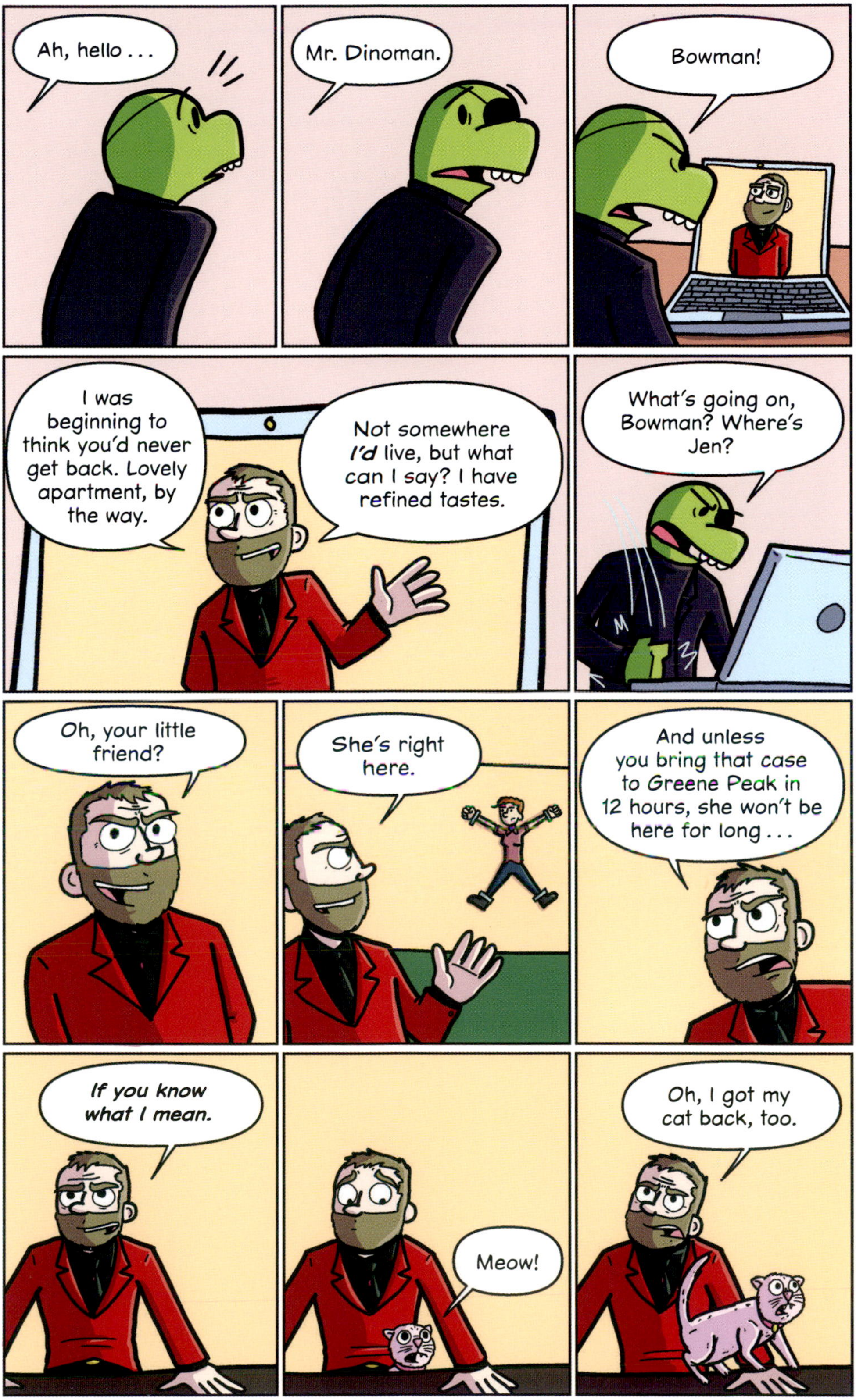

Ah, hello . . .
Mr. Dinoman.
Bowman!
I was beginning to think you'd never get back. Lovely apartment, by the way.
Not somewhere *I'd* live, but what can I say? I have refined tastes.
What's going on, Bowman? Where's Jen?
Oh, your little friend?
She's right here.
And unless you bring that case to Greene Peak in 12 hours, she won't be here for long . . .
If you know what I mean.
Meow!
Oh, I got my cat back, too.

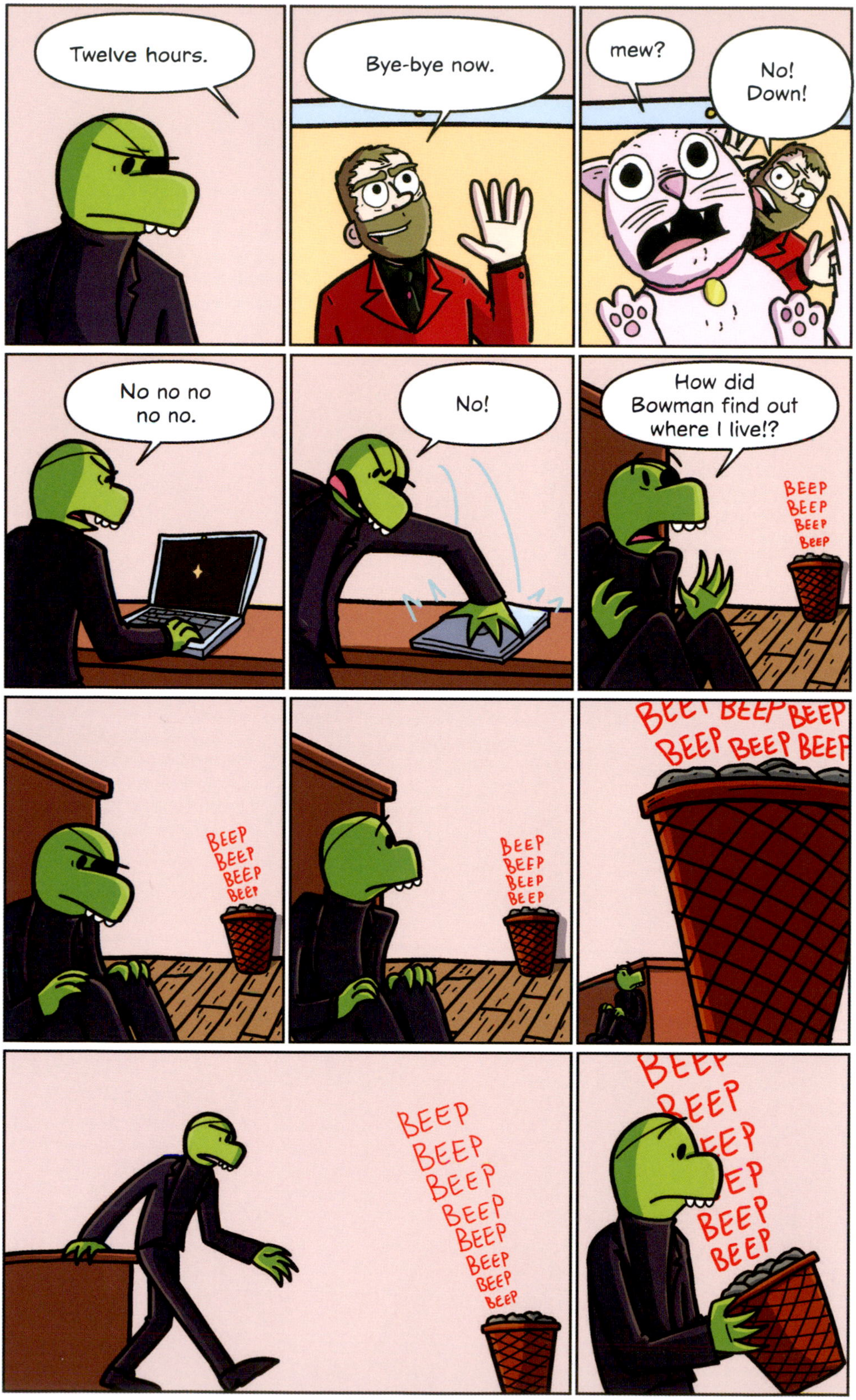
Twelve hours.
Bye-bye now.
mew?
No! Down!
No no no no no.
No!
How did Bowman find out where I live!?
BEEP BEEP BEEP BEEP
BEEP BEEP BEEP BEEP
BEEP BEEP BEEP BEEP
BEEP BEEP BEEP BEEP BEEP BEEP BEEP BEEP
BEEP BEEP

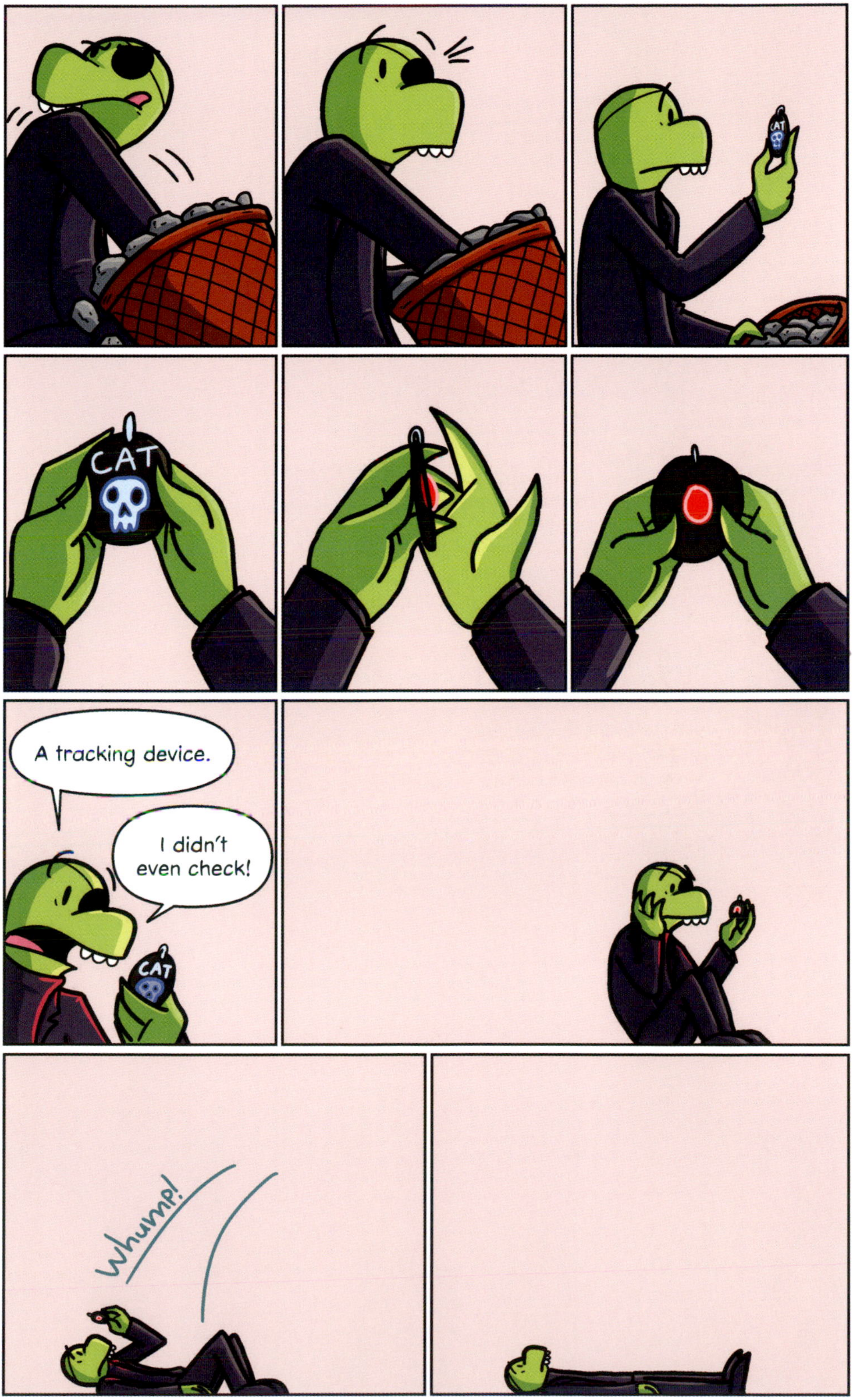
CAT
A tracking device.
I didn't even check!
Whump!

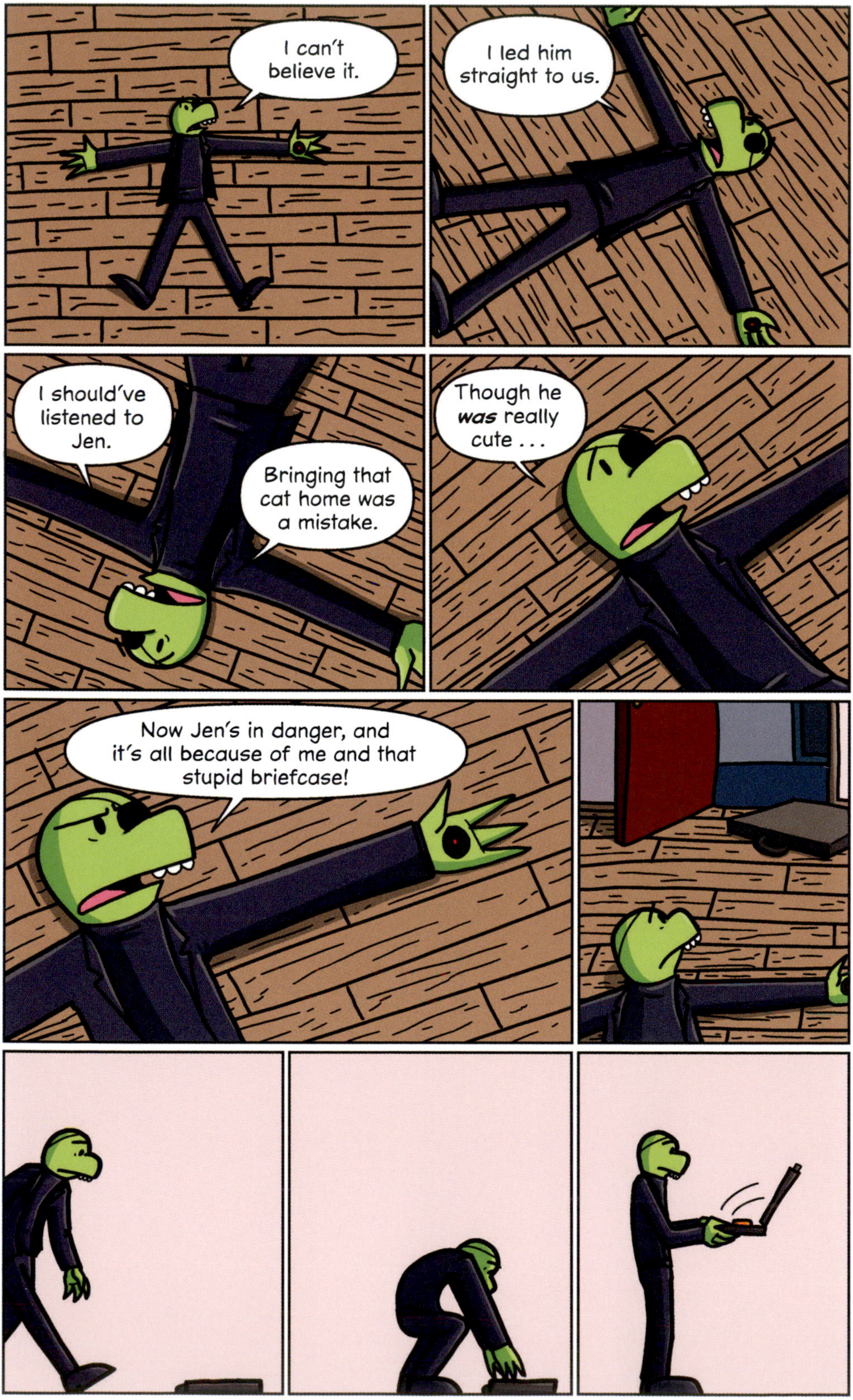
I can't believe it.
I led him straight to us.
I should've listened to Jen.
Bringing that cat home was a mistake.
Though he *was* really cute . . .
Now Jen's in danger, and it's all because of me and that stupid briefcase!

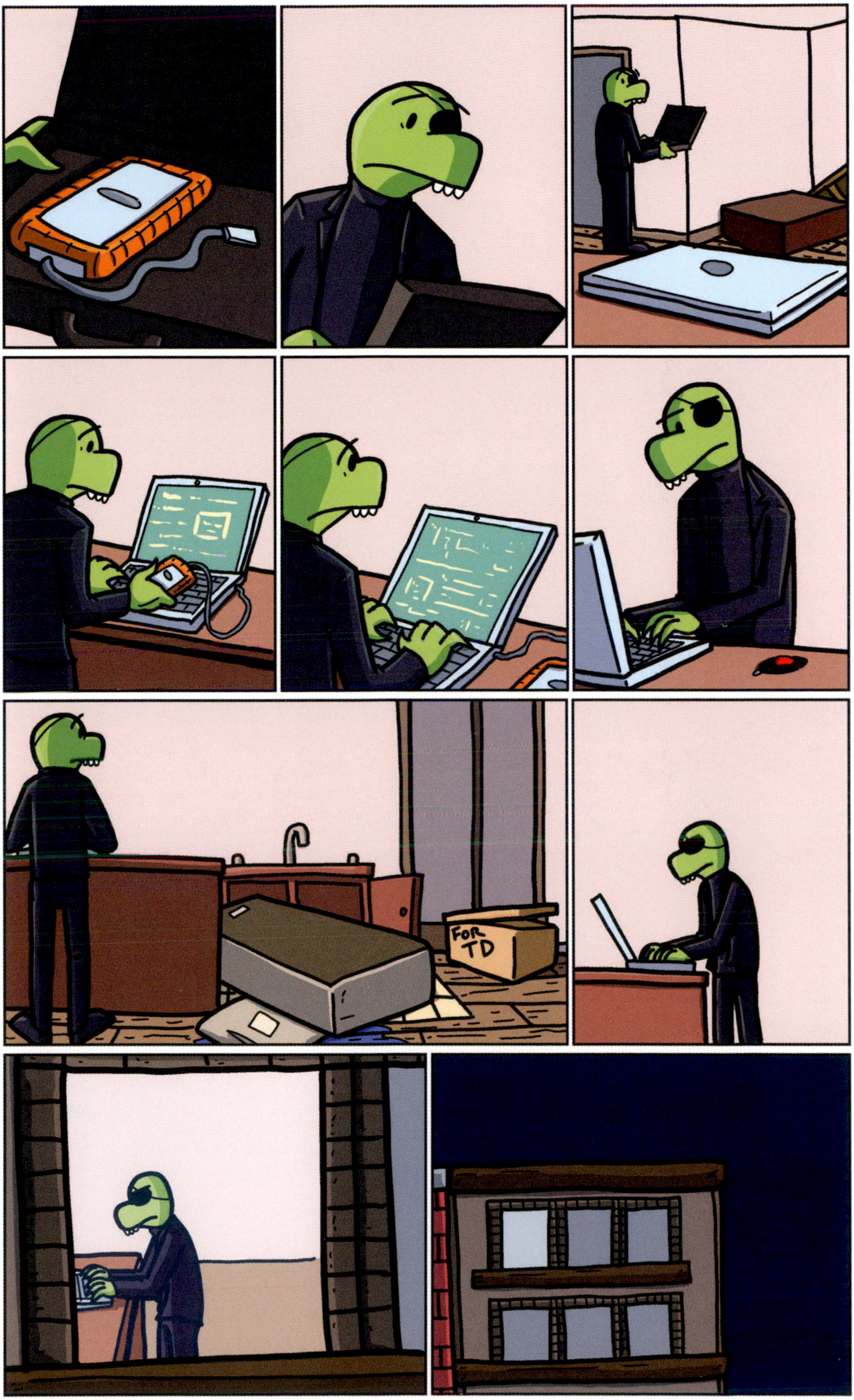
FOR TD

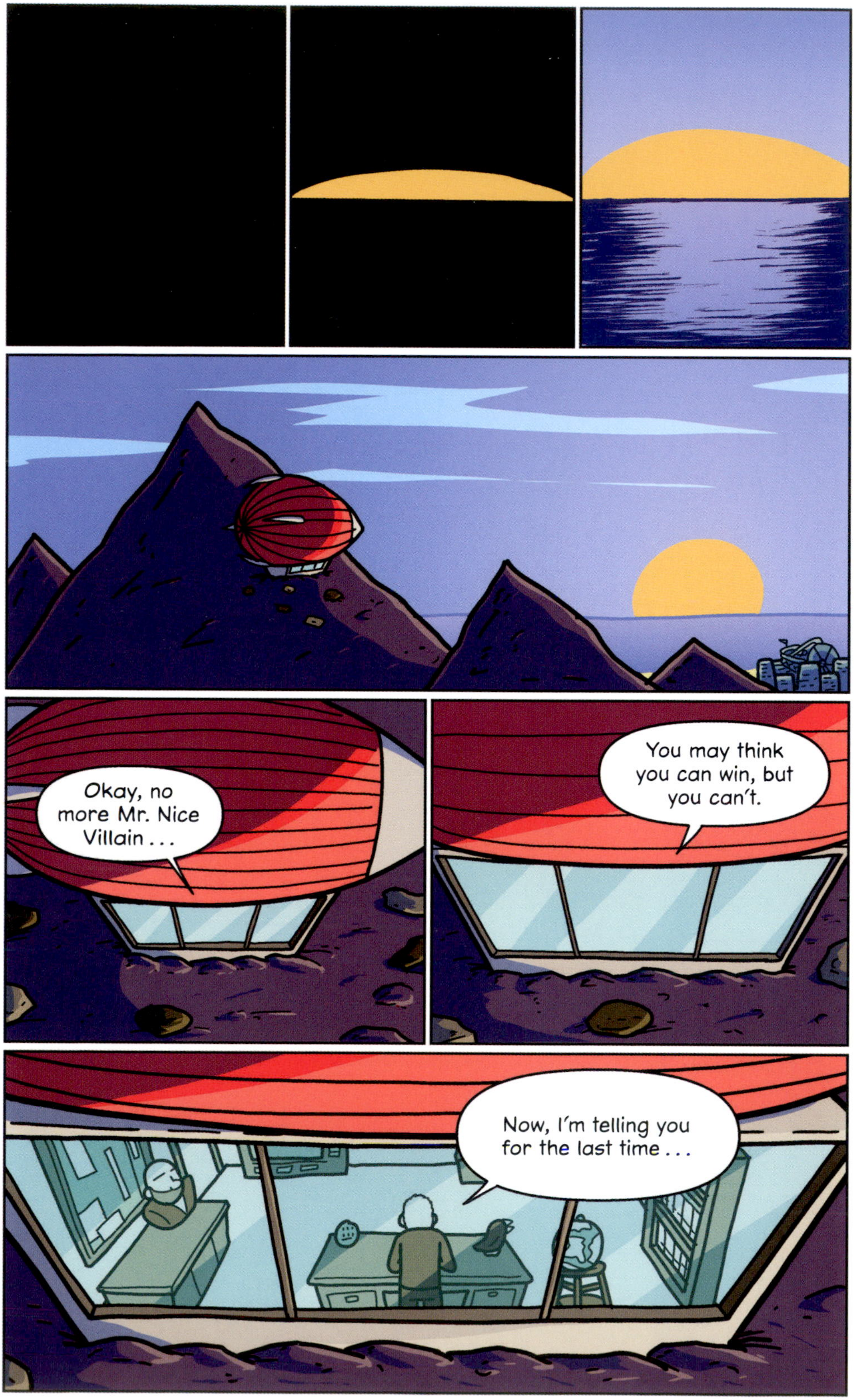
Okay, no more Mr. Nice Villain . . .
You may think you can win, but you can't.
Now, I'm telling you for the last time . . .

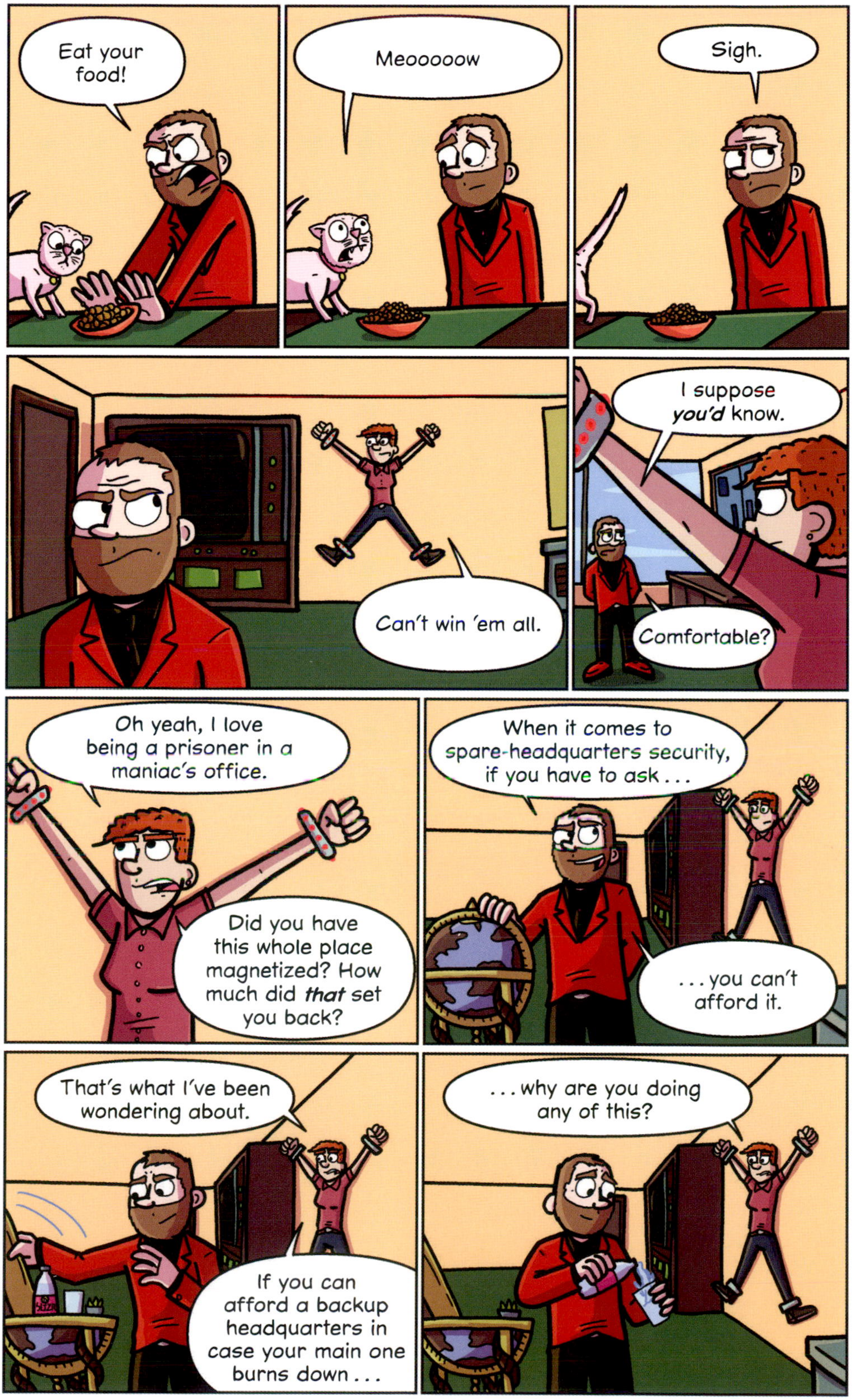
Eat your food!
Meoooooow
Sigh.
Can't win 'em all.
I suppose *you'd* know.
Comfortable?
Oh yeah, I love being a prisoner in a maniac's office.
Did you have this whole place magnetized? How much did *that* set you back?
When it comes to spare-headquarters security, if you have to ask . . .
. . . you can't afford it.
That's what I've been wondering about.
If you can afford a backup headquarters in case your main one burns down . . .
. . . why are you doing any of this?

You see . . .

From the first moment I had money . . .

I've always wanted more money.

And?

And . . . now I'm about to have more money? I think it's all pretty clear.

But what's with the satellite, the headquarters, the henchman, the general supervillainy?

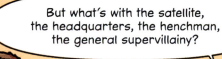

Well, everyone's afraid of a supervillain.

And the easiest way to take people's money is to make them afraid.

CRUNCH

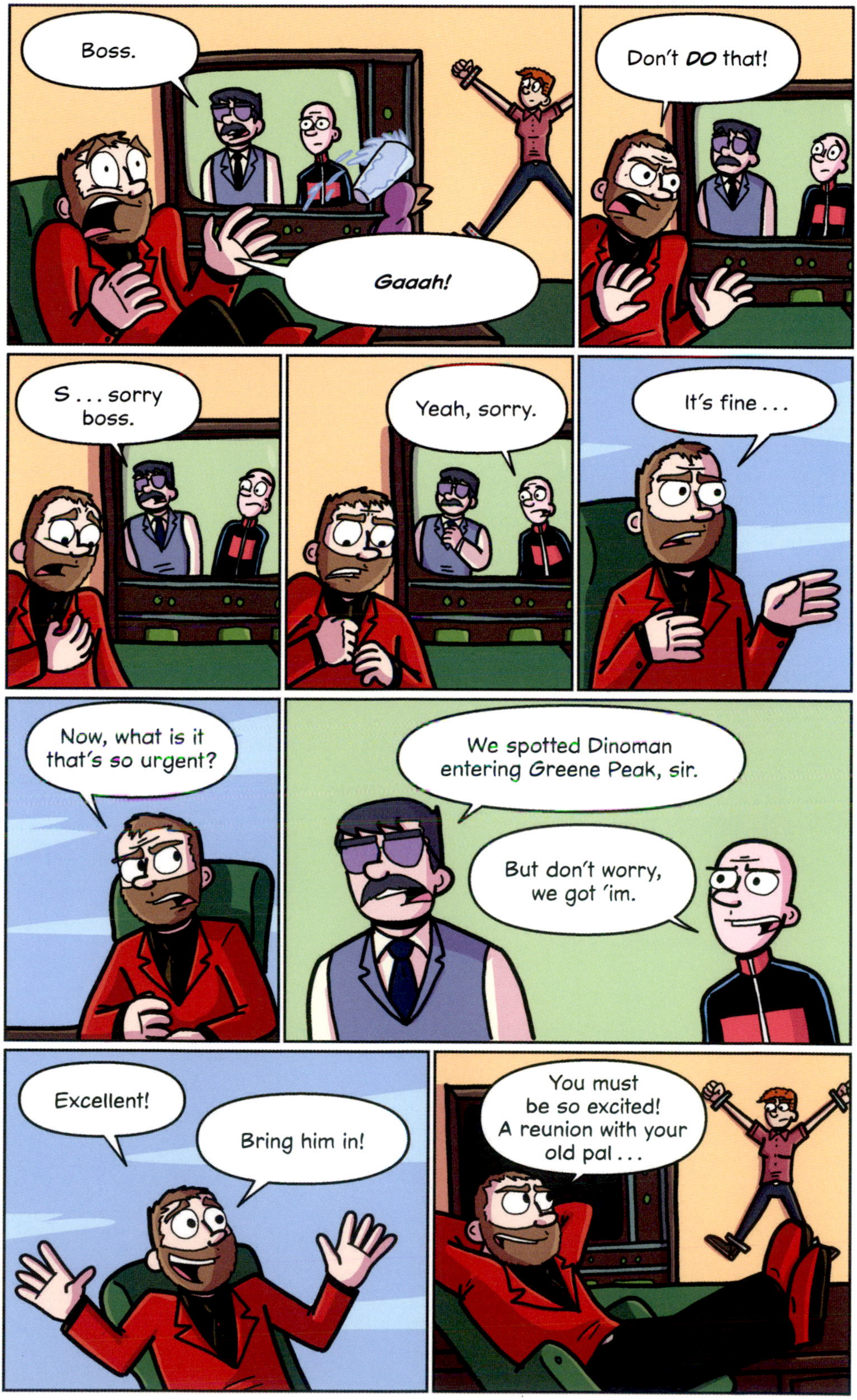
Boss.
Gaaah!
Don't DO that!
S . . . sorry boss.
Yeah, sorry.
It's fine . . .
Now, what is it that's so urgent?
We spotted Dinoman entering Greene Peak, sir.
But don't worry, we got 'im.
Excellent!
Bring him in!
You must be so excited! A reunion with your old pal . . .

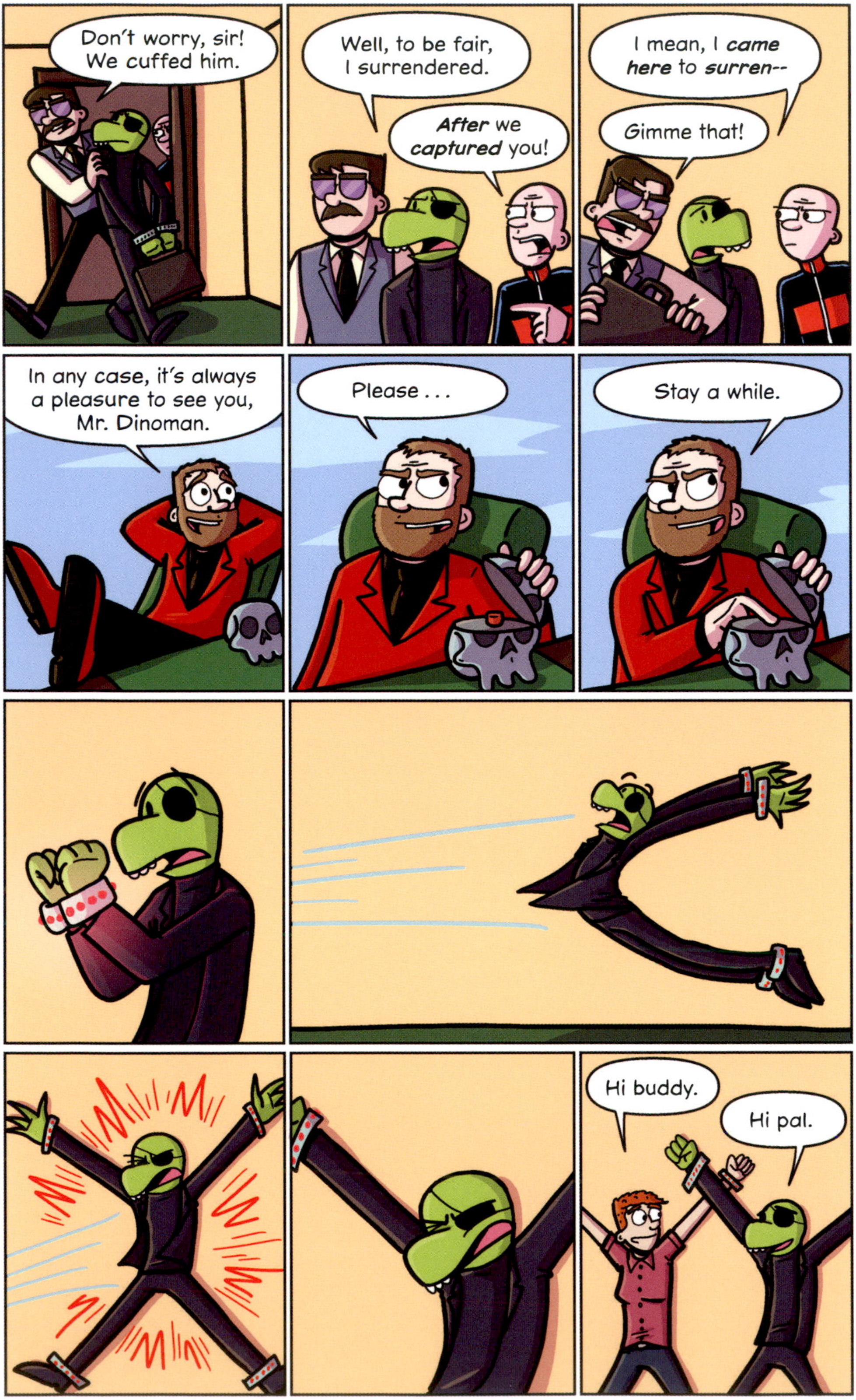
Don't worry, sir! We cuffed him.
Well, to be fair, I surrendered.
After we *captured* you!
I mean, I *came here* to *surren--*
Gimme that!
In any case, it's always a pleasure to see you, Mr. Dinoman.
Please . . .
Stay a while.
Hi buddy.
Hi pal.

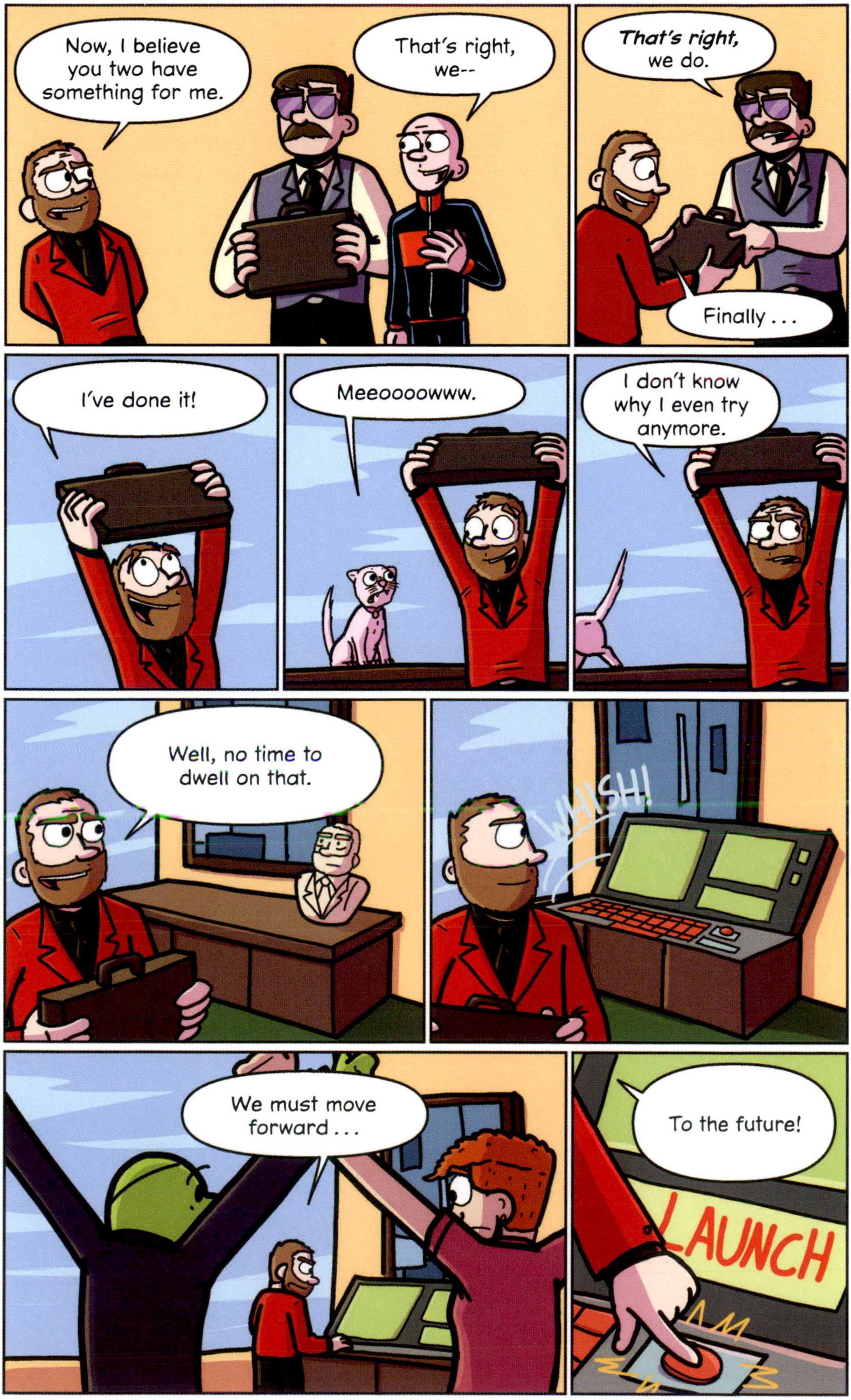
Now, I believe you two have something for me.
That's right, we--
That's right, we do.
Finally . . .
I've done it!
Meeooooww.
I don't know why I even try anymore.
Well, no time to dwell on that.
WHISH!
We must move forward . . .
To the future!
LAUNCH

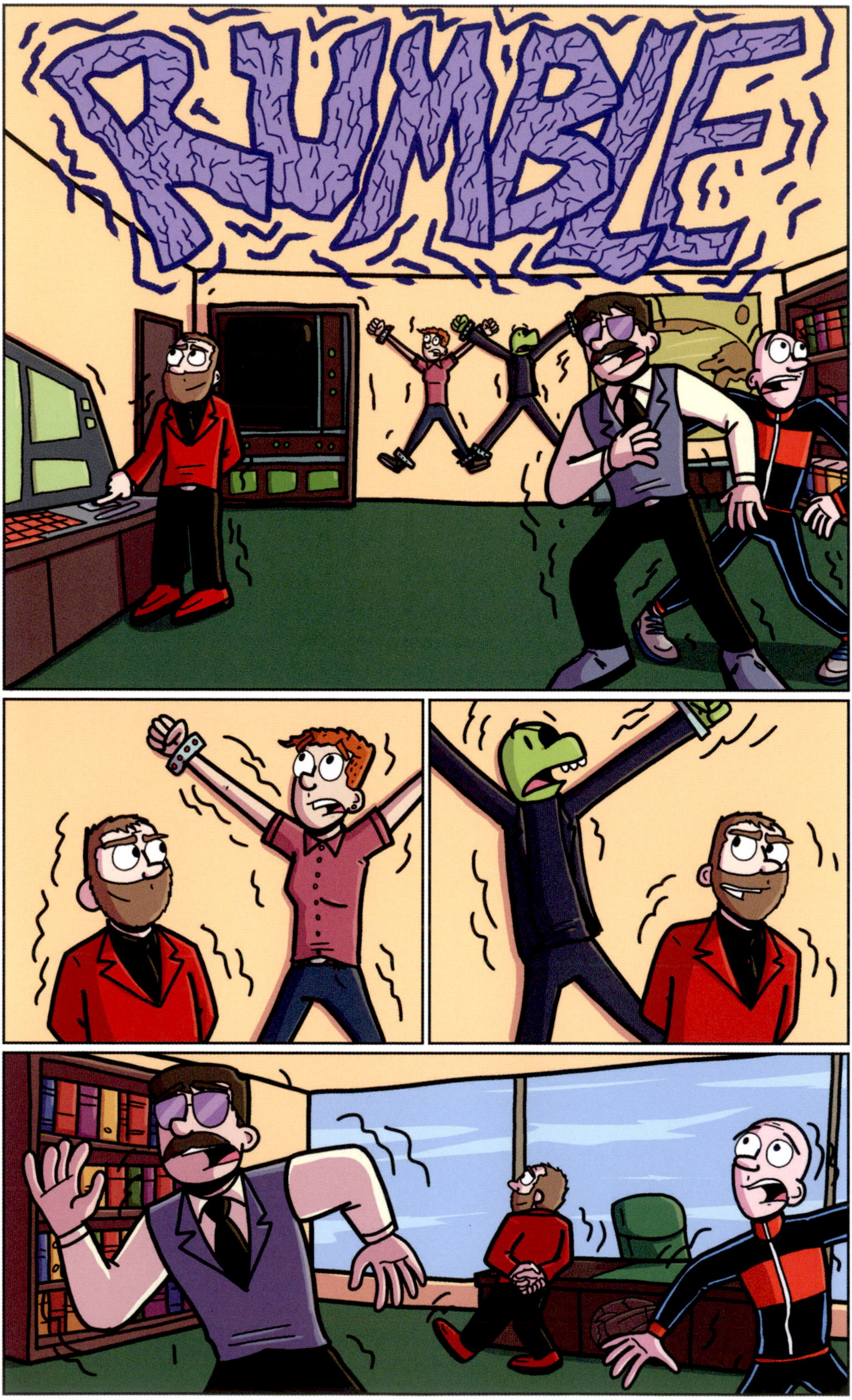
RUMBLE

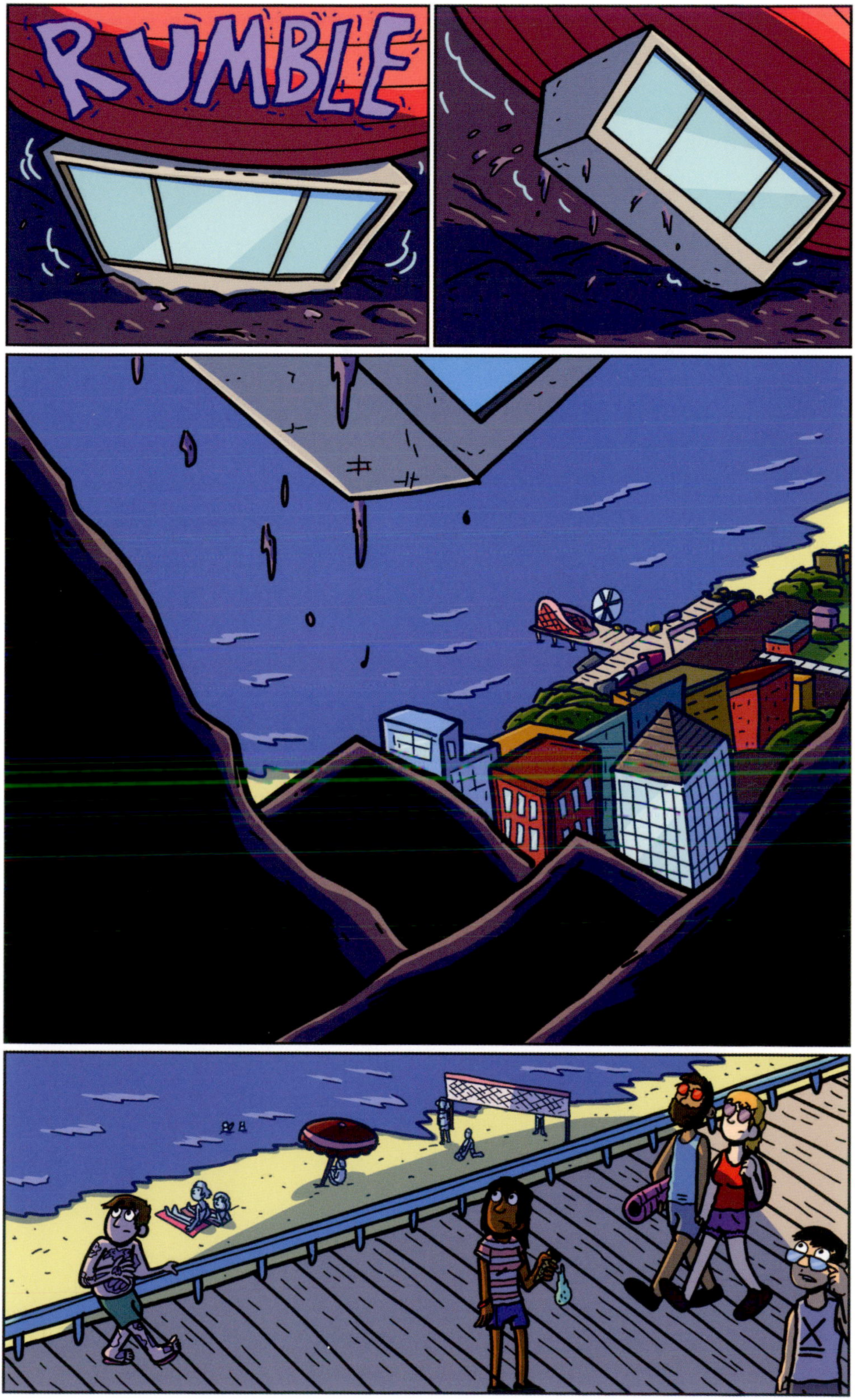
RUMBLE

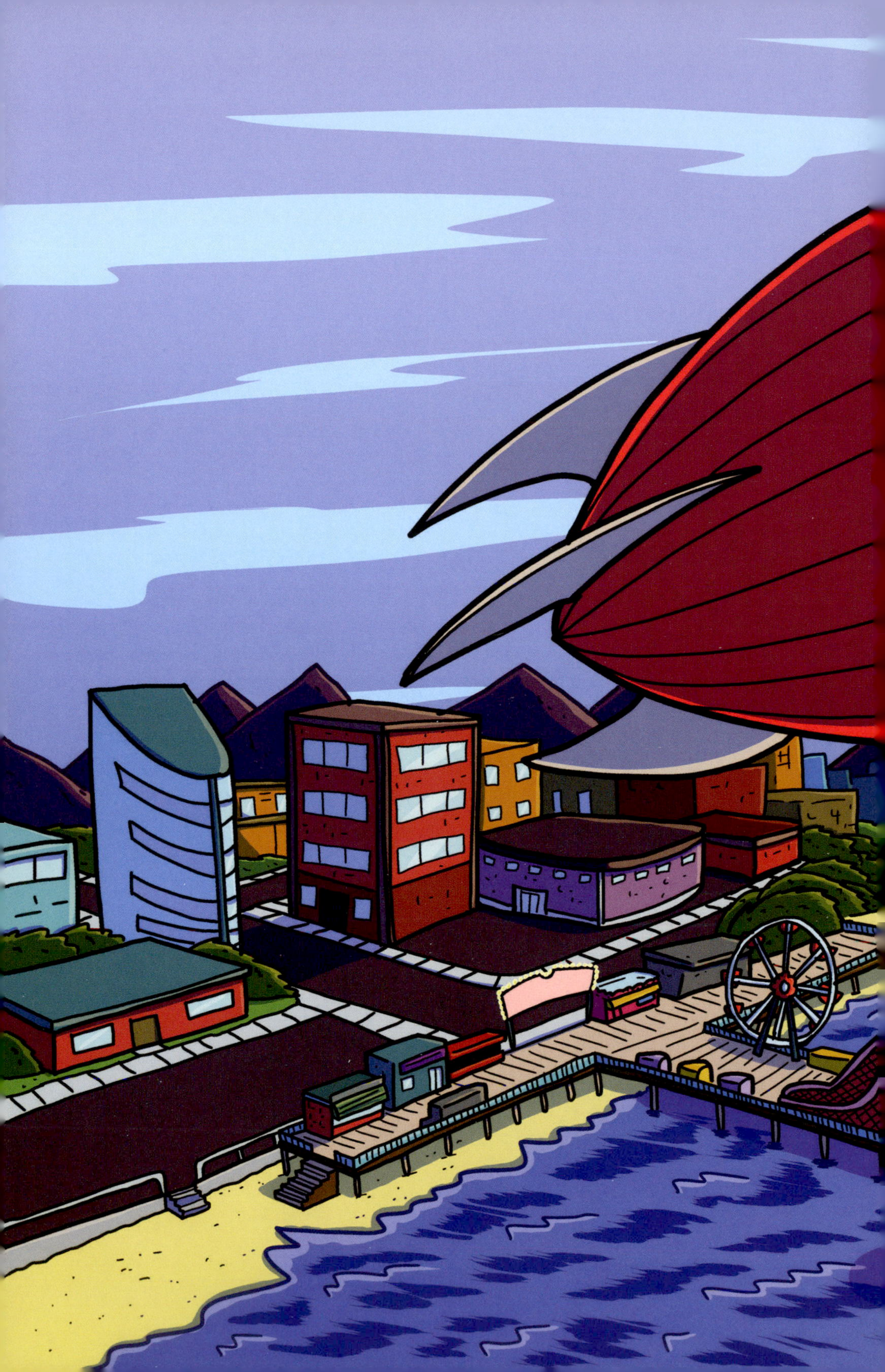

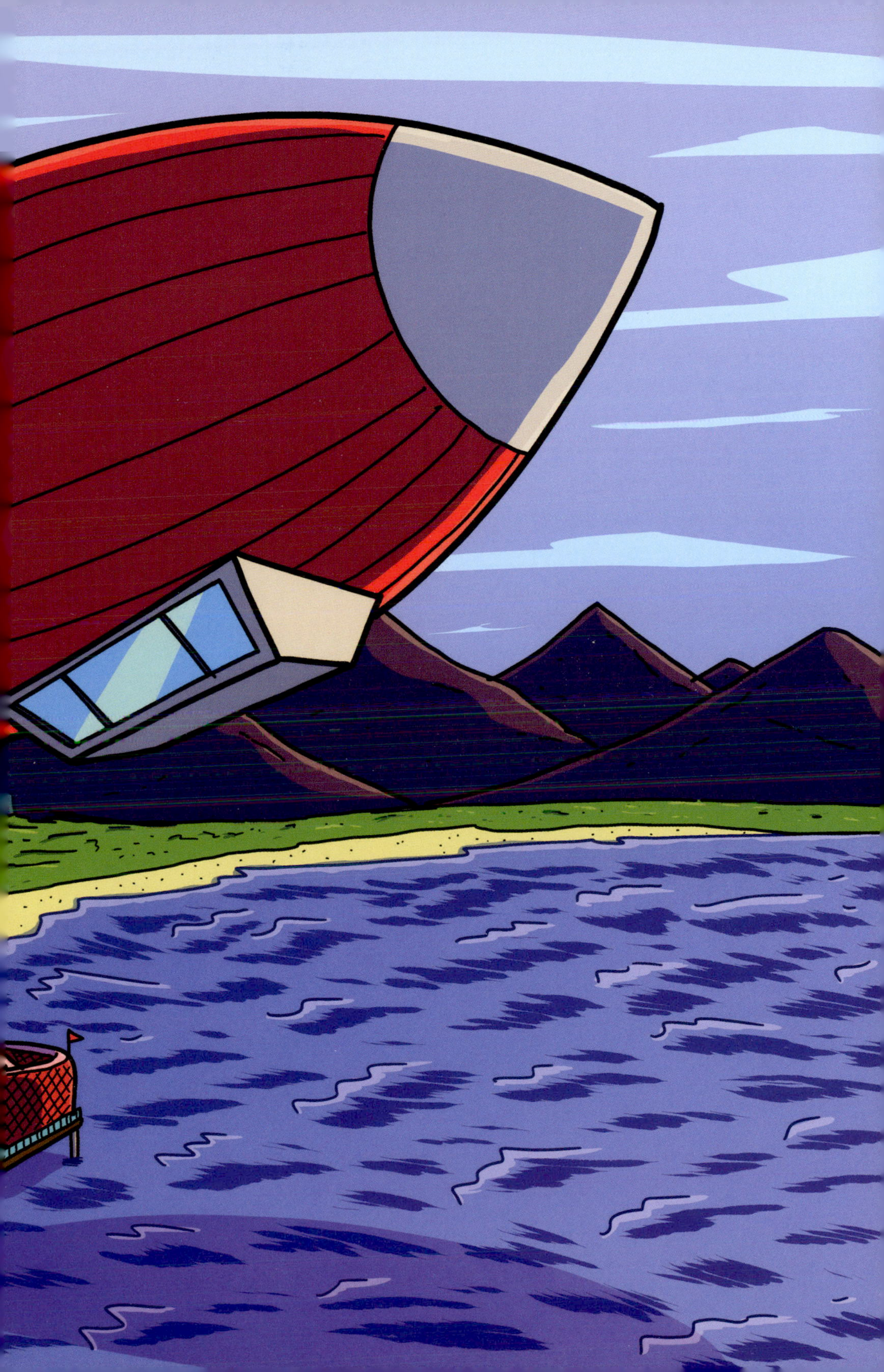

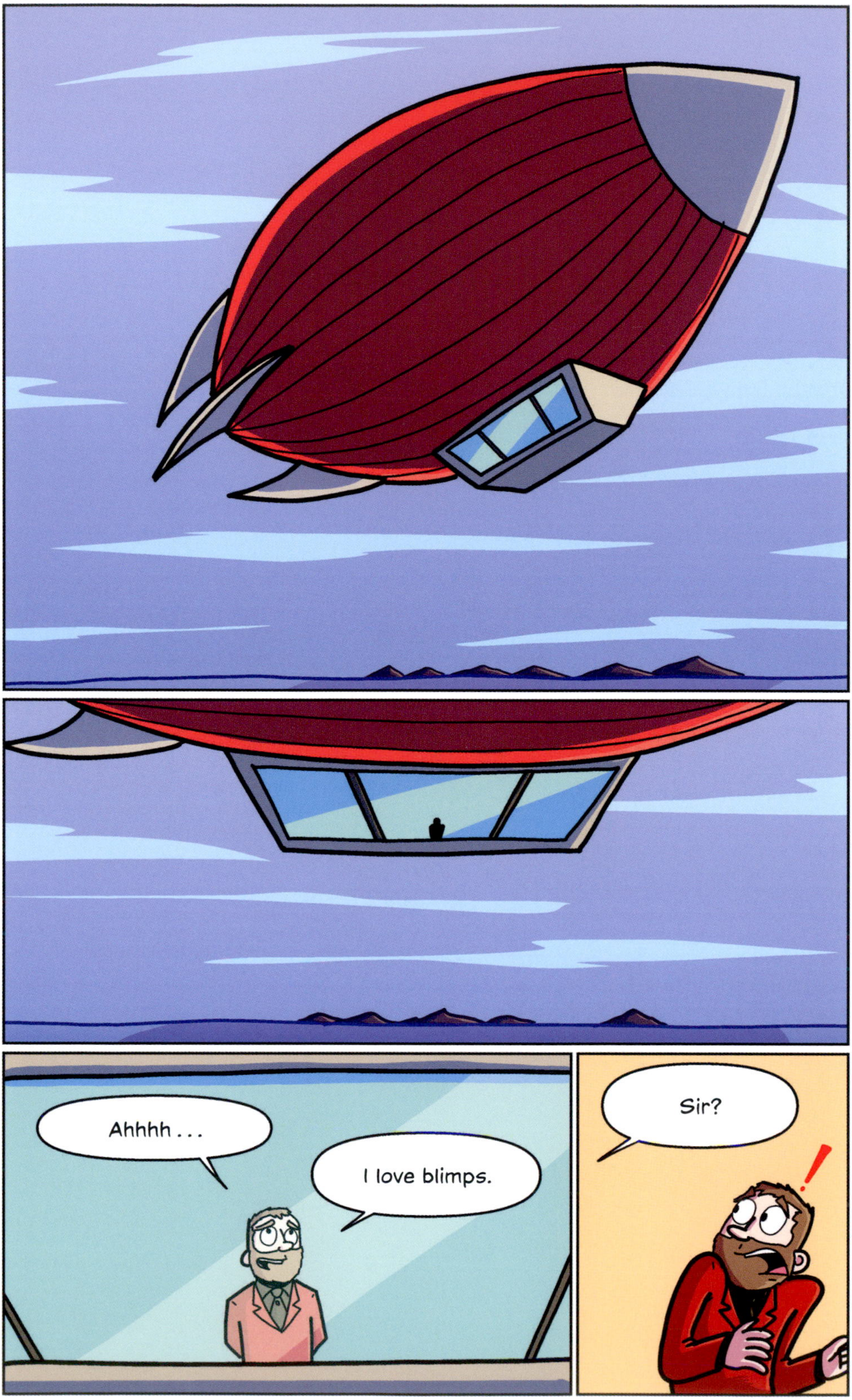
Ahhhh . . .
I love blimps.
Sir?
!

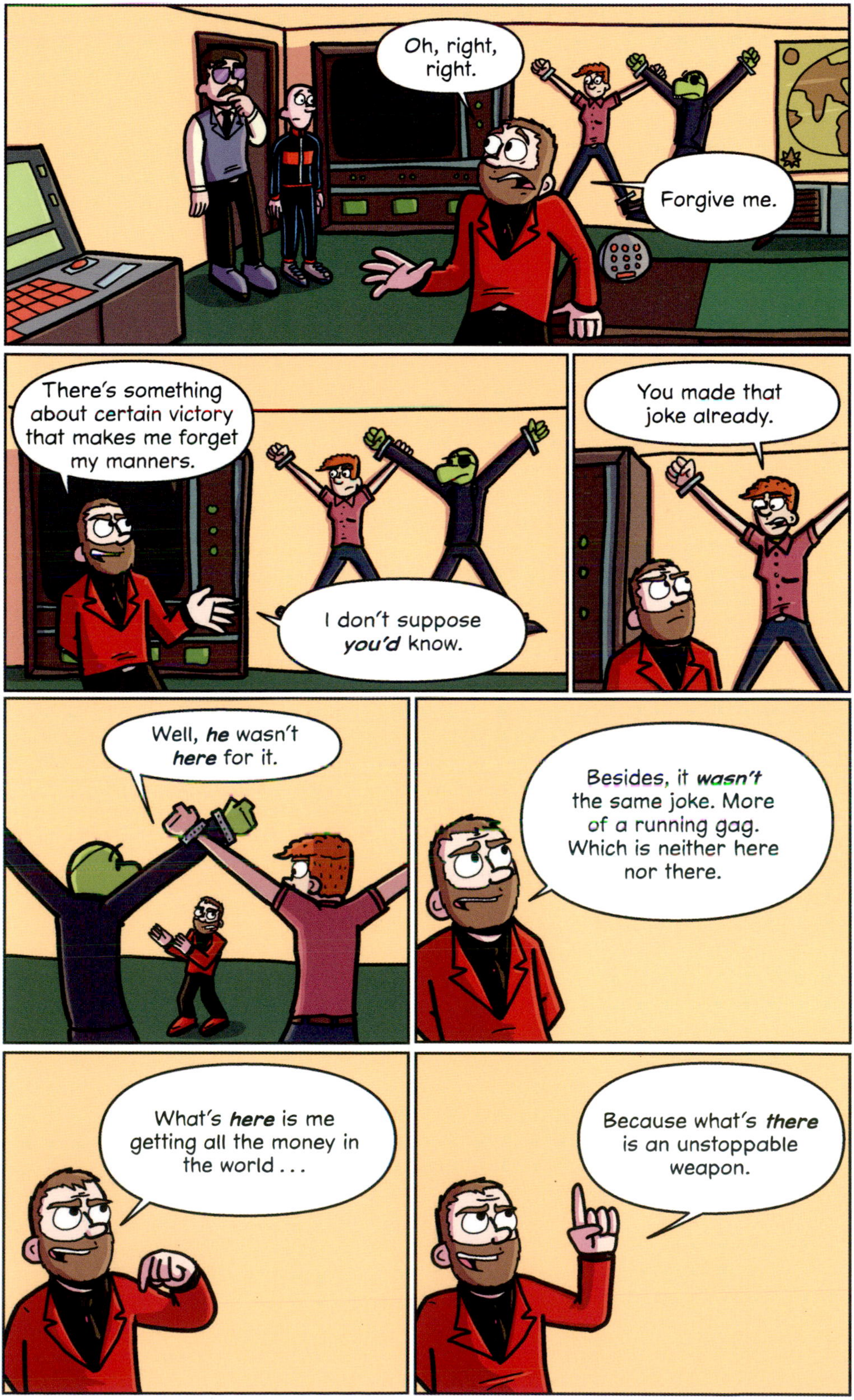
Oh, right, right.
Forgive me.
There's something about certain victory that makes me forget my manners.
I don't suppose *you'd* know.
You made that joke already.
Well, ***he*** wasn't ***here*** for it.
Besides, it ***wasn't*** the same joke. More of a running gag. Which is neither here nor there.
What's ***here*** is me getting all the money in the world . . .
Because what's ***there*** is an unstoppable weapon.

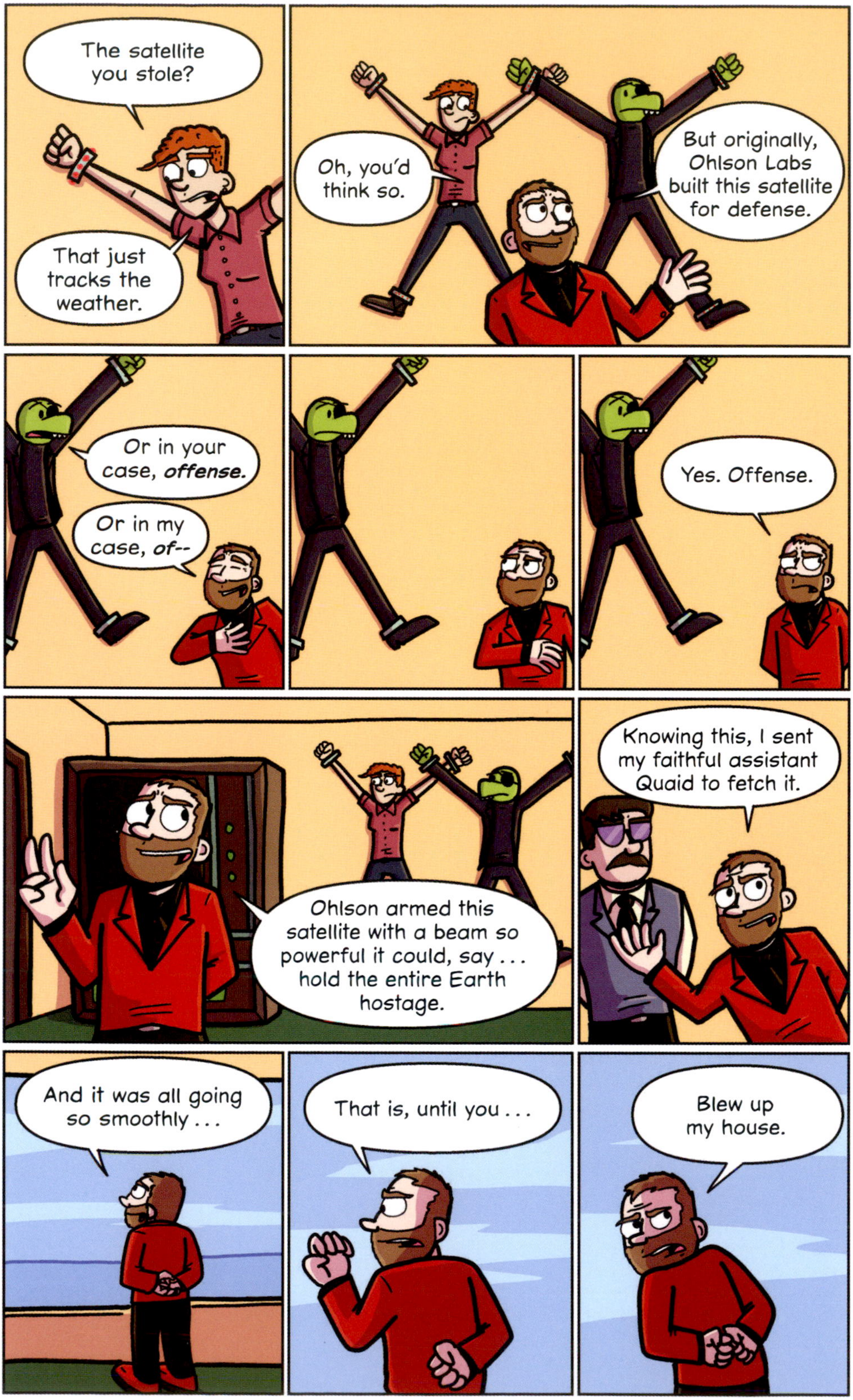
The satellite you stole?
That just tracks the weather.
Oh, you'd think so.
But originally, Ohlson Labs built this satellite for defense.
Or in your case, *offense.*
Or in my case, *of--*
Yes. Offense.
Ohlson armed this satellite with a beam so powerful it could, say . . . hold the entire Earth hostage.
Knowing this, I sent my faithful assistant Quaid to fetch it.
And it was all going so smoothly . . .
That is, until you . . .
Blew up my house.

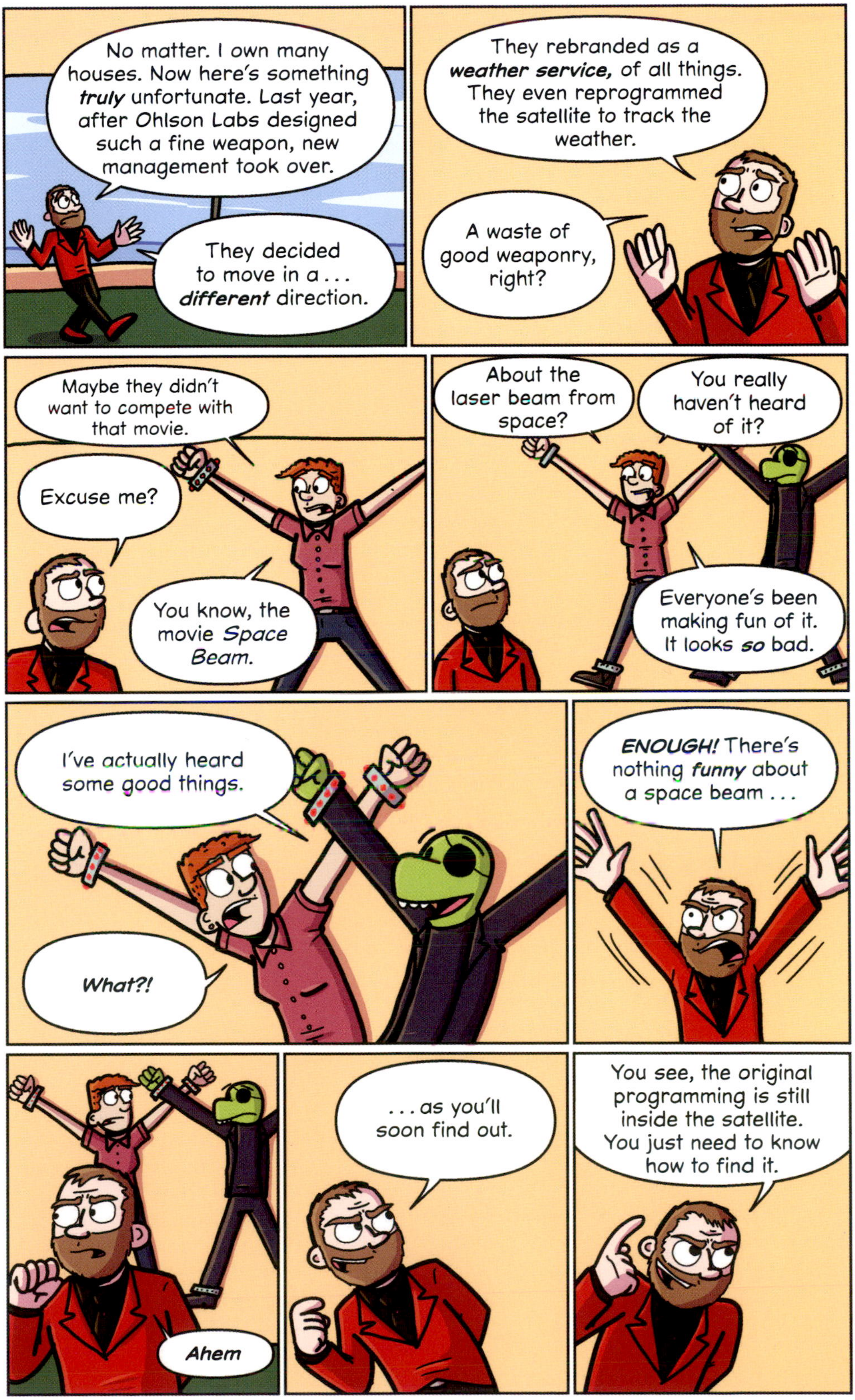
No matter. I own many houses. Now here's something *truly* unfortunate. Last year, after Ohlson Labs designed such a fine weapon, new management took over.
They decided to move in a . . . *different* direction.
They rebranded as a *weather service,* of all things. They even reprogrammed the satellite to track the weather.
A waste of good weaponry, right?
Maybe they didn't want to compete with that movie.
Excuse me?
You know, the movie *Space Beam.*
About the laser beam from space?
You really haven't heard of it?
Everyone's been making fun of it. It looks *so* bad.
I've actually heard some good things.
What?!
ENOUGH! There's nothing *funny* about a space beam . . .
Ahem
. . . as you'll soon find out.
You see, the original programming is still inside the satellite. You just need to know how to find it.

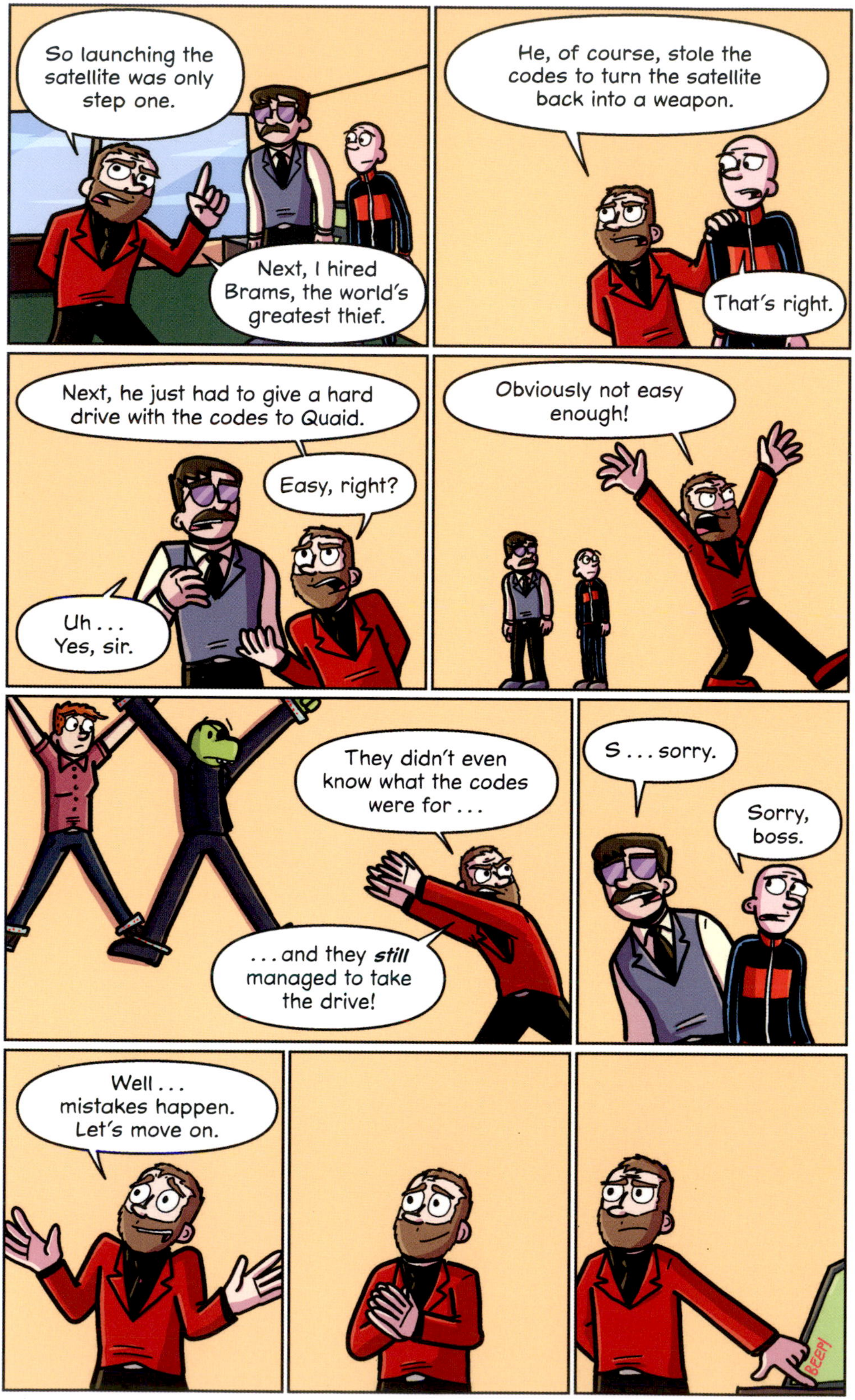

So launching the satellite was only step one.
Next, I hired Brams, the world's greatest thief.
He, of course, stole the codes to turn the satellite back into a weapon.
That's right.
Next, he just had to give a hard drive with the codes to Quaid.
Easy, right?
Uh . . . Yes, sir.
Obviously not easy enough!
They didn't even know what the codes were for . . .
. . . and they *still* managed to take the drive!
S . . . sorry.
Sorry, boss.
Well . . . mistakes happen. Let's move on.
BEEP!

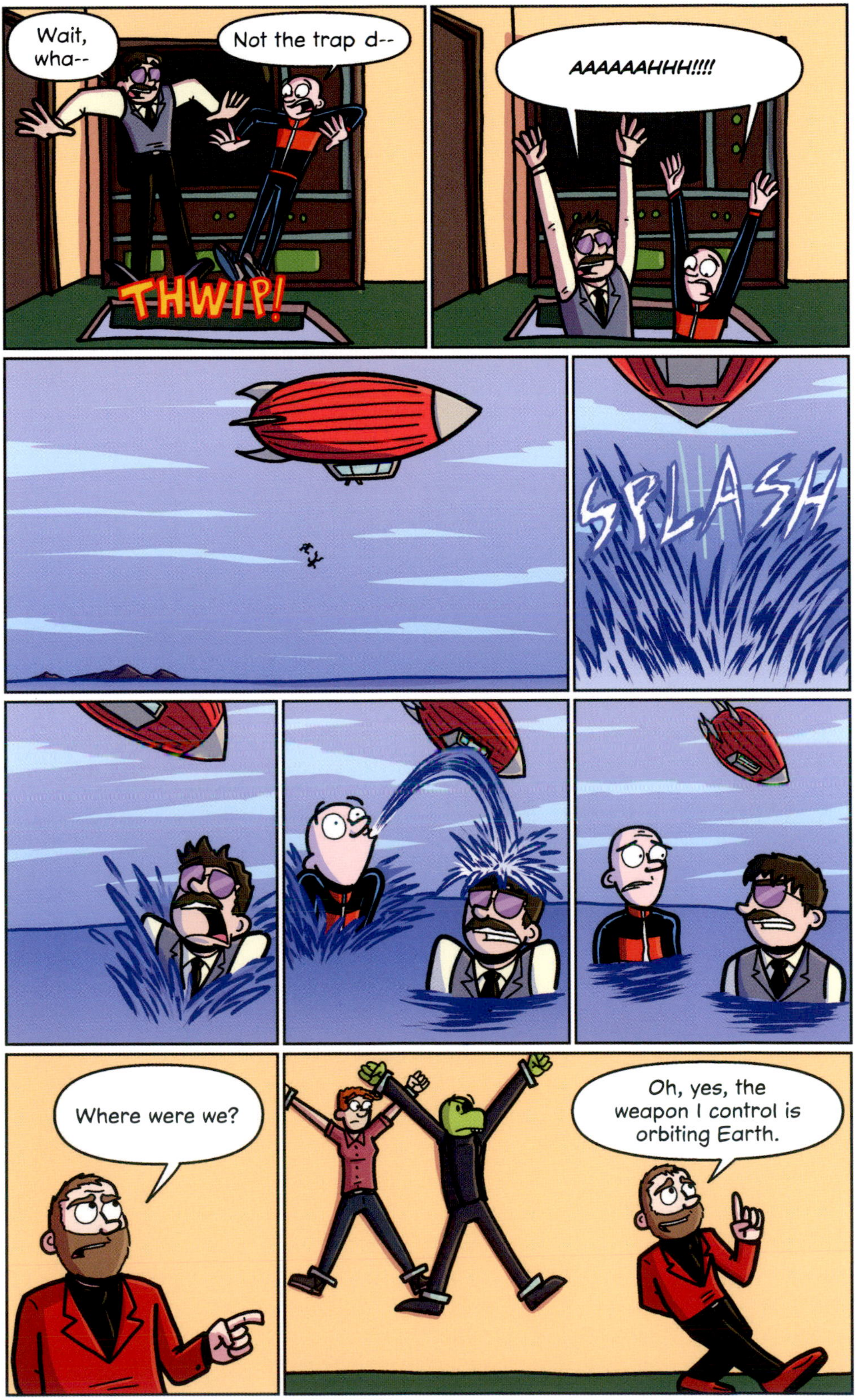
Wait, wha--
Not the trap d--
THWIP!
AAAAAAHHH!!!!
SPLASH
Where were we?
Oh, yes, the weapon I control is orbiting Earth.

But a weapon's only good if it **works**...

So we're going to do a quick test.

CLICK!

Test?

What kind of test?

Um...

The evil kind?

Surely you didn't think we were in a blimp just because it's a luxurious way to travel.

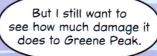

We need to get out of the blast radius...

But I still want to see how much damage it does to Greene Peak.

Hence the blimp! It's just the best.

Once the city is destroyed, the world will know I **mean** business.

No! You can't!

Oh, I can.

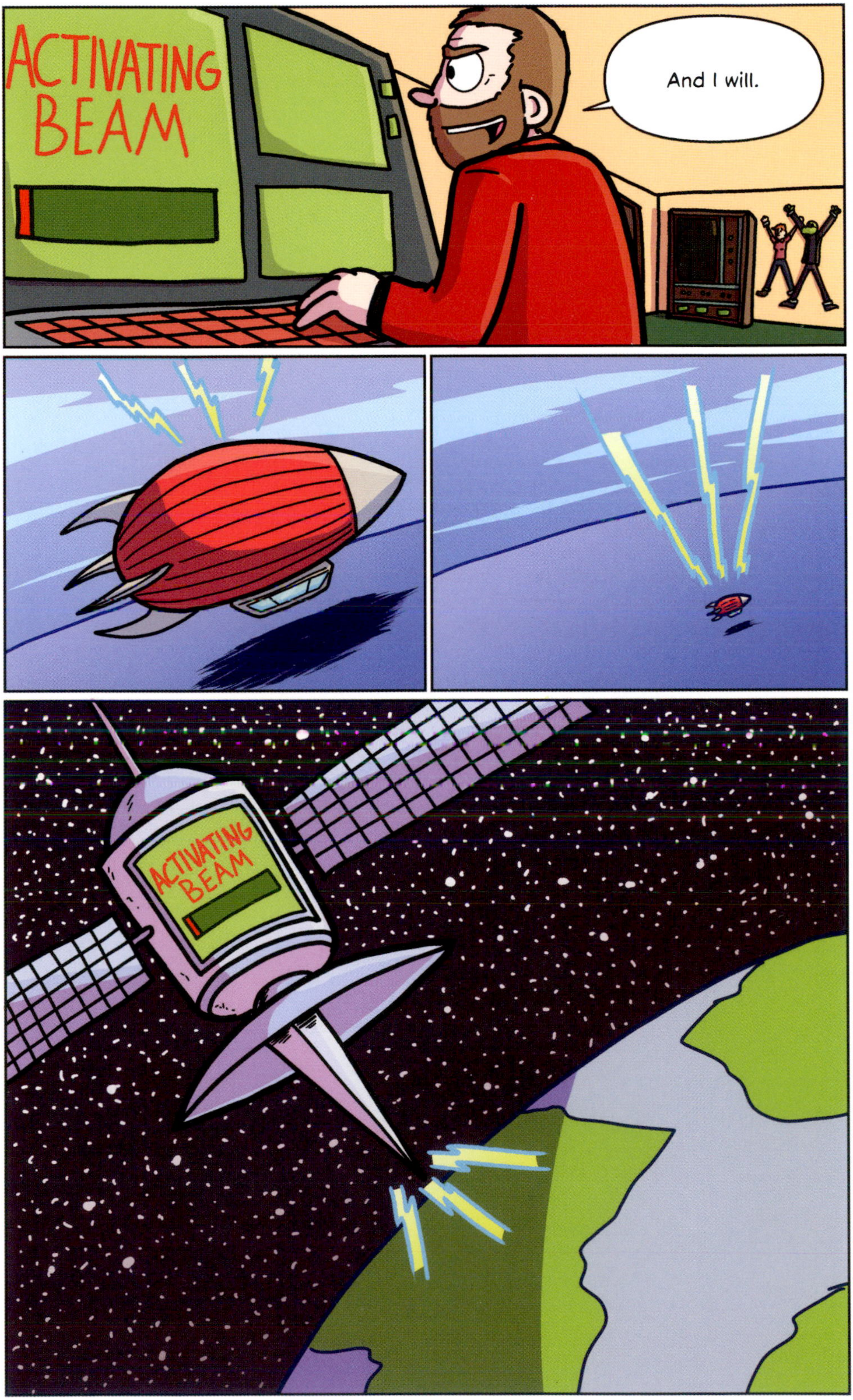
ACTIVATING BEAM
And I will.
ACTIVATING BEAM

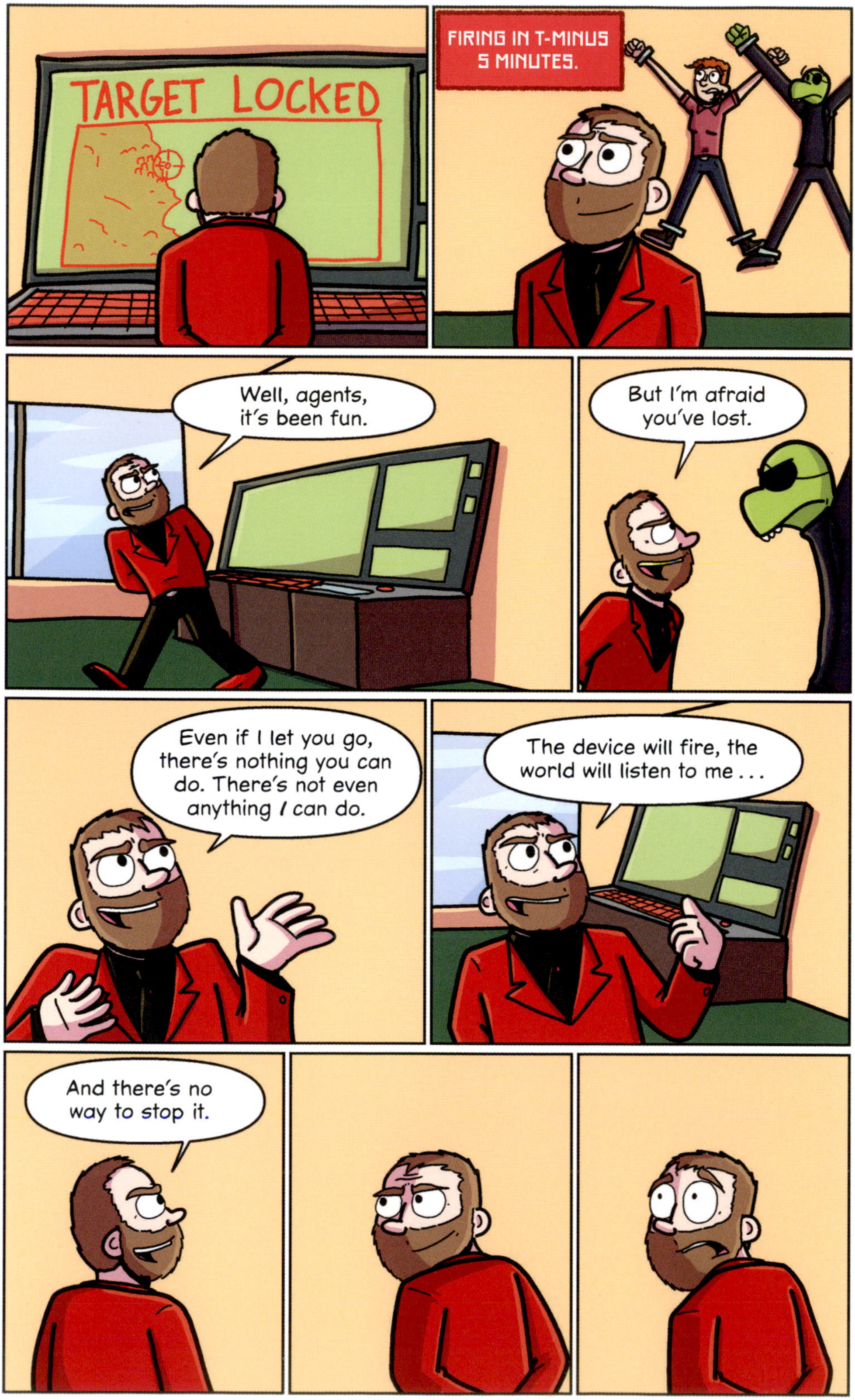
TARGET LOCKED
FIRING IN T-MINUS 5 MINUTES.
Well, agents, it's been fun.
But I'm afraid you've lost.
Even if I let you go, there's nothing you can do. There's not even anything *I* can do.
The device will fire, the world will listen to me . . .
And there's no way to stop it.

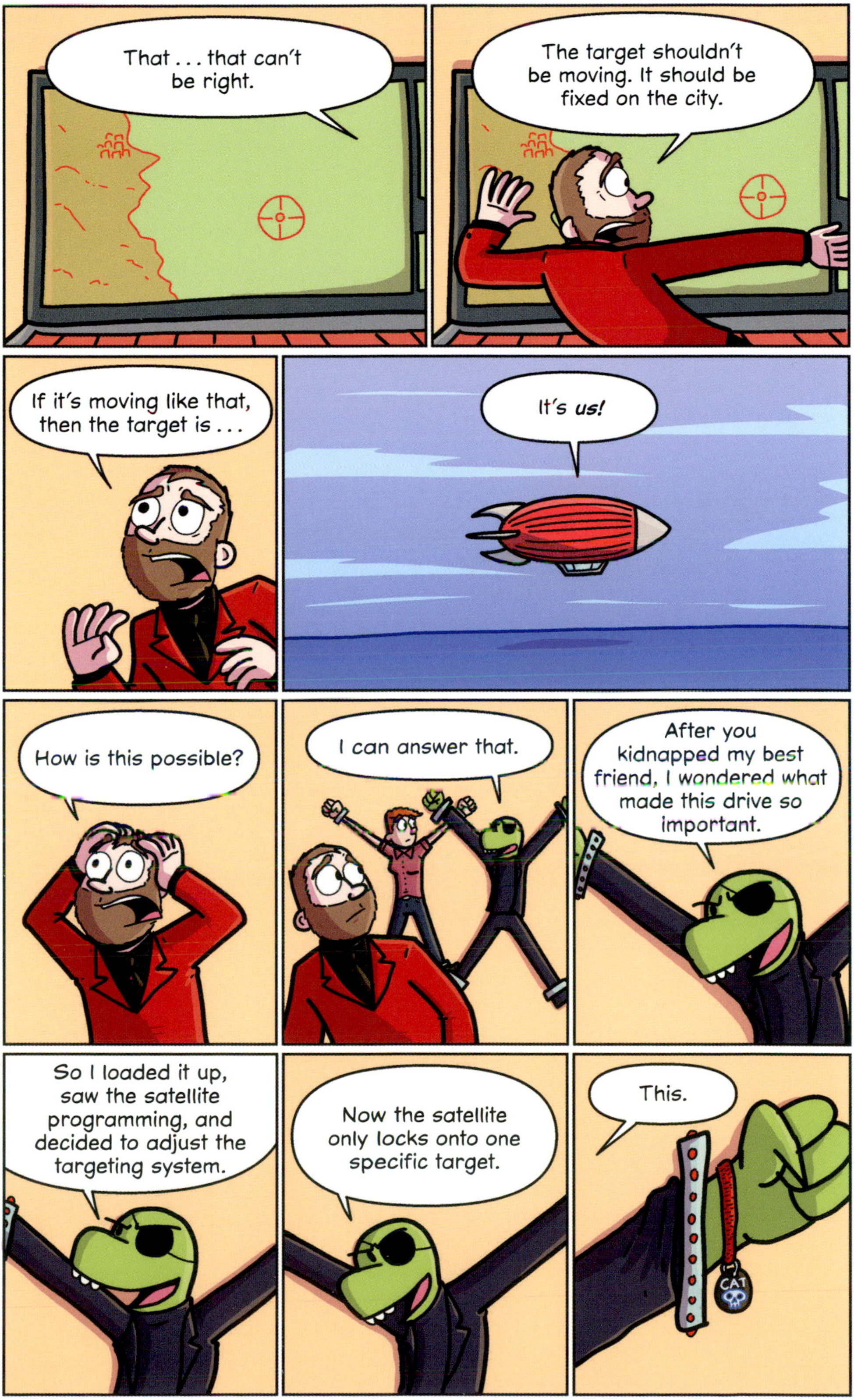
That . . . that can't be right.
The target shouldn't be moving. It should be fixed on the city.
If it's moving like that, then the target is . . .
It's *us!*
How is this possible?
I can answer that.
After you kidnapped my best friend, I wondered what made this drive so important.
So I loaded it up, saw the satellite programming, and decided to adjust the targeting system.
Now the satellite only locks onto one specific target.
This.
CAT

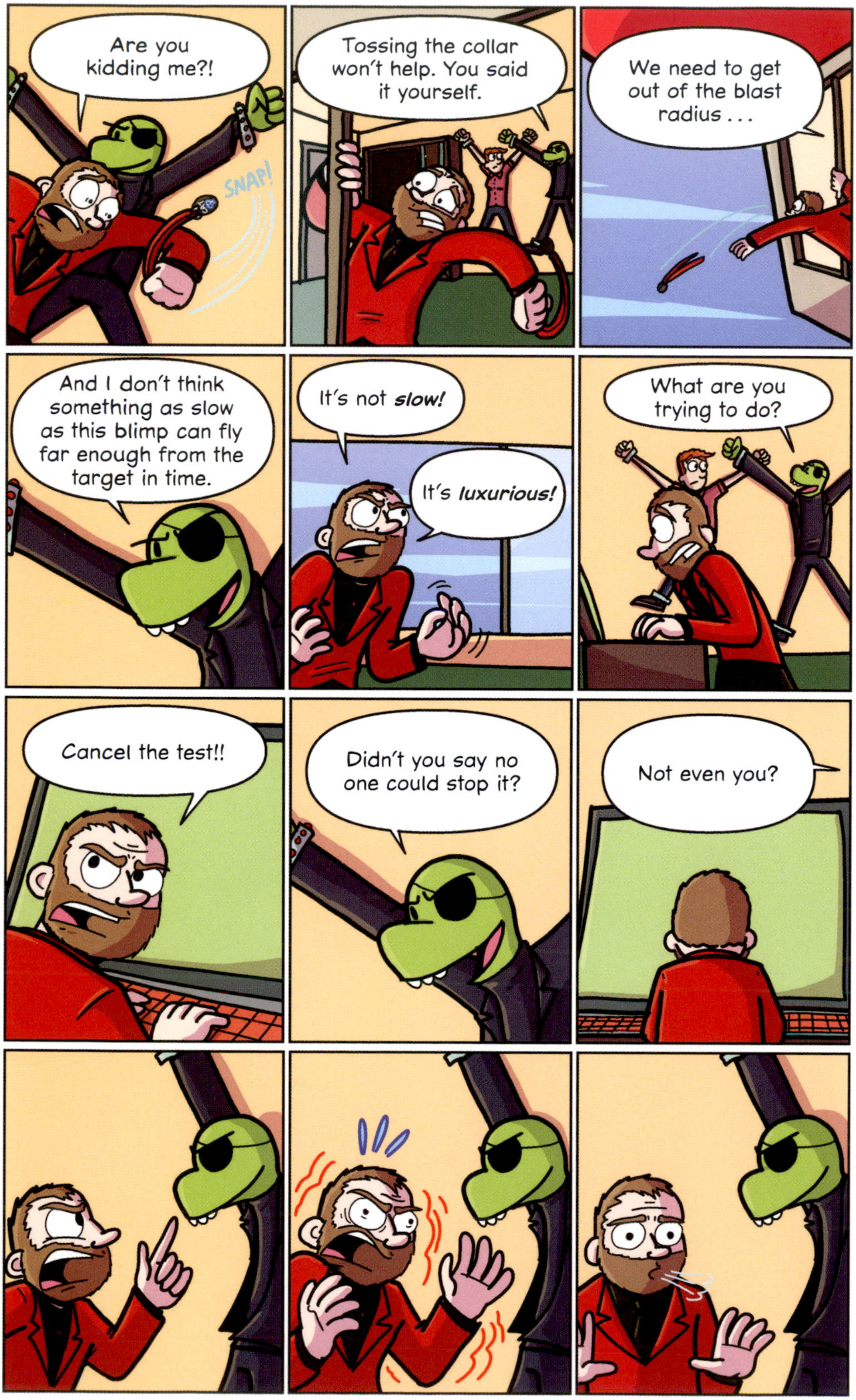
Are you kidding me?!
SNAP!
Tossing the collar won't help. You said it yourself.
We need to get out of the blast radius . . .
And I don't think something as slow as this blimp can fly far enough from the target in time.
It's not *slow!*
It's *luxurious!*
What are you trying to do?
Cancel the test!!
Didn't you say no one could stop it?
Not even you?

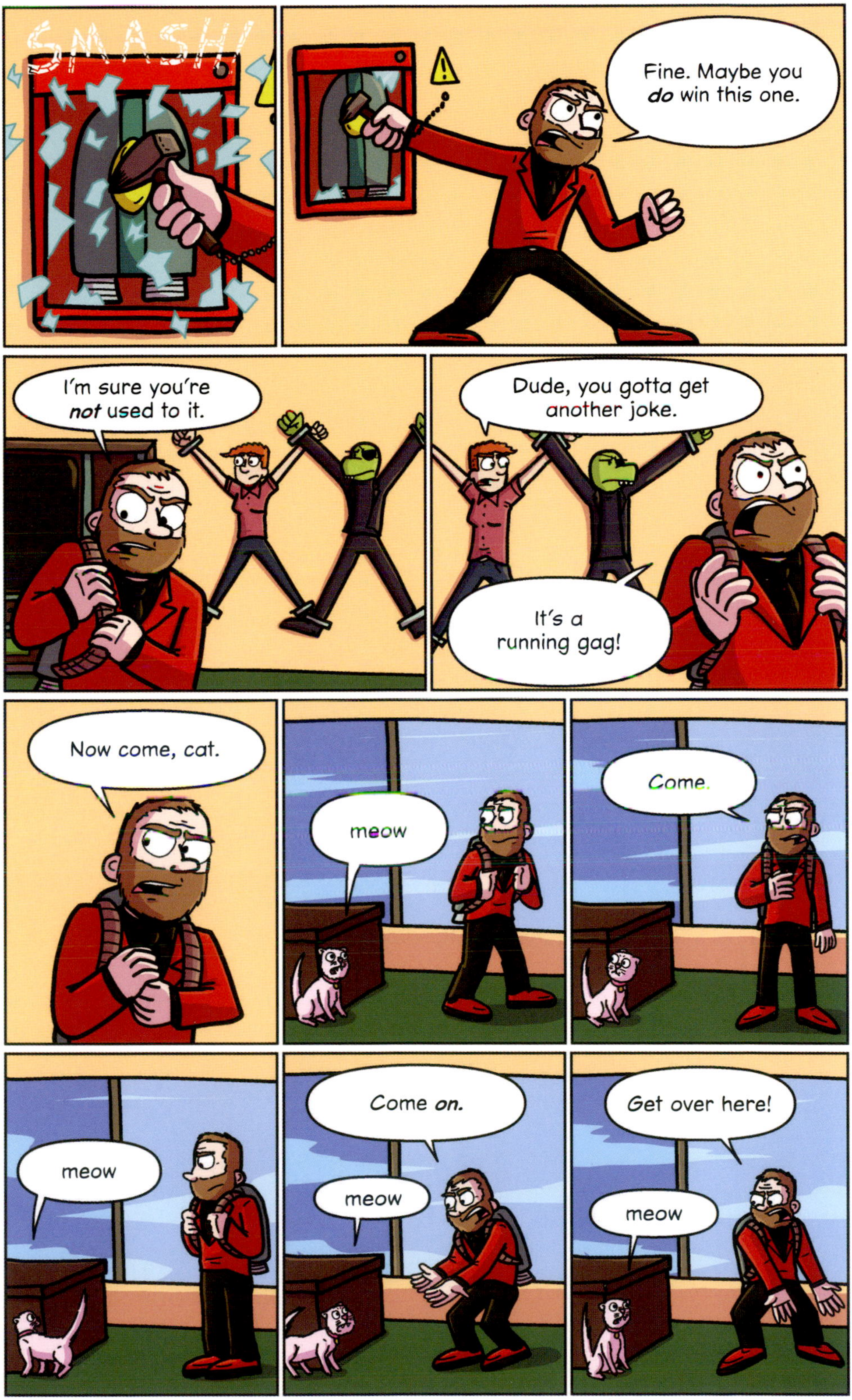
SMASH!
Fine. Maybe you *do* win this one.
I'm sure you're *not* used to it.
Dude, you gotta get another joke.
It's a running gag!
Now come, cat.
meow
Come.
meow
Come *on.*
meow
Get over here!
meow

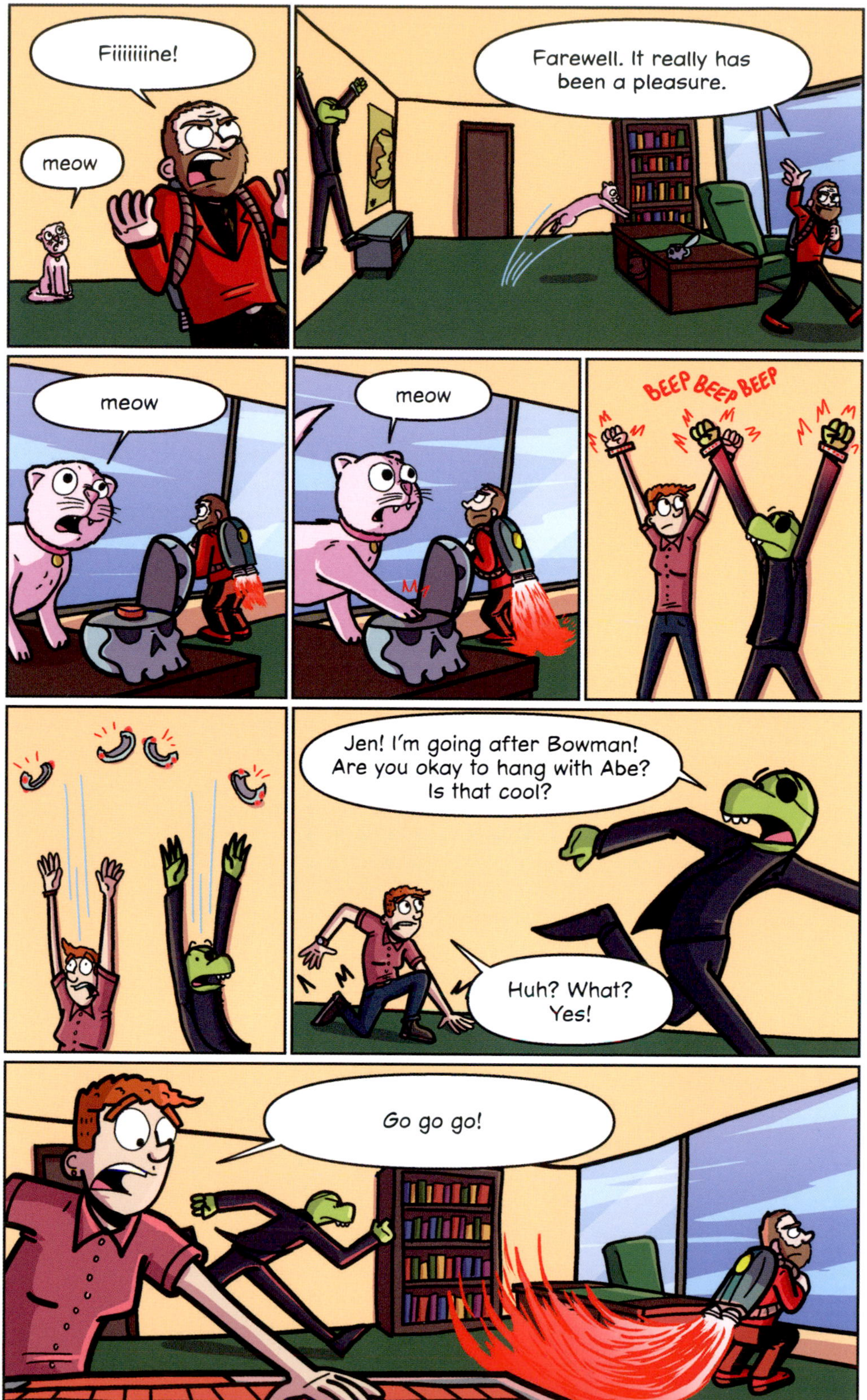
Fiiiiiiine!
meow
Farewell. It really has been a pleasure.
meow
meow
BEEP BEEP BEEP
Jen! I'm going after Bowman! Are you okay to hang with Abe? Is that cool?
Huh? What? Yes!
Go go go!

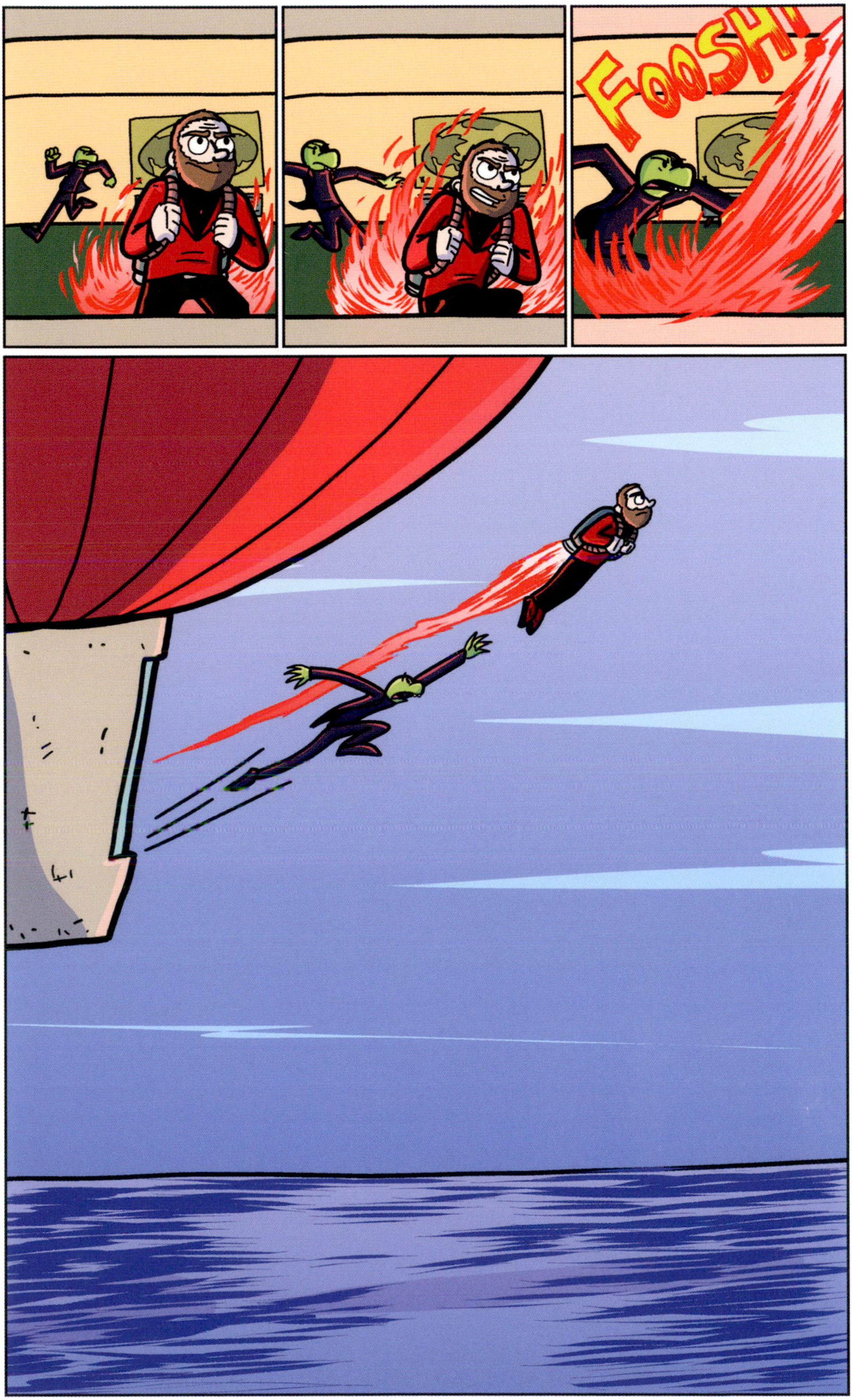
FOOSH!

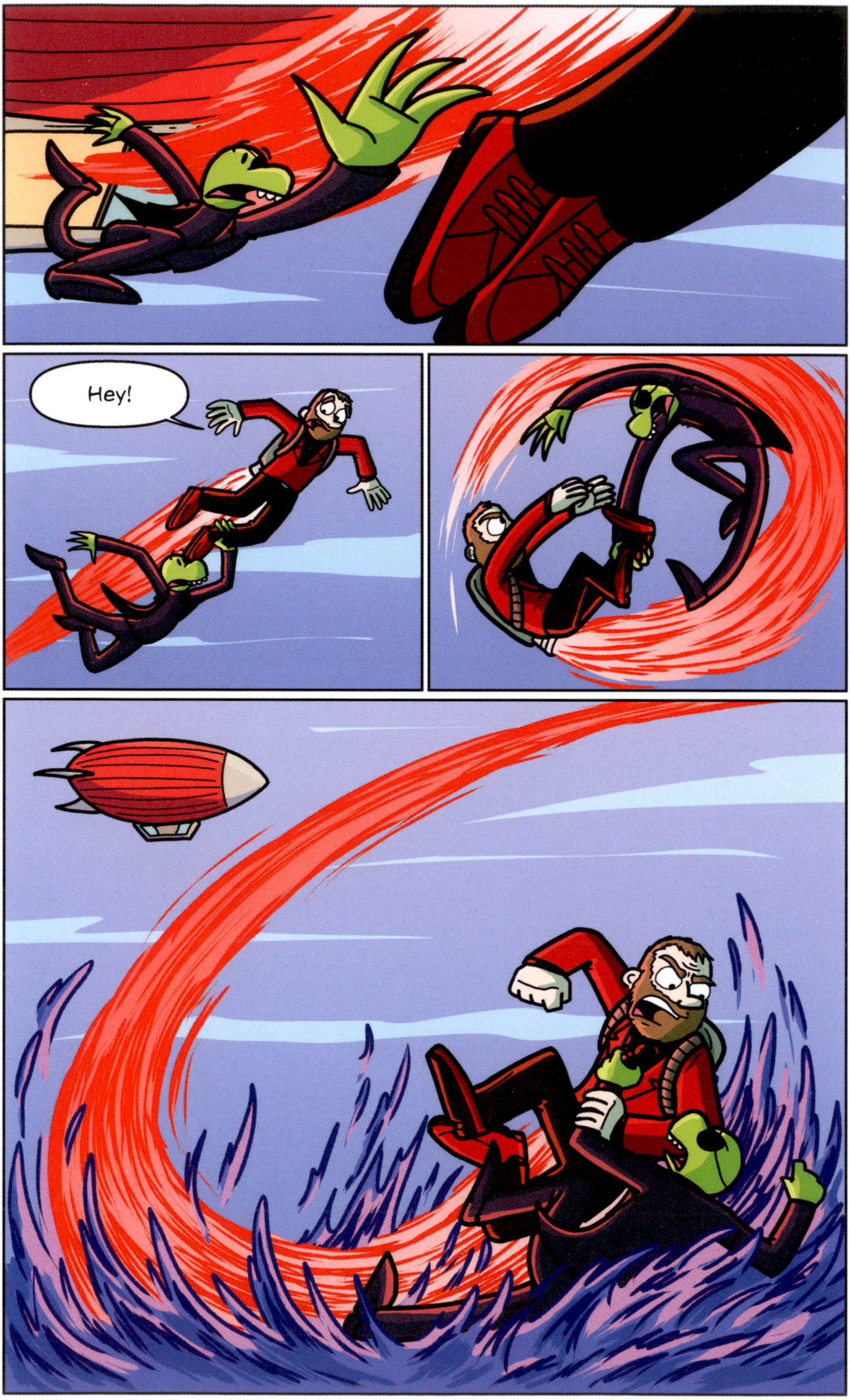
Hey!

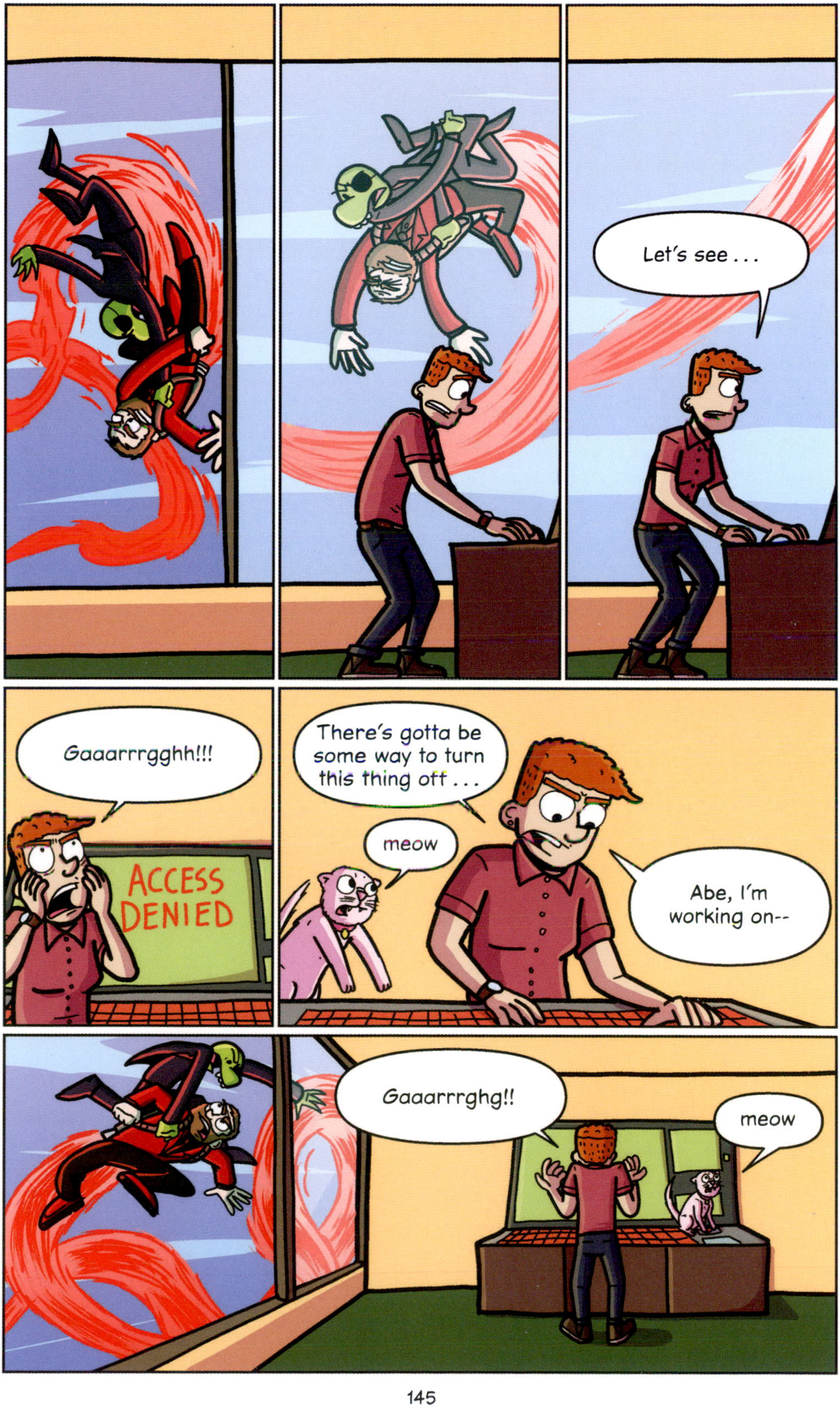
Let's see . . .
Gaaarrrgghh!!!
ACCESS DENIED
There's gotta be some way to turn this thing off . . .
meow
Abe, I'm working on--
Gaaarrrghg!!
meow

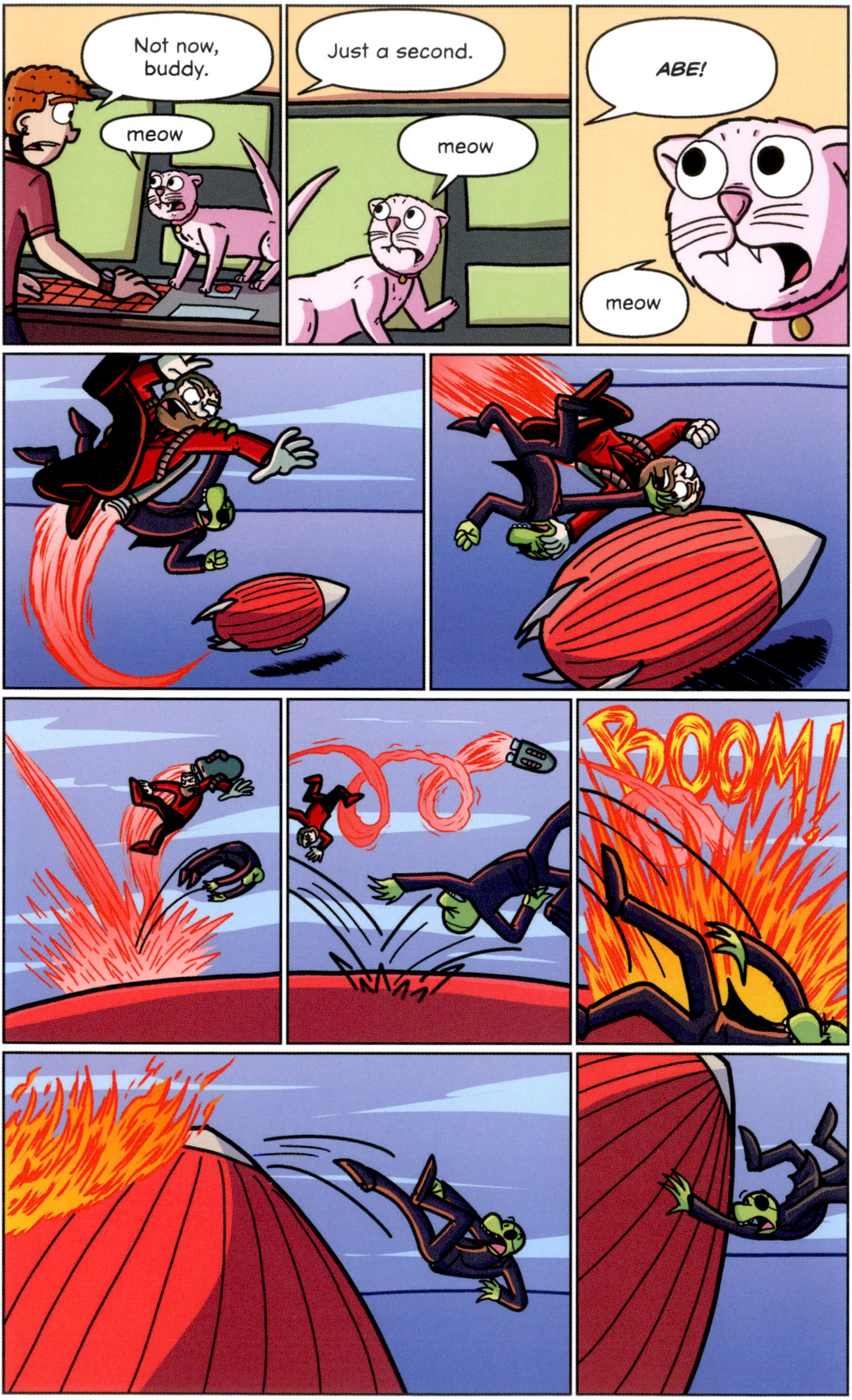
Not now, buddy.
meow
Just a second.
meow
ABE!
meow
BOOM!

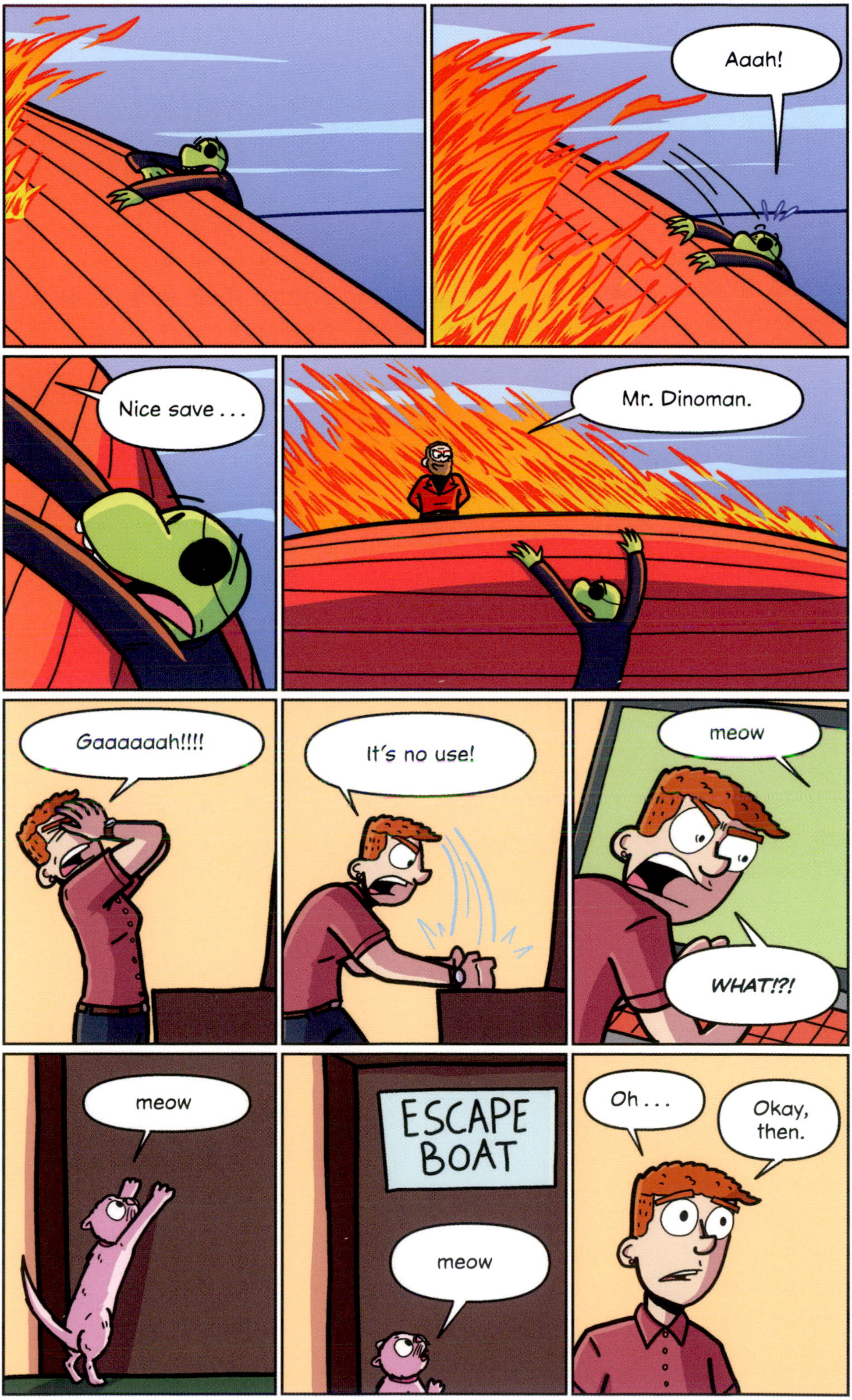
Aaah!
Nice save . . .
Mr. Dinoman.
Gaaaaaah!!!!
It's no use!
meow
WHAT!?!
meow
ESCAPE BOAT
meow
Oh . . .
Okay, then.

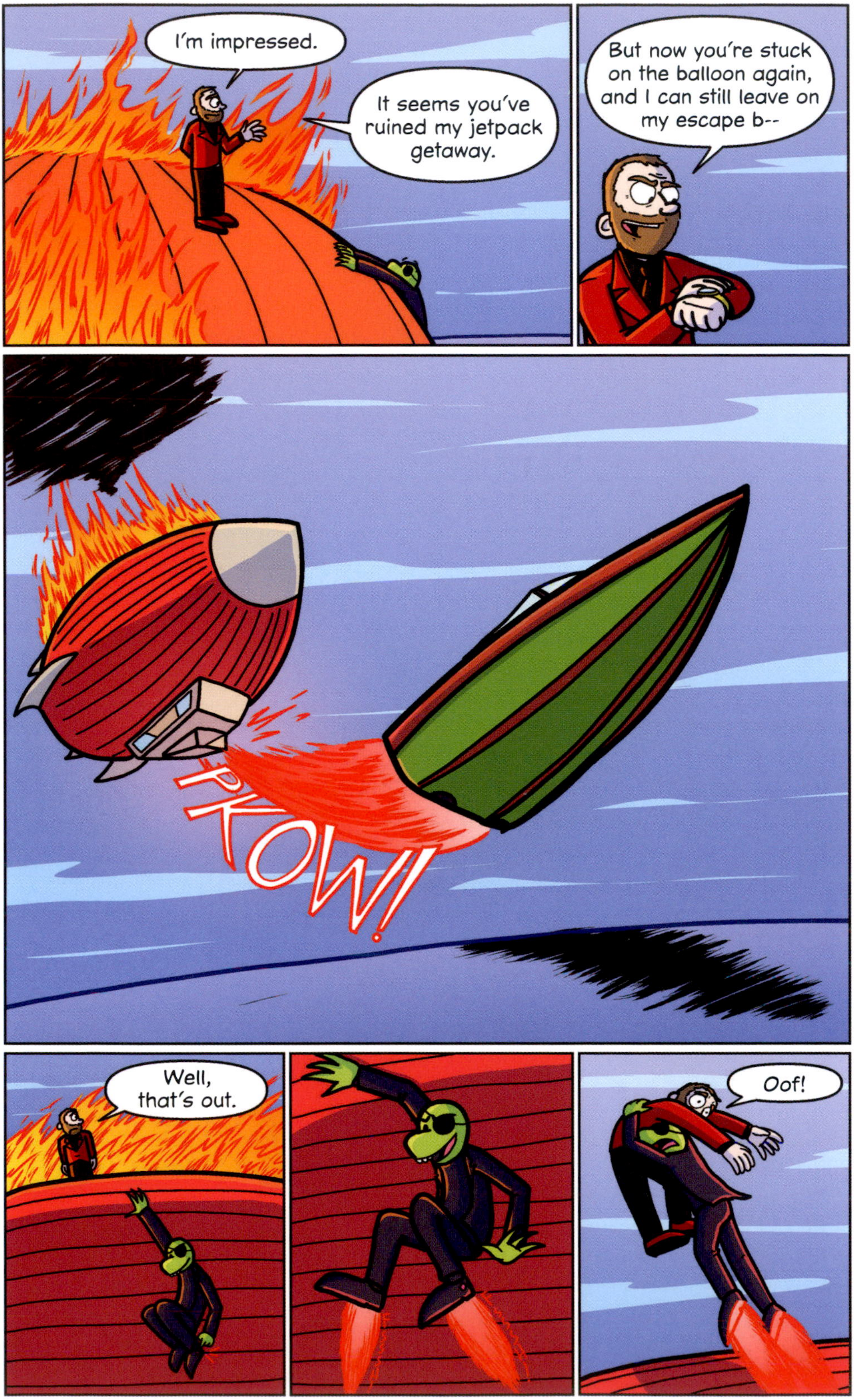
I'm impressed.
It seems you've ruined my jetpack getaway.
But now you're stuck on the balloon again, and I can still leave on my escape b--
PKOW!
Well, that's out.
Oof!

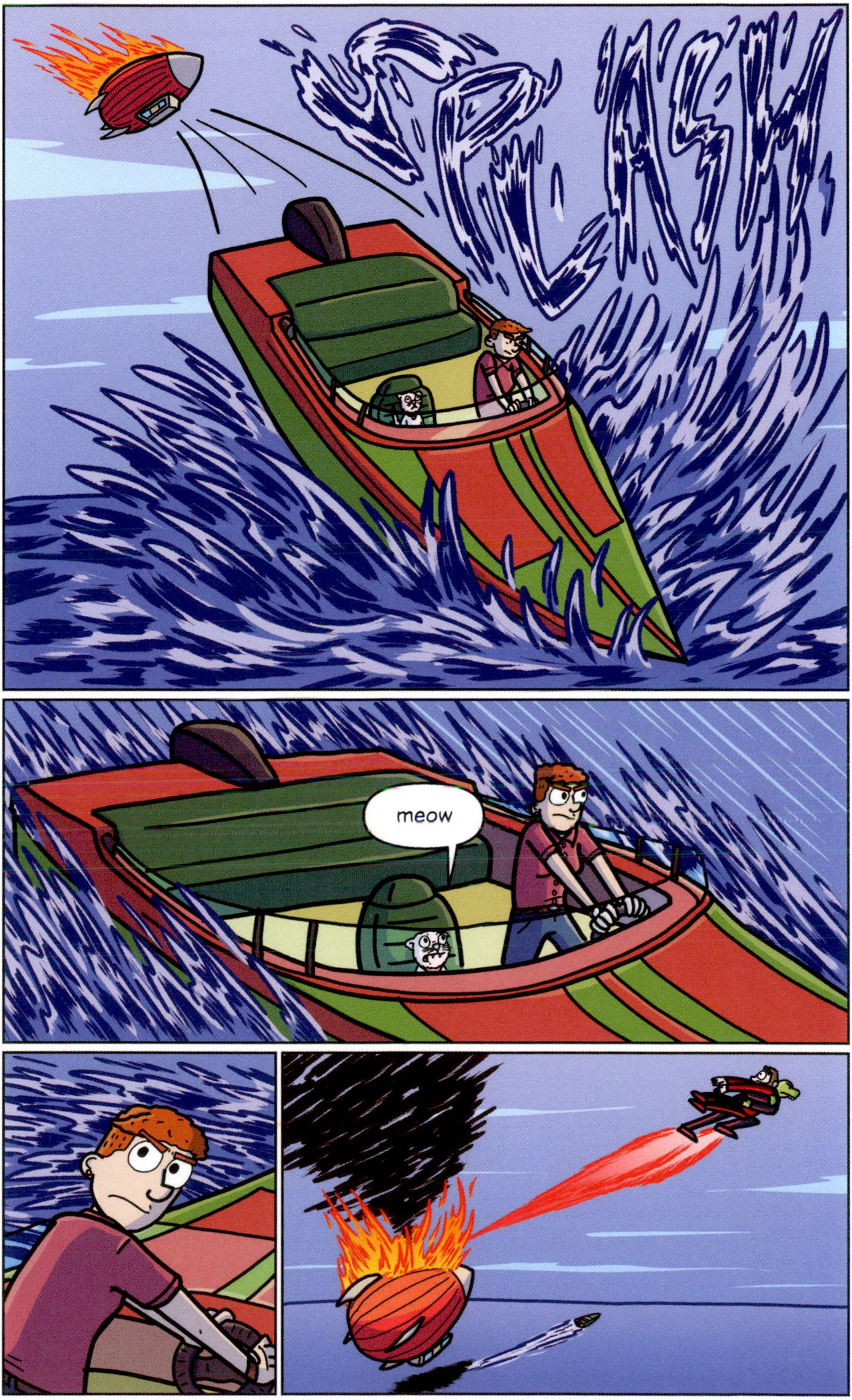
SPLASH
meow

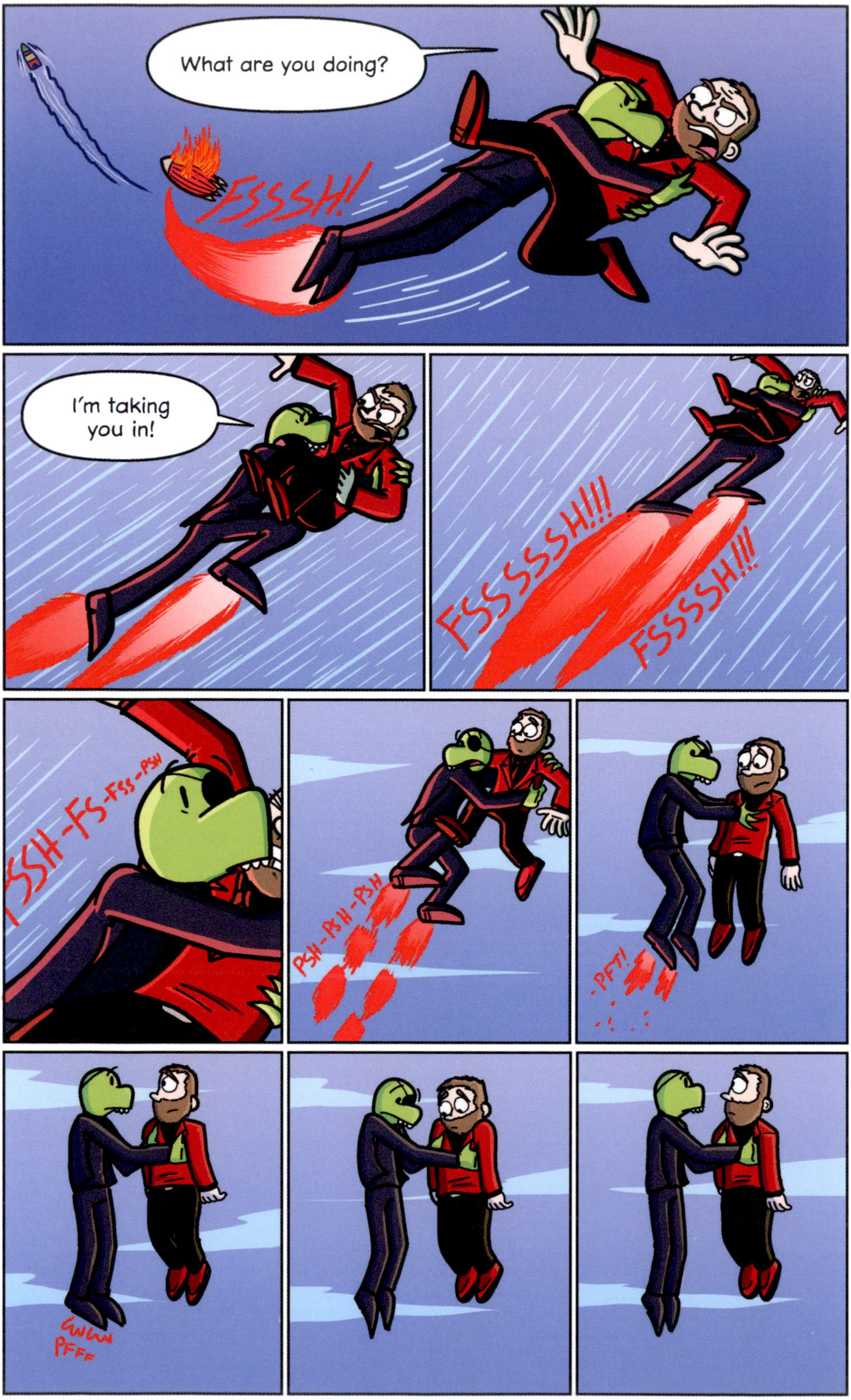
What are you doing?
FSSSH!
I'm taking you in!
FSSSSSH!!!
FSSSSH!!!
SSH-FS-FSS-PSH
PSH-PSH-PSH
PFT!
GWAN PFFF

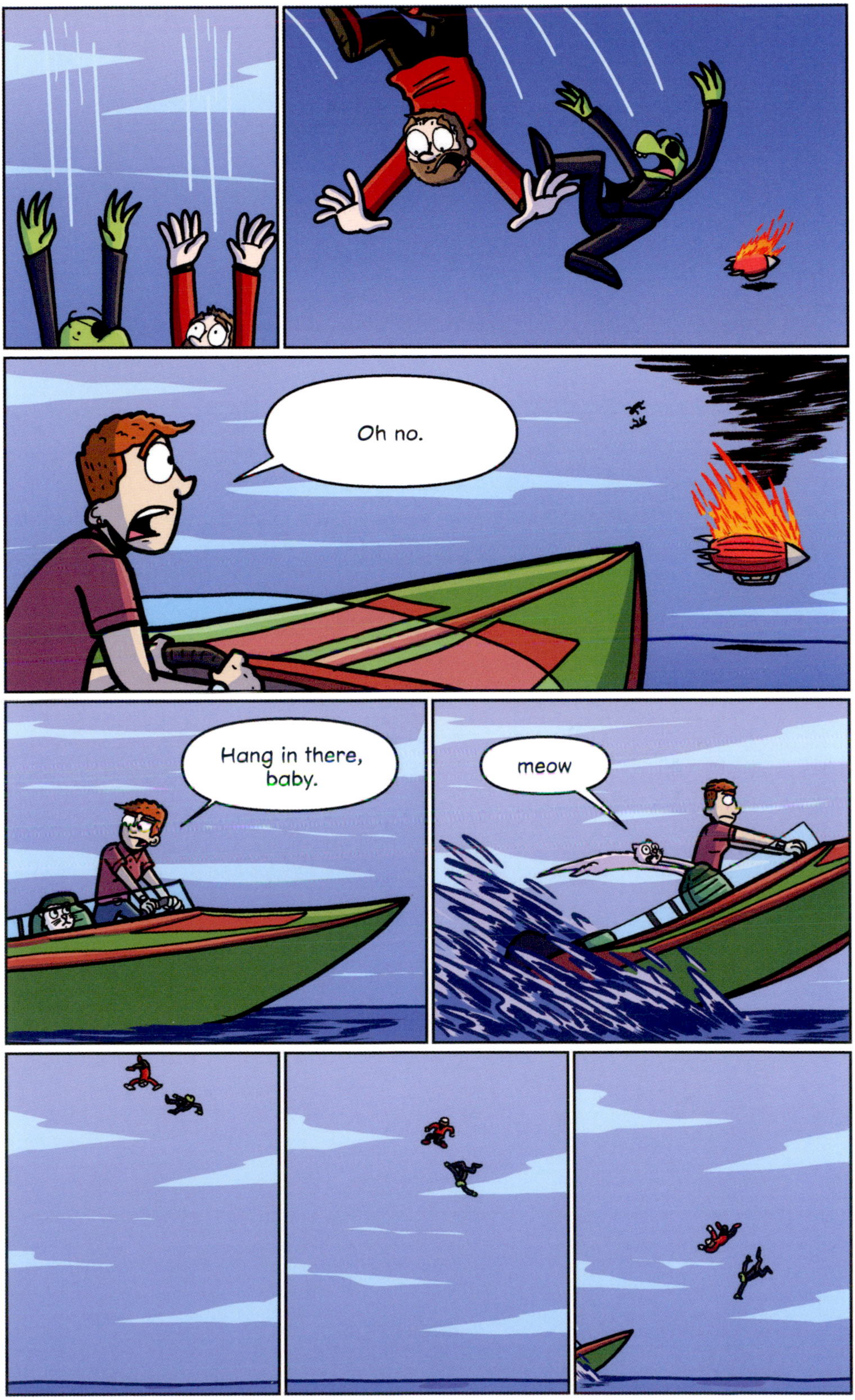
Oh no.
Hang in there, baby.
meow

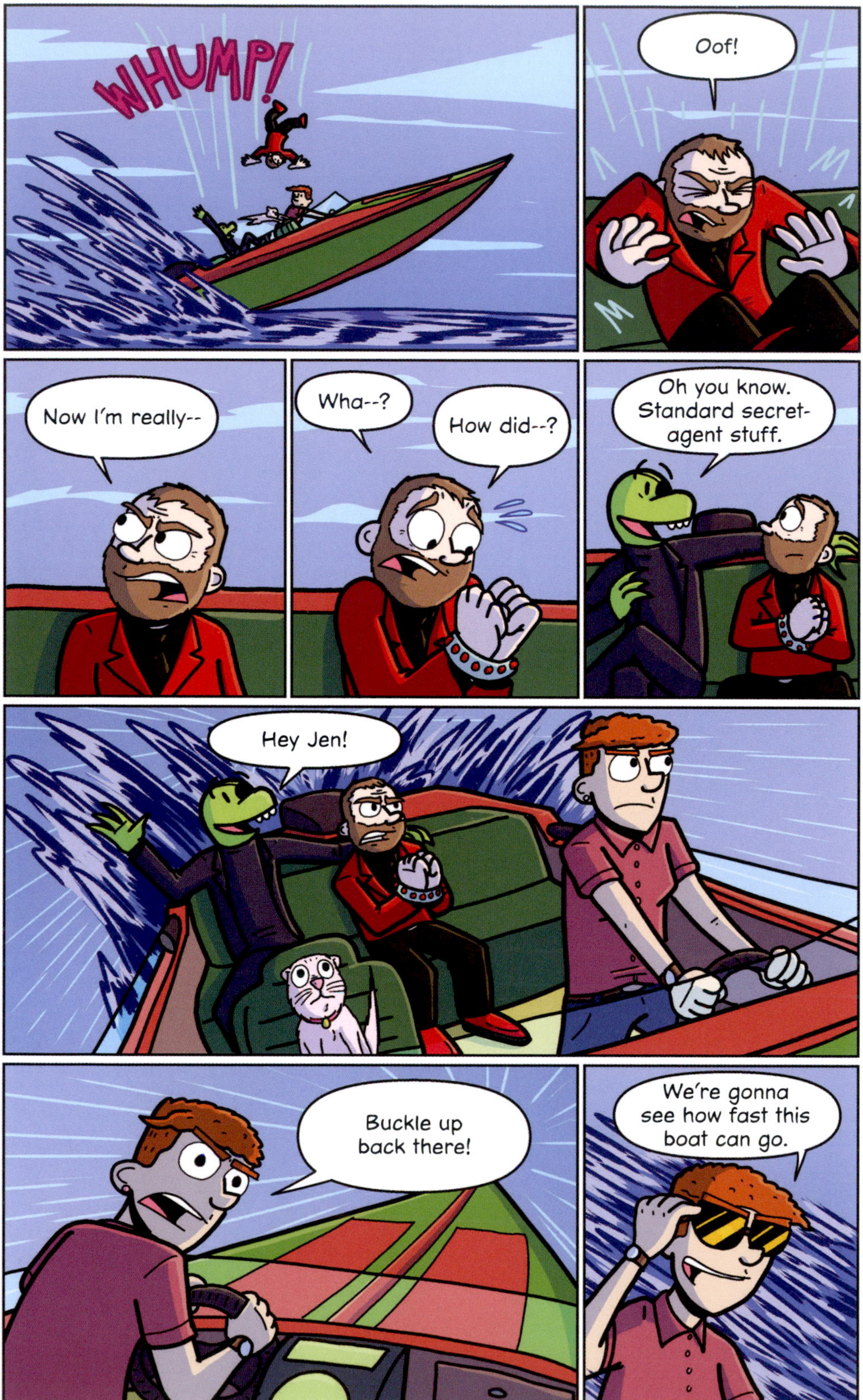
WHUMP!
Oof!
Now I'm really--
Wha--?
How did--?
Oh you know. Standard secret-agent stuff.
Hey Jen!
Buckle up back there!
We're gonna see how fast this boat can go.

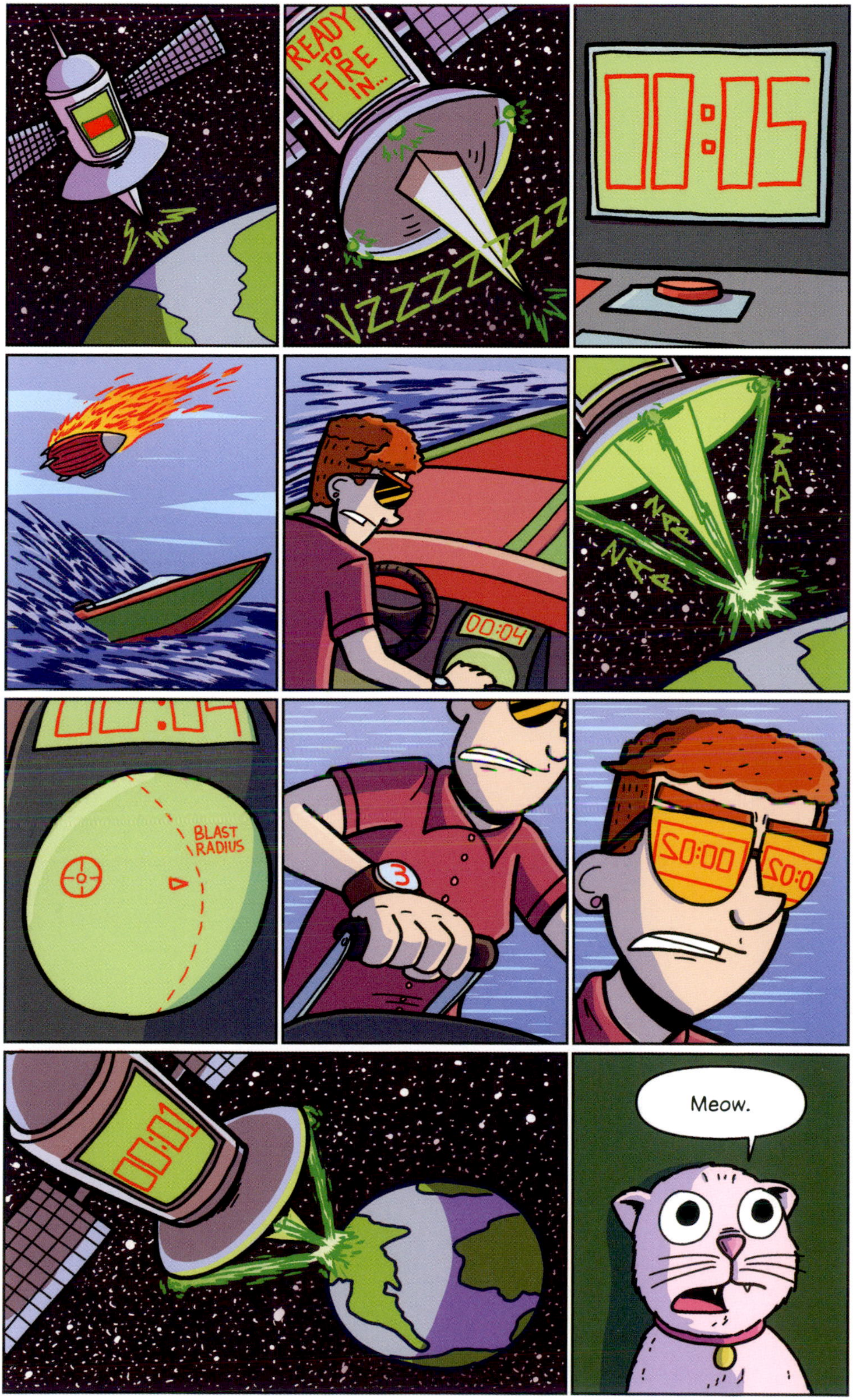
READY TO FIRE IN...
VZZZZZZZZZ
00:05
00:04
ZAP
ZAP
ZAP
BLAST RADIUS
3
00:02
00:01
Meow.

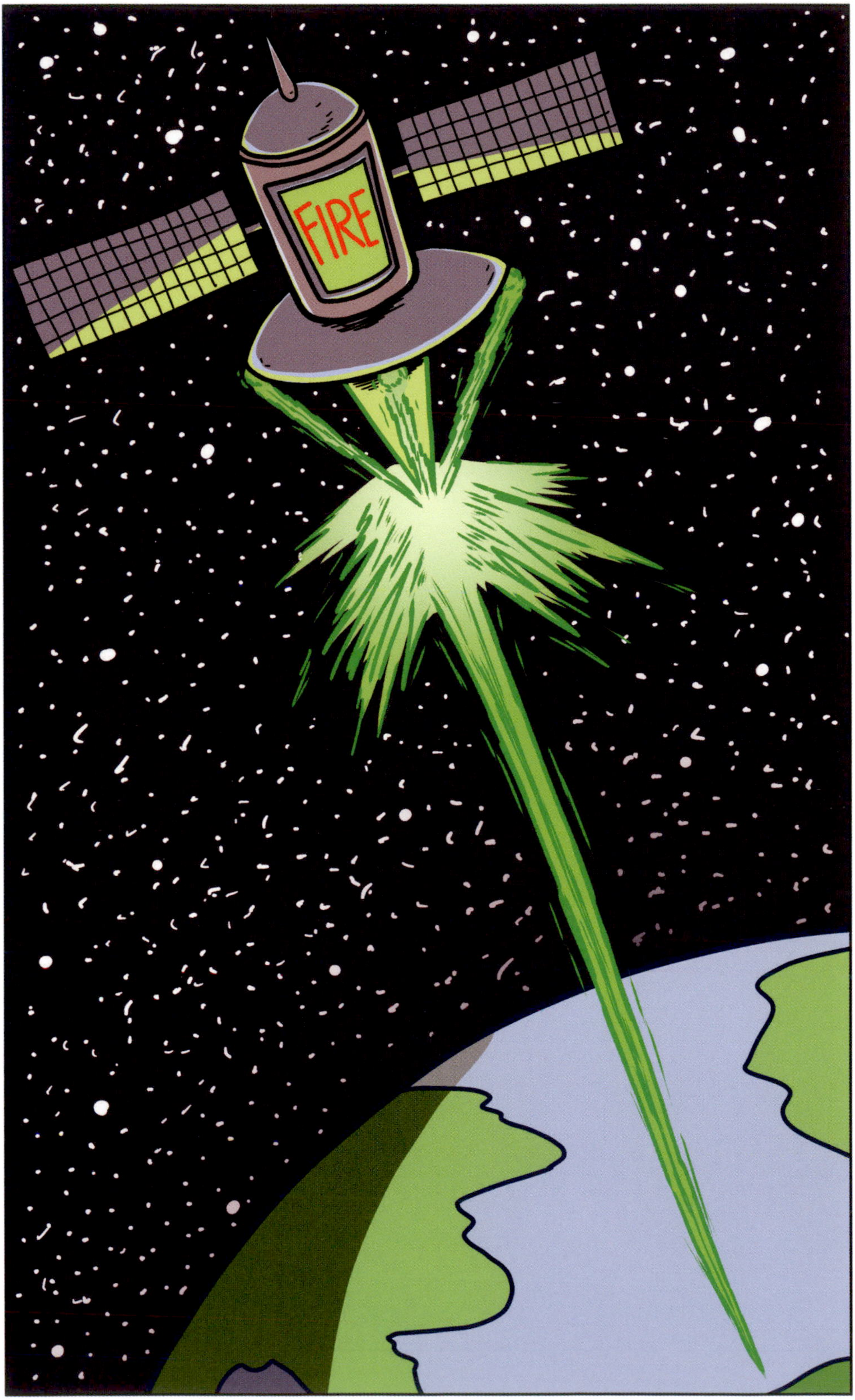
FIRE

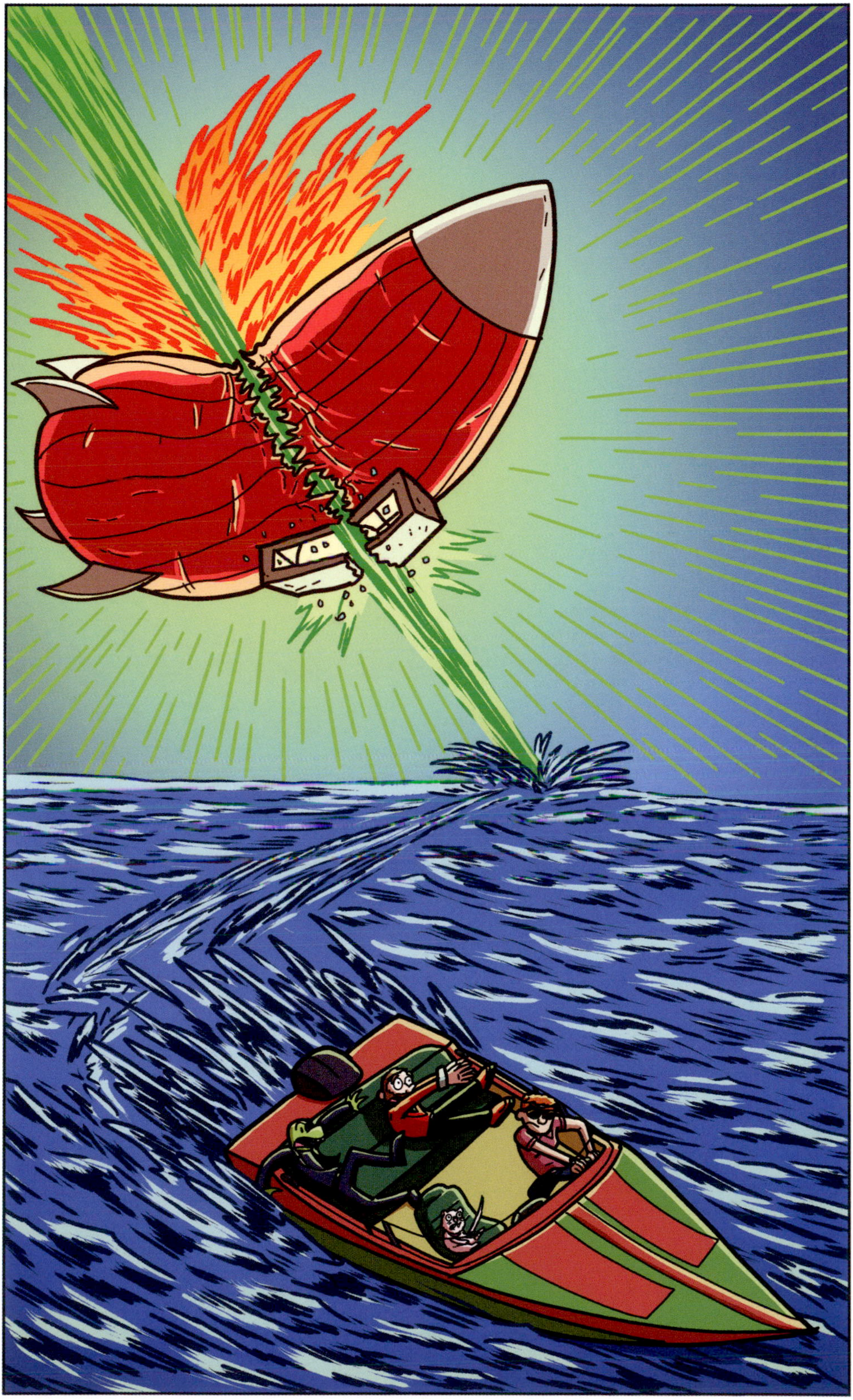

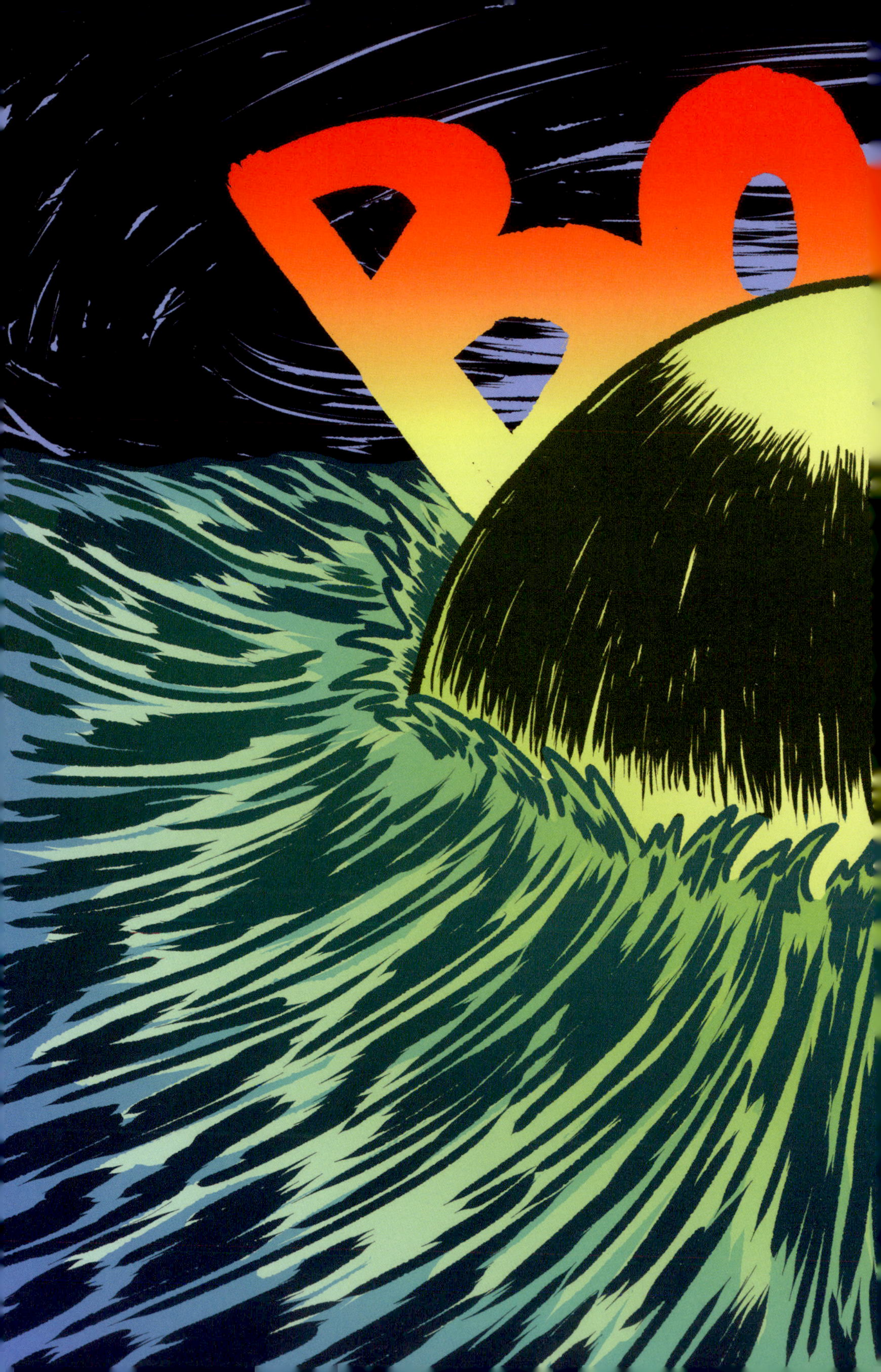
BO

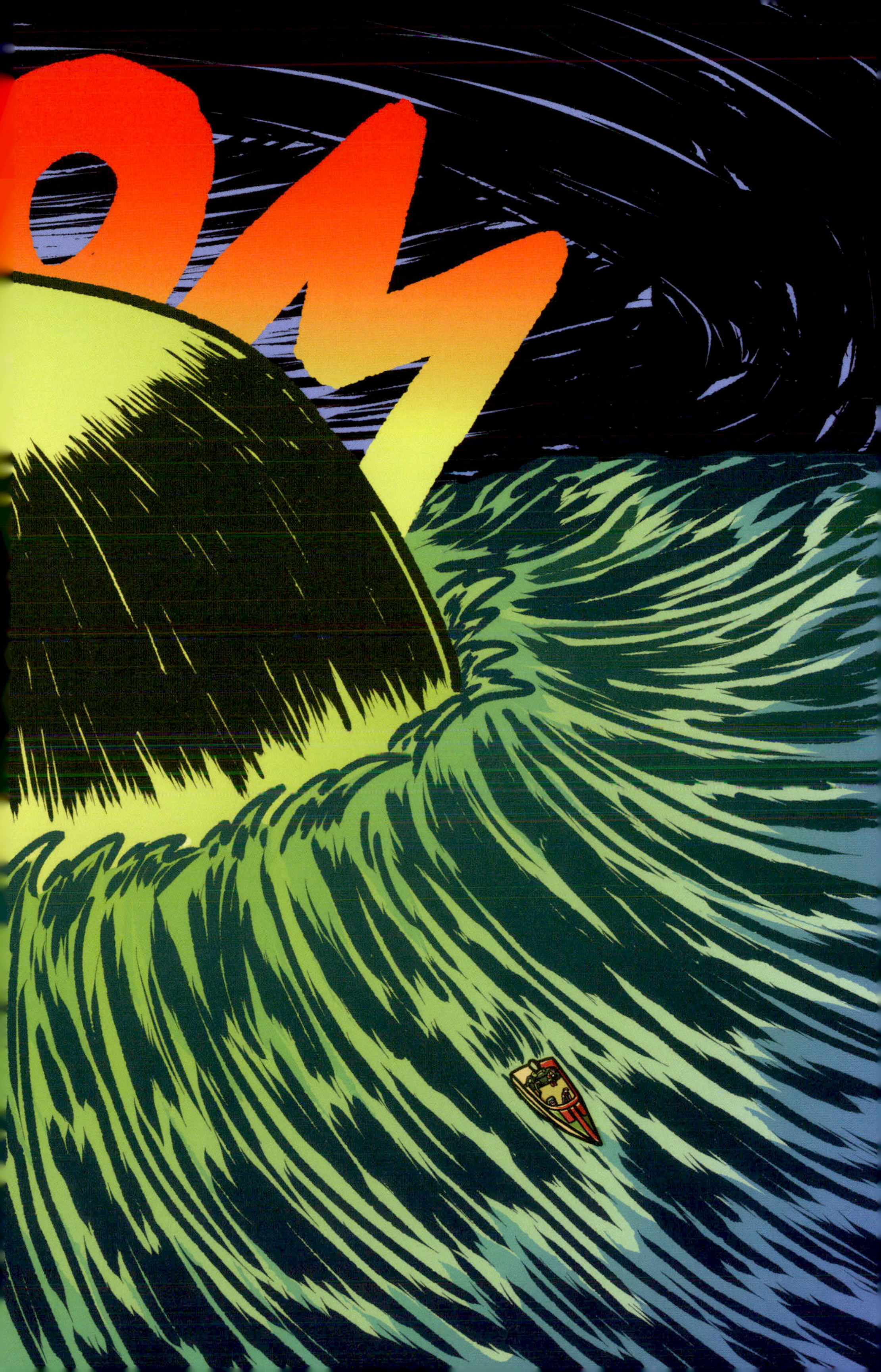
OM

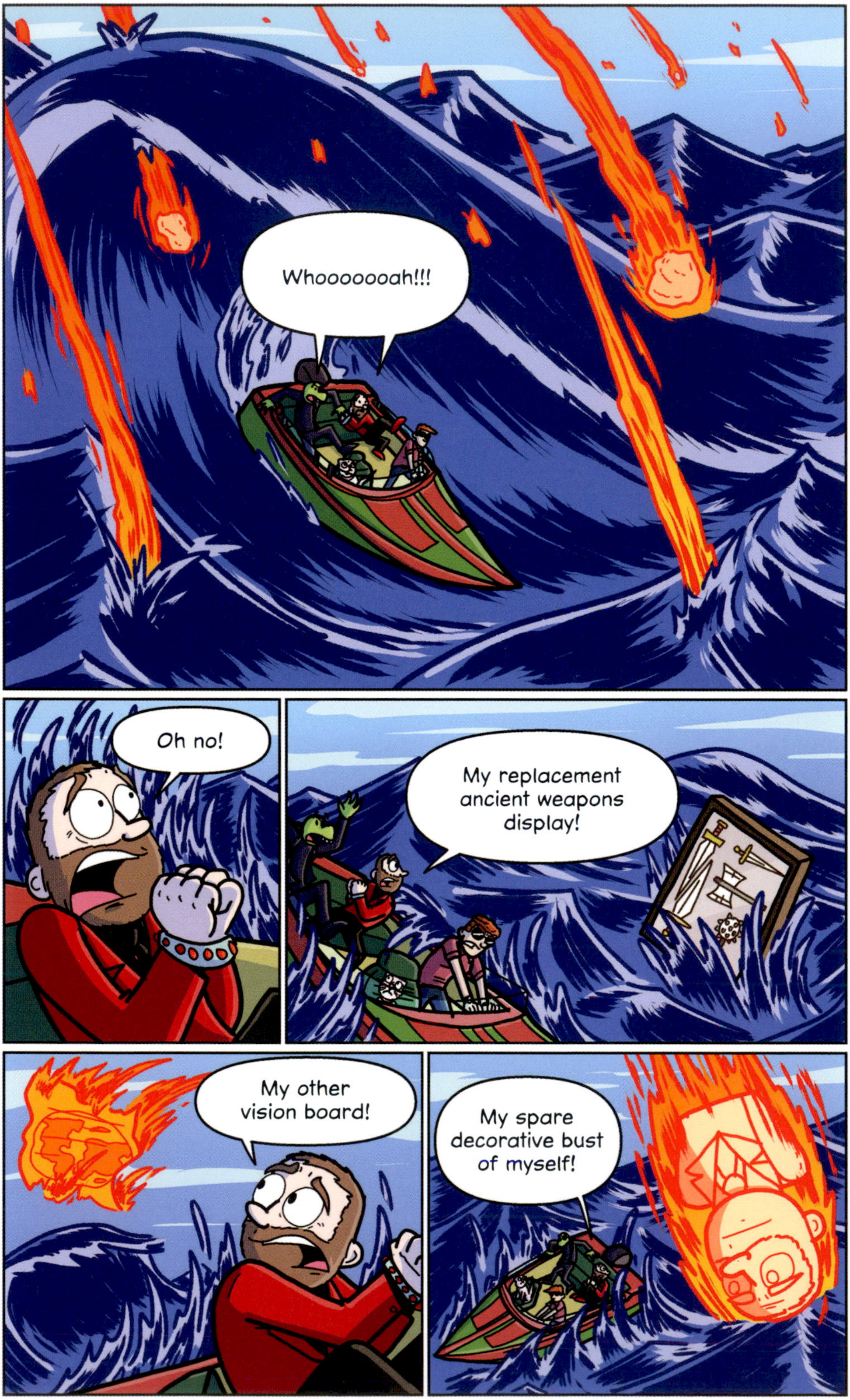
Whoooooooah!!!
Oh no!
My replacement ancient weapons display!
My other vision board!
My spare decorative bust of myself!

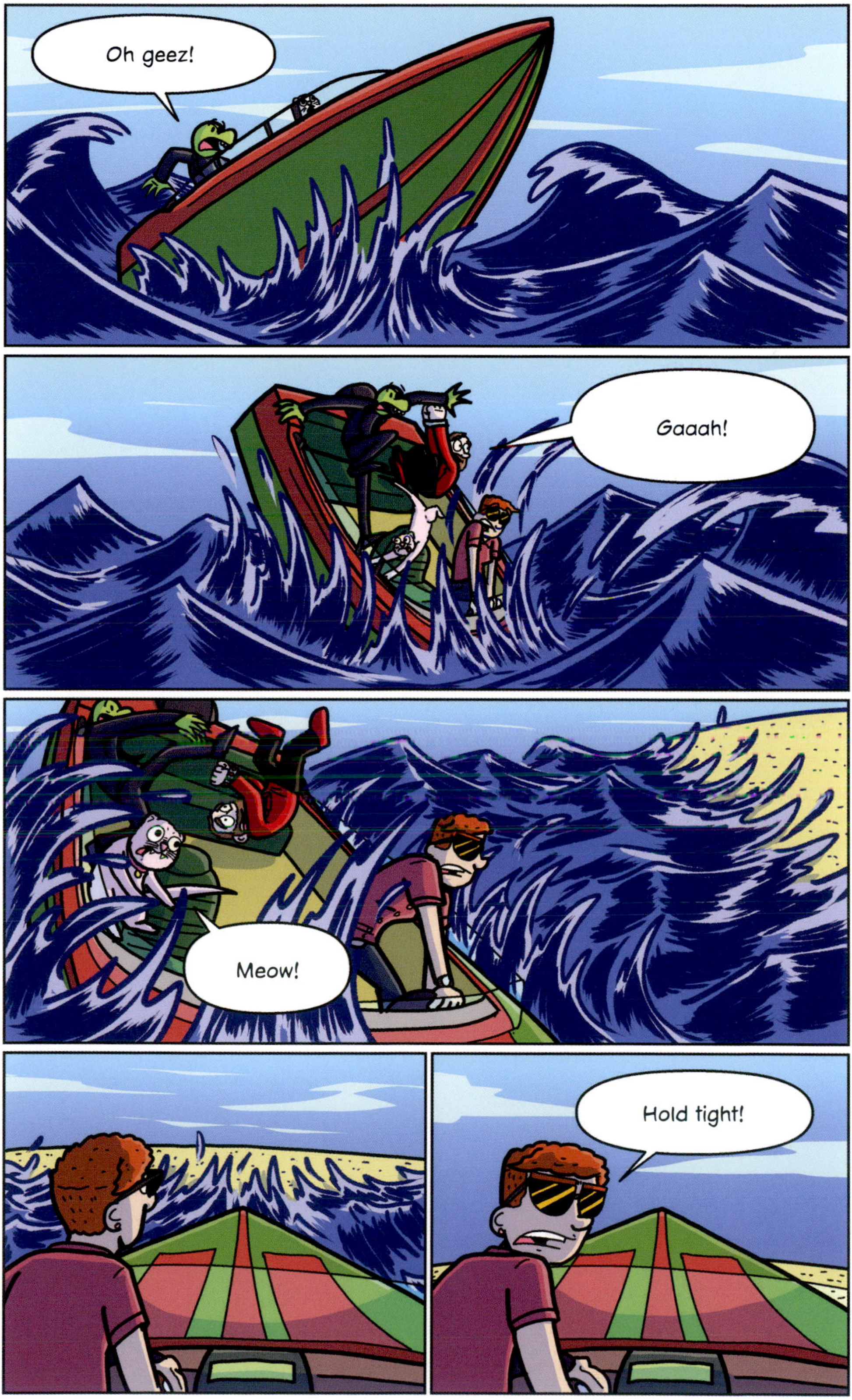
Oh geez!
Gaaah!
Meow!
Hold tight!

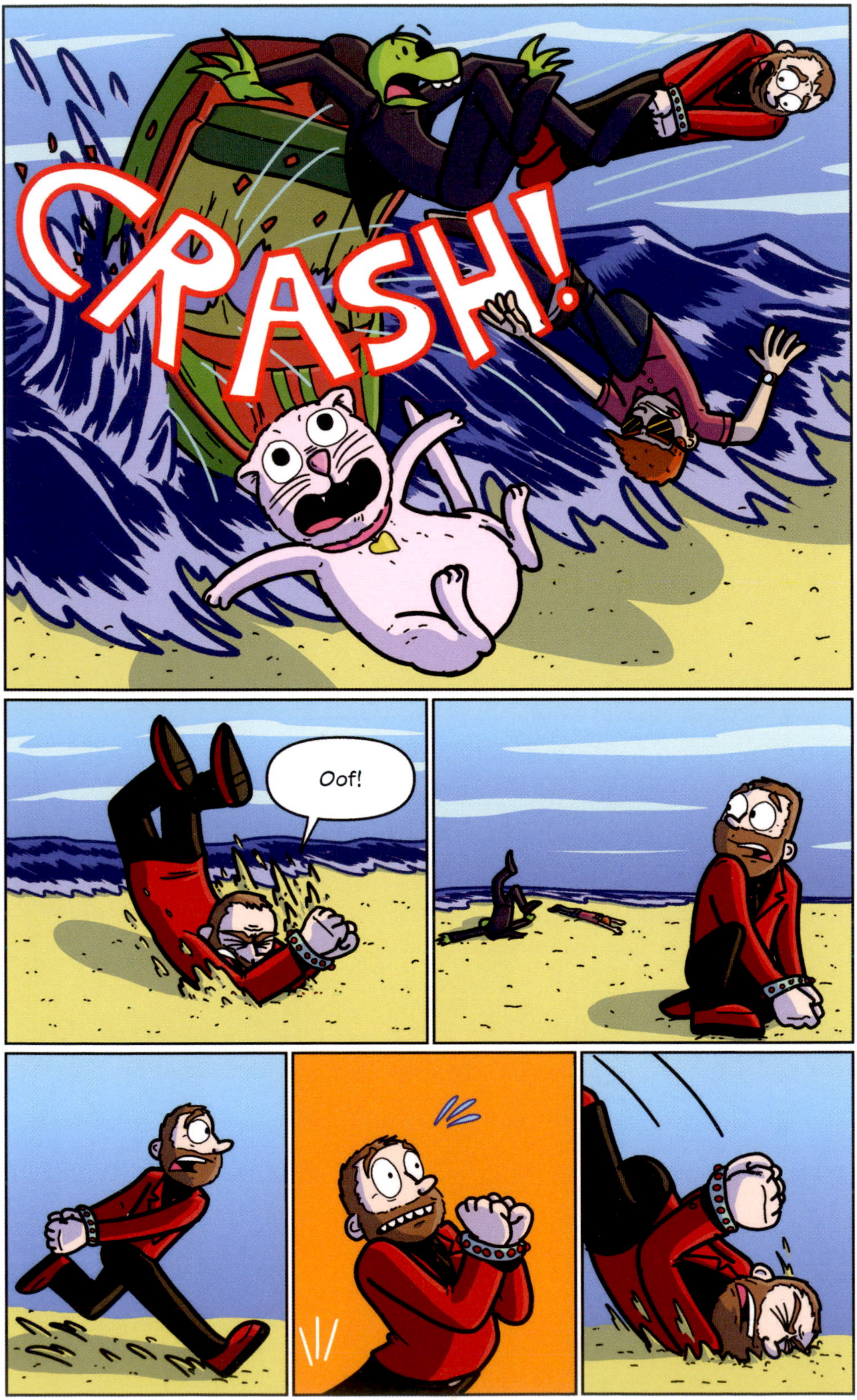
CRASH!
Oof!

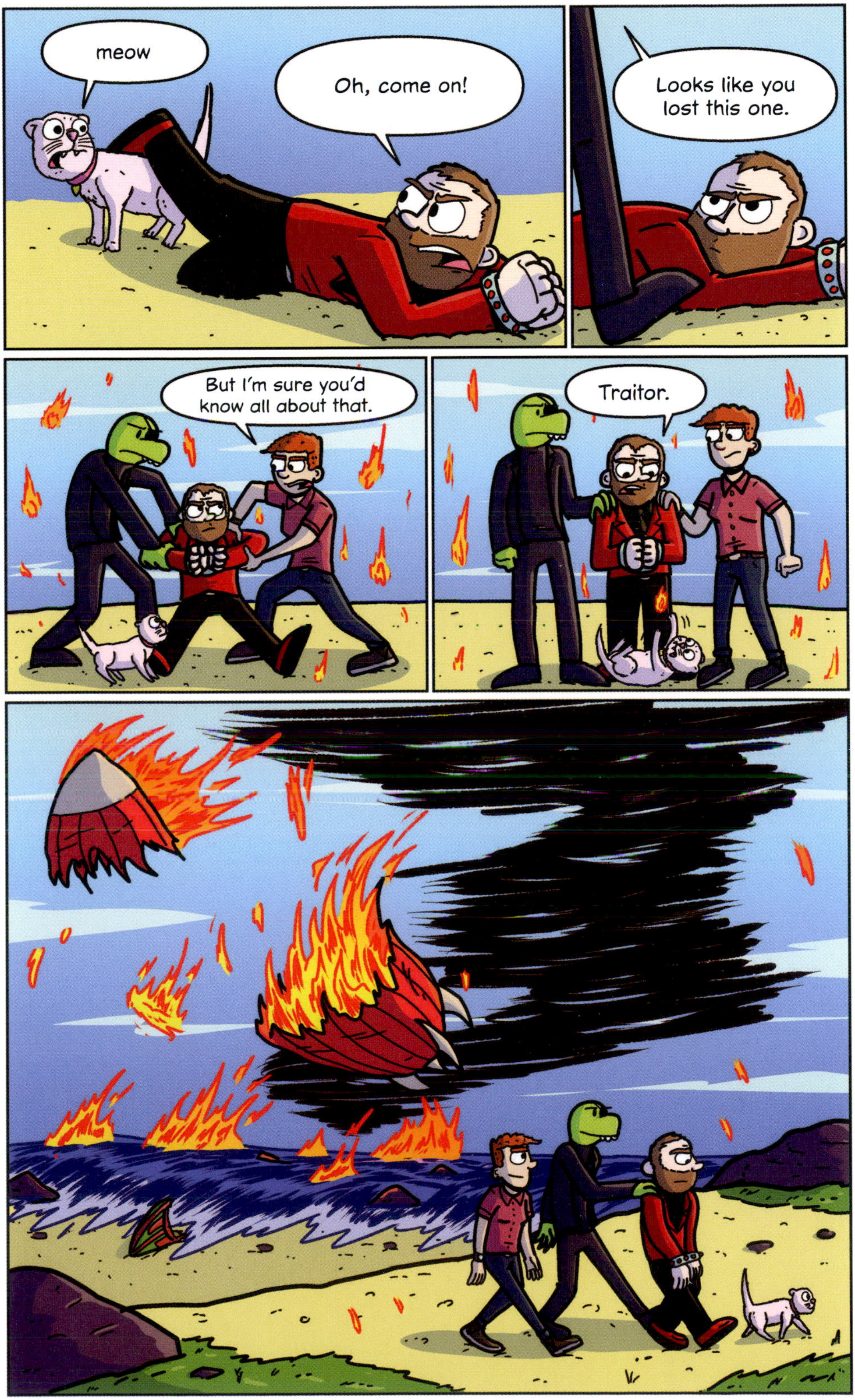
meow
Oh, come on!
Looks like you lost this one.
But I'm sure you'd know all about that.
Traitor.

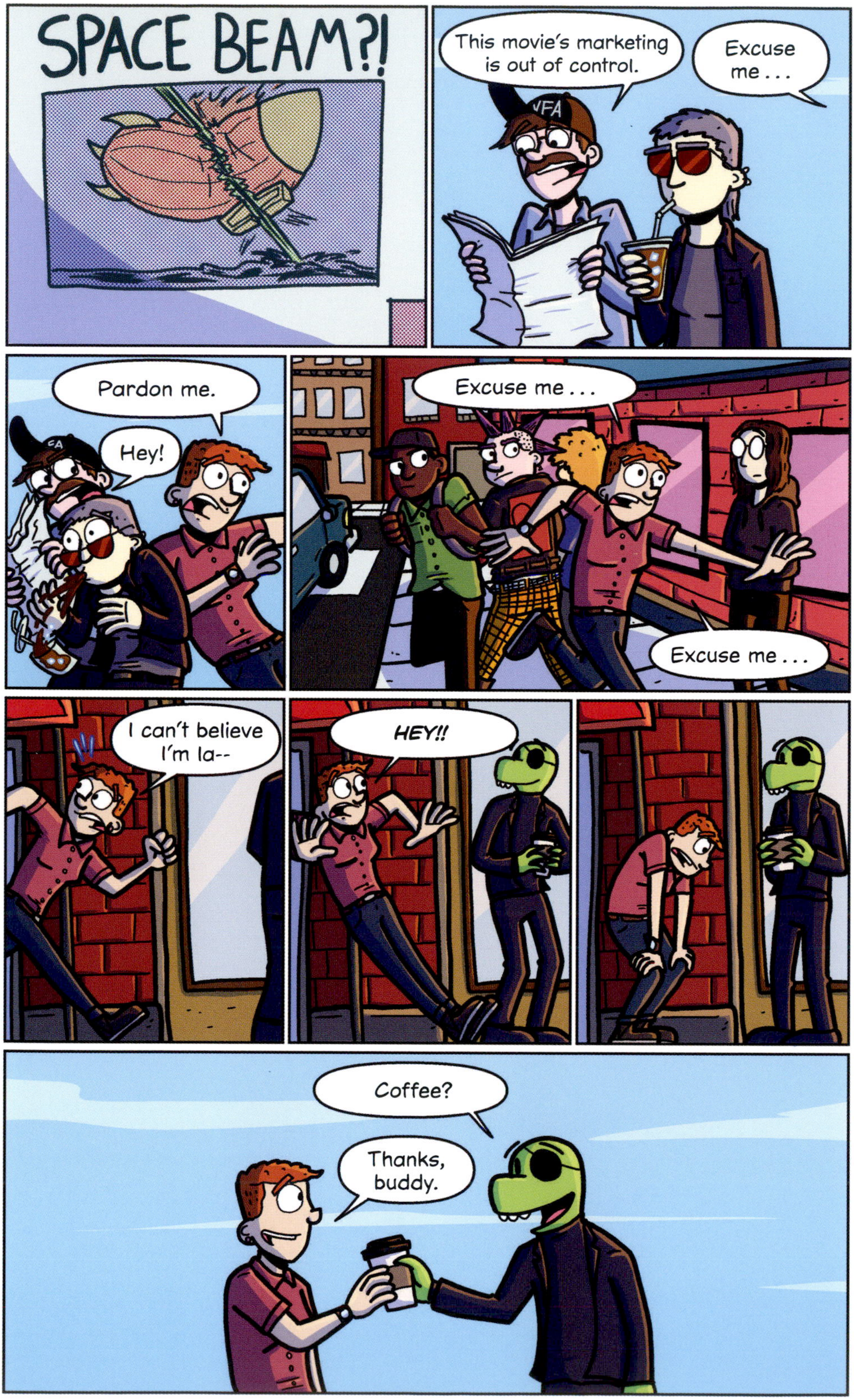
SPACE BEAM?!
This movie's marketing is out of control.
Excuse me . . .
NFA
Pardon me.
Hey!
Excuse me . . .
Excuse me . . .
I can't believe I'm la--
HEY!!
Coffee?
Thanks, buddy.

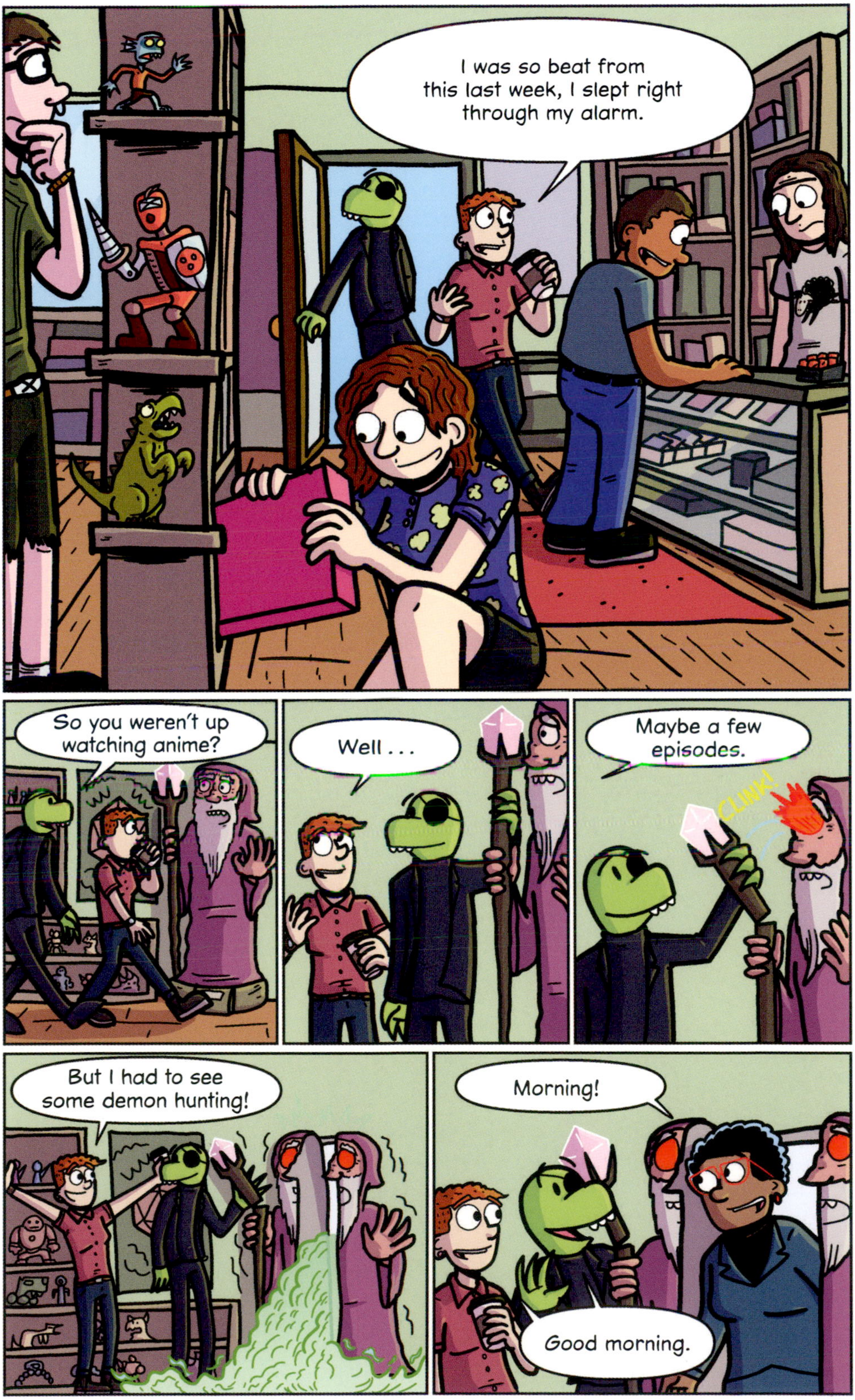
I was so beat from this last week, I slept right through my alarm.
So you weren't up watching anime?
Well . . .
Maybe a few episodes.
CLINK!
But I had to see some demon hunting!
Morning!
Good morning.

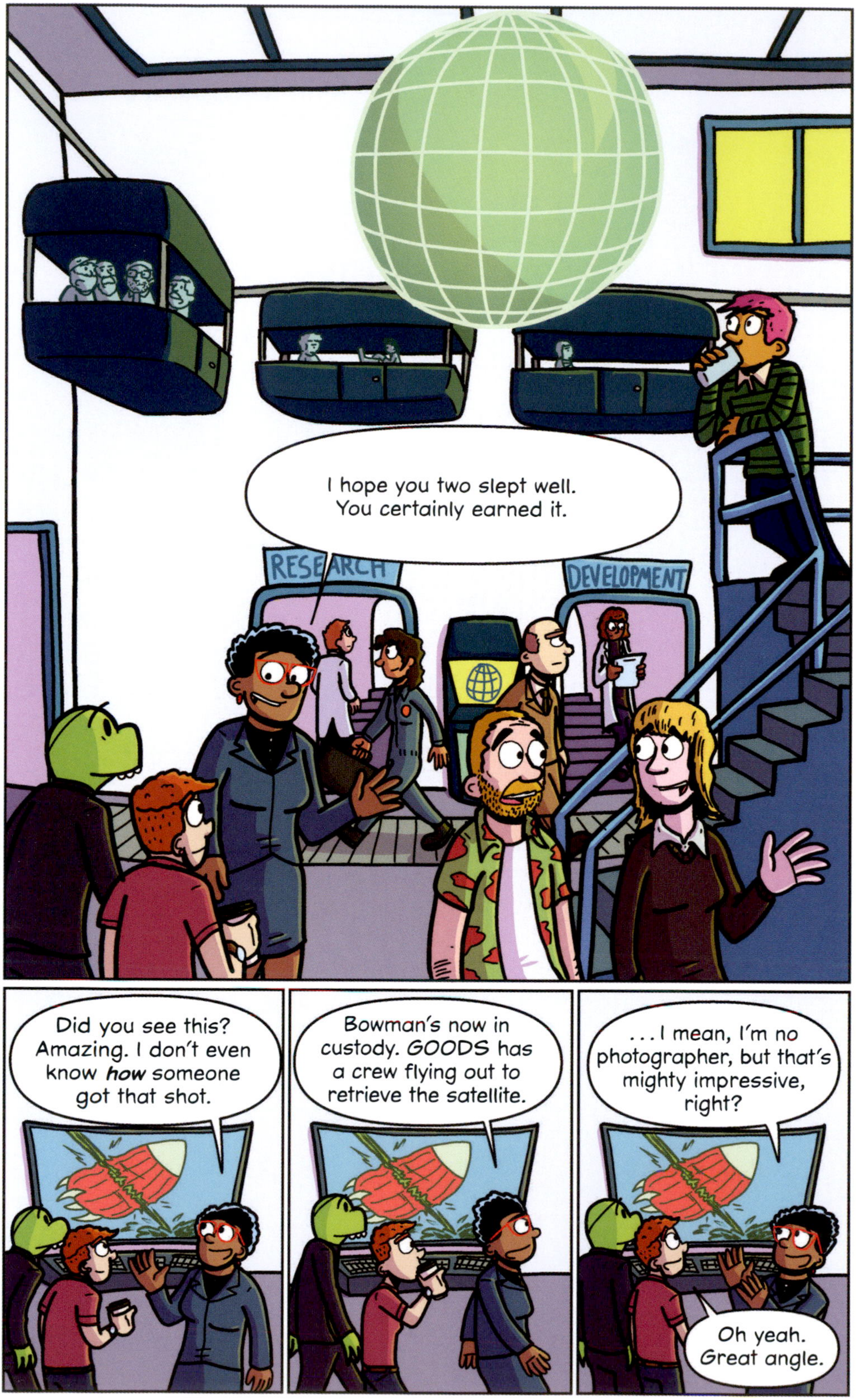
RESEARCH
DEVELOPMENT
I hope you two slept well. You certainly earned it.
Did you see this? Amazing. I don't even know *how* someone got that shot.
Bowman's now in custody. *GOODS* has a crew flying out to retrieve the satellite.
. . . I mean, I'm no photographer, but that's mighty impressive, right?
Oh yeah. Great angle.

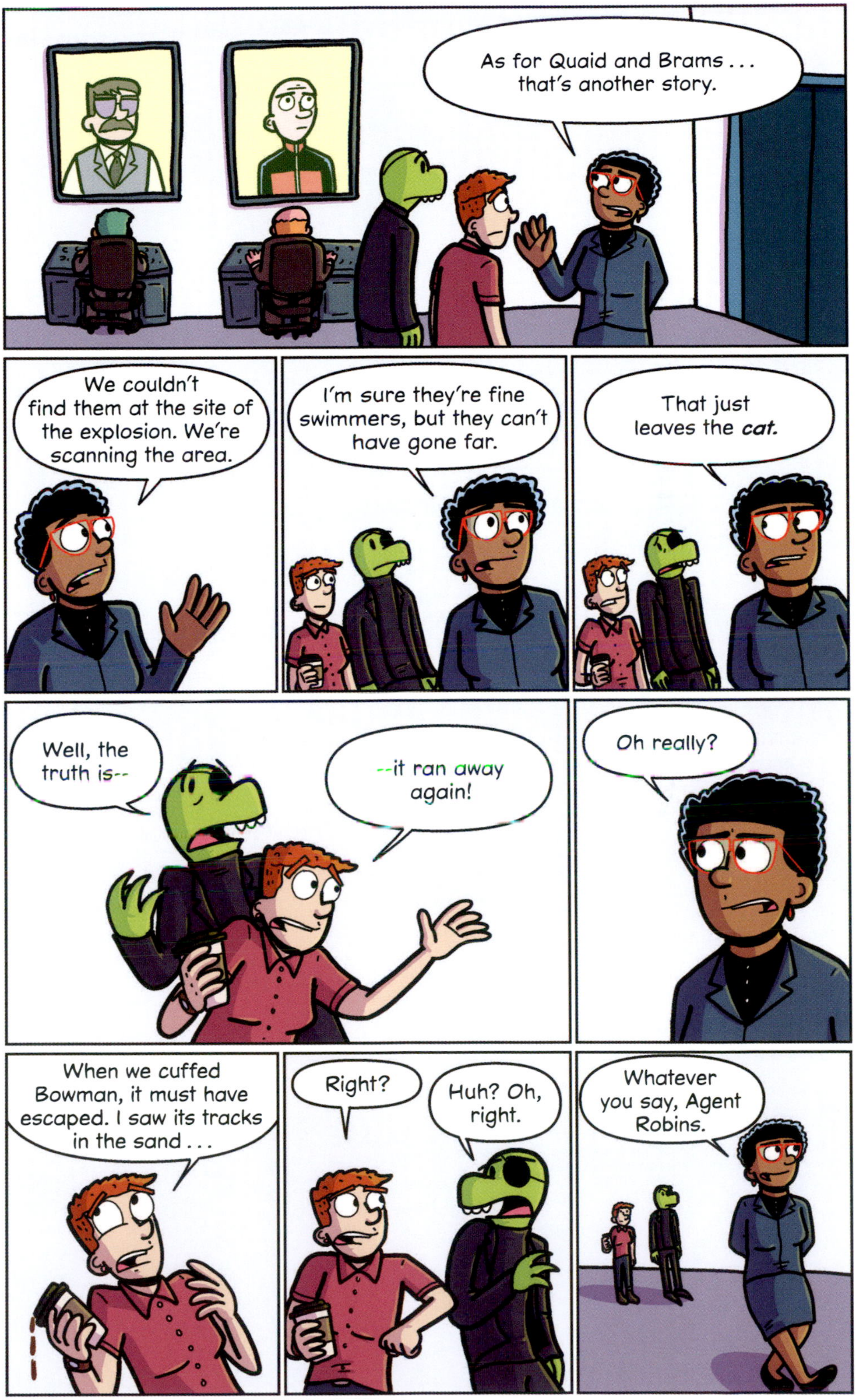

As for Quaid and Brams . . . that's another story.
We couldn't find them at the site of the explosion. We're scanning the area.
I'm sure they're fine swimmers, but they can't have gone far.
That just leaves the *cat.*
Well, the truth is--
--it ran away again!
Oh really?
When we cuffed Bowman, it must have escaped. I saw its tracks in the sand . . .
Right?
Huh? Oh, right.
Whatever you say, Agent Robins.

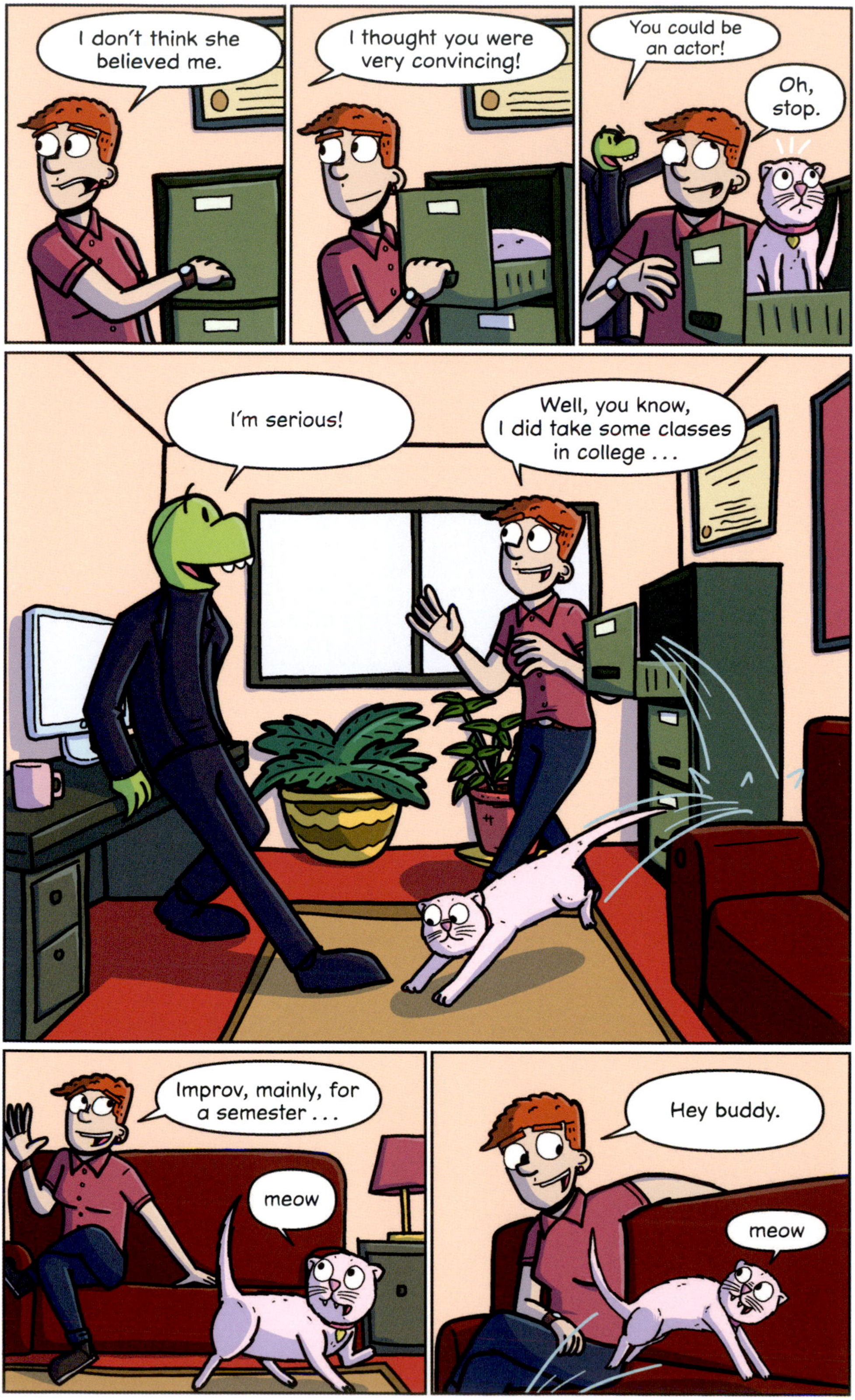
I don't think she believed me.
I thought you were very convincing!
You could be an actor!
Oh, stop.
I'm serious!
Well, you know, I did take some classes in college . . .
Improv, mainly, for a semester . . .
meow
Hey buddy.
meow

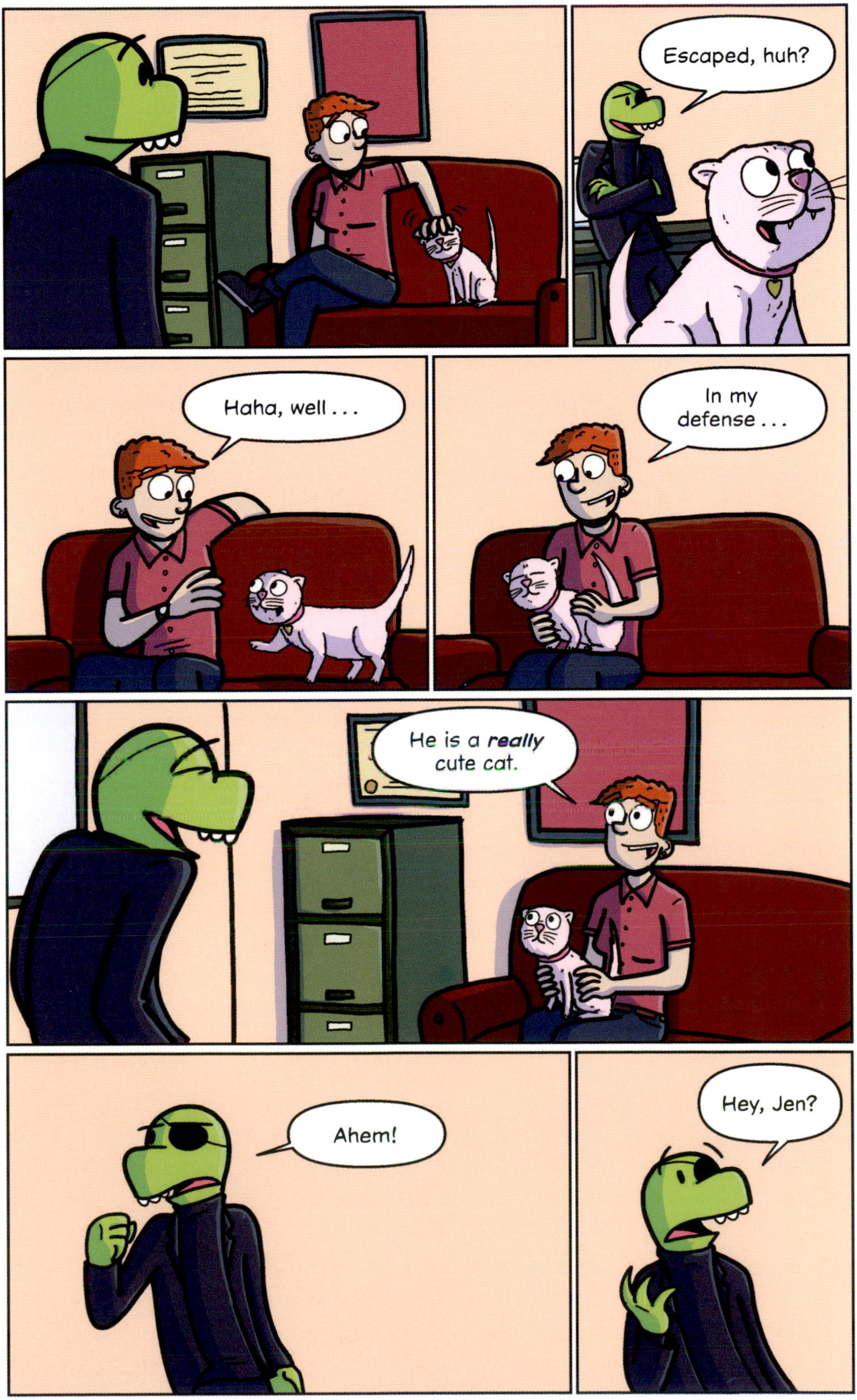
Escaped, huh?
Haha, well . . .
In my defense . . .
He is a *really* cute cat.
Ahem!
Hey, Jen?

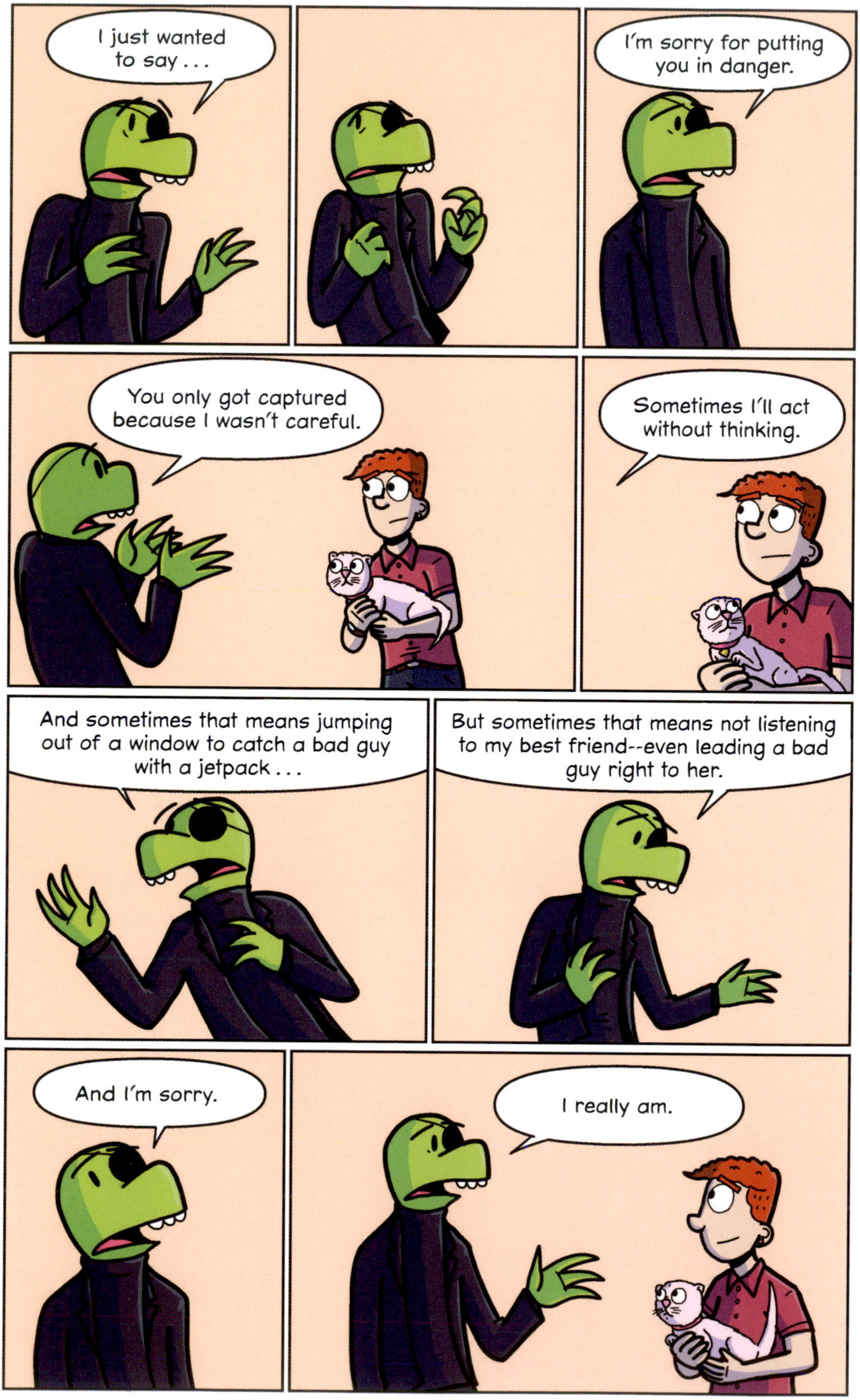
I just wanted to say . . .
I'm sorry for putting you in danger.
You only got captured because I wasn't careful.
Sometimes I'll act without thinking.
And sometimes that means jumping out of a window to catch a bad guy with a jetpack . . .
But sometimes that means not listening to my best friend--even leading a bad guy right to her.
And I'm sorry.
I really am.

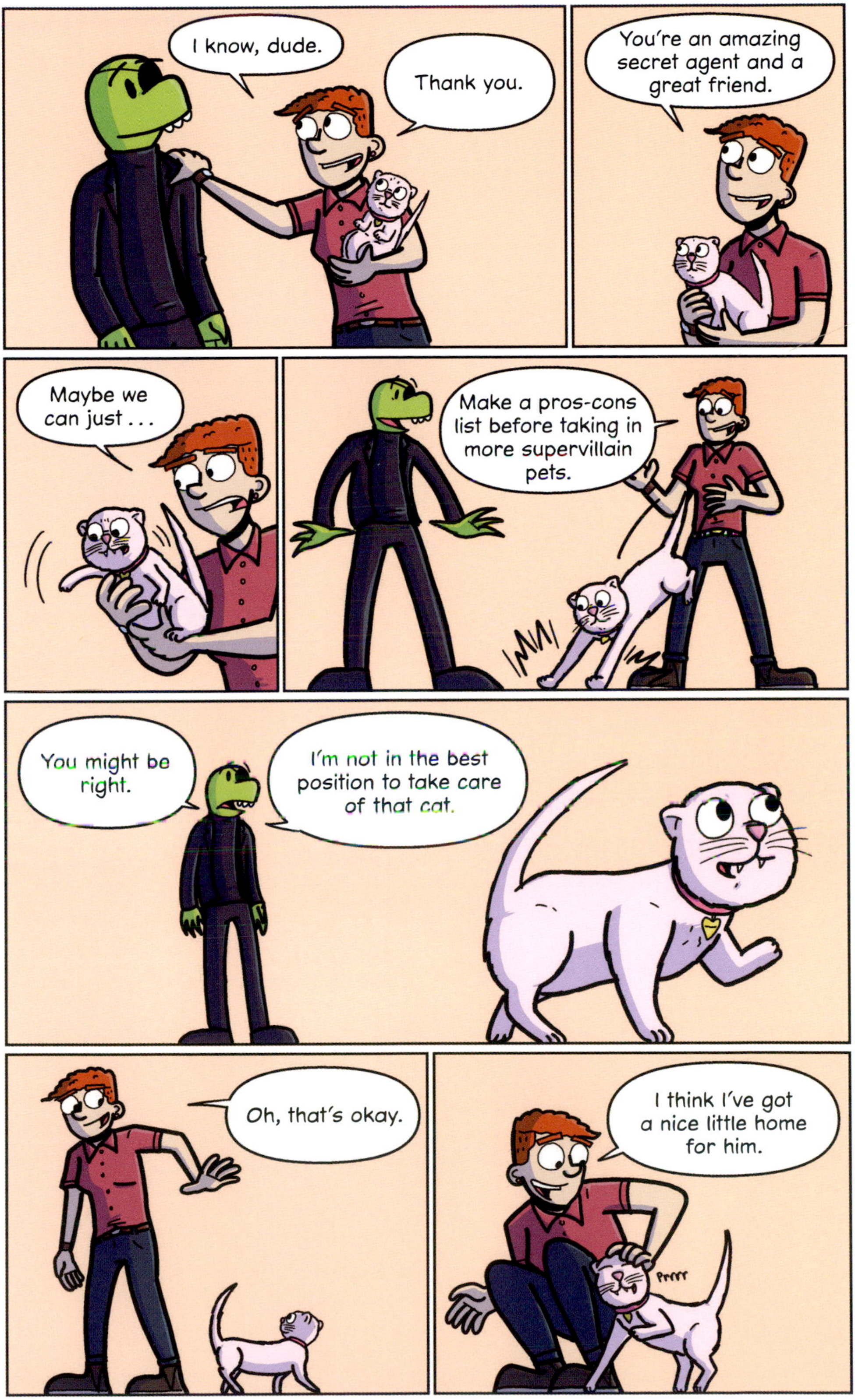
I know, dude.
Thank you.
You're an amazing secret agent and a great friend.
Maybe we can just . . .
Make a pros-cons list before taking in more supervillain pets.
You might be right.
I'm not in the best position to take care of that cat.
Oh, that's okay.
I think I've got a nice little home for him.
Prrrr

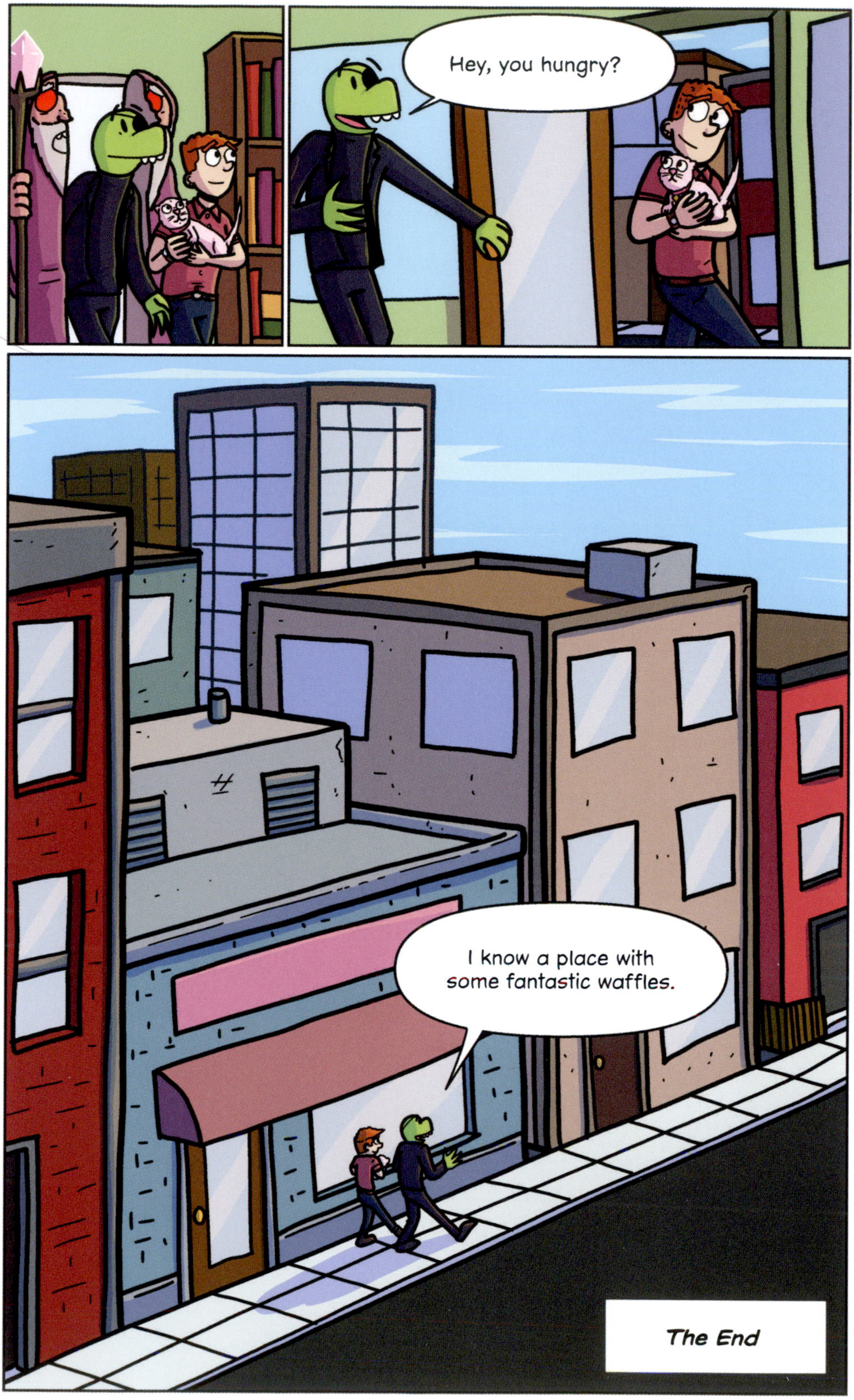
Hey, you hungry?
I know a place with some fantastic waffles.
The End

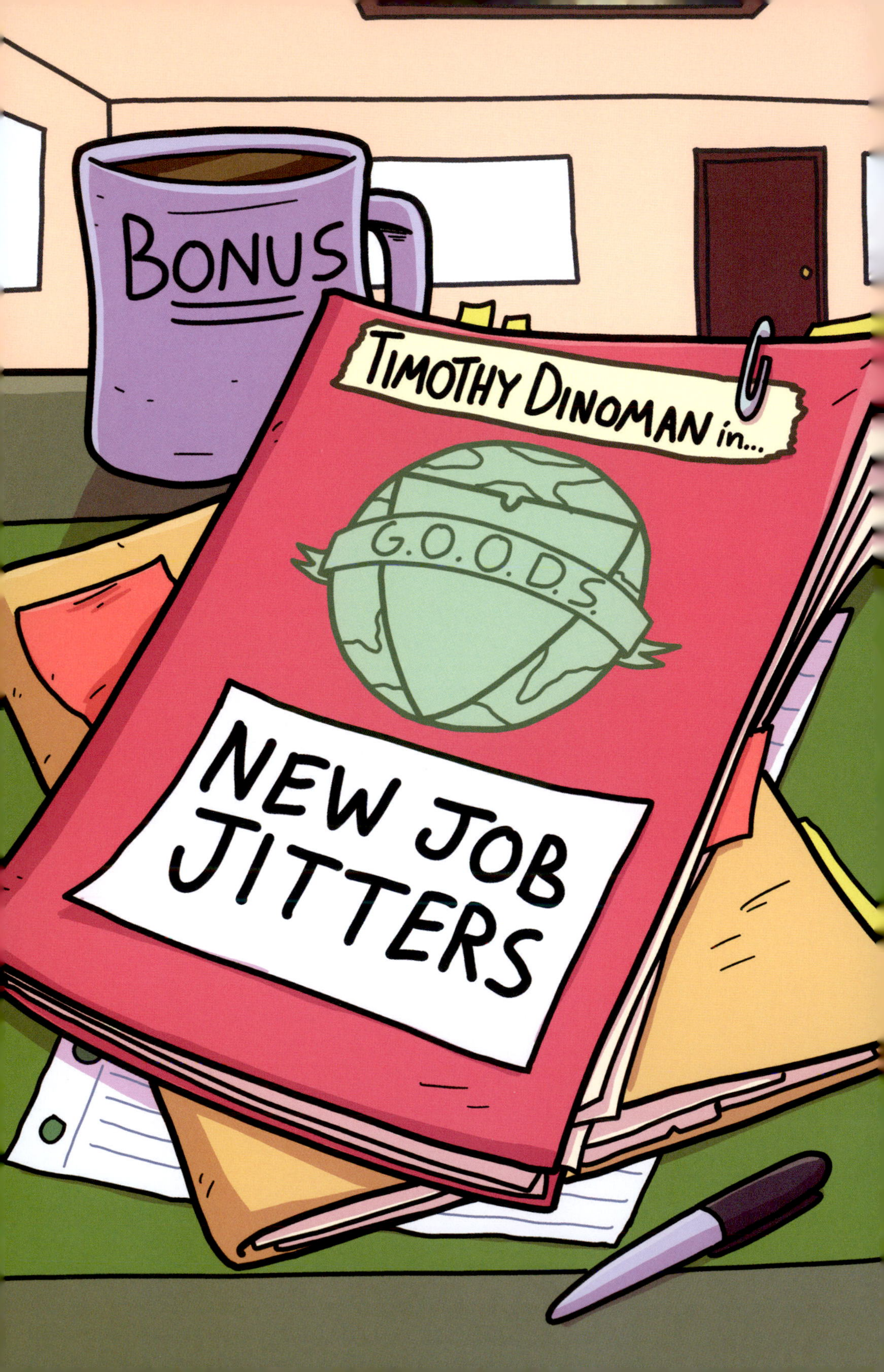
BONUS
TIMOTHY DINOMAN in...
G.O.O.D.S.
NEW JOB JITTERS

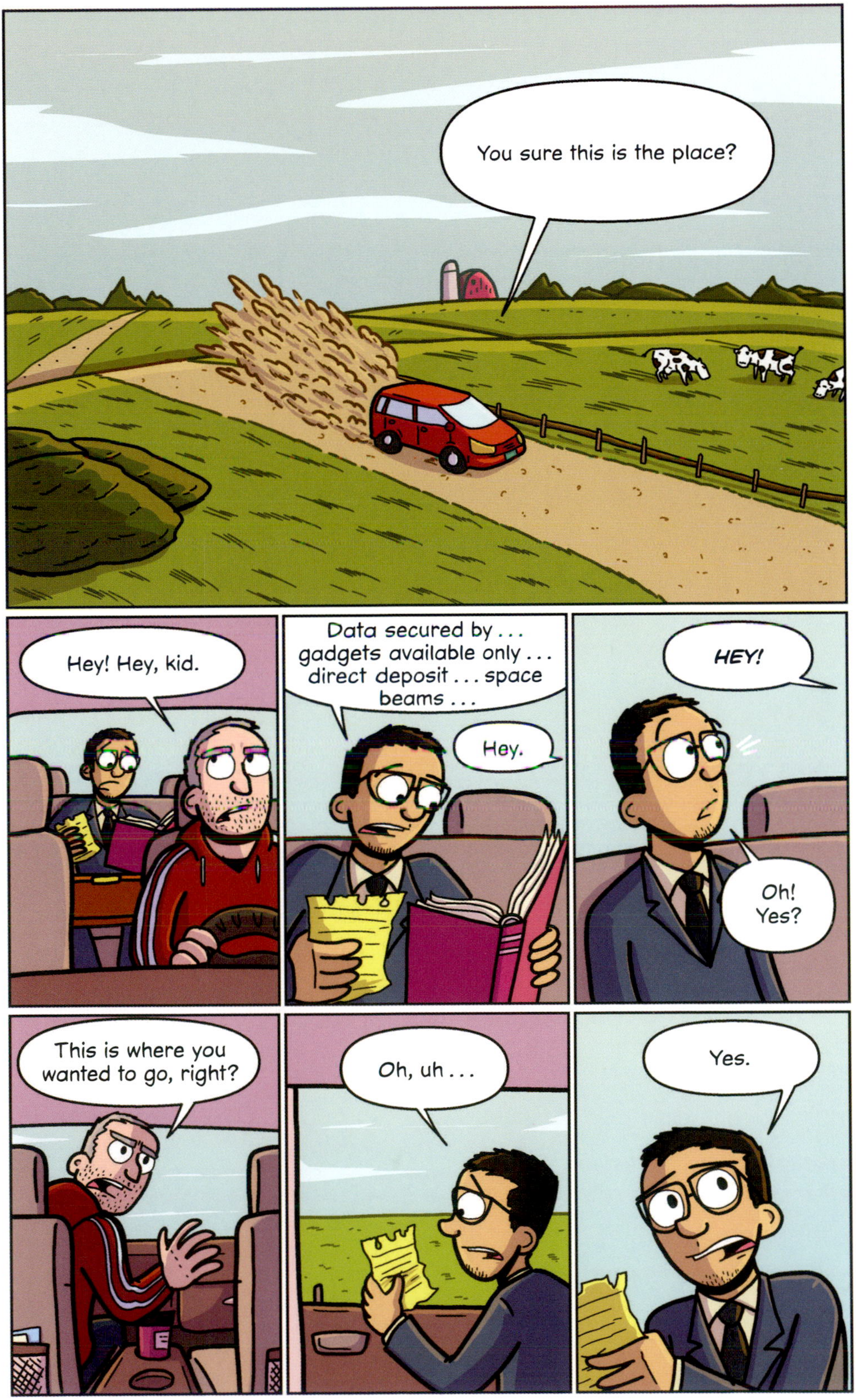
You sure this is the place?
Hey! Hey, kid.
Data secured by . . . gadgets available only . . . direct deposit . . . space beams . . .
Hey.
HEY!
Oh! Yes?
This is where you wanted to go, right?
Oh, uh . . .
Yes.

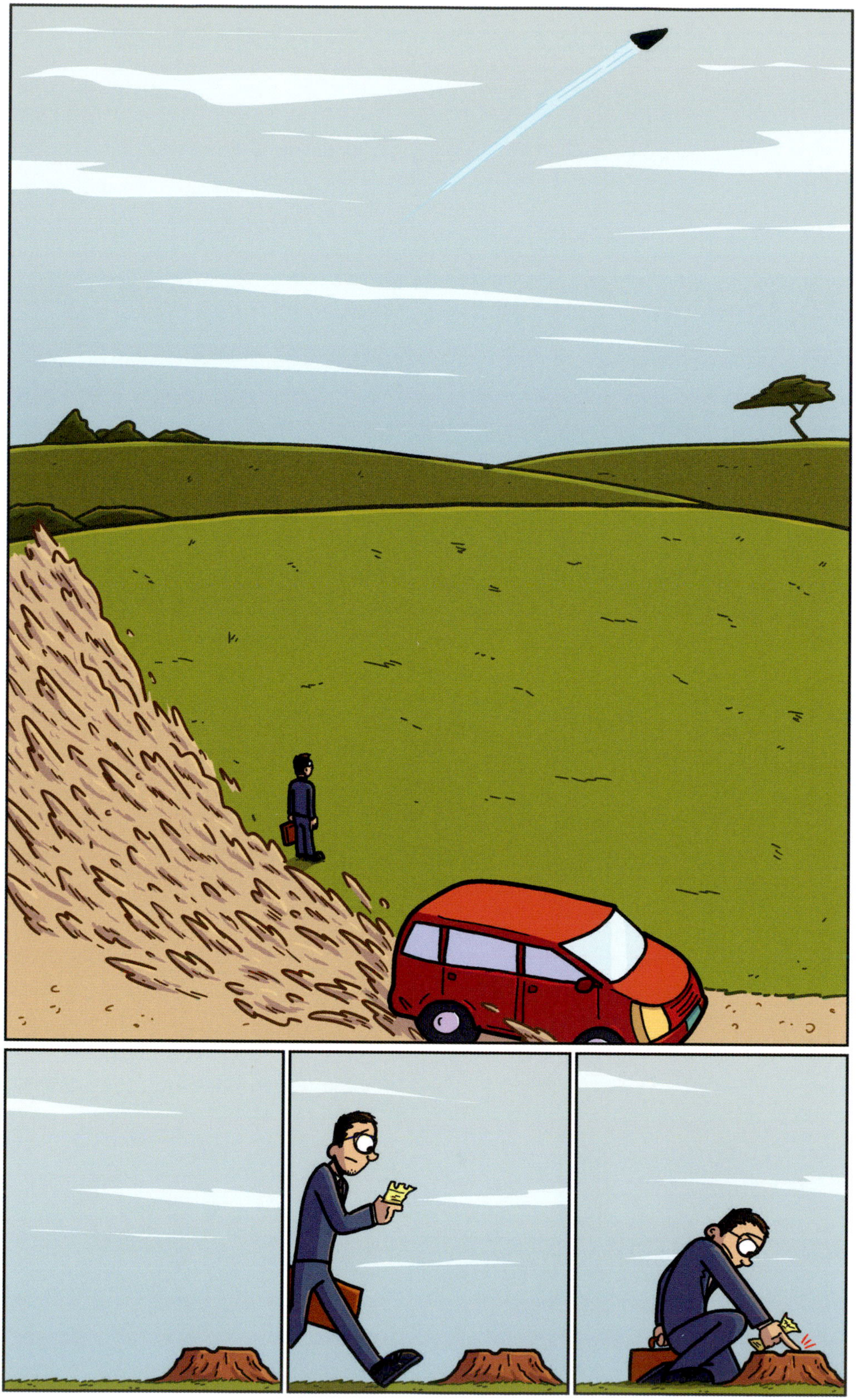

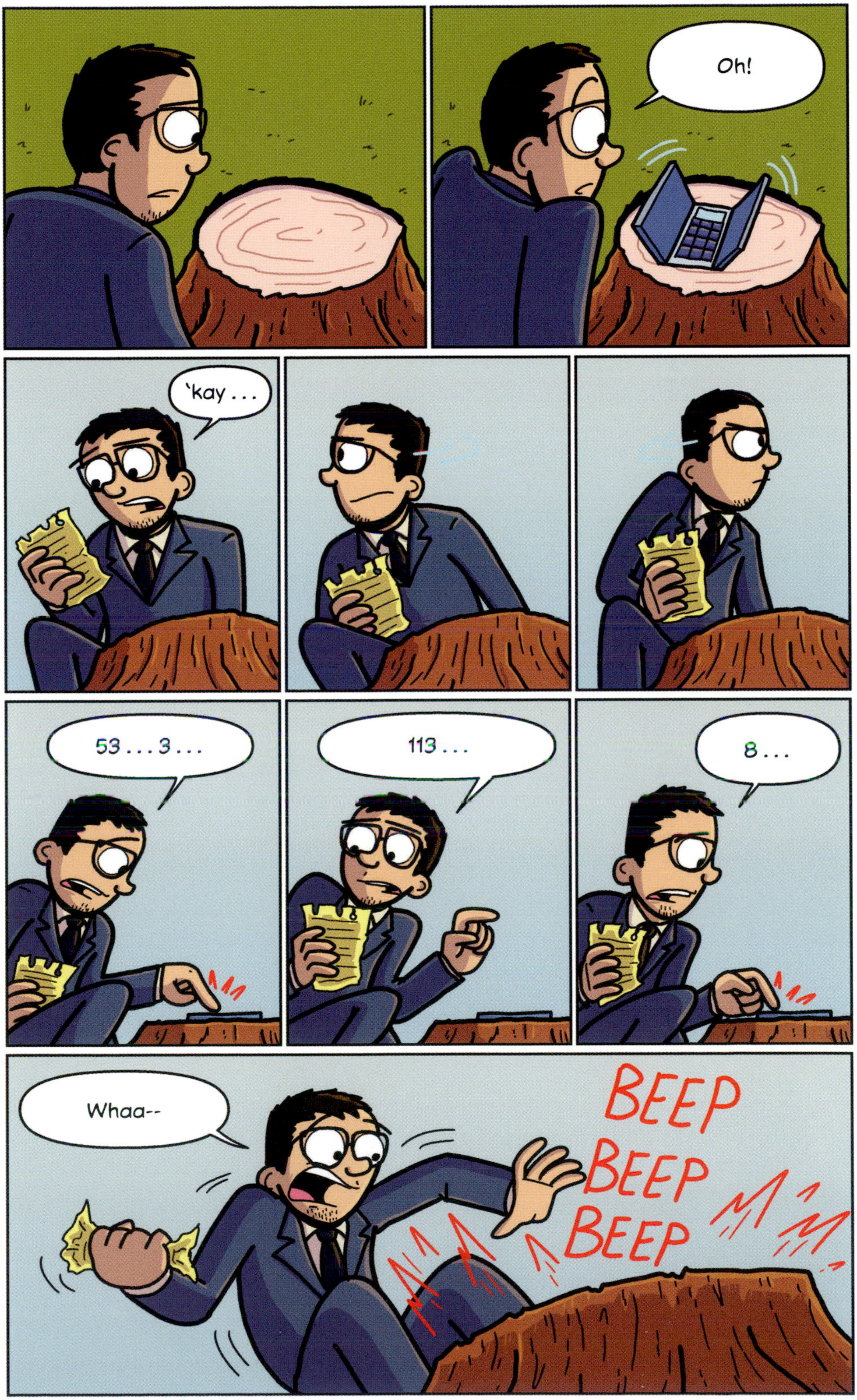
Oh!
'kay . . .
53 . . . 3 . . .
113 . . .
8 . . .
Whaa--
BEEP
BEEP
BEEP

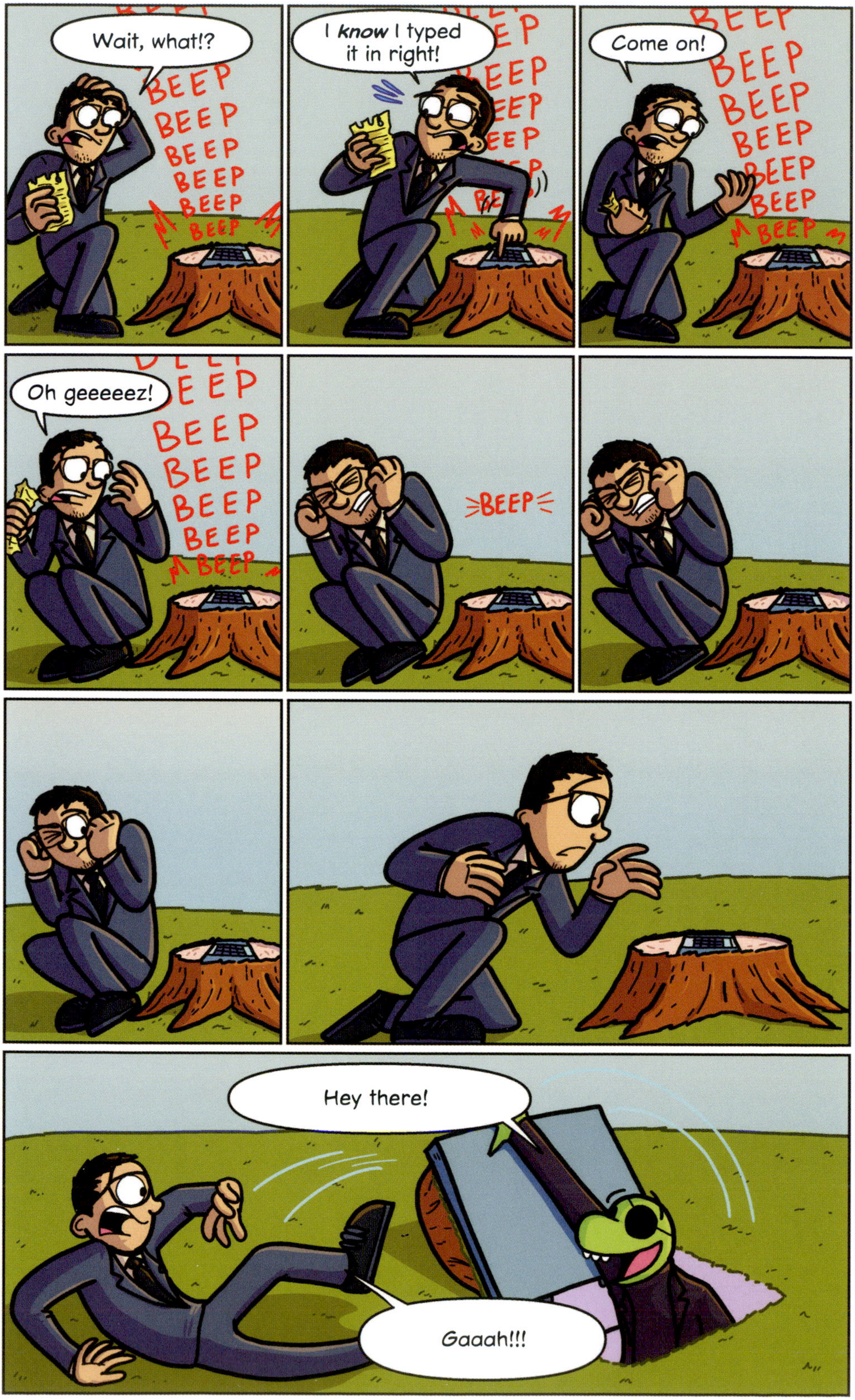
Wait, what!?
BEEP BEEP BEEP BEEP BEEP BEEP
I know I typed it in right!
Come on!
BEEP BEEP BEEP BEEP BEEP BEEP
Oh geeeeez!
BEEP BEEP BEEP BEEP BEEP
BEEP
Hey there!
Gaaah!!!

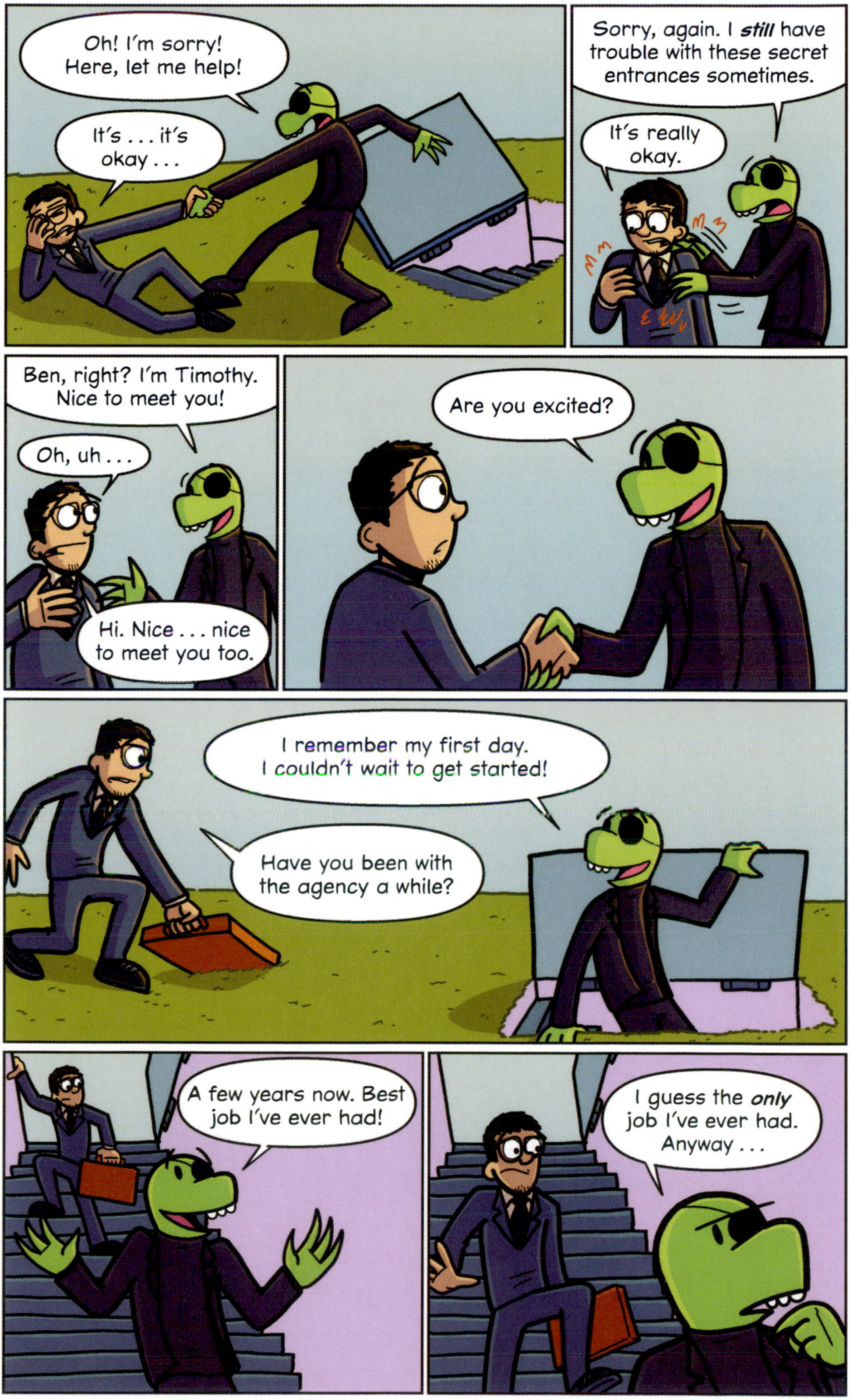
Oh! I'm sorry!
Here, let me help!
It's . . . it's okay . . .
Sorry, again. I *still* have trouble with these secret entrances sometimes.
It's really okay.
Ben, right? I'm Timothy. Nice to meet you!
Oh, uh . . .
Hi. Nice . . . nice to meet you too.
Are you excited?
I remember my first day. I couldn't wait to get started!
Have you been with the agency a while?
A few years now. Best job I've ever had!
I guess the *only* job I've ever had. Anyway . . .

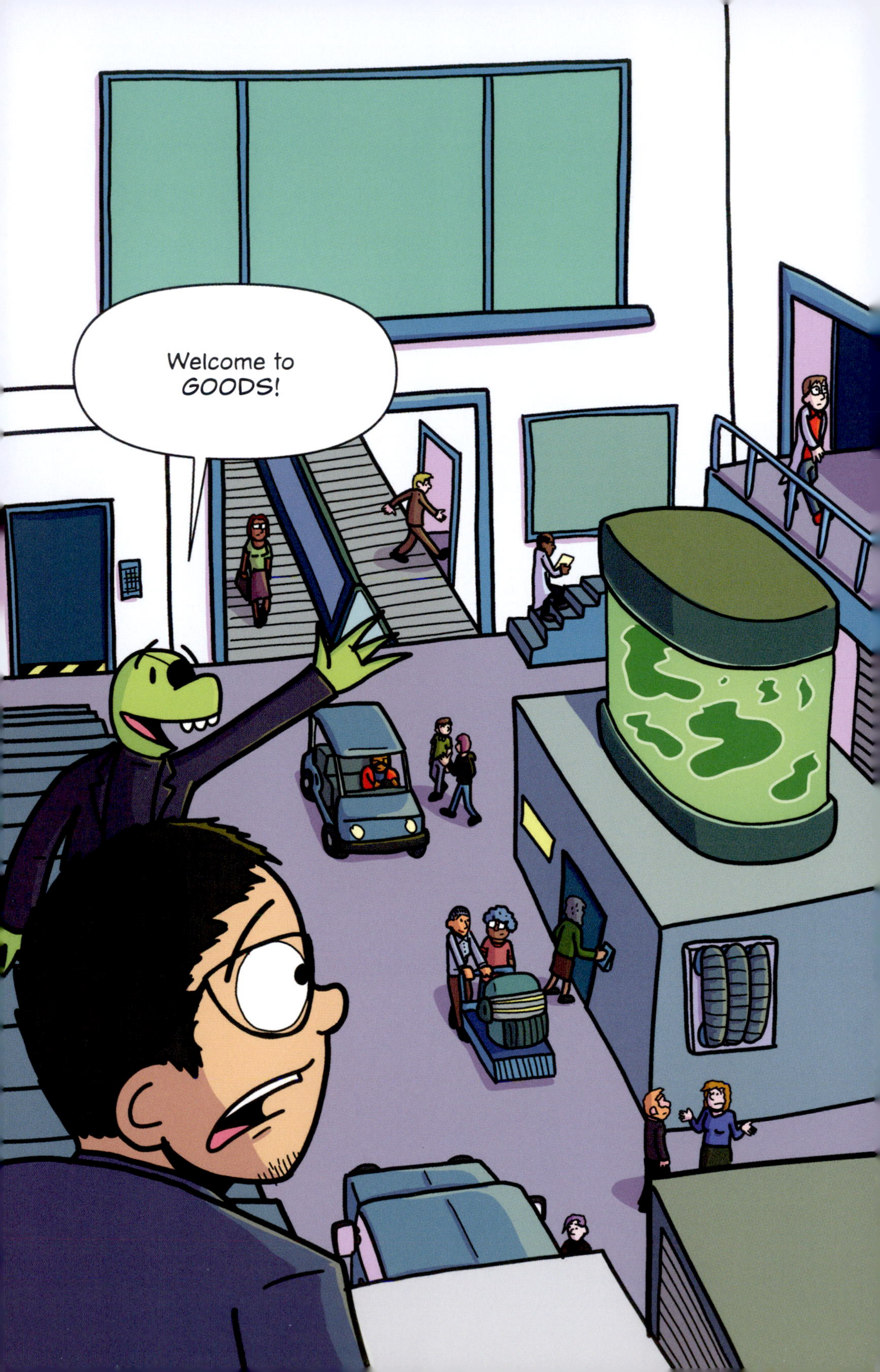
Welcome to GOODS!

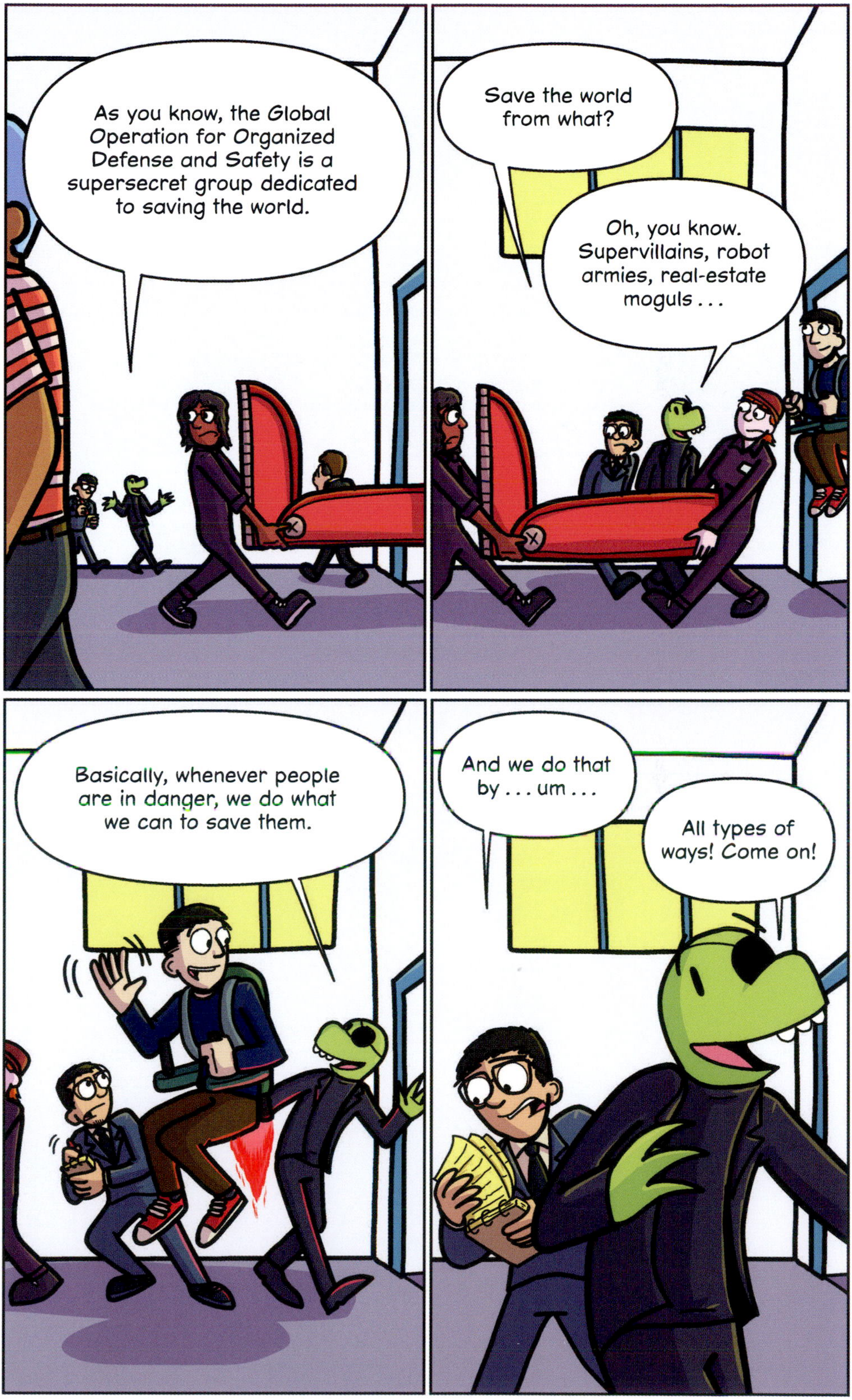
As you know, the Global Operation for Organized Defense and Safety is a supersecret group dedicated to saving the world.
Save the world from what?
Oh, you know. Supervillains, robot armies, real-estate moguls . . .
Basically, whenever people are in danger, we do what we can to save them.
And we do that by . . . um . . .
All types of ways! Come on!

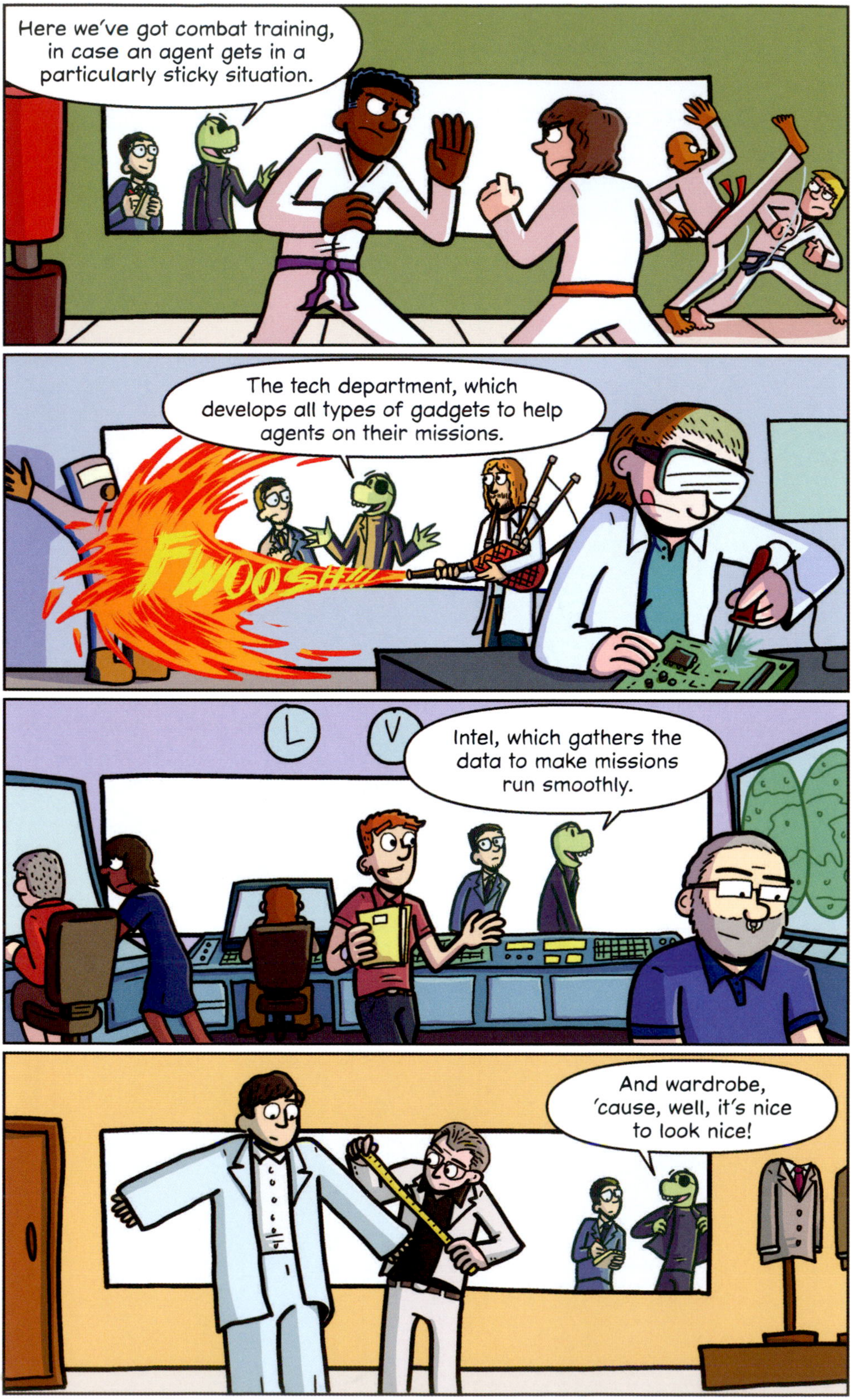
Here we've got combat training, in case an agent gets in a particularly sticky situation.
The tech department, which develops all types of gadgets to help agents on their missions.
FWOOSH!!!
Intel, which gathers the data to make missions run smoothly.
And wardrobe, 'cause, well, it's nice to look nice!

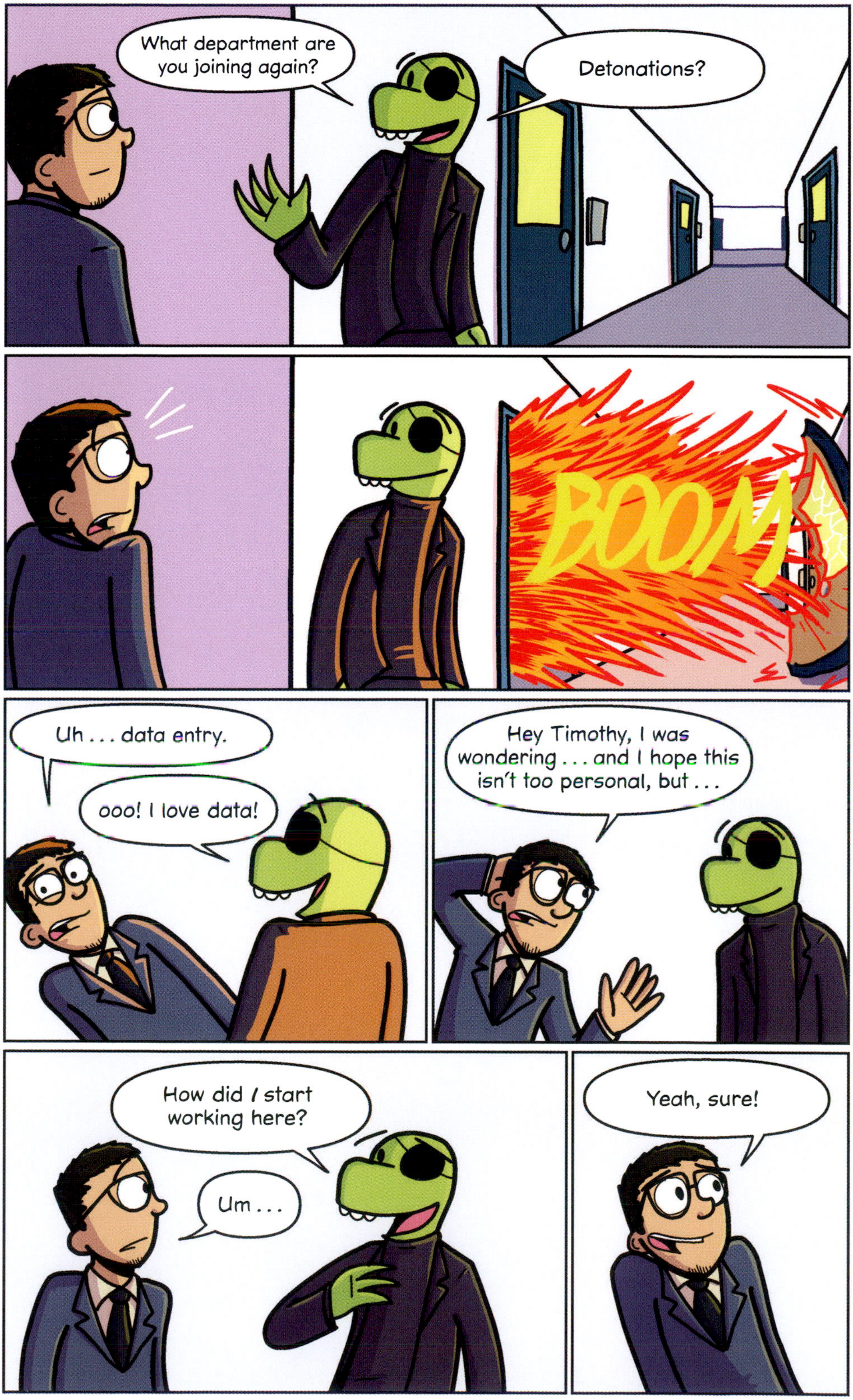
What department are you joining again?
Detonations?
BOOM
Uh . . . data entry.
ooo! I love data!
Hey Timothy, I was wondering . . . and I hope this isn't too personal, but . . .
How did I start working here?
Um . . .
Yeah, sure!

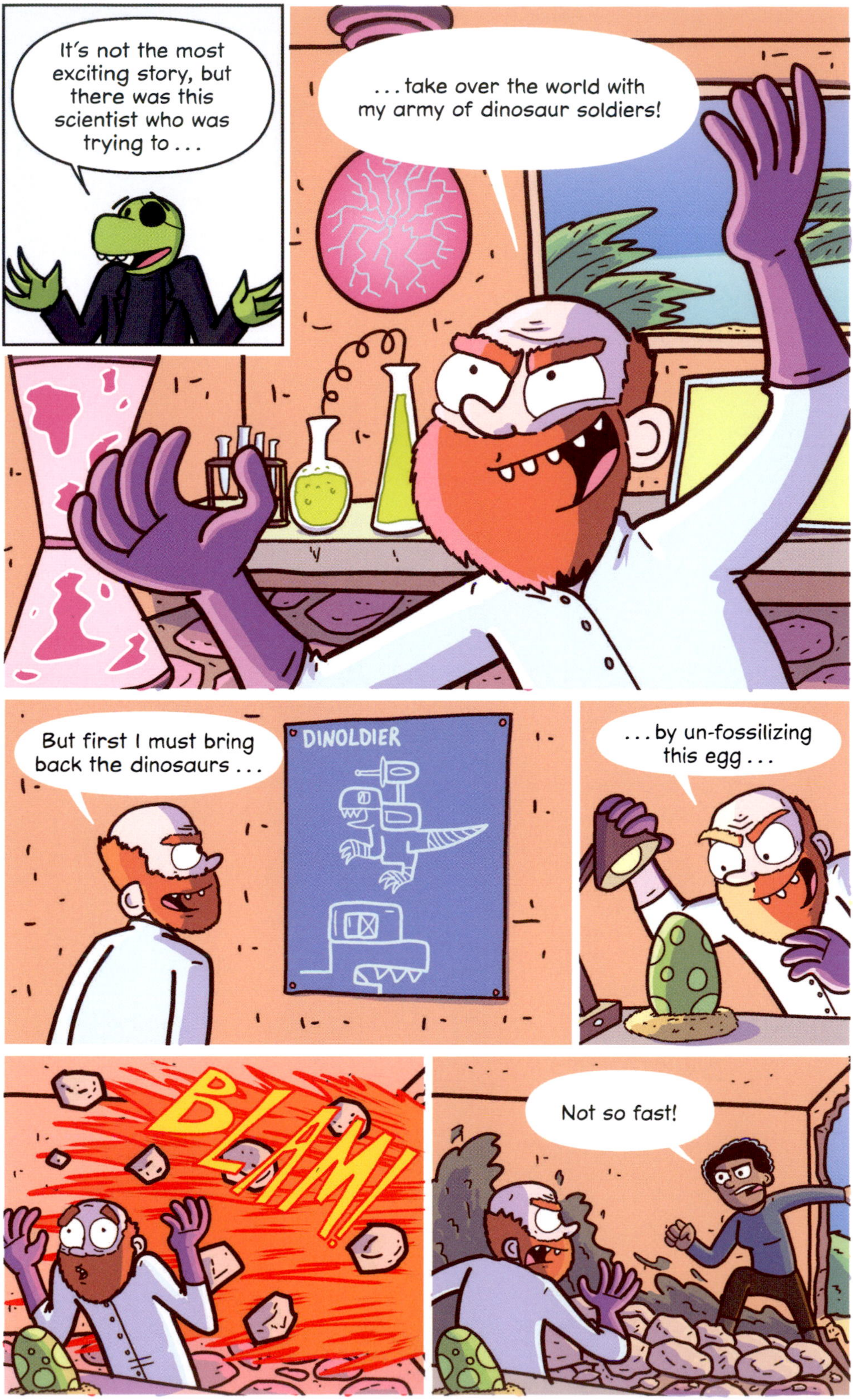
It's not the most exciting story, but there was this scientist who was trying to . . .
. . . take over the world with my army of dinosaur soldiers!
But first I must bring back the dinosaurs . . .
DINOLDIER
. . . by un-fossilizing this egg . . .
BLAM!
Not so fast!

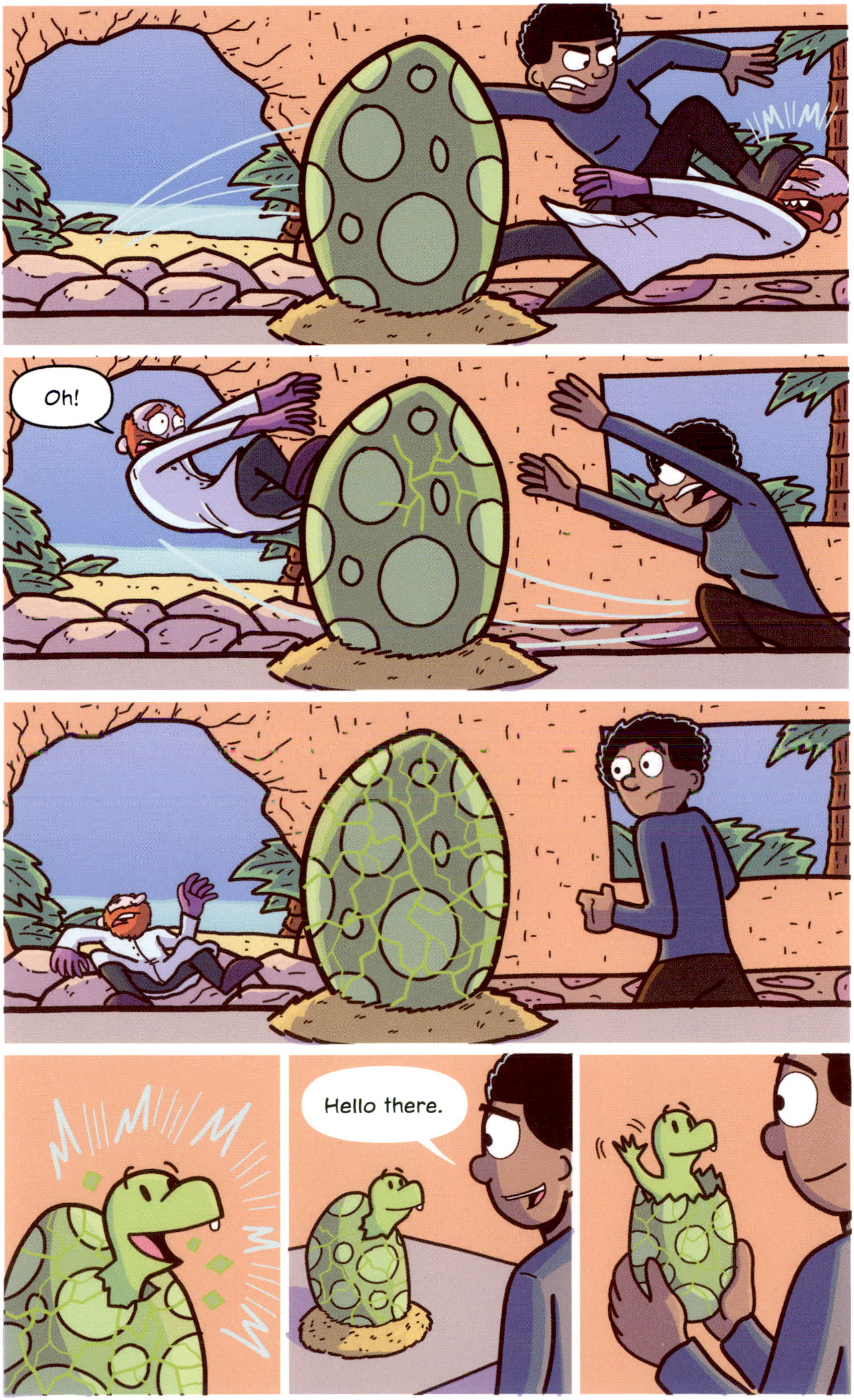
Oh!
Hello there.

Now just sit tight.

We're going home.

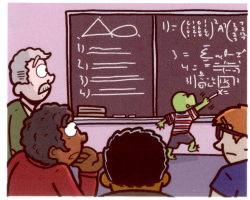

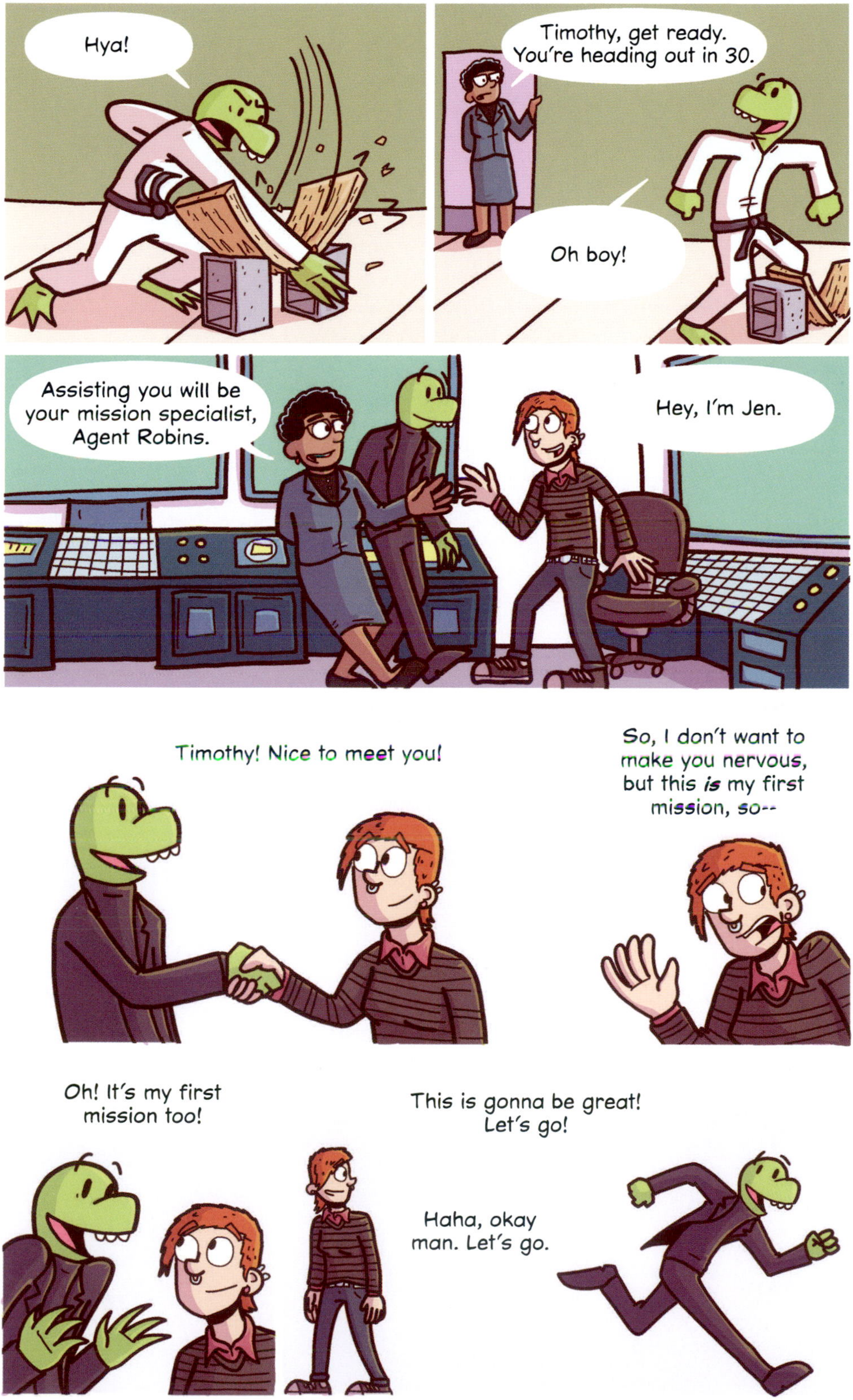
Hya!
Timothy, get ready. You're heading out in 30.
Oh boy!
Assisting you will be your mission specialist, Agent Robins.
Hey, I'm Jen.
Timothy! Nice to meet you!
So, I don't want to make you nervous, but this *is* my first mission, so--
Oh! It's my first mission too!
This is gonna be great! Let's go!
Haha, okay man. Let's go.

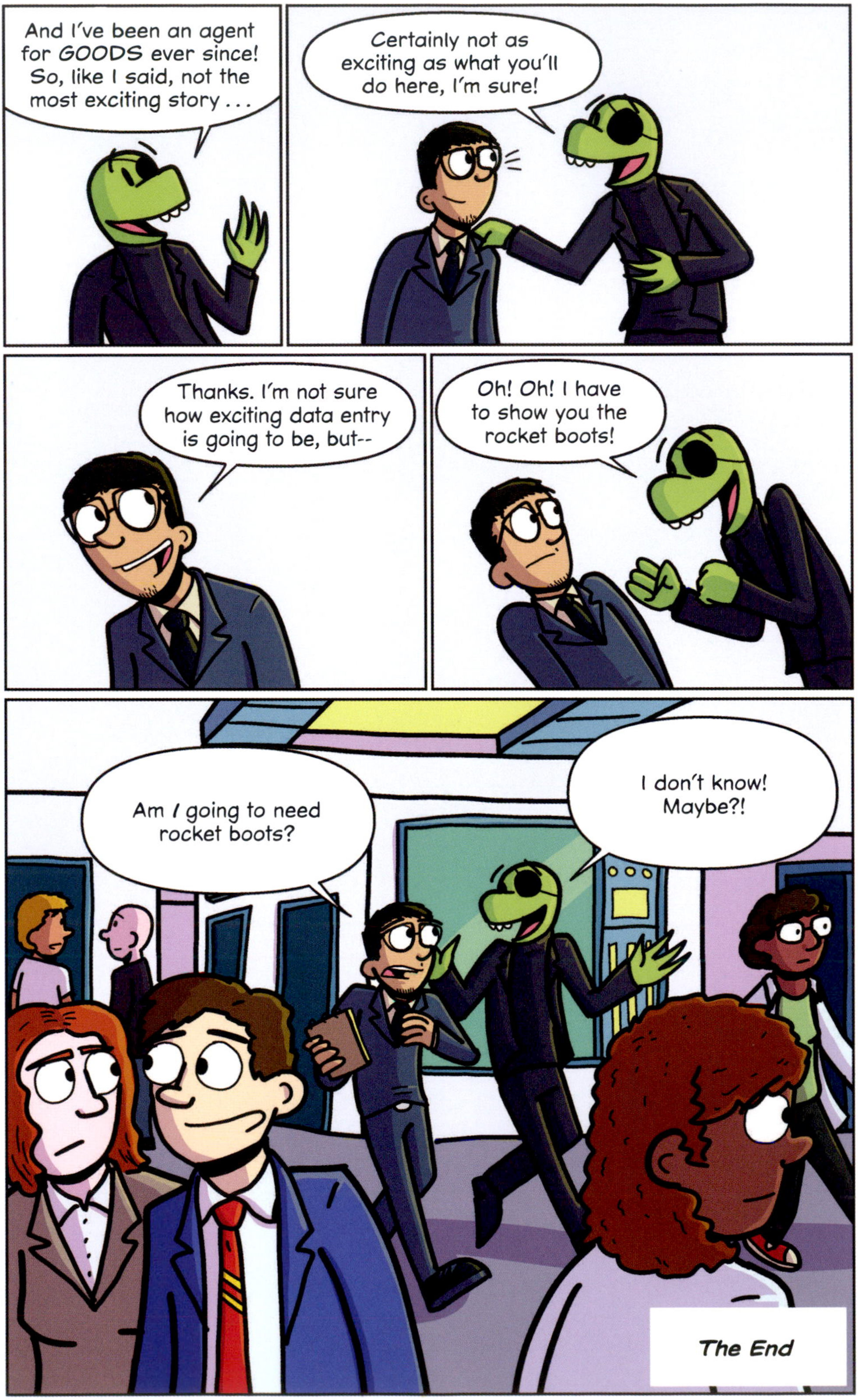
And I've been an agent for *GOODS* ever since! So, like I said, not the most exciting story . . .
Certainly not as exciting as what you'll do here, I'm sure!
Thanks. I'm not sure how exciting data entry is going to be, but--
Oh! Oh! I have to show you the rocket boots!
Am *I* going to need rocket boots?
I don't know! Maybe?!
The End

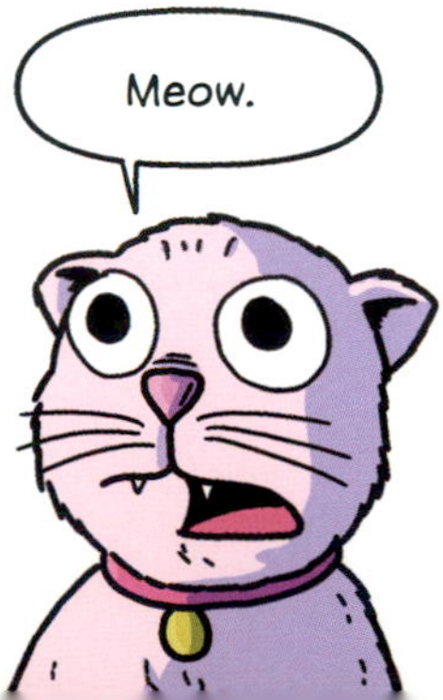
Meow.

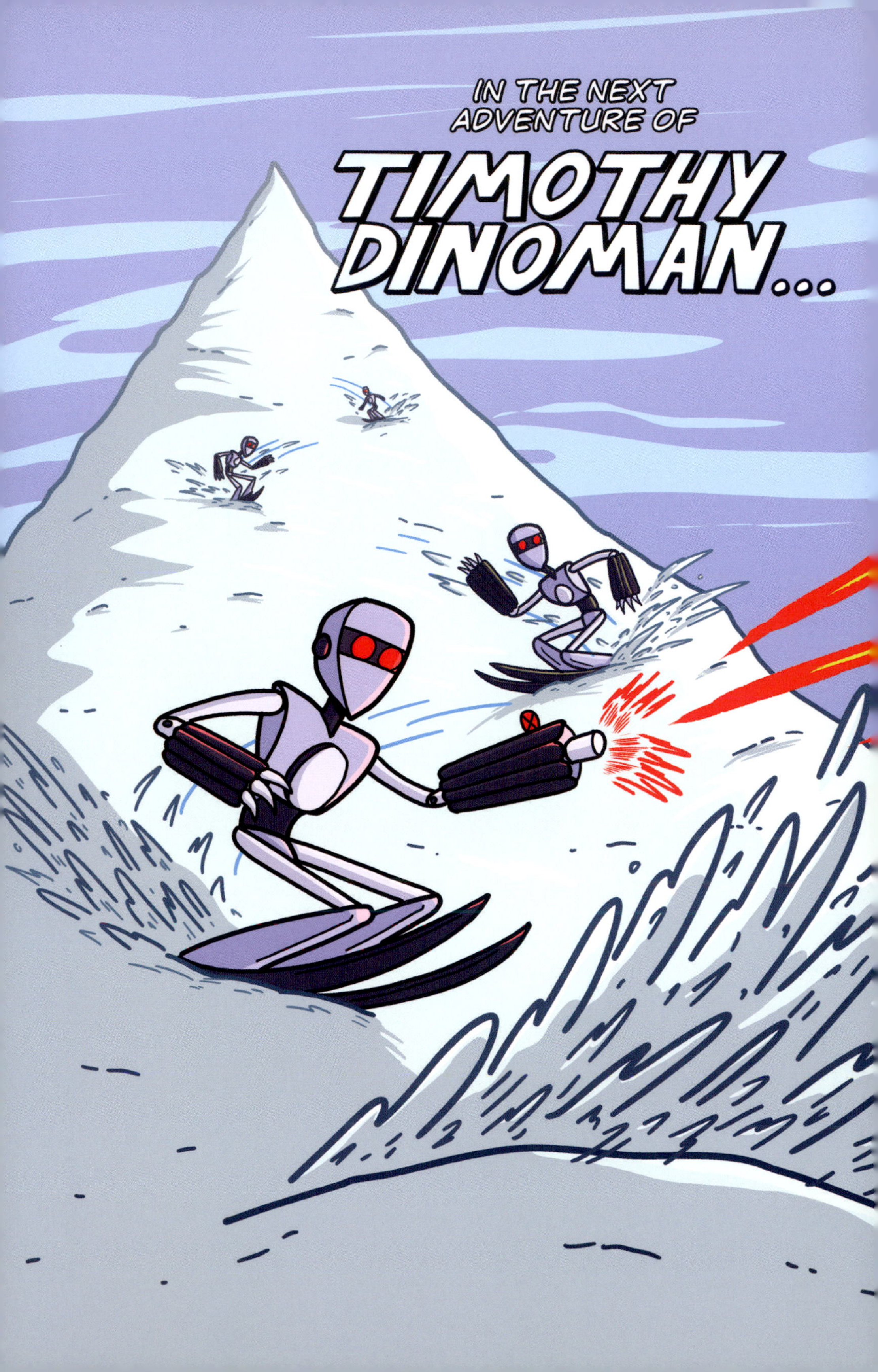
IN THE NEXT
ADVENTURE OF
TIMOTHY
DINOMAN...

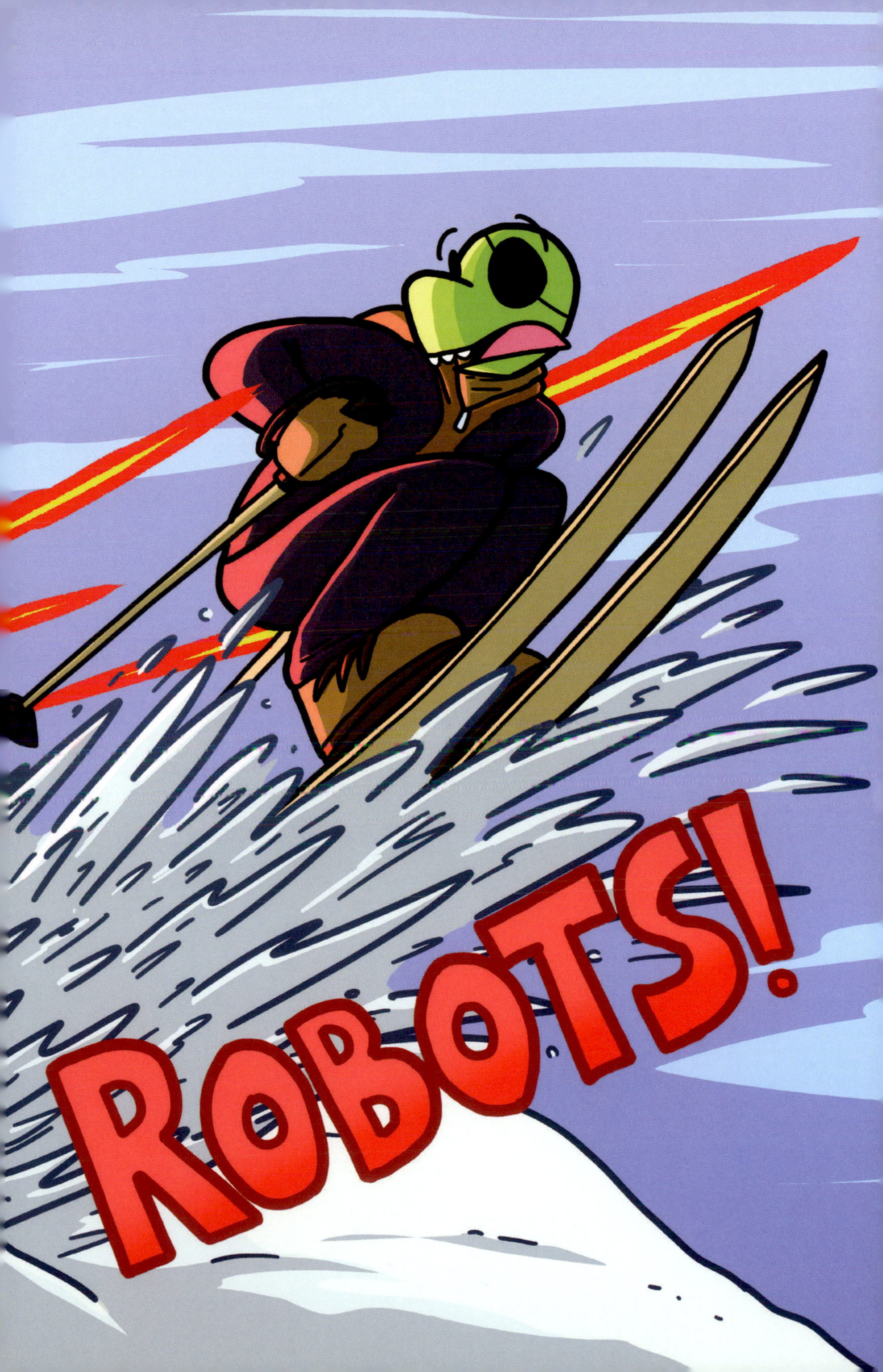
ROBOTS!

Acknowledgments

Thank you so, so much to Rachel for the love and support through every step of this process. Thanks to Greg Hunter for reaching out to me and being the world's greatest editor and collaborator. Thank you to Viet Chu for the book's design. This would have been impossible without Robyn Smith, Jarad Greene, Sophie Yanow, Rachel Dukes, Avi Ehrlich, Michael Sweater, Benji Nate, Christine Larsen, Ben Passmore, Josh O'Neill, Anna McGlynn, Alec Longstreth, David Ohlson and Donna Baluchi, the Dottie's Donuts Crew, Gene and Mymble, my family, and all 141 movies that played in the background while I was drawing.

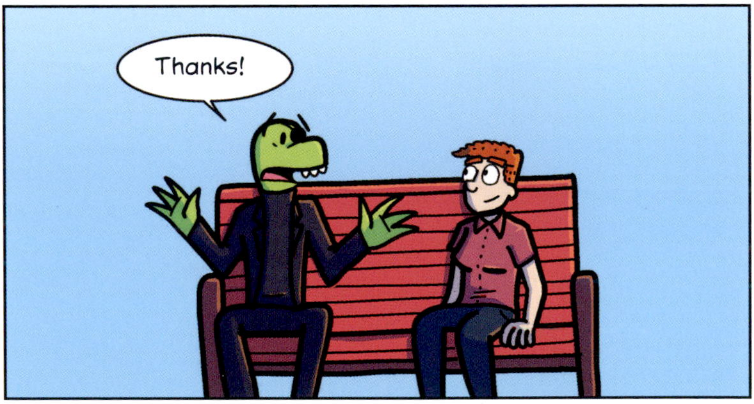
Thanks!

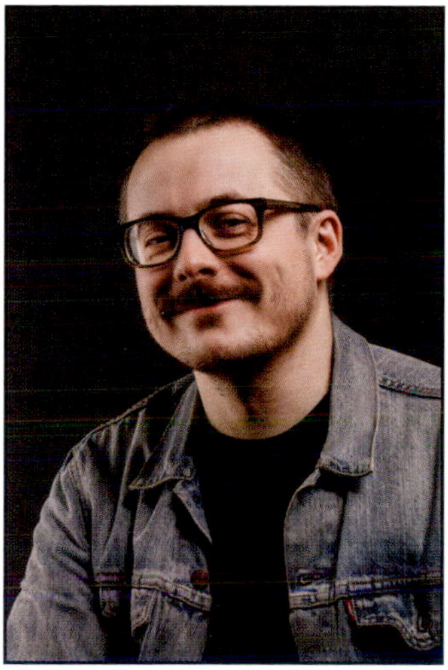

Photo by Michael Messina

About the Author

Steve Thueson is a cartoonist from Salt Lake City, Utah. They received an MFA from the Center for Cartoon Studies in 2017. In addition to Timothy Dinoman, they have made the series Quest Mania, as well as comics for *Good Boy Magazine*, Silver Sprocket, and Birdcage Bottom Books. When they're not drawing, they're selling donuts or watching movies. They live in Philadelphia with their wife and two cats.

Graphic Universe™
An imprint of Lerner Publishing Group, Inc.
241 First Avenue North
Minneapolis, MN 55401 USA

For reading levels and more information, look up this title at www.lernerbooks.com.

Main body text set in CCDaveGibbonsLower.
Typeface provided by Comicraft.

Library of Congress Cataloging-in-Publication Data

Names: Thueson, Steve, author, illustrator.
Title: Timothy Dinoman saves the cat / by Steve Thueson.
Description: Minneapolis : Graphic Universe, [2022] | Series: Timothy Dinoman ;
    book 1 | Audience: Ages 9–14 | Audience: Grades 4–6 | Summary: "Some
    suspected supervillains have stolen outer-space tech! To learn why, Timothy
    Dinoman will visit a mountain fortress, a giant blimp, and a diner with excellent
    waffles. He'll even meet a really cute cat" —Provided by publisher.
Identifiers: LCCN 2021051392 (print) | LCCN 2021051393 (ebook) |
    ISBN 9781728401775 (library binding) | ISBN 9781728463094 (paperback) |
    ISBN 9781728461038 (ebook)
Subjects: CYAC: Superheroes—Fiction. | Humorous stories. | Graphic novels. |
    LCGFT: Superhero comics. | Humorous comics. | Graphic novels.
Classification: LCC PZ7.7.T536 Tim 2022 (print) | LCC PZ7.7.T536 (ebook) |
    DDC 741.5/973—dc23/eng/20211110

LC record available at https://lccn.loc.gov/2021051392
LC ebook record available at https://lccn.loc.gov/2021051393

Manufactured in the United States of America
1-48243-48811-2/2/2022